The Inn at Misty Lake

Margaret Standafer

THE INN AT MISTY LAKE

By Margaret Standafer

Copyright © 2015 by Margaret Standafer

ISBN-13: 978-1518625039

This book is a work of fiction. Names, characters, places, and incidents are either the product of the author's imagination or are used fictitiously. Any resemblance to actual persons, living or dead, business establishments or locales is entirely coincidental.

For Claire
For Dylan

Your stories are unfolding in amazing
ways…far better than I could have ever
written.

1

Susan blew the hair out of her eyes, wiped the sweat from her forehead, and wondered, not for the first time, if she was in over her head. She looked at the mess surrounding her and almost gave in to despair. Almost. Instead, she allowed herself five minutes to sit in front of the fan and gulp a bottle of water before turning the music up a little louder and getting back to work.

She could have the rest of the kitchen floor torn out by evening, she told herself, then swore as her hand slipped off the crowbar she was using to pull up faded yellow linoleum and landed a nice uppercut on her jaw. She rubbed her chin, moved her jaw back and forth a couple of times, and as the sting subsided, had to laugh at herself. She'd learned a lot in the few weeks she'd been in the 'remodeling business,' but she thanked God daily she didn't have to make a living at it. It was hot, dirty work.

But, all the sweat would be worth it when she turned the old farmhouse into the best bed and breakfast in Northern Minnesota.

To think that only a few months ago she'd still been working at the Billingsley Hotel in Chicago and putting up with the pompous and utterly worthless Stephen Billingsley. Once he took over the day-to-day operations from his father, Susan had known she needed to get out. He had asked her out repeatedly and, when she refused, made her life at work miserable. Besides, she was tired of Chicago, tired of the Billingsley, and tired of working for someone else.

She knew her parents, her brothers, her friends—everyone, really—thought she was crazy. Her cousin Sam hadn't said much and had even invested in Susan's dream, but Susan knew she had her doubts, as well. She'd show them, she promised herself. She already had so many ideas she had started writing them down…in a notebook she kept well hidden in her dresser at Sam's place. She wasn't ready to share everything just yet. She needed to work on her friends and family gradually, let them warm to the general idea of a bed and breakfast before springing too many details on them.

As she attacked the floor with renewed vigor, she silently prayed that the heat would give way to cooler, October-like temperatures soon. So far, the blazingly hot summer they had endured was holding tough, apparently unwilling to let go, and forcing most of the upper Midwest to sweat through the early days of autumn. Certainly not the weather she would choose for the work she was doing. The heat seemed to surround her, sapping her energy and making the job all the more difficult. Not to mention the fact that the high temperatures served to intensify the odors that the one hundred and fifty-year-old house sitting vacant for forty years had developed. Susan sneezed as dust billowed when a section of floor splintered under the force of the crowbar then wrinkled her nose against the smell. She had swept and shoveled and done everything she could to clean out the mess left behind by animals that had sought refuge in the house over the years. It wasn't as bad as it had been, but the smell was still unpleasant. Riley had assured her pulling up the old flooring would help, another reason she couldn't wait to have the job behind her.

Riley McCabe. She didn't know whether to smile or curse when she thought of him. When she first met him, it had been his work that had grabbed her attention. A series of framed photos proudly displayed at his parents' house and showcasing before and after pictures of remodeling and restoration work he'd done had intrigued Susan. Even through photos, the quality of his work and the care and conscientiousness he put into it was apparent. She had peppered him with questions to learn about this business and, in the process, found the man to be interesting, thoughtful, and funny. And, at times, infuriating.

When she'd approached him about working for her he'd been hesitant. She'd walked him through the place, given him an overview of her ideas, and his advice had been to tear it down. The front porch was crumbling, the roof was almost beyond repair, the plumbing, wiring, and heating systems were long outdated, and it was filthy. Susan, however, had pointed out the hardwood floors hidden beneath ragged carpets, the beautiful floor-to-ceiling windows and the huge, cozy-looking fireplace in the parlor, and the intriguing brick wall behind the rusted cabinets in the kitchen. Knowing Riley had been itching to flip a house after years working as a contractor doing additions and remodels, Susan had pressed. She had used the fact that taking the job would mean he'd have steady employment to her advantage. He needed work and she needed someone she could trust to do it right. While restoring an old farmhouse might not have been exactly what he'd had in mind, in the end, he hadn't been able to refuse the challenge...or the guarantee of months of work. And if Jake, Riley's older brother and Sam's fiancé, had added his two cents and had helped convince Riley to take the job as she suspected, fine by her. Riley wasn't due to officially start for a couple more weeks, but he had been stopping by to lend a hand and give advice when he could.

It was funny how a trip to Misty Lake to visit Sam and get a look at the house she had inherited from their grandfather had turned into a life-changing adventure. A little bit at loose ends after having quit her job just before the trip to Minnesota, Susan wasn't sure where life was going to take her next when Kathleen Melby, the local realtor who had helped Sam out with the paperwork on her house, had mentioned an old farmhouse going up for sale on the lake. From there, things had started to fall into place. Susan had already decided she wasn't going back to Chicago, the house was listed at a reasonable price, opening a bed and breakfast would finally give her the chance to be her own boss, and hiring Riley McCabe to do the work would give her a chance to get to know him better. Win-win-win.

She headed outside to the dumpster with yet

another load of old linoleum just as Riley's truck pulled into her driveway. "Well, speak of the devil."

"Talking to yourself again, Red? You really should see someone about that, seems like it's getting to be a problem," Riley answered as he slammed the door of his truck closed.

"Figure of speech, McCabe," she snarled as she looked at her watch. "I didn't expect you this early."

"The inspector was actually on time and since he can't ever find fault with my work, it was a quick visit." He looked her up and down, taking in the sweaty, stained t-shirt, the reddish gold hair that, he'd learned, tended to curl when she sweat, and the shockingly green eyes that were right now narrowed to slits and glaring at him. She was stunning. Not that he'd ever admit it.

"Are you here to help or to waste my time?"

"Easy. What's gotten into you today? You're even more unpleasant than usual."

Susan blew out a breath and mumbled, "Sorry. I'm hot, sweaty, and tired and that damn kitchen floor is going to be the death of me."

Riley noticed the nicks and cuts on her arms and, if he wasn't mistaken, a bruise forming on her chin. He'd have to ask her about that later when she was in a better mood. Feeling sorry for her as he knew very well how miserable tearing out an old floor could be, he grabbed his tool box, threw an arm around her shoulder, and said, "Let's see if I can't take care of it before it does you in."

Two hours later the last of the ugly yellow linoleum was gone and Susan and Riley were sitting on the dusty kitchen floor savoring the ice-cold beer Riley had miraculously produced from the cooler he had stashed in his truck. Susan had stopped snapping at him about an hour before, Riley figuring she was simply too tired to put in the effort. Right now, as she leaned against the wall, eyes closed and the cold can held to her neck, he was betting she was close to falling asleep sitting up.

"I think we should call it a day. The floor is out, that's a big step. You look exhausted and, besides, it's going to get dark soon."

Susan ignored most of what he said and didn't bother opening her eyes. "That reminds me, when is the electrician going to be here? Have you heard back from him? I'm going to need to be able to work here after dark and obviously the days are getting shorter. I need some working lights run into the different rooms."

Riley just shook his head. He wasn't sure if he'd ever met a more stubborn woman. "Actually, I did hear back," he began slowly, "there'll be an electrician here tomorrow."

Susan's eyes flew open and she was on her feet. "What? Tomorrow? Are you serious? Why didn't you tell me earlier? I thought it was going to be a couple of weeks, at least."

"I called in a favor. You're welcome," he added when she just stared at him.

"Oh, Riley, that's wonderful! Thank you. Really…thank you. I can't believe you were able to arrange it."

"No problem, I'm anxious to get things going here, too. Which reminds me of a little more news."

She waited, shifting from one foot to the other

and her eyes dancing, all tiredness seemingly forgotten. When he pulled a notepad from his pocket and made a couple of notes, picked up the empty beer cans and tossed them in a garbage pail and still didn't say anything, she threw her hands in the air and shrieked, "What?"

Grinning and paging casually through his notepad he began ticking off on his fingers. "Well, like I said, the electrician will be here tomorrow, looks like the plumber will be here on Monday, the roofing crew by the middle of next week...oh, and I can start full-time on Thursday."

He almost pulled out his phone to capture the moment. It was the first time he had seen her at a loss for words. Her eyes were wide; her mouth opened, then closed again as she turned away, taking a deep breath and running her hand through her hair. After a minute she turned back to face him.

"It's really happening," she said softly, looking a little dazed. "I mean, I knew it was happening, it's about the only thing I've thought of for the past two months, but this just makes it so real."

"It's really happening. You're not going to change your mind, are you?"

"No, of course not," she brushed the idea aside then wrinkled her forehead. "All the permits are ready? Is there anything else that needs to be done right now?"

"I have the permits. I stopped and picked up everything on the way over here. You're ready to go."

She blew out a deep breath then slowly smiled. "Oh, Riley." She walked to him and hugged him. "Thank you for everything. Thank you for making everything happen so quickly. I know you thought I was nuts when I said I wanted to try to get some of the big stuff done before winter and I know I've driven you crazy already and you haven't even officially started working here, but you still made all this happen. I appreciate it."

Riley was surprised. He'd never seen this side of her. Teasing, irritable, bossy, and determined he'd seen plenty of, but appreciative? Humbled? No. That he hadn't seen. He supposed she showed it to others but never to him. He found he kind of liked it. And, he found he enjoyed the feeling of her in his arms.

"You're welcome," he mumbled, his words getting lost in the hair that seemed to be surrounding him and flooding his senses. It was both a relief and a curse when she moved away and began twirling around the kitchen. He had been about to reach for that hair, to finally feel the fiery golden waves between his fingers, but he quickly realized that would have been a mistake. A little more flustered than he cared to admit, Riley watched as Susan moved around the kitchen, then into the dining room and parlor, all the while talking and imagining the finished product. He couldn't help but smile at her enthusiasm, her dreams, and visions. The simple hug had been a thank you, nothing more, and he was glad he hadn't made a fool of himself.

She was excited, and a little scared. The doubts that had been there all along but she had done her best to smother, once again reared their ugly heads and she wondered if it wasn't all a big mistake. This was a huge undertaking, expensive, time-consuming, and with no guarantee of success. She stared out the window at the lake, picturing in her mind the way it would look when everything was done, with people enjoying the beach, the canoes and paddleboats she planned to have available, relaxing in the garden with lemonade in the summer or in front of the fire with hot cocoa in the winter. Or, maybe gearing up for the night's events. Which reminded her…

"Um, Riley," she began, heading back to the kitchen.

He was still leaning against the wall, looking at her with a funny expression as if he couldn't quite figure something out. She ignored it and continued. "I was thinking…the old barn out back?"

Susan didn't like the way Riley narrowed his eyes at her. She liked his low, hesitant voice even less.

"What about the old barn? I thought we agreed it was coming down. Or, maybe we'd turn it into a garage for guests."

"Well, yes, we did talk about that but don't you think it would make more sense to really use the space? I think turning it into an event center would be much more logical, and better for business. Just think. I could host wedding receptions, family reunions, all kinds of parties, even girls' weekends. The space could be reconfigured to suit just about any sort of gathering. We'd just need to run plumbing out there, probably do some work on the electrical, put in a bar—oh, I already have something in mind for that—maybe section off a couple of smaller rooms, not really a big deal."

"Not really a big deal? Are you kidding? Do you know how much additional work you're talking about?" His voice was rising now and he appeared anything but pleased.

"Calm down, calm down. It doesn't all have to be done at once. I just thought since the electrician and the plumber would be here soon, it would only make sense to have them do the work in the barn at the same time."

As Riley watched her, smiling and apparently quite proud of herself, he wondered what in the world he had gotten himself into. He had done some difficult jobs over the years, some painstakingly tedious ones, some, in his opinion, downright ridiculous ones, but this one might fall in a category all its own. He eyed her, tapping his fingers on his thigh and considering, as he took a deep breath.

Susan nervously waited for his reaction. She hadn't planned on springing the barn on him so soon but when he told her the schedule for the subcontractors, she realized it really couldn't wait. She had figured he wouldn't like it, but she was confident she could convince him. It was her place, after all, she had the final say. But, she knew she needed him on board. If he refused to tackle the extra work she'd have to look for another contractor and that was something she didn't want to think about.

Finally, Riley gave a huge sigh, shaking his head and looking towards the ceiling. "Fine, let's go walk through and you can tell me what you're thinking. We'll have to draw up more plans, see what kind of additional permits we need."

She threw her arms around his neck again, jumping up and down while she did so. "Thank you, thank you, thank you! You'll see. It's going to be amazing. I have so many ideas."

They headed to the barn with Susan barely able to contain her excitement. "Just so you know," Riley warned, "if I think your ideas are stupid or impractical, I'm going to tell you."

"Sure, sure, then you'll tell me how to fix it so it's not stupid or impractical," she said with a grin.

Riley didn't know whether to be annoyed or impressed by the fact that her ideas were neither stupid nor impractical. He made a few suggestions, a few changes, but mostly just for form's sake. He found himself swept up in her vision and felt as if he could see the finished event center as clearly as she could. They talked, argued, negotiated, and finally agreed on some of the details. When it got dark enough that the small lantern they'd carried with them to the barn didn't do much more than create some shadows, Riley knew it was time to call it a night.

"All right, that's enough for tonight. I'll draw some of this up, run it by you in a day or two, and I'll talk to the electrician and the plumber about the additional work. Right now, I need a shower and something to eat. And you need some sleep." He couldn't see the dark circles around her eyes in the dusty, gray light of the barn, but he knew they were there.

As they left the barn, Susan started to worry. "What do I need to tell the electrician tomorrow? I'm not sure I understand all the blueprints well enough to explain what I want. What if he has questions I can't answer?" She was biting her lip and twisting her hair.

"Don't worry, an electrician knows how to read blueprints and I'm only a phone call away."

"Okay. What if we haven't thought of everything? What if I want to change something or add something later?"

"Relax, Red. The subs aren't going to finish everything at once. There's some work they need to do initially then they'll be back later on as the work progresses." Riley climbed into his truck and started the engine. "Everything will be fine. I'll try to stop by some time during the day to check on things."

"Thanks, that would make me feel better."

"Okay then, see you tomorrow." He gave a little wave as he started to back out, then stuck his head out the window and added, "Oh, by the way, electrician's name is Cindy." With a devilish wink, he revved the engine and sped off.

2

"So, Cindy should be arriving soon," Susan muttered to herself as she glanced at her watch while tackling the orange shag carpeting in one of the upstairs bedrooms. She had spent the better part of the night wondering who Cindy was and what kind of favor Riley had called in to get the electrician out to the house ahead of schedule. She had spent the rest of the night wondering why she cared. All in all, for as tired as she had been, sleep hadn't come easily. She had tossed and turned and when she did drift off, images of a beautiful, blonde, and buxom Cindy fawning over Riley filled her dreams.

She better know what she's doing, Susan thought. She wasn't going to put up with some ditzy girlfriend of Riley's who played at being an electrician. She'd fire her, that's what she'd do. When she screwed up, or asked too many stupid questions, or wasted time talking on the phone, she'd fire her. Riley would just have to find someone else. Satisfied, she gave the carpet a good tug and was rewarded with a particularly stubborn section in the corner finally coming loose and sending her falling onto her backside.

Susan was still fuming when she heard a vehicle pulling into her driveway. Ready to let Cindy know she wasn't going to accept anything but professionalism and quality work, she stomped down the steps and out into the yard. The small, trim woman heading toward her with a quick, purposeful gait had a clipboard in one hand and the other extended in a greeting. Her hair was short and black but showed more silver than black; her face was small with bright, keen eyes, and Susan put her age at about fifty-five. She must have looked confused because the woman laughed a little as she shook Susan's hand and introduced herself.

"Hi, Susan Taylor? I'm Cindy Fossen."

"Hi. You're the electrician?"

"Riley didn't tell you to expect a woman, did he? He likes to do that, likes to see what sort of a reaction I'll get."

"Actually, he did tell me your name was Cindy. I guess I…" She didn't know what to say, she felt like an idiot. Recovering somewhat, she finally said, "Well, thank you for coming so quickly. Riley only told me yesterday that you'd be able to start today."

Cindy looked around, taking in the old house and barn. "I guess it's a good thing we're getting started, it looks like we've got our work cut out for us. Care to show me around?" With that, she headed for the house leaving Susan to follow behind.

It took only about five minutes for Susan to

decide she liked Cindy. The woman was friendly, honest, open, and intelligent. Susan learned Cindy had become an electrician in order to work alongside her husband. "We built a business and a family and after thirty years still each think we're the luckiest person on the planet. Guess you can't ask for much more than that."

"No, I guess not," Susan agreed.

"Now, Riley showed me the plans and the inspector's report so I have an idea of what I'm working with. Anything you'd like to add before I get started?"

"You're ready to get started? Just like that?" Somehow Susan thought the process would be longer, that there would be more talking, more looking around, but Cindy seemed eager to get going.

"I don't see any reason to waste time. You get back to that orange carpet and I'll get my things moved in and set up." In a flash, she was out the door and Susan was again left trying to catch up.

"How's it going, Red?" Riley asked when he arrived later that afternoon. She was hard at work again tearing out more old flooring. This time, it was a ragged, faded, multi-colored shag carpet. She stopped to look up at him.

"Having a blast, McCabe, can't you tell?"

"Getting along okay with Cindy?" he smirked.

Deciding not to rise to his bait, she answered calmly. "She's wonderful. I can't claim to understand all of what she's doing, but it seems like she's done a lot of it. She's taken down fixtures, pulled out old wiring, basically just dug right in."

"Yes, I find she likes to dig right in."

She just glared at him then turned and went back

to yanking on the edge of the carpet, taking care to stay on her knees in order to avoid taking a tumble in front of Riley.

"I talked to her about the barn," Riley said in a tone intended to pique Susan's interest enough to get her to turn around. It did.

"What did she say? I didn't bring it up with her, thought it should come from you since you're technically the one who hired her."

"She's fine with it, said she can fit it in her schedule."

A smile spread across her face. "Perfect. I knew it would all work out." But she hadn't known, had been worrying about it for hours, and was relieved that, once again, Riley had found a way to make everything fall into place.

He nodded, looked like he wanted to say something, but turned and walked out. Just as quickly, he was back. "You're working in town tomorrow?" It was more a statement than a question since he knew her schedule as well as she did.

"Yes, I have the nine to four shift. If Cindy can have some decent light rigged up, I plan on coming out here tomorrow night to start removing some of the doorknobs and hardware, stuff we talked about reusing. Sam and Jake said they'd help."

"You don't have to get everything done at once and besides, I can do that when I start on Thursday. For God's sake, Susan, you're going to kill yourself. Why don't you just quit that job if you're going to be here every day?"

She heard worry in his voice and, she thought, anger. She took her time answering. "I'm not trying to get everything done at once but there is a lot to do and I figure the more I help with things that I'm able to help with, the easier it will be for you. Besides, it's exciting to finally be inside here after all the waiting for the sale to be finalized. And I can't quit my job yet, I have to earn some money somewhere since I'm not going to be seeing any income from this place for a long time. Once you really get started there probably won't be as much for me to do, for a while anyway. I can handle my job and this place. Not that I think I owe you an explanation," she added.

"Sorry," he said, his eyes not meeting hers. "It just seems like you're putting in some pretty long hours, but it's your business. I need to go over a few things with Cindy before I head out."

Susan watched his back as he headed down the hall. What the heck was that? she wondered. She wanted to be angry with him for telling her what to do, but she was touched that he noticed, that he cared. Still, she wasn't sure what to make of it. She turned it over in her head as she got back to the carpet.

That evening, she brought it up with Sam while they ate dinner. "Who does he think he is, telling me to quit my job, to work less on the house?"

"I've been telling you the same things, Suze."

"That's different."

"How?"

"I don't know, it just is." Over the last few hours she had decided she was more angry than touched. She didn't need anyone telling her what to do or when to do it.

"Well, I guess he's just worried about you. You have been putting in some pretty long hours between the shop and the house."

"I know, but I just can't quit yet. Emily needs me at It's a Lake Thing. Her maternity leave is starting soon and I can't leave her short-handed. Besides, I'm months away from being able to open the inn and until then I'll be bleeding money trying to get the place in shape."

"I can help you," Sam said tentatively, as if anticipating Susan's response.

"No, you can't. You've already done enough," Susan answered automatically.

"I haven't done that much."

"You invested in the B&B, you helped me get the loan, you've done more than enough."

"Susan, I want to help. I have the money from Granddad. I still don't think it's right he left almost everything to me."

Susan knew she felt guilty, but wished she wouldn't. Their grandfather had raised Sam and her brother, Danny, after their parents died. It was only right that the majority of his estate went to Sam, he had been more like a father than a grandfather. If Danny were still alive Susan knew half of what Sam received would have gone to him. As it was, Susan was glad the lake home and most everything else that had been their grandfather's was now Sam's.

"It's yours, you need to stop feeling guilty. No one worries about it but you, you know."

Sam sighed. "I know. Promise me, though, that you'll tell me if things start getting tight financially. I'm more than willing to help."

"I know, and thanks. But let's change the subject," Susan said as she bounced with excitement. "How are the wedding plans coming?"

Sam's face softened and her eyes took on a dreamy expression. "Oh, Susan, it's so wonderful but so overwhelming at the same time. I can't believe all the things I'm supposed to be thinking about. We need to pick a date, find a place for the reception, think about food, music, flowers...I haven't even looked for a dress."

"And I haven't been much of a maid of honor. I'm sorry, Sam. I've been so consumed with the inn I feel like I haven't helped you at all."

"Don't worry about it. Jake and I were supposed to get serious and hash out some details last night. We didn't get anywhere. I don't know why it's so hard. I'm worried he's starting to think I'm stalling."

Susan studied Sam. Her cousin seemed somewhat lost, unsure, and had been that way since her engagement a couple of months ago. Susan had put it off to excitement, to love, to all the things that go along with getting engaged, but now she wondered if there wasn't something more. Her mind started churning and the idea blossomed sending a slow smile across her face.

"Why are you looking at me like that?" Sam asked.

Susan knew she had to tread carefully. She was convinced she knew what Sam needed, but convincing Sam would be another matter. "Have you talked to Mom and Dad much about your plans?" she asked casually.

Sam immediately looked away and tension seemed to creep into her very being. "I called Uncle Ben and Aunt Caroline after Jake proposed, you know that."

"I talked to Mia the other day," Susan said, referring to her pregnant sister-in-law. "She said she's getting big and is eating everything in sight. Apparently

Hawaiian pizza and chocolate milk shakes are her current favorites."

Sam gave a little half smile then looked down at her hands clasped tightly in her lap, but not before Susan saw the longing, as well as the fear, in her eyes. She needed to go home, Susan knew, needed to visit her family and friends and face the past.

"Do you remember Lindsay? My friend from high school?" When Sam looked up and gave a little nod Susan continued. "She runs this shop now, wedding dresses, bridesmaids dresses…I think we should go check it out. What kind of a maid of honor would I be if I didn't help you find a wedding dress?"

Sam opened her mouth to argue but then closed it again and was quiet for a long time. Finally, she said, "You think I should go home."

"Sam, I think you need to go home. It's been a long time, I know you miss everyone. I think a trip back to Chicago will help you finally get the closure you need and make it easier for you to think about what's ahead." Susan saw the pain in her eyes and wished she could say something to take it away.

"I do miss everyone and I want so badly to see Mia while she's pregnant." Sam got up and paced around the room. "I've been thinking about it, thinking about making a trip back."

"Really? Why didn't you say anything?"

"Because just about the time I tell myself I'm going to do it, I chicken out. I haven't even mentioned it to Jake. I know he'd go with me but I don't think he should, not the first time. It would be too easy to lean on him and to avoid facing the things I need to face. Do you think he'll understand that?"

"I know he will. He loves you, Sam. I'm sure he's figured out there's something that isn't quite right, some reason you're holding back just a little with the wedding plans, and I'm sure he's frustrated that he can't fix it."

"You're probably right. I need to talk to him."

"Well, do that later. Right now, let's pick a weekend to go home."

Relief washed over Susan as Sam nodded. She knew Sam couldn't move forward before she went back. Susan had more plans, more ideas, but they could wait. One step at a time, she told herself.

The woman sat staring out the motel window at the dead, brown grass that ringed the pot-holed parking lot. A cigarette hung loosely between her fingers, the ash growing until it finally fell to the shabby, stained carpet. The woman never noticed.

The little boy crawled across the bed using the lines on the frayed bedspread as roads for the small car he held tightly in his hand. When he made his way to the end of the bed he sent the car flying off in dramatic fashion, delighting in how far it flew before crashing mightily into the dresser and coming to rest on the floor. Scrambling down, he retrieved the car and headed back to the bed, ready to replay the scene.

He peeked at the woman and in a small, hopeful voice asked, "Wanna play, Mommy?"

"No."

"My car can drive all the way down this road then fly over the river." He moved the car along the bed as he spoke thinking that maybe if he showed her how fun it

21

was, she'd want to play.

"See? It goes real fast then when the road ends, it has to try to jump over the river—"

"I said no!" she screamed and the boy sank back into the pillows.

He looked at her for a minute, waiting for her to say she was sorry like she usually did when she yelled at him, but she didn't say anything, just stared out the window. Eventually, he resumed his game, driving the car back and forth over the bedspread, but being careful not to make any noise.

The woman raised a shaky hand to her mouth and took a long drag on the cigarette before dropping it on the floor and absently crushing it out with the toe of her tennis shoe. She leaned against the window hoping it would cool her aching head, but was met with glass heated to blistering by the desert sun.

3

By ten o'clock the next night Susan was exhausted. She knew Riley was watching her, as were Sam and Jake, so she fought the yawns and tried to keep up some lively conversation. It had been a long, long day. It's a Lake Thing had been busy with customers and with a shipment that had come in and needed pricing and displaying. After her shift, she had grabbed a quick sandwich and coffee then headed to the B&B where she had been taking down doors, removing doorknobs and hinges, and working at the last of the carpet for the past five hours.

"I don't know how long Cindy was here today but she seems to have gotten a lot done. Having some good temporary lighting is wonderful. I was worried for a while that I'd be limited by the daylight." Had she already talked about Cindy getting lights in? She couldn't remember. Probably. Dammit. What else could she talk about? She racked her brain then was grateful when Sam spoke up and she could stop thinking for a minute.

"Do you want help moving these things to the barn?" Sam asked referring to some boxes and furniture that had been left behind by the previous owners, as well as the doors and hardware they were currently working on. Susan hadn't wanted to toss anything without looking it over thinking there may be some things she could use and she hadn't gotten to everything yet. She had already decided some of the wooden furniture and maybe a couple of bedframes could be salvaged with a little work.

Susan looked at Riley before answering. He raised his eyebrows at her, obviously wondering why she hadn't told Sam about her plans for the barn. Rather than giving a direct answer, Susan did her best to sidestep the question.

"I still need to look through some of the boxes and check out some of the furniture. I'm going to try to get it done by this weekend."

"It seems like it will be in the way when Riley starts tomorrow, though. Shouldn't we haul it out to the barn and just stash it in there so it's out of the way?"

Susan was grateful when Riley spoke up, figuring it would buy her some time.

"I can work around things for a while. My first step will be demo, I've got to knock down some walls, get down to the framing. I'll take it one room at a time so we can move things out as Red goes through them."

Susan gave Riley a quick nod and was relieved when Sam accepted his explanation. "Maybe what we can do yet tonight is box up some of the hardware and label the boxes so I know what's what later on."

"You've got some nice looking things here to work with, Susan," Jake said turning a glass doorknob over in his hand. "Is the plan to keep everything fitting with the time period of the house?"

"To some extent, yes, I'd like to try. But, I'll mix in some modern, up-to-date features as well. My idea is to give people a relaxing experience with a little taste of the past, but to keep them comfortable with things like air conditioning, mini-fridges, and Internet access, if they want it."

"How about the whole themed thing?" Jake continued. "Seems like the B&Bs I've seen have whole rooms centered around a quilt or something." The regret registered on his face before he finished speaking the words.

Sam gave him a questioning look. "Seen a lot of B&Bs, have you?"

Jake looked panicked, but Sam came up behind him and reached her arms around him. "Maybe you'll take me one of these days?"

"Whenever you want," he answered, turning and kissing her on the top of the head.

"Maybe Mom still has brochures for the places the two of you stayed." Riley barely got the words out before doubling over with laughter.

Jake's eyes shot daggers at his brother as Riley laughed even harder. "Shut up, Riley," he snarled.

Sam did her best not to laugh but Susan had joined Riley and was chuckling as she asked, "You and your mom? At a B&B? Care to explain?"

"Not really," Jake mumbled as the blush climbed up his neck to his cheeks.

"Come on, Jake, tell them all about your night in the honeymoon suite."

Sam couldn't hold back any longer and the laughter bubbled out as she squeaked, "The honeymoon suite?"

Jake's voice was low and menacing. "I swear, Riley, you're going to pay."

"Oh, come on, Jake, you have to tell us now," Sam prodded.

Jake took a long, slow breath while staring at Riley, an internal debate raging on whether to slug him now or later. Eventually, he shrugged, defeated. "It's really not a big deal. My junior year of high school mom took me to look at colleges. We drove from here to Colorado stopping at schools along the way. We ran into some bad weather and our schedule was thrown off so we didn't have hotel reservations." He sighed and glared at his brother again. "A couple of times we couldn't find any place with a vacancy except a bed and breakfast."

When he didn't say anything more, Sam coaxed, "And…the honeymoon suite?"

"It wasn't the honeymoon suite." Jake said, looking at Riley and willing him to keep his mouth shut, but Riley could hardly get the words out fast enough.

"Okay, not the honeymoon suite, but what was it called? Cupid's Delight? I think that was it."

"It was the only room they had left," Jake said resignedly.

"The old woman who ran the place and was checking them in looked Jake up and down then whispered to Mom, 'Good for you!'"

Sam clapped her hand over her mouth and turned away, but Riley and Susan broke out in renewed fits of laughter. Jake let them have their fun then finally said, "So, about the quilts?"

Half an hour later the four had accomplished everything that Susan had asked of them, and more. Susan thanked Jake and Sam, teased Jake once more about the B&B, then sent them on their way.

Riley noticed an instant shift in her mood. Doubt seemed to creep into her eyes and her hands fluttered as she tried to busy them. "What's up, Red?"

"Oh, nothing." Clearly a lie, but before he could respond, she added, "Do you think we should start on these walls?"

She really was crazy, he decided. "No, I don't work twenty-four-hour days. It's almost eleven o'clock. I want to go home so I can come back tomorrow."

"Okay, I just thought if we got some done tonight you'd have a head start tomorrow."

She seemed tense, tying and retying her hair in a ponytail as she paced around the room. Walking to her, Riley grabbed her hands, quieted them, and looked her in the eye. "Susan, tell me what's wrong."

Using her real name and, he liked to think, the fact that her hands were in his, had the desired effect and he had her attention. She stared at him for a minute then dropped her gaze as she muttered, "I guess I'm a little scared."

Riley put a finger under her chin and lifted it. "Hey, that's normal. I've had customers tackling much smaller projects than this call me in a panic the night before I was set to start. Any big decision is a little scary. I'd worry about you if you weren't scared."

"Really?"

"Really. Once I had a job remodeling a bathroom. At about ten o'clock the night before I was scheduled to start work, the woman called me crying, saying she'd changed her mind. I listened to her babble incoherently for several minutes before her husband realized she was on the phone and picked up an extension. Then I listened to the two of them argue. The husband told her over and over it was the right thing to do; she cried, said it was a mistake. At some point the tables turned and he was saying maybe they shouldn't go through with it while she tried to convince him they should. It was madness. Every so often one of them would say something to me or ask me a question but for the most part, they continued as if I wasn't there. Eventually, I just hung up, showed up at their house in the morning, and got to work as if nothing had ever happened."

By the time he finished, Susan was smiling. "So, I'm not crazy?"

"I didn't say that."

"Sometimes it just hits me that I have taken on this huge project and that I really don't know what I'm doing. I have all these ideas but how do I know if it will work?"

"There are never any guarantees, but that doesn't mean we stop trying. Plenty of people thought I was nuts when I started my business. I heard over and over that I should look for something with more security, something where I'd know what my paycheck was going to be every week. In spite of all that, or maybe because of it, I was determined to make it work. So far, so good," he shrugged.

"I'm pretty sure Sam thinks I've made a mistake."

"Sam wants what you want. I think she's a little

worried about you, worried that you're going at this too hard, but she'll support you no matter what you decide."

Susan nodded but Riley still saw the doubt in her eyes. Gently, he ran a knuckle down her cheek. "Hey, you can do this."

Before he could change his mind, he leaned toward her and softly pressed his lips to hers. He saw her eyes widen before he closed his and lost himself in her.

She first stiffened, remaining firmly rooted in place, but before Riley could try to make sense of her reaction, she began to relax into him. The lips that started out shocked and stiff softened and moved against his. Then it was as if someone reached in and slapped him upside the head, telling him to come to his senses. She needed a friend, not someone to take advantage of her. He pulled away, pulse racing and much less steady than he'd ever admit.

When he opened his eyes, he found Susan tipped forward, eyes still closed, and lips slightly pursed. Almost before the image registered, she began blinking furiously in, what he guessed, was an effort to clear her head...if her head felt anything like his.

Gathering herself, she said, "Well. Thank you for the pep talk. I guess I'll see you tomorrow?"

Riley considered a smart reply but, instead, just grinned. "See you tomorrow, Red."

4

"What do you mean he kissed you?" Sam was squinting against the light and trying to make sense out of what Susan was saying.

It was late, but Susan had gone straight to Sam's room and thrown herself on the bed replaying the events of the night for her cousin.

"What's not to understand? He kissed me."

"Okay, but I'm not clear on the details. Was it a friendly kind of good night kiss? Was it a 'this is just the beginning' kind of kiss? Did he say anything before he kissed you?"

"I don't really know what kind of kiss it was. We were talking, he was actually trying to calm me down since I'd had something of a breakdown, so maybe it was just a 'calm down, you're going to be fine' kind of kiss."

Sam looked alarmed. "Wait a minute, what do you mean you had something of a breakdown. What's wrong?"

Susan threw her hands up in the air. "It was nothing, just some nerves, but that's getting away from the main issue here. Riley McCabe kissed me. What the heck?"

Sam still wanted to get to the bottom of the breakdown or nerves or whatever Susan wanted to call it, but she leaned back and studied Susan. She knew her well enough to know that she didn't react to a simple kiss the way she was reacting right now. She had a thing for Riley.

"Well," Sam began, "Riley's a good guy. He might act tough, but he wouldn't deliberately hurt you or take advantage of you. And, since he looks a lot like his brother, I can honestly say the man is drop-dead gorgeous. That's a heck of a combination. My guess is he's either interested in you or he's deeply concerned about you. Maybe a little of both. I think you need to figure out how you feel and then let him know. Subtly, of course."

"Of course. But what if I don't know for sure how I feel?"

"You have time. The two of you are going to be spending a lot of time together, things will work their way out."

"Maybe." Susan didn't seem convinced.

"Trust me. I know a thing or two about McCabe men," Sam winked. "They don't stay dark and mysterious for long."

"You're in love. You're biased."

"That, my dear cousin, is true. But, I'm still right. You'll figure Riley out sooner rather than later."

The next morning, Susan tried her best to act as if nothing had happened. She failed miserably. Every time she'd try to talk to Riley she'd stumble over her words and blush, unable to meet his eyes. Riley, for his part, acted the same as always. He started tearing out walls in the kitchen and worked comfortably with Cindy. Susan fumed as she sorted through boxes and pulled cast off things from closet shelves.

Much of what she found was worthless. Moth-eaten, stained linens and clothing filled several boxes. She found some cracked and chipped dishes and glasses that were useless, stacks of old newspapers and magazines that definitely were not, and various knick-knacks, some of which were cheap and broken, but some which delighted her. It was hard not to sit down with the newspapers and page through the stories of fifty years ago but she fought the temptation and, instead, boxed up what was still in good condition to pull out later when she had time.

As she carried load after load to the dumpster, her mind began wandering and she wondered about the people who had lived there. What had their lives been like? Were they happy? Why had they left so many things behind? Had they planned to return? She imagined births, deaths, prosperity, and hardship and longed to know the true stories. When she finally had the garbage cleared out, she knew she couldn't put it off any longer and would have to ask Riley what he wanted done with those things she had decided to save.

"Hey, McCabe, do you have a minute?" she called to him from upstairs. Easier than facing him, she decided. Her pulse quickened as she heard him tromping up the stairs. Fool, she chided herself, get it together.

He stuck his head in the room and looked around. "You're making some progress."

"Do you think we can put some of these things in

the cellar?" she asked, indicating the boxes sitting around her.

"I hate to do that, I'm afraid it's too damp down there. Why don't we move things to the attic? Nothing much is going on up there right now, we'll just need to reinforce some of the floor boards and replace the windows later on."

She had been afraid he was going to suggest the attic. She debated with herself on whether to just go along with him and haul things up there or to tell him another one of her ideas.

"Actually, I was thinking about the attic. I think we should put another room up there, it's really just wasted space otherwise." She kept her back to him as she spoke, but could sense his reaction without seeing him.

"Another room."

"Well, yes. It's huge, we might even be able to split it into two rooms, but I'll leave that up to you to figure out."

"Leave it up to me."

She turned to face him, not liking the way he was quietly repeating what she said. His eyes were dark and dangerous and his hands were opening and closing in fists.

"You can't argue that the space is perfect. The sweet little dormer windows and the sloped roof would make such a cute, cozy room. Or two. I think I'd keep it rustic up there, use log furniture, darker colors, but we'll see…"

When he didn't speak at all this time, she continued. "But, I suppose we could move things up there now and just move them again when you get started on the room. Or rooms. We really need to decide if it will be one or two. Or do you think it could be three? That might be tricky with the stairs, though. Oh well, you know best."

"You can't…" he sputtered. "It's not…plans are done…" He glared at her for a minute then said, "Leave this crap here, I'll talk to you later." With that, he spun around and stormed back down the stairs.

"That could have gone better," Susan muttered. But then she smiled as she realized things were indeed back to normal with Riley.

Later that evening, after Cindy was gone and Susan was thinking about heading home, Riley came upstairs with a scowl on his face. "I've been thinking about the attic."

Susan waited but he didn't elaborate. "What about it?"

"I wish you'd just tell me every crazy idea you have all at once rather than prolonging the agony. I can't keep making changes to the plans. I have to schedule people to come in and help, I need to know what I'm dealing with."

"I suppose you're right," she conceded. "I was just worried if I sprang too big a job on you all at once you never would have agreed to it."

"You may be right about that."

"Do you think the attic could work?"

"Of course, it could work. Whether it makes sense is another question entirely. Have you thought all this through? You were talking six rooms with one of them being for you. Now you want to add one, two, or even three more? You're talking about the potential for up to eight rooms filled with guests. That's a lot of work."

"I know that and yes, I haven't done much but

think things through. I can't guarantee I've always come to the right decision, but I can guarantee I've put a lot of thought into things."

"When you say things…tell me now if there are more things I need to know about."

Susan balked. There were more but she didn't like the way Riley was looking at her. She busied herself taping boxes and tried to figure out how to best answer.

"I'm waiting."

"Okay, okay." She stood up straight, mustered her courage, and let fly. "I want to put an addition off the kitchen with a room for me. I don't want to be so close to the guests, I think a little distance would be a good thing. I'll need another bathroom there, of course."

"Of course," Riley replied stonily.

"I think there should be a gazebo down towards the lake. People like to be outside in the evening but you know how bad the bugs are."

"Can't have bugs bothering the guests."

Susan was looking at him sideways now, a little frightened by his quiet, monotone voice, but since she had started, she'd continue. "Now, some of these things don't have to be done right away, I could always add things as I go, but since you asked, I'd like a shed to store a few outdoor games, things for people to do while they're here—I'm thinking with a little work one of the small outbuildings would be perfect for that; I'll need a dock, that goes without saying; a fire pit down on the beach would be good; and a chicken coop."

Riley didn't respond, Susan didn't think he even blinked. She was worried he was going to throw his tool belt down and walk out. But, she wasn't quite done. "One more thing…the barn will need to be done by September because I want to have Sam and Jake's reception here and I'm pretty sure they've decided on Labor Day weekend."

After what seemed like an eternity, Riley finally growled, "Is that all?"

"Well, there are some more things in my notebook, but it's mostly inside stuff, ideas for décor, food, and so on, so nothing you need to worry about." She attempted a weak smile but Riley didn't return it.

"Your notebook?"

"I've been jotting things down waiting for the best time to talk to you about them."

He just shook his head. "A chicken coop?"

"Well, think how nice it would be to have fresh eggs. People up here from the city would probably get a kick out of feeding the chickens, collecting eggs, that kind of thing." When she saw his icy stare she backed off. "But I guess that's something I could do without. I mean, what do I really know about raising chickens?" Her laugh died on her lips when he continued to scowl at her.

Susan twirled her hair around her finger and chewed on her lip as she waited for Riley to respond. Twice he opened his mouth as if ready to say something, but then closed it again without making a sound. Finally, he took a deep breath, leaned his head against the wall, and pinched the bridge of his nose. She prepared herself for the worst.

"Here's what's going to happen. You are going to go out to dinner with me tomorrow night. You're going to bring that damn notebook and you're going to show me every single page. We will discuss every page. I will tell you what I will and what I won't agree to. If you don't like it, you can find another contractor. Any questions?"

"Nope. All clear."

"Good. Now I'm going home." He began heading towards the stairs.

"Wait, just one more thing."

He stopped and waited without turning around.

"What should I wear?"

5

Susan worked in town on Friday and was grateful for the steady stream of customers in and out of the shop that helped keep her mind off her upcoming dinner with Riley. She was nervous and excited at the same time. Nervous, because she was afraid of how he'd react to her notebook. She had given serious consideration to rewriting it, toning it down and only including some of the ideas that were in the real notebook. But, in the end, she figured she might as well face the music. Excited, because an evening out with Riley, albeit under less than ideal circumstances, was intriguing.

She hadn't had a date for months. Not that she was considering this a date, even though he had kissed her. Maybe it was a date? No, Riley had barely grunted that they'd get pizza when she had asked what to wear. He hadn't made it sound like a date. But maybe…the bell above the door jingled and she was relieved to focus on something other than Riley McCabe.

After work, Susan headed home to change and ready herself for the evening. She was disappointed Sam wasn't home but remembered she was delivering a cocktail table and end tables to a client. Susan had wanted to talk things out with her knowing Sam would know what to say to calm her nerves.

Instead she played with Rigi until the dog was tired out, then, when she couldn't find anything else to do, grabbed her notebook and climbed back in her car deciding to head to the B&B for a while until Riley finished working for the day. She pulled in to find several vehicles in the driveway and a man she didn't recognize operating some sort of machine and digging around the foundation.

She found Riley inside, dusty and sweaty and, at the moment, seemingly swearing at the wall. She couldn't help herself, she watched as he stretched to pull at a high section of plaster. His broad shoulders pulled his t-shirt taut and muscles rippled down the length of his outstretched arms. His jeans hung low on his hips and, with the bandana he had tucked in his back pocket, made for quite the sight. The late afternoon sunlight caught his wavy brown hair and the auburn highlights she had noticed the first time she met him were more prominent than ever. She knew when he turned around his piercing blue eyes would be focused and intent. She started to sigh before catching herself.

"That wall giving you a hard time, McCabe?"

Riley hadn't heard her come in and was surprised, and a little annoyed, by the jolt that rocked him at the sound of her voice. He yanked the bandana from his pocket and wiped sweat from his forehead as he slowly ran his eyes over her. She wore her hair down. Fiery waves tumbled over her shoulders and on down her back. Her green sweater made her eyes intensely green. The tight jeans she wore disappeared into knee-high black boots with heels that brought her within a few inches of his height. When she started to grin he realized he was staring.

"Not really dressed for a day on the job," he managed. "I thought I was picking you up?"

"I had some time, thought I'd stop by and see how things are going. What's that guy doing digging around the house?"

He was relieved when she moved so easily into shoptalk and ignored his obvious leering. "He's checking the foundation. I don't like the dampness in the cellar, I want to make sure the foundation is secure and find out if we need to do some waterproofing."

"Hmmm." There were noises coming from different areas in the house. "What about all the other vehicles out there? How many people do you have here today?"

"I've got a couple guys in helping tear out walls. It's not difficult work, just dirty and time consuming. These guys have helped me out in the past, they know what they're doing. Cindy's here and has someone helping her today, too. It's a full house but they should all be heading out before long."

"Okay. I think I'll just putz around a little, check out some of the dressers and wardrobes to see if they seem worth hanging on to. I know you're anxious to have things cleared out."

"The sooner the better, but we're still okay working around some of it."

"All right. Well, I'll be around. And don't worry," she said anticipating his next comment, "I'll stay out of the way."

There were a few pieces of furniture they had pushed into a corner that Susan wanted to get a better look at. They had been emptied, where necessary, but she hadn't really taken time to look closely for warping, structural damage, things that would make a piece useless.

She admitted to herself she didn't know a lot about antiques so had no idea how old some of the things left behind might be. Some of it looked old to her but as far as any value, she really couldn't guess. It would make sense to have someone look at it, she figured. If there was something worth keeping, Sam could probably fix it.

She pulled at drawers, opened and closed doors, and checked for sturdiness. She found missing knobs on a couple of dressers. One was cracked and warped and wobbled at the slightest touch. Probably not a keeper. A particularly interesting wardrobe had water damage and seemed warped on one side. Too bad. It was a beautiful, three-door design with glass on the door in the center. The ornate pulls and keys made Susan think it was most likely quite old. She really needed to get someone out there who knew about this stuff, she told herself again.

The last dresser she checked out had a drawer that wouldn't budge. She yanked and pulled and wiggled but it didn't want to open. Just as she gave it one more try, Riley came in to tell her everyone had cleared out and he was ready to head home.

"Will you see if you can get this thing open first?"

He pulled at the drawer. "It's caught on something." He removed the drawer above which enabled him to see down behind the stuck drawer. "There's something wedged in here, looks like some kind of book."

He finagled it a little until it came free then handed it to Susan while he put the drawers back in place.

It was a composition-type notebook with a paperboard cover. She began flipping through the pages. "Look at this. It's some kind of journal," she said in awe, looking for dates. "Maybe I'll learn more about the house's history."

Riley leaned over to look with her. "Here," he pointed. "It says 'Graduation Day, May 22, 1949.'" Together they read the account of stiff black graduation robes, speeches, hymns, and prayers that were part of the ceremony.

"This is so amazing, I can't wait to read all of it," Susan said, carefully fanning the pages. "Oh, there's a name here in the back. Charlie Walker." She continued paging slowly through the book. "I wish there were pictures. I would love to know what it used to look like here, both inside and out."

"You should check some of the old town records. There may be some pictures or at least some more information on the family who owned the property if you don't find what you're looking for in there."

"I might do that," Susan mumbled as she flipped to the beginning of the journal and began reading.

Riley busied himself for a few minutes looking over the furniture. "Have you made a decision on all of this?"

"What? Oh, no, not all of it. I was thinking I should find someone who knows something about antiques and see if any of it is worth trying to save." She went back to looking at the book.

"Shauna would do it for you."

"Shauna would do what?"

"Look at this stuff," he answered, taking the book from her hands so as to have her attention.

"Really? I thought she worked at the bank. Does she know about this kind of thing?"

"She's got some kind of art history degree, she loves antiques. I'm sure she'd be thrilled to get a look at all this."

"That's perfect. If I had known, I would have asked her to come out here weeks ago."

"It's Friday, she'll probably be around town tonight. If we don't run into her I'll talk to her tomorrow. Now, we should get going, I'm starving."

"Right. The pizza. Okay." She was suddenly nervous again and couldn't quite figure out why.

"How do you want to do this? Should I follow you home so you can drop off your car? Or do you want to leave it here and I'll drive you back out here later?"

"No, no, I'll just follow you."

He gave her a look. "You're not going to follow me and then drive yourself home later. Let's drop your car off, that seems like the best plan."

She wanted to argue but decided against it figuring it would be a waste of her time. "Fine," she said with a shrug and followed him outside.

The evening was still warm but there was finally a hint of fall in the air that seemed to promise cooler temperatures. "I hope the forecast is right and we get some cooler weather." She didn't know what to say and weather seemed like a safe topic.

Knowing Riley must have picked up on her nervousness, she hoped he'd attribute it to her having to show him the notebook and nothing more. She was still determining how to make him believe that when something caught her eye and she stopped in her tracks and pointed.

"Look," she cooed.

Riley followed her outstretched finger and spotted the puppy. He was sniffing around the dumpster, slightly crouched and shaking.

"Oh, Riley, he looks so scared." She bent down low and held out her hand calling softly to the dog.

The dog hesitated then looked around frantically. He took a couple of tentative steps before changing his mind and darting off down the road.

"Oh, no. I hope he's okay." Susan watched him run until he turned into the trees and was out of sight. "He didn't have a collar. I wonder where he came from."

"Probably belongs to someone right around here," Riley said.

Susan hoped so, but doubted it. By the tone of Riley's voice, he concurred. The dog, which had appeared to be a young black lab, was dirty and not much more than skin and bones. He didn't look like he'd seen a home of any sort for a good long while.

"Let's get going, we'll keep an eye out for him as we drive."

Susan appreciated Riley's attempt to sound encouraging. There was no sign of him though as they drove the few miles to Sam's house. As Susan climbed into Riley's truck after parking her car, she said, "I don't like just leaving him."

"I don't either but there's not a lot we can do. It's going to be awfully hard to find him in the dark. He may turn up back at your place, we'll keep an eye out for him."

Hating the helpless feeling but resigned to it, Susan settled back and listened as Riley pointed out some places on the lake and told her stories about growing up in the area. When they pulled up to the house he shared with his twin brother Frank, Susan hesitated.

"Well, aren't you coming?" Riley asked when she made no move to get out of the car.

"I could just wait here." Her eyes were flitting around, landing everywhere but on Riley's.

He got out of the car and circled around to her door, opening it and leaning his forearms on the roof. Peering in the car at her he teased, "You're not afraid to be alone with me, are you, Red?"

"Don't be ridiculous." She pushed him aside, his smug tone enough to have her climbing from the car and heading for the door without looking back at him.

Riley laughed out loud. Susan's shoulders tensed as she hesitated for the briefest moment before throwing her chin in the air and continuing the walk to the house. Riley jogged a few steps to catch up with her.

What was it about this man that had her going from intrigued to nervous to infuriated in less time than it took to tie her shoes? she wondered. Normally she was fun, confident...herself, around men. Either she was interested and let them know or she wasn't and let them know. With Riley, she couldn't seem to make up her mind.

As she mulled it over, she realized Riley had the door open and was talking to her.

"I'll just be a few minutes. I need a quick shower and a change of clothes. Make yourself at home. Frank might be showing up before long, I think he said he'd be home for a while this evening. But maybe that was yesterday." He shrugged and headed down the hall leaving Susan standing in a living room dominated by a TV, a black leather sectional sofa, and a cocktail table stained with several water rings. Apparently coasters were optional at the Brothers McCabe abode. She rubbed a little at the water rings. It was a nice table and she hated to see it damaged. She could give him a few suggestions to get rid of the marks, she thought idly.

She wandered around, realizing she was curious about how Riley lived. The house appeared to be very clean, which surprised her, and was dominated with sports-related paraphernalia, which didn't. Hockey seemed to be the brothers' sport of choice. She found everything from Minnesota Wild beer glasses to a framed, autographed jersey to some curious looking oven mitts hanging from magnets on the side of the refrigerator.

She listened for a second and when she heard the shower still running, took a quick peek in the fridge. It was well stocked with what seemed to be a variety of fruits and vegetables, several condiments beyond the expected ketchup and mustard, and an extensive selection of yogurts and cheeses. Hmmm. Not at all what she'd expected.

As she continued her self-guided tour, she came to a hallway full of framed photographs. Frank's, she assumed. To say they were stunning wouldn't do them justice. He had captured dramatic sunsets, magnificent fall colors, and what she guessed to be a street in town the morning after an ice storm.

A door opening down the hall made her jump but when she realized Riley wasn't coming just yet, she wandered on. A series of family photos taken with obvious care and loving detail dominated the next section of wall space. She stopped when she came to a grouping of pictures and newspaper clippings of Riley and Frank dressed in hockey gear. She glanced at some of the headlines from the local paper touting the 'dynamic duo' of Frank and Riley McCabe, co-captains of the high school team. Susan had just started to read when Riley reappeared.

"You never told me you played hockey."

"It's not what I usually lead with."

Susan laughed. "Point taken." Indicating the article she had started to read, she added, "Apparently you were pretty good."

He seemed embarrassed. "I don't know…"

Susan scanned the article then, with a trace of admiration in her voice said, "You set the school record for most goals scored?"

"Yeah, I guess."

"Why don't you like to talk about it?"

"It's not that I don't like to talk about it, I do…sometimes." When she gave him a confused look he sighed and continued. "I know a few guys who seem to have never gotten over their high school glory days. Every time I run into them we have to rehash the same old stories. Honestly, none of them have done much with their lives since high school. It's almost as if wearing a letter jacket for a couple of years was as good as it's ever going to get for them. I guess I don't want to wind up like that so I tend to avoid the subject."

Susan cocked her head and gave a slow nod. "That's deep, McCabe." Putting up a hand to stop the retort she saw forming on Riley's lips she added, "But I get it. Although, I don't think you have to worry about never accomplishing anything worthwhile past your school days."

"Well...thanks."

"Still, I'd love to learn more about the dynamic duo. Maybe over pizza? I can tell you all about my glory days, too. But, I have to admit, there's really not much to tell."

He gave her a warning look. "Oh, no, you don't. You're showing me that notebook, Red."

"Relax, I'll show it to you."

Riley muttered something under his breath as he made his way to the door. With a last glance at the pictures on the wall, Susan followed.

6

The Brick was crowded and they had to wait for a table. The smell of hot baked pizza had Susan's stomach growling in anticipation. As she scanned the restaurant, she spotted Shauna at a table, laughing with a group of girls who all seemed close in age. Good, she'd get a chance to talk to her about checking over some of the furniture left behind at the house. Shauna spotted them and, after looking at the two of them with narrowed eyes as if trying to decide how she felt about seeing them together, gave a little wave.

Once they were seated and had ordered a pizza and a pitcher of beer, Riley put his elbows on the table and rested his chin on his folded hands. Giving a quick nod to the bag Susan had tucked into the corner of the booth, he said, "Shall we get started, Miss Taylor?"

"So formal. I guess you're not in the mood for small talk?"

"Let's get this over with and then see if we can't enjoy the rest of the evening."

"Okay, fair enough." Reaching for her bag, she pulled out the notebook and laid it on the table, hands protectively on top. She wanted to ease into it. "Now, some of what's in here is vague, just ideas, concepts, that would come to me and I'd jot down. Some of it is a little more concrete with sketches, color and fabric swatches, maybe the name of a website or two." She snuck a peek to judge his reaction, but was met with a steady gaze and an impassive expression.

"Hmmm, let's see, where should I start?" She was talking to herself more than to Riley, but he answered her.

"Start at the beginning and go through to the end. I seem to remember saying I want to see the entire notebook."

"Yes, I guess you did say that, didn't you?" With a deep, fortifying breath, she began.

"The first thing is a sketch I did for the addition I mentioned. I really think it would be a good idea to have some distance from the guests, as I said before, and it seems to me like there would be plenty of room to build on behind the kitchen. Now, I don't claim to have your skills when it comes to drawing up plans, but you should be able to get the general idea."

Riley glanced at the paper but didn't say anything. Susan flipped a couple of pages showing Riley more on the addition. "Here's the stuff I jotted down about the event center in the barn. We've already talked about a lot of this." She turned the page again and added, "This is the idea I had for the bar."

Riley put his hand over hers when she made to

flip the page again and looked more closely at the sketch and notes she had jotted down regarding the bar. He pulled his small notepad from his pocket and wrote something quickly before nodding, indicating she should move on. Susan flipped through pages showing ideas for the attic rooms, beach, dock, gazebo, fire pit, chicken coop, and storage shed. There were photos of detailed porch railings, an ornate doorknob, shutters, and even a mailbox.

Susan skipped over a few blank pages and took a break for a slice of pizza before opening further back in the notebook. "That was my outside section. Back here I have ideas for inside." She showed him paint strips, fabric swatches, and china patterns. She had cited several websites on the pages with notes next to them. She had sketched built-in shelves surrounding the stone fireplace. There were several pages devoted to trim work, crown molding, stair railings, and newel posts as well as kitchen cabinets and appliances.

When she paused and looked up at him, Riley asked, "Those pages you skipped over? You're sure they were blank?"

"Yes, McCabe, they were blank."

"So is that everything?" He reached for the notebook but she slapped her hand down on it.

She hesitated just a moment then said, "Well, there's just one more thing, I haven't even gotten it in here yet, but I was wondering about adding fireplaces to some of the bedrooms."

"Gas fireplaces I hope?"

"I was thinking the real thing. I know it would be a lot of work and they're messy, but they're so romantic."

She watched as Riley closed his eyes in what seemed to her to be an especially long blink, before beginning. "First, you have some very good ideas." She brightened and sat a little higher in the booth. "But, there are some things I really think you should forget about. Just wait," he cautioned when she started to speak. "Next, we need to discuss your planned opening date. If you're sticking with the time frame we talked about when you first approached me with all this, you're going to have to forget about most of your new ideas. Otherwise, you'll have to push that date back."

"I guess that makes sense," Susan snuck in before Riley could continue.

"And I need to ask, when did you do all this?" He sounded totally perplexed and was shaking his head.

"I don't sleep much."

"Apparently not. You know, Susan, this is a long process. I understand the excitement that comes with undertaking a project like this and I understand how it can be tempting to try to make everything perfect, but you need to realize that scaling back on, or at least postponing, some of these ideas is going to be necessary. If you try to do all of this," he waved a hand toward the notebook, "you're going to have to wait a long time until you'll feel like it's done."

"Okay."

"Now, some of your ideas, if you really want to go through with them, should be done at the outset. The attic rooms, for example, would be difficult to do later. Not that it can't be done, but it would be an inconvenience having construction going on in the house when you have guests."

Susan nodded in agreement and Riley continued. "Personally, I think the event center could wait. It's away from the house, construction there wouldn't be such a problem sometime down the road. But, if you're set on having it ready for Sam and Jake's wedding then I'll figure out a way to get it done."

Susan felt happier by the moment and silently toasted herself with her glass of beer. Things were going better than she had expected. Riley hadn't ripped the notebook to shreds and he was actually complimenting her on some of her ideas.

"By the way, do Sam and Jake know they're having their wedding reception there? I meant to ask you why you avoided the subject of the event center with Sam the other day."

"Um, not exactly. Or, just no, I guess. I haven't brought it up with Sam yet. She's got some things she still needs to work through. We're going back to Chicago soon and after she puts some of her past behind her once and for all, I'll ease her into it."

Riley's attitude changed at the mention of Sam's past and he looked concerned as he asked, "Is she okay? I thought things were going well for her. Once that nut job was caught last summer and after she and Jake got engaged, she seemed to be a different person. When I first met her she had so much sadness inside her and was so closed off to everyone around her, but that seems to have all changed."

"You're pretty perceptive, McCabe." Susan gave Riley an approving nod. "She is so much better. If you had known her a year ago, you wouldn't believe it's the same person. Losing Danny and then Granddad and dealing with everything that came about after his death was almost more than she could bear. But, I think that now, with the wedding plans facing her and realizing that she really is moving on, things have been a little difficult. I'm confident going back to Chicago is what she needs and that she'll come back here ready to tackle the wedding planning. That's when I'll tell her my plans." Susan grinned smugly.

"Well, you have to know, I guess. Now, moving on. About the addition. I think that needs to wait. Hear me out," he said as she jumped to interrupt. "I'm not saying you should never do it. I think having a separate space for yourself is a very good idea. Maybe a sanity-saving idea. But an addition like you're talking about will be a big expense and will take a lot of time and manpower. Hold off a year and see how business is going, then make your decision. Building off the kitchen won't be too disruptive, work won't even be visible from the front of the house."

Susan was quiet, her mind working as she chewed on her lip and frowned. "I suppose you're right. I know I need to watch my budget, I sometimes forget about that part. But if everything goes well business-wise, maybe I can do it down the road." She forced a smile.

"What I can do is turn that weird extra room off the kitchen into a bathroom. I know you were planning on storage there but once I get the cellar waterproofed, I think you'll be fine using that for most of your storage. Then, with the bathroom and assuming you take the main floor bedroom for yourself, you'll still have some privacy."

"Oh, that's perfect! I hadn't thought of that. See, I knew there was a reason I hired you."

Riley chuckled. She was like no other woman he

had ever known. She wore her emotions very close to the surface. Whether she was angry, frustrated, or pleased about something was never in question. He sensed someone would never be on the receiving end of the silent treatment from her. He had known plenty of women, some he was related to, who would get upset or angry but never give a clue as to why. As if he was supposed to read their minds? With Susan, he figured, there would be some spirited discussion, some yelling, then it would be over and they would make up and move on.

Riley drew in a quick breath and blinked hard. How had his thoughts moved so seamlessly to picturing he and Susan arguing and making up? He stared at her trying to figure out what she had done to put such ridiculous thoughts in his head. It had to be her fault, he reasoned. She said something, did something, that had him imagining a life with her. His eyes bored into her searching for some way to place blame until she cleared her throat.

"Hey, McCabe, are you listening to me?"

"Huh?" It seemed to be all he could manage.

"I said, are you listening to me? I asked you what other plans of mine you're going to nix."

"Oh, um…" He struggled to remember what he had been telling her. Fireplaces, that was it. They were going to have a fireplace in their bedroom. No! Damn, he needed to get away. "I'll be right back," he mumbled and dashed from the booth to the men's room.

Susan stared after him wondering what had just happened. Before she had a chance to think too hard on it, Shauna sat down in Riley's just-vacated spot.

"What's with my brother? He almost sprinted

across the room. I hope he's not already so impossible to work with that you slipped him something in his beer."

Laughing, Susan answered, "No, I did not do that. Although, it's a good idea. I'll hang on to that one in case I need it later. I don't really know what got into him. We were talking about plans for the inn and all of a sudden he just kind of spaced out. Weird, really."

"Well, my brothers can be weird."

Changing tracks, Susan said, "I'm glad you stopped by, I want to ask you something."

"Shoot."

"Riley tells me you're into antiques, that you know what's what, and whether something may be valuable."

"I love antiques. I can't claim to know everything, but I've studied up on some things. Why?"

"Quite a bit of furniture, some knick-knacks, some other things were left behind at the farmhouse. I wouldn't know an antique table from one in Ikea's clearance bin. I was wondering if you'd be willing to come take a look, see if you think any of it is worth holding on to."

Shauna's face lit up. "I'd love to! Tomorrow?"

"Wow, really? You could come that soon?"

"Sure, I can't wait to see what you have."

"I can't promise there's anything of value but, like I said, I really don't know so you'd be doing me a big favor. I'm curious about the history of the house and about how far back some of the things might date. Oh, and I found a journal today from someone who lived there, I assume, and graduated from high school in 1949. It made me even more curious. I was telling Riley I wish I'd have some pictures of what it used to look like."

"You should talk to Frank. He did some research a few years back for Misty Lake's anniversary celebration. He found some old photos. I don't know if he has any of your place, but it'd be worth asking him."

"I'll do that," Susan answered as Riley reappeared. He seemed himself again and chatted for a few minutes with Shauna before she left with her friends.

Once they were alone again he picked up as if nothing had happened. "The last big thing I wanted to discuss with you is your idea for fireplaces. I know wood-burning sounds cozy and romantic and everything, but I really hope you'll listen to me when I tell you you're far better off with gas."

Riley hoped he sounded normal, he thought he did, but after what happened a few minutes ago, he wasn't sure of anything. He'd had to splash cold water on his face and give himself a serious talking to about his crazy fantasy, or whatever it had been, before he'd dared come back to the table. He had even considered he may be drunk, but then realized he'd only had one glass of beer so couldn't blame the alcohol. In the end, he'd decided with he and Susan spending so much time together, talking house, even coming across the old journal and imagining what life must have been like, it was only natural his mind had wandered a little. No big deal. It wouldn't happen again.

"Are you saying it wouldn't be possible to build wood-burning fireplaces or that you just don't want to?"

"Of course it would be possible, almost anything is possible, and it's not that I don't want to, but it's just a bad idea. Think about it. You've got the mess to deal with, you've got to be hauling wood in all winter long and, worst of all, you've got people who may have never used a fireplace trying to start a fire in their room. You're going to have embers burning holes in the rugs, smoke filling the house when someone doesn't do things correctly, and, who knows? You get a couple drinking a bottle of wine or two and deciding they want a little ambiance. Next thing you know the whole place is on fire."

"That's a little dramatic, don't you think?"

"Not entirely. Do you know how many house fires are the result of fireplaces? A lot. Just let them flip a switch and get almost the same effect."

"Okay, I'll go with gas. I'm letting you win most of the arguments tonight, in case you haven't noticed."

"You're not letting me win, my side is just the right side. But, thank you. Thank you for not putting up too big a fight. It makes me think we might be able to see this thing through. I was starting to have my doubts."

"Not me, I knew we'd make a good team." Riley coughed over the alarm that bubbled up in his throat, but Susan continued. "Now, you said 'the last big thing.' Are there more little things?"

Riley eyed her carefully, trying to be certain she was just talking about them as a business team and not something more, but couldn't decipher her expression. He was becoming paranoid, he decided. "Just a few. I think we already agreed the chicken coop is a no-go, right?" When she gave a half-hearted nod, he continued. "Some of the little details I'll leave to you. I'm not going to help you choose linens and china."

"Fair enough. Anything else?"

"I'm curious about something." He pulled out his

notepad and glanced at it. "The sketches you did for the event center were…interesting. What exactly do you have in mind out there?" They had already discussed some of the basics of the construction, but her sketches had grabbed his interest.

"I just thought it should have a little of the same feel as the main building. I don't think it would work to keep a lot of the original feel to the inn and then have some ultra-modern design in the event center, so I was playing around with ideas. I was thinking a bar top of reclaimed wood. I probably didn't do a very good job of sketching it."

"Reclaimed wood. Huh."

"Do you think it's a bad idea? I know granite is popular and I could go that route, but I just was thinking I could sort of design everything around the bar. I'm thinking old, or at least old-looking, brick on some of the walls with some of the original wood exposed, a reclaimed wood floor."

Riley was mystified as he responded. "I think it's a good idea. Strange, though, as I've been toying around with the idea of building a bar top from reclaimed wood. I haven't been able to talk a client into it yet so haven't been able to try it, but I've been itching to."

"Seeeee," Susan deliberately drew out the word while waving her finger back and forth between the two of them. "We've got a connection, McCabe."

He was afraid she was right. And it scared the hell out of him.

7

All Saturday, while Susan worked with Shauna sorting and sifting, she struggled to keep her mind from wandering. If she wasn't thinking about her evening with Riley, she was peeking out the window hoping to catch a glimpse of the lonely looking puppy she'd spotted nosing around the dumpster.

Shauna was in heaven and kept Susan hopping. She quickly got down to business and established three rigid categories: garbage (get rid of it now), potentially useful but not valuable (I'll leave it up to you to decide what to do with it), and treasure (don't you dare get rid of it). She ruthlessly assigned every item to one of the categories and surprised Susan more than once when an item Susan had been sure would be headed for the garbage pile elicited oohs and ahhs and was deemed treasure. Thank goodness for Shauna.

With every trip to the dumpster, Susan kept her

eyes peeled for the puppy. She filled a small bowl with dog food and set it where she and Riley had seen him. On her fourth trip outside she caught sight of him greedily devouring the food. Susan stopped in her tracks and quietly waited. After eating every bit of food and then licking the bowl until it flipped over at which point no amount of batting with his little paw was going to right it, he began sniffing around the dumpster, his tail wagging furiously. Slowly, Susan lowered herself to the ground and sat, leaving about fifteen yards between herself and the pup.

She watched for a few minutes, her heart melting, as he entertained himself with a small section of PVC pipe, rolling it, chasing it, barking at it, and, when it disappeared under the dumpster, plopping down on his backside and cocking his head as if wondering why the game had to end. Determined not to scare him off this time, Susan further lowered herself until she was lying on the ground, head resting on her folded arms, and making just the smallest amount of noise so as to get the puppy's attention. She watched out of the corner of her eye as he studied her, inching slowly closer.

Susan took a couple of pieces of paper from the box she'd been carrying and gently crushed one into a ball. Tossing it lightly into the air, she caught it and watched as the puppy quivered with excitement. She tossed it again, this time forward a bit, before crawling and scooping it up. After a few more tosses she was closer to the dog who was now unable to contain himself and was jumping up and down in place, yipping enthusiastically. Ever so gently, she rolled the paper ball to him. He pounced on it, clenched it in his mouth with all his might, and swung his head back and forth prepared to do whatever it might take to vanquish that particular enemy.

"Oh, so ferocious," Susan crooned, as he happily shredded the paper. She crumpled another piece and immediately had the puppy's attention. Unable to control himself, he charged at Susan and launched himself into her lap. He licked her face and bit at her hair while she laughed and hugged him tight.

That's how Riley found her, rolling around on the ground and giggling while the dog jumped on her and over her. He couldn't tell who was having more fun. Susan looked so carefree, the stress and worry that went along with the remodel forgotten for the moment, and it pulled at Riley's heart. He wanted to fight it, even tried to tell himself it was more about the puppy than about her, but he couldn't. When she spotted him and her face lit up even more, he knew he'd do whatever he could to keep her looking just that way.

"Look, he came back!"

"I see that," Riley said, taking a seat beside her and getting a dose of puppy love for himself.

"Why are you here on a Saturday? You're always accusing me of working too much."

"I don't know, a little bored, I guess." And, he realized, he had wanted to see her. "Frank's working so the house was quiet. I thought I'd see how you and Shauna are doing then maybe put in a couple of hours."

"Hmmm." Turning her attention back to the puppy she asked, "How old do you think he is?"

"He doesn't look very old, I'd say a few months. It looks like he still has his puppy teeth," Riley added as the pup chomped playfully on his finger.

"Do you think he's lost? Abandoned?" Susan asked hugging him protectively.

"From the looks of him, it seems like he's been on his own for a while. He's thin, dirty, and apparently starving." They watched as he tried to eat the cardboard box Susan had been hauling outside. "If someone was trying to find him you'd think they would have. It doesn't seem like he's roaming too far."

"I suppose we should check?"

Riley guessed she wanted to hear that it wasn't necessary, but he knew it was. "We can check with Doc Fischer. If someone is missing him, they probably contacted the vet. We can ask Jake, too. Sometimes people will call the sheriff's office to try to find out if a stray has been picked up."

"Okay," Susan answered half-heartedly. "Well, I'm not going to think about it right now." She scooped up the puppy and stood. "I'm going to take him inside until I'm done here. I don't want to take the chance he runs off again." She nuzzled him and he buried his head under her chin. Riley found himself hoping there wasn't a little boy somewhere crying for his lost puppy.

After Shauna had her chance to fuss over him and he lapped up a bowl of water, Susan got a blanket from her trunk and settled the puppy into a corner where he promptly fell asleep. Work continued around him but not even Riley's electric saw roused him.

Inquiries to the vet, the sheriff's office, the nearby animal shelter, as well as online searches all turned up nothing. Susan had taken the pup to Dr. Fischer who determined he didn't have a microchip then checked him out, gave him a clean bill of health, and put his age at around three months. Susan knew she'd have to wait a bit longer to see if anyone responded to the lost pet notices she had posted in town and online, but with every passing day, he felt more and more like hers.

Sam was more than happy to welcome the puppy but her dog, Rigi, was nothing short of ecstatic. Rigi took it upon herself to train the puppy in the house rules and soon had a willing and able partner to help patrol the yard and keep it safe from all unwanted birds and squirrels. The fact that the puppy had to work twice as hard as Rigi to run the same distance was a blessing. He was usually so tired after a romp with Rigi that he was more than ready to climb in his crate and sleep, continuing the war on critters in his dreams.

Frank clicked and explained. "So you just drag the photo you want into this box and it will show up on your home page. You'll be able to add photos later on if you want to have, say, a separate section for each room or for special events, whatever you decide."

"It's really that easy?" Susan was skeptical. She could use a computer, but building her own website seemed daunting. When Frank had volunteered to spend an afternoon helping her get started, she had jumped at the chance.

"It really is. I didn't know much when I started either, but with this web page builder, a lot of the work is already done for you. It's really just a matter of adding photos, adding content, details that make it your own. For the B&B, I would guess you'd want a number of photos to showcase the property and the different rooms. You'll want to add pricing information, and here," he pointed to the upper right-hand corner of the screen, "you'll put your contact information."

"Wow. I think I can do this." Susan beamed as she clicked on the contact information tab and added a link for email. "I'm not going to put a phone number in yet since I only have my cell phone and I don't want to give that. As I get closer to opening, I'll set up a business line." She kept talking as she keyed in information and continued to browse photos in an attempt to decide what to put on the home page.

"You're right about your cell number, you definitely don't want that on the website. With the email address you've created for the inn, people will be able to contact you easily enough."

"I can't imagine getting inquiries into the B&B before it's even ready to open."

"I bet you do. Maybe even a reservation."

Susan's stomach gave a little lurch at the thought. It was exciting and terrifying in equal measure. She allowed herself a few minutes to fantasize then asked, "So, what do you think? Put the conceptual drawing of the inn on the front page or this one?" She indicated a stunning photo Frank had recently taken of the lake from her property with the fall color at its peak, lining the shores and reflected on the clear, smooth surface of the lake.

"I guess I'm partial to my photo," he grinned.

"It is incredible, definitely a contender." Turning, she studied him. So much like his twin. From the way they walked to the way they both tended to run a hand through their hair when frustrated to the rich sound of their laughter, it was clear they were twins. But there were subtle differences, she was learning. Riley liked to think about things, to take his time before answering or making a decision. Frank tended to go with the flow, a little more easy-going than his brother. But, at the same time, something told Susan Frank might be the more softhearted of the two. Frank also seemed to have more patience as evidenced by him sitting with her for hours teaching her how to set up and manage a website. She couldn't picture Riley sitting still for so long. It fit, she figured. A photographer needed patience, needed to be willing to wait for the perfect shot. For a contractor, on the other hand, it wouldn't do to spend much time waiting.

Physically, there were differences as well. Susan had seen pictures of the two as children when they had been, in her opinion at least, identical. Now, as men, each had his own look. Where Riley's brown hair leaned toward auburn, Frank's was a slightly lighter shade, with, she noticed, a few golden tints. Susan guessed their heights would be within a fraction of an inch of the other but Riley had a few pounds on his brother. Frank's face had sharper angles; Riley's was fuller. The eyes, however, were identical in their dark, almost navy blue, intensity.

She noticed him looking at her, probably wondering why she was staring. "Frank, I really can't thank you enough for everything you've done. The pictures you're taking of the inn as it moves through different phases of reconstruction are amazing. I'm going to use them on the website and also plan on having some framed to hang once the place is done. And now you're helping me get my website up and running…it's just so much. I am truly grateful."

"No problem. Since I went through setting up my website not that long ago, it only makes sense I pass on what I learned. Besides, you gave me your okay to use some of the photos in my advertising, that helps me out, too." He seemed to debate with himself for a moment before continuing. "There's another project I've been tossing around in my head and I may ask you for permission to use some of the before and after photos I'm taking of the inn for that, as well."

"Oh, of course. What is it?" she asked. Then backing off some, added, "Or don't you want to talk about it yet?" She didn't want to push too hard but, as usual, curiosity was eating at her.

"It's in the very beginning stages, I haven't even mentioned it to my family. There's this magazine, a very famous one, that approached me about submitting some photos as a sort of audition for a feature they're doing on restoring and reviving old farmhouses and barns, like what you're doing here. The editor who contacted me said he had come across my work from an advertising shoot I did a year or so ago, that brought him to my website, and when he saw the early photos I took of your place, he contacted me. If they want me, and if I do it, it could open up a lot of doors."

"That's fantastic, Frank. You must be so excited." She couldn't miss the guarded look in his eyes. "But you're not sure you want the exposure?" she guessed.

"I'm not sure. If they like my work, I'd be traveling all around the country collecting photographs for their story. It's an incredible opportunity. Not only would I be on their radar for future projects, but having my name attached to this publication would virtually ensure I'd be known in all the biggest photography circles."

"Which would mean leaving Misty Lake, probably heading to New York or Los Angeles or somewhere, and adopting a completely different lifestyle."

"That's about right. I'm not sure it's me. A few years ago I would have jumped at the chance. When I first started out I dreamed of an opportunity like this. Now? I do a good business, I'm near my family, I'm happy, content. Makes me sound old and boring, doesn't it?"

"No, it makes you sound like you know what you want, what makes you happy."

Frank shrugged. "I have some time to think about it. My submission wouldn't be due until spring."

Susan laid a hand on his arm and smiled. "Then think about it. I'm sure you'll come to the right decision."

"You really need to give him a name," Riley said as they watched the dog race in circles trying to catch his tail.

"I know, I've just been afraid to. If I name him it seems permanent and I've been so afraid someone is going to claim him." It had been almost two weeks and though she was cautiously hopeful, Susan still couldn't shake the feeling that she'd wake up one morning to a message that someone had lost a dog matching his description.

"Doc said two weeks, we're almost there."

"You're right. Let's name him right now. I can't keep calling him puppy and sweetie."

"No, you can't. He's going to start to be embarrassed in front of his friends."

That got a chuckle out of Susan. "Do you have any suggestions?"

"I don't want to influence you. What have you

been thinking?"

"Well, I've tossed around a couple of ideas." She hesitated then said, "I was thinking Chewie after Chewbacca and because that's what he seems to love to do, but I've kind of already talked myself out of it."

Riley nodded in agreement. "What else?"

"Barney, but he seems to have too much energy for a Barney."

"Agreed. Next?"

"I've considered Marvin, Finley, Harley, and Gus but nothing sounds quite right."

Riley watched the dog that had now lost interest in his tail and was racing in circles in the yard for no discernable reason. "He does have a lot of energy." Riley thought for a moment. "What about instead of Gus, Gusto?"

"Gusto." Susan tried it out, repeated it a couple of times, then called the dog. "Gusto, come!" He looked up, stumbled a little, his racing in circles apparently having left him slightly dizzy, then bounded toward Susan and ran headlong into her legs.

"He seems to like it," Riley laughed.

"I think you're right. We have a winner, Gusto it is." Susan bent to pick up the dog, already more difficult than it had been a couple of weeks ago, and held him towards Riley. "Give him a kiss and tell him thank you for your name."

The dog obediently nuzzled Riley and licked his chin. "He sure loves you," Susan said to Riley who now had the dog in his arms.

Riley could tell by the tone of her voice she was

building up to something. He waited her out. She kicked at some dried leaves, picked up a stick and broke it in half, zipped up her jacket, and pulled her phone out of her pocket to snap a picture of Riley holding Gusto before finally speaking again.

"I was wondering, since he likes you so much and since you're here so much during the day...I know it would be a lot of work and I understand you're busy, but he's so comfortable around you and I hate to leave him at a kennel so soon after taking him in..."

He finally took pity on her. "Do you want me to keep him while you go to Chicago?"

The tension seemed to dissolve from Susan's shoulders. "Oh, Riley, would you? Jake's going to be staying at Sam's to watch Rigi and Sam said I could leave him there, but Jake will be gone long hours sometimes. Rigi can handle it but Gusto's just a baby and still getting used to everything. I hate the thought of leaving him in his crate all day. Not that you can't put him in the crate when he's here, you can, he likes it fine, it would just be good if he didn't have to stay in there for too long at one stretch. He—"

"Red, take a breath, I said I'd do it." Setting the dog down, he wrapped his arm around her shoulder and pulled her close. "He'll be fine, I've taken care of dogs before."

Susan looked up at him, relief in her eyes. "Thank you, Riley. I'll feel so much better knowing you have him. Maybe you can take him over to Sam's once or twice and let him run with Rigi, he likes that. Or, maybe Jake would bring Rigi over here. Either way, it would be nice if they could get together. And I'll write down when he eats and how much so you don't have to worry about that."

"I'll make sure he cleans his plate and I'll schedule play dates for him," Riley teased. "And I'll read to him before bed and make sure he listens to classical music."

"Okay, okay, very funny. I know I'm a little crazy when it comes to him but he had such a rough start, didn't you boy?" She bent down to rub his ears. Gusto leaned against her legs savoring every moment.

"I'll take good care of him," Riley assured her. "I like him too, you know." He joined her on the ground and the three wrestled until the dog finally tired.

When he woke up he was in the backseat of the car and they were driving again. He couldn't remember getting in the car, Mommy must have carried him while he was sleeping. The last thing he remembered was his mom giving him some chicken nuggets and orange soda then turning on the TV and making him promise not to go anywhere while she was gone. She hadn't told him where she was going and he'd been scared. He had almost started to cry, but he knew she'd get mad so he'd squeezed his eyes shut tight. He'd eaten his nuggets and finished most of the soda then curled up on the couch to watch SpongeBob while he waited for her to come back.

Even though he didn't know where they were going, he was glad they left that man's house. He was mean. Mommy said he was her friend but he was mean to Mommy, too. And Mommy kept leaving with him and then he'd be alone. He wasn't going to think about it any more because he hoped they wouldn't have to go back.

Right now, though, he had to pee. He was afraid to ask his mom to stop, but he didn't think he could wait much longer. "Mommy, I have to pee," he said softly.

"What?" It seemed to take a minute for her to remember he was in the back seat. "Oh, hey buddy. Did you have a good nap? We'll stop soon, I promise. Are you hungry?" She turned and smiled back at the boy.

The boy nodded but didn't say anything. Sometimes it was scarier when Mommy was happy. She'd be nice and talk to him and play with him but then get mad again and he never knew why. And sometimes she got mad just because he talked. She said it made her head hurt. He couldn't tell if this was one of those times so he decided not to say anything yet. He fidgeted in the seat and hoped she would stop soon.

8

"So, how was the trip?" It was the first time Susan and Riley had had time to catch up since Susan's return from Chicago. She had agreed to the extra shifts on her schedule in exchange for her time away, but they were turning out to be draining.

"Exactly what I had hoped for." Susan smiled as she looked around at the progress Riley had made on the house. "I knew it would do Sam wonders to go back. She was nervous on the drive down, she almost convinced me to turn around once, but, in the end, she agreed it was just what she needed."

"Good. She's seemed at ease since getting back."

"She is. She visited some of her friends, spent some time talking things out with the family, and made a trip to the cemetery. I think she found the final little bit of closure she needed. And it's full steam ahead with the wedding plans. She bought a dress while we were there and now she's talking flowers, cake, and all the details."

"Have you discussed having the reception here yet?"

"No, but soon. The time hasn't been quite right."

"Don't wait too long or she'll make other arrangements."

"Don't worry, I've got it all under control," Susan grinned. "Did you hear everyone is coming for Thanksgiving?"

"I did. I was told Thanksgiving dinner will be at Sam's this year and that the McCabe clan will be dining with the Taylors. My mom already sat us down and told us she expects our best behavior. It's like she thinks we're still kids and are going to start a food fight or something," he grumbled.

"Oh, McCabe, I've seen you and your brothers in action. I don't blame your mother in the least."

"Hah! I bet you and your brothers do the same thing."

"Well, I can't deny that. You know, I wouldn't be surprised if my mom has the same talk with my brothers before they come."

"Should be an interesting day. Do you think everyone will be afraid to talk?"

"I think we'll manage. Mia and Karen will have plenty of baby stuff to talk about. They're due just about the same time and from what I've seen from the both of them, it's their favorite topic, hands down. Brad and Joe will have a couple of drinks, realize they're both secretly terrified of becoming dads, and will end up admitting their deepest, darkest fears to one another. The rest of the guys will watch football and bond over sports, that's a no-brainer. And our moms? They are so much alike I give it ten minutes until they're acting like long-lost sisters. Just be prepared for my mom to pull every McCabe family secret out of your mom. She's got some sort of weird magic she wields and people are helpless. They tell her everything."

Riley just shook his head. She had hit it on the head, he figured, and could envision the day going exactly as she predicted. "I guess I'd better steer clear of your mom."

Susan laughed. "I'll try to get her to go easy on you. Besides, once I put my plan into action, our moms will be busy with wedding business."

"Your plan?"

"Sure, I told you I have it all under control. My plan is to get Sam and Jake to firm up their date when everyone is together. Then I'll mention the event center and that the B&B will be almost ready to open and that I would love to have everyone stay there as a trial run kind of thing. No one will be able to say no." Susan was grinning proudly, obviously pleased with her grand scheme and, like usual, not seeing any potential flaws.

Riley hated to burst her bubble, but felt he needed to be the voice of reason. "Okay, Red, back up for just a minute and let me be sure I'm understanding this. You want to not only have the reception here, but also host everyone at the B&B? Your first guests and your first event all at the same time? Do you think Sam is going to be understanding if everything she has been planning comes crashing down around her?"

"You have that little faith in me?"

She seemed genuinely hurt and Riley regretted his

words. Softening his tone, he tried a gentler approach. "I'm just worried that both your first guests and your first event are going to be such major milestones that maybe it would be better to space them out a little. You could have the reception here but let everyone find someplace else to stay. That way you could devote all your attention to the reception and not have to worry about keeping everyone comfortable and fed."

She still seemed hurt, but now some of the hurt was replaced by the all-familiar fighting spirit. "I look at it this way. Having family here means if I make a mistake or two I won't have disappointed guests leaving bad reviews on my website. With family, I'd like to think I'd be allowed a misstep without ramifications. What better way to test everything out?"

"Who's going to do all the work? You're the maid of honor. I would guess there are some things in that job description that will require your attention."

"True, but I've already thought about that. Obviously I'll need to hire some help here, someone who knows the hotel business, who knows her way around a kitchen, and who's good with people. I talked to my friend Cassie when I was back in Chicago. She's interested. I think."

Again, her ability to look forward and plan left him impressed. "You've already talked to someone about working for you?"

"Sure. Cassie is amazing, I need her here so I'm not going to wait around too long. She has experience working at both small and large hotels. She more or less ran a resort for a couple of years where she did everything from working in the kitchen to tracking and ordering inventory to planning guest activities to cleaning rooms. She's still at the Billingsley right now and hates it as much, or more, than I did. She's admitted she wants out, I just have to convince her Misty Lake is the right place for her."

"That might not be so easy if she's used to Chicago."

"Oh, I know, but I'm persuasive," Susan grinned.

"That, I'll give you. But back to my original argument. There will be bugs to work out during your first run at hosting an event. Is Sam going to be okay with that? It's her wedding, after all."

"Sam's pretty easy going, but I don't plan on taking advantage of that. I'll have everything running smoothly, you'll see."

He wanted to argue more, to get her to see she was putting too much pressure on herself, but could tell she wasn't going to back down. Maybe Sam would have something to say about her plans. Deciding to change the subject to something he knew would catch her interest he said, "Frank didn't have any luck finding old pictures of this place. He looked through his files from when he did the research for the town's anniversary celebration and also checked out a few other sources. Sorry, I know you were hoping for some photos."

"He did all that? That's so sweet of him. Too bad he couldn't find anything, though. I read through the journal and am more curious than ever. I haven't had a chance to tell you everything I learned." Her eyes were sparkling and thoughts of wedding receptions were forgotten for the moment.

"Did he turn out to be a bank robber or something equally as exciting?"

Susan gave him a condescending look and a tsk before continuing. "No, it would seem our Charlie Walker was a pretty normal teenager. He wrote about life on the farm, about school, and about his girlfriend Rosemary. It sounded like they were so much in love. There were entries about their dates, about sharing ice cream at the church picnic, and about his plans to save up enough money to marry her after she graduated from high school. Then the entries just stop until one last entry scribbled in the back of the book where he talks of leaving Misty Lake and moving to California with his new wife Martha. There's no date so I don't know how much time passed, but somehow it seemed it was months rather than years. The entry is short but so sad. I could tell he was heartbroken. He wrote about how he hated leaving everything behind. I know it was more than his home and the town, I know he was thinking of Rosemary, although there's no mention of her by name. I wonder what happened?"

"I don't know. I guess people can fall in and out of love. Maybe Rosemary found someone else."

Susan shook her head. "I didn't get that feeling. I don't suppose I'll ever know what really happened, but it seems like there's more to the story. The fact that he left the journal behind is telling, too, I think. Something must have happened that left him changed somehow and not wanting to document his life any longer. Almost like he was starting over but not necessarily in a good way."

"Or maybe you're just reading too much into it?"

Susan snorted. "Men. You're all hopeless."

Riley laughed. Gusto chose that moment to decide it was time to go outside and began racing from Riley and

Susan to the door. Obliging, the two followed the rambunctious dog out into the yard and watched as he chased leaves in the waning daylight.

"I guess I need to be careful what I wish for, it's freezing out here." Susan pulled her jacket tighter around her neck. The wind was strong off the lake and was forcing loose many of the leaves still clinging to the trees, sending them twirling through the air.

Riley watched as the wind took hold of Susan's hair and lifted it, swirling it wildly, like golden flames unable to settle in one spot. As she chased the puppy around the yard, the color rose in her cheeks and her eyes danced. She gathered leaves into a pile and tossed them in the air for Gusto to chase. Riley simply couldn't resist. Sneaking up behind her, he grabbed her by the waist and dumped her in the leaves. Susan squealed as she went tumbling, coming to rest on top of Riley in the pile of leaves.

She pulled leaves from her hair and sputtered, "What, may I ask, did I do to deserve that?"

"Nothing in particular. It just seemed like it needed to be done."

She couldn't hide her grin. "Just needed to be done. I see. Keep that in mind if you happen to find yourself suddenly going for an unplanned swim or, better yet, face down in a snow bank." She held up her arm as the first few snowflakes settled on her jacket sleeve.

"I'd like to see you try."

"Oh, you'll do more than see me try, McCabe," she warned. Then, curious, she asked, "Does it always snow here before November? Seems like that would make for an awfully long winter."

"Not always, but often. And yes, winter can be long. Very long. But there are good things about winter in Misty Lake. Ever been ice fishing?"

"Can't say as though I have. It sounds horrible."

"Actually, you'd be surprised. A nice fish house, some music, a stocked cooler, and a good stove? Magic. If the fish are biting it's a bonus."

"Hmmm. That's all you've got? Ice fishing?"

"No, there's snowmobiling, cross country skiing, snow shoeing, pond hockey, broomball…the options are endless."

"I think you've lived here too long."

"You'll see. Besides, you're going to have to believe in all the fun Misty Lake has to offer in the winter if you expect to attract guests year round."

"I guess you're right about that." Then, getting a devilish look in her eyes, she added, "Well, then this is probably a good time to tell you about that page in my notebook I didn't show you at The Brick."

Riley drew back and said, "Now wait a minute, I specifically asked and you promised me you showed me everything."

Susan fought mightily to keep the smile off her face and said timidly, "Just one page, at the back, that I was afraid to show you." Riley's eyes darkened as he sat up straighter. "It was just the page I called 'Riley teaches Susan how to love winter in Misty Lake.'" With that, she scooped up a pile of leaves, tossed them in his face, and was off like a shot before he could fully grasp that she'd only been yanking his chain.

9

Riley worked later than he had planned and Susan hung around helping when she could, but mostly trying to stay out of the way. She enjoyed watching the progress and was intrigued by the work that took the ideas she had envisioned and brought them to life. She asked a lot of questions of Riley and, to his credit, he was patient and explained the process in as much detail as she seemed to want. Sometimes he needed a hand holding something in place and she was more than willing to help. When he let her operate the nail gun and help erect a section of wall, she was thrilled.

Eventually, he began packing up and, taking a look at the time, started moving quicker.

"I thought maybe we could go grab something to eat," Susan said.

"Sorry, I don't have time tonight. I need to be somewhere."

"Oh." She wanted to ask where, whether he had a date, but decided it was really none of her business. She watched him for clues, to see if his eyes would give anything away, but he kept his back to her.

"Actually, I have a hockey game."

Not at all what she had expected to hear, it was relief that hit her first followed quickly by curiosity. She'd have to give the feeling of relief some more thought later but for now, curiosity won out. "A hockey game? You mean you're playing in a hockey game? Or you're going to watch a hockey game?"

"I'm playing. Frank and I play in a men's league, we have for years, tonight's our first game of the season."

"Ooh." The idea of watching Riley play hockey fascinated her, something else she'd have to think about later, and she thought back to the articles she'd seen on the wall at his house. "Where do you play?"

"There's a rink next to the high school. Usually we get stuck with the latest ice times, but somehow we got a pretty decent one tonight. I wasn't really watching the time so I need to get moving if I'm going to be able to grab a sandwich and not be late."

Susan watched him hurry to straighten up, no doubt wanting everything in order for the morning. He didn't seem anxious to invite her along to watch and she vacillated between inviting herself and hoping he would do it. In the end, she figured waiting for a man to read her feelings was an exercise in futility so she asked, "Do you ever have an audience? I'd love to watch the dynamic duo in action."

Riley struggled with how to answer. The only

women who came to watch were wives or serious girlfriends. And even then, not often. He knew that if he brought Susan along he'd face a barrage of questions as well as heckling from the team. He wasn't sure he was ready, or willing, to deal with it. But when he saw her waiting hopefully for his answer, he knew there was only one he could give her. "Sure, you can come watch if you want. I can't promise great hockey, but you're welcome to come along."

Susan gave a little clap and beamed. "Wonderful. How about if I meet you there? I'll drop off Gusto, grab a warmer jacket, and head over."

"Okay, Red, game's at eight." With that, he headed out and mentally prepared for the thrashing he knew he'd face once the guys spotted Susan in the stands.

"You should have seen them," Susan raved, "they were unstoppable." She and Sam were in their pajamas, each curled up in front of the fire with a glass of wine and a blanket, their dogs dozing at their feet. "It was like they always knew where the other one was without even looking."

Sam smiled. Susan had been telling her about Riley's three goals off Frank's three assists since she came home. "I'll have to come watch some time."

"I don't know, I got the feeling they aren't used to an audience. I think Riley took quite a bit of heat for letting me tag along." She shrugged. "Whatever. I'm glad I went, but I took the hint when Riley said the team was going out for a beer and he *supposed* I could come along if I really wanted."

"Subtle," Sam said. "I guess they need their guy

time."

Susan brushed it aside. "Sure, I get it. Riley said it was their first game this season, I'm sure there was catching up to do."

They talked a bit longer about the hockey game with Sam asking questions at the appropriate times before changing the subject. "Tomorrow's Halloween. I don't expect there will be any kids here so I'm going to Jake's to hand out candy with him. Do you have plans or do you want to come along?"

"I hadn't really thought about it. Time is going so quickly. If I had stayed in Chicago I'd have already planned out the holiday decorations at the Billingsley and instead I didn't even realize that tomorrow is Halloween. A different way of life, that's for sure."

"But better, don't you think?"

"Definitely better. You know, I thought I'd be homesick and that I'd miss the excitement of the city, but I don't. Not at all. I love staying busy with the work at the B&B, working at It's a Lake Thing is so fun it hardly seems like a job some days, and this fellow," she gave Gusto a little nudge with her toe, "keeps me hopping. I'm happier than I've been in a long time."

"How much of that has to do with one Riley McCabe?" Sam asked.

Automatically, Susan opened her mouth to deny Sam's insinuations but then closed it. She couldn't fool her cousin any more than she could fool herself. Probably less so. "I've been trying to figure that out. Tonight I asked him if he wanted to go get something to eat when he finished working and when he told me he had plans, this weird feeling hit me. I'm not sure if it was jealousy, hurt, or just plain curiosity, but whatever it was, it wasn't something I've felt before and I didn't know what to do with it."

Sam nodded knowingly. "I think it's called love, sweetie."

"Oh, I don't think so, I hardly know him and mostly we drive each other crazy."

"There's no set time frame, these things just have a way of happening."

"Listen to you, all of a sudden you're an expert? I seem to remember just a few months ago I was trying to get you to believe you were in love with Jake and you were denying it."

"See? My point exactly. These things have a way of just happening whether we're ready for it or not."

Susan turned and watched the snow fall. She definitely had some things to think about.

10

The autumn that had taken its sweet time arriving in Misty Lake chose not to stick around for long. Winter took a firm grasp and showed no signs of letting go. As Thanksgiving approached, the snow piled up and the temperature dropped. Thankfully the roof was completed and enough electrical and plumbing work done that the house was relatively comfortable in spite of the weather. Progress moved quickly and there were changes every time Susan stopped by. She had started narrowing her choices on appliances, linens, and stain colors. The whole process was more real with every passing day.

Susan had kept in touch with Cassie and felt like she was getting closer to convincing her to make the move. According to Cassie, Stephen Billingsley had become even more impossible and Cassie had to force herself to go to work each day. Susan was confident it wouldn't be long before Cassie at least agreed to come and check out Misty Lake.

Susan's family arrived the day before Thanksgiving and, with the exception of Kyle who had seen Sam's home the previous summer, were all amazed and somewhat dumbfounded at the place William Taylor had built without letting any of them in on the secret. There was a great deal of reminiscing about times spent on Misty Lake. At that time, there was nothing more than a small cabin on the lot but, for the joy it brought, it could have been ten times the size of the home now occupying the spot. Susan could tell Sam enjoyed the trip down memory lane and, unlike it would have done just months ago, it brought her much more happiness than pain and sadness. She watched as Sam leaned into Jake and smiled, relaxed and in love, and free from the nightmares that had haunted her for so long.

Thanksgiving. The house was full of people, laughter, and food, exactly as it should be, Riley thought as he took in the crowd around him. Dinner was over, the dishes washed, the television tuned to football, and every available seat filled. He made his way across the room to Susan who was standing slightly outside the group, seemingly taking in the surroundings much as he had been doing. As he approached, she waved her arm to encompass the room.

"Didn't I tell you? Exactly as I predicted."

Riley had been thinking the same thing. The men, with the exception of Joe and Brad, were all glued to the football game and had begun a friendly argument over their Super Bowl predictions. A laugh broke out from the corner of the room and he turned to see Karen and Mia with their hands on one another's baby bumps. Nodding towards the women he said to Susan, "You were right about those two, that's for sure. They've hardly talked to anyone else."

"They have a lot to discuss. First baby for each of them, I'm sure it's comforting to talk with someone who's in the same position." She lowered her voice. "And even though they both refused to tell their baby's gender or give any hint as to names they're considering, I'm pretty sure they told each other."

Riley gave her a doubtful look. "I don't know, they were both pretty adamant during dinner. Shauna tried every trick in the book to get them to spill the beans."

"They told each other, I can tell. Some kind of pregnant woman bond of secrecy, I suppose." Then, pointing subtly to Joe and Brad who were standing as far away from the rest of the group as possible, she said, "Look at those two. Sometimes I think they seem a little more relaxed then it's as if one brings up something the other hadn't thought of yet and panic sets in again."

Riley watched as the fathers-to-be both sipped nervously on their drinks, glanced over at their wives, then lowered their heads together again, apparently discussing some newly realized terror. Riley laughed when Joe's head jerked up, his eyes wide as he looked over at Karen and Mia, then ran a hand through his hair and tipped his glass to his lips only to realize there was nothing left but ice. He snagged Brad's glass and headed to the bar.

"Our moms are in the kitchen with Sam looking at catalogs and talking wedding plans." Susan gave Riley a satisfied grin and repeated, "Exactly as I predicted."

"Speaking of wedding plans, I thought you were

going to bring up the reception. Aren't you worried they're making plans for it right now?"

"Soon." She glanced at the television. "Actually, just a few minutes now. Halftime, when I have everyone's attention."

"I hope you know what you're doing."

"I always do."

Riley gave her a skeptical look but refrained from commenting. Instead he pointed to a sunny spot in front of the windows where his great aunts Kate and Rose had made themselves comfortable. "Maybe we should give Shauna a break."

"You're probably right."

Shauna had been sitting with the women, attempting to keep up with their stories and serving as waitress, refilling their drinks when requested. She looked up gratefully when Susan and Riley approached and made a speedy exit.

"Did you enjoy the dinner?" Riley asked as he and Susan sat down.

"It was nice, dear," Rose answered, then turning to her sister said, "A turkey dinner is never quite the same without Mother's stuffing though, don't you agree?"

"I know how to make Mother's stuffing, you just won't admit that it's just as good."

"There's something different when you make it, I've told you that countless times."

"It's exactly the same, Rose, you just don't remember what Mother's tasted like."

"Of course I remember what Mother's tasted like!"

"It's been almost forty years."

"I remember it, Kathryn," Rose said slowly and forcefully, eyeing her sister as if daring her to contradict her again.

Riley spoke up, not wanting to have to mediate an argument between the two. "Susan found some recipes at the old house she bought."

"What's that, dear?" Kate asked looking at Riley as if trying to figure out when he had arrived.

"I was just saying that Susan found some recipes and some other things left behind at the house she bought. Remember I told you I'm working there doing the remodel?"

"That's right, you said you have a big job ahead of you." Kate turned to Susan and asked, "Now, where is that house? Is it on the lake?"

"Yes, not too far from here. It used to be a farm. The house is big and there's a barn, as well. I have plans to turn it—"

"Rosie, do you remember that big house that used to sit on the corner of Main Street? What was the family's name?"

"Do you mean the Meachams?"

"That's it. Oh, remember that nasty Doris Meacham? She thought she was so much better than the rest of us with her shiny shoes and her silk hair ribbons."

"I remember the time you pushed her in the mud puddle after school and she ran all the way home crying. When her mother came marching up to our door I thought for sure you were going to get whooped," Rose laughed at the memory.

"I'll never forget how Mother told Mrs. Meacham that if she would teach her daughter some manners maybe things like that wouldn't happen." Kate gave a hoot and slapped her hand to her leg. "Mother was strict but she didn't let anyone take advantage of us, no matter how much money they had."

"And mother made the best turkey stuffing," Rose mumbled.

Riley intervened before Kate could respond. "Maybe you remember who used to live in the house that Susan bought. She's curious about the family that lived there."

"What house is that, dear?" Kate asked Riley.

Patiently Riley replied, "Susan bought an old farmhouse on the lake, I think it's the last farmhouse still standing out here. It's just a couple of miles west. Do you know who used to live there?"

"I found an old journal," Susan added. "It made me curious about the history of the place. The boy who wrote the journal was named Charlie Walker. Does that sound familiar?"

Rose seemed to tense and Kate looked down at her hands clasped tightly in her lap before looking back up at her sister. "I don't recognize that name," she said quickly.

"How about you, Aunt Rose, do you remember anyone with that name?"

Rose stared straight ahead then said, "I wonder whatever happened to that Doris Meacham? She probably ended up marrying some rich man who bought her everything she could ever want. But I'll bet she's never been happy a day in her life."

Susan gave Riley a questioning look but before either could ask anything else, Rose pushed slowly to her feet. "Excuse me for a moment, won't you?"

"Sometimes Rosie gets mixed up," Kate said forcing a laugh. "Be a dear and refill our drinks, Riley. That will give me a chance to tell Susan about the time your mother was under the weather and I took you to the dentist." Turning to Susan she continued, "He got mad at me and threatened to jump out of the car. He fiddled with the door handle long enough that it finally opened and he fell right out while we were moving." Kate continued telling her story, but kept an eye on her sister as she slowly made her way across the room.

Susan wanted to ask more questions about her house but just as Riley returned with fresh drinks, the group watching football started moving from their spots, stretching, and some heading to the kitchen in search of leftovers. It was halftime and Susan was the halftime act.

11

"I'm not sure why we're doing this on a Sunday," Riley grumbled as he and Susan made their way across the snowy yard to the barn. Gusto ran in front of them, jumping up to try to catch the snowflakes falling heavily all around.

"You're always so busy during the week, people are asking you questions and you have a dozen different things going, you'd never have time go over all this uninterrupted," Susan smiled up at him. "Seriously though, thank you for meeting me here. I'll feel better when we iron out all the details."

Susan had given everyone the run-down of her plans on Thanksgiving and, somewhat surprising to Riley, Sam and Jake had agreed to hold their reception at Susan's proposed event center. Not that there hadn't been questions and concerns, especially from Susan's parents who were convinced she had bitten off more than she could chew, but, as Riley had come to expect from her, Susan had managed to convince everyone she had things well under control.

"I think your mom had a valid point when she said people who come to a B&B will be expecting quiet and relaxation, not a bachelorette party raging across the lawn."

"She's right. I had given that some thought before, but after hearing everyone's opinion, I've decided that in order to use the event center, the group will need to book all the rooms, as well. I think it makes sense. If they have a group big enough to use the facility, they should be able to fill up the inn. If not, I can provide alternatives in town."

They were brushing snow off their jackets and stomping to clean off their boots. "I hope my family beat this storm," Susan said, worriedly looking up at the gray, swirling sky.

"They left early, didn't they? They should be ahead of it."

"I hope so," Susan mumbled. "I didn't realize we were supposed to get this much." The snow was falling at a rapid pace and piling up while the wind continued to pick up speed.

Riley switched on the space heaters in the barn to try to take some of the chill out of the air. "The forecast seems to keep changing. The last I heard we could get anywhere from ten to twenty inches depending on how the storm tracks." He gave a shrug. "We'll see."

"Well, let's try to get done here so we can head home before it gets too much worse. Now, what do we need to iron out?"

Switching to business mode, Riley outlined the remaining decisions Susan needed to make before he got too much further into his plans for the barn. "Okay, we need to talk about these support beams."

"You said after the remaining stalls are removed, the beams will need to stay for structural reasons, right?" When Riley nodded, she continued. "I picture them framing a walkway of sorts around the main part of the room. Depending upon the event, we could set up tables for seating in the walkway leaving the main area open for a dance floor or display area. Or, the alternative—tables throughout the main area with the walkway left open or used for display. Now, for the reception, I envision tables in both areas initially then once dinner is over, removing tables from the center to clear an area for a dance floor."

Riley was nodding along, picturing what she was describing to him. "And you're still thinking a permanent bar over here?" He indicated the area towards the back of the barn.

"Yes, I think that's best. Here, let me show you something." Susan pulled out her phone and after a moment held it out for Riley to see. "I found these pictures of a refurbished barn and I think some of the ideas could work well here." She pointed to the small screen on her phone and continued. "See how this one has a bar in the back with stairs directly behind leading to the loft? I love how the loft wraps around part of the barn and leads to private rooms upstairs. If we wall off that area," she said pointing, "we could make rooms that could be used for a bridal party, or prep rooms for a presentation, even rooms for parents to use if kids need a nap."

"That will work. Now, about all the exposed

beams along the walls and ceiling…I explained that if you want the place insulated so it can be used year round, you're going to lose some of that."

"I know," she pouted, "I just can't stand the thought of covering up all that beautiful wood."

"We won't cover all of it up, that would be almost criminal," Riley said, running his hand along the aged wood. "There are a few options, but since I'm not an expert on this, I found someone who is. I was talking with a friend and he knows someone who does barn restoration so I called him and he's coming out next week to consult. He should be able to answer some questions about how best to insulate and whether it makes sense to try to make it usable year round."

"Perfect. Not that I doubt your abilities, but from what I read online, there are a lot of things to consider when trying to refurbish a place like this."

"And like I said, I don't claim to be an expert. I'm curious to hear what he has to say. Are you prepared to listen and to take his advice?" Riley asked with a sideways look at Susan.

"Yes, I'll listen."

"And?" Riley prompted.

"And I'll take his advice. I'm prepared to hear that we shouldn't try to use it in the winter. If that's what he recommends, I'll go along with it. I've already seen how cold it gets here and we're not even into December. I can't imagine what it would take to keep it heated all winter."

Susan shivered a little and Riley moved quickly to the next points he needed to cover with her so they could finish up and get out. The space heaters weren't doing much against the wind that was battering the walls.

As they walked around the barn hashing out details, Susan began filling Riley in on some of the plans she had for the wedding reception. "It's going to be so beautiful in here, I can just picture it with little white lights twined through the ceiling beams, candle light, sparkling china and crystal, white linens. Oh…" she sighed dreamily.

"So Sam didn't change her mind once she had some time to think things through?"

"Of course not," Susan scoffed. "She's excited about it. I think she really likes the fact that the space isn't huge and won't be able to hold the whole town. She was concerned about the guest list. Since your family seems to know everyone, she and Jake were struggling with where to draw the line. With the limited capacity here, it helps them figure that out. We talked and planned. I know at first she thought it would be too much but once I told her I'm not going to handle the decorating or the food, she relaxed some."

"I was glad to hear that part, too. Who's going to do it though?"

"I've already found a couple of catering outfits nearby that do wedding receptions. They'll provide food, linens, tableware, everything, really. One will do the decorating too, and the other gave me the name of a company that they work with that handles decorating. Sam and Jake—actually, probably Sam and I—are going to check them out in the next few weeks to get an idea of what they have to offer. When I told them what I'm doing here they were plenty excited. The possibility of me sending business their way should have them motivated to put their best effort forward and to give Sam a good deal."

"Have you made any progress with your friend

Cassie?"

"I called her yesterday to see how Thanksgiving went at the Billingsley. It was a nightmare," Susan happily reported. "Stephen drove her crazy fussing with the buffet menu up until the last minute and then insisted she find a table for his group of twelve after they were booked solid. Then, on Thursday afternoon, he told her he needed a suite for his aunt and uncle who had decided to stay overnight. She'll be here before you know it, mark my words."

While in Riley's mind the likelihood of a young woman with a wealth of experience under her belt leaving Chicago to come to work at an inn in Northern Minnesota seemed remote, he figured Susan would end up being right about that, too. He was coming to realize there wasn't much that didn't go as she planned. When he considered how she was juggling her job in town, Sam's wedding plans, and a puppy, not to mention the huge B&B project, he wondered if there was anything she couldn't handle.

Riley was just about to tell Susan they had covered everything on his list when his phone rang. Glancing at the screen, he saw it was Jake. "What's up?"

"Well, my frustration level, for one thing. Where are you?" Jake barked.

"Out at Susan's. Why are you yelling?"

"Have you looked outside?" Jake asked, clearly exasperated.

"Not recently. I assume it's still snowing?" Heading to the door, Riley gave it a shove and was surprised when it moved only a couple of inches.

"Still snowing? Are you kidding? Riley, we've got eight inches on the ground already and it's not showing any signs of letting up. I was hoping you were home and could get over to Mom and Dad's to shovel before Dad decides to do it. I'm not going to get away any time soon, there are accidents all over the place and we're stretched thin. But if you're out at the lake, you should probably stay put. The highway's closed already and the streets in town are in terrible condition."

Riley had managed to push the barn door open against the snow that had drifted in front of it. Everywhere he looked he was met with swirling white. Susan, coming up behind him, drew in a sharp breath. He heard her mumble, "Oh. Wow."

"Where the hell is Frank? Tell him to get over to Mom and Dad's."

"I don't know, I tried you first. Will you try calling him? I've got to check on Sam then deal with everything here."

"Sure, I'll call him. Let me know if Sam needs anything, I'm closer than you are."

"Thanks, Riley," Jake said as he hung up.

Turning to Susan as he pulled the barn door closed Riley said, "I guess we've been in here a while."

"I guess. We should probably call it a day, though, if we want to make it out of here. I suppose the roads are pretty bad..." Susan wrapped her arms around herself and glanced about nervously as if expecting the snow to start falling inside the barn.

Riley could tell she was scared and tried to lighten the mood. "Not a fan of winter driving? I would expect a girl from Chicago would be able to handle a little snow," he teased.

"I just don't like—" Her voice hitched and she

turned away hugging herself tighter.

Alarmed, Riley quickly came up behind her and put a hand on her shoulder. "Hey, Red, I was just joking. No one likes driving in the snow." He saw the tears streaming down her cheeks and panic gripped him. "Hey," he repeated, wrapping her in a hug.

"I'm sorry, I don't usually let it get to me," she began, but buried her head in his shoulder and hung on tightly to him.

Riley ran a hand down her hair and tried to calm her, still unsure what had caused her reaction. "Don't apologize." Riley held her tight as she trembled in his arms, her breath catching as she tried to get her emotions under control. When she calmed some, he led her to a bench and sat down with her, keeping her close. "What is it, Susan?" he asked.

She didn't answer for a long time and Riley started to think she wasn't going to, but then she started softly. "I was just a kid, but I'll never forget the day my grandmother and Sam's parents were killed. I was excited because it was snowing and I couldn't wait for school to end so I could get outside and play. When the principal came to my classroom to get me, I knew immediately something was wrong."

Riley closed his eyes, wishing he could take back his comments about driving in the snow. He had forgotten about the accident that had claimed the lives of those she loved. He squeezed her shoulders and mumbled his apology.

"It's okay," Susan said in response then continued with the story she seemed to need to tell. "My brothers and I waited in the office for a few minutes until my mom got there to pick us up. We didn't know what had happened, but we were scared. No one would tell us anything. I remember the secretary in the office was hardly able to make eye contact with us. We went to the hospital, Sam and Danny were already there, huddled together with my dad and grandfather. Granddad's eyes were red and he seemed unsteady, as if he would collapse if he tried to stand. I had never seen him look like he did that day. Sam and Danny were sitting on either side of my dad, one of his arms wrapped tightly around each of them. Sam was staring straight ahead, I don't think she even noticed us arrive. Danny looked confused, his eyes jumping from one person to the next as if waiting for someone to explain to him what was really happening."

Riley could feel the tension in her as she moved closer to him. He watched as she unconsciously twisted and untwisted her hands while her leg bounced up and down. It was as though she needed an outlet for the emotion building inside her.

"My dad seemed so strong when I first saw him. I looked at his face and there was nothing there, no grief, no fear, nothing. I started to tell myself it was all a mistake, that my dad knew the truth, and that any minute he was going to tell us everything was okay. But then I watched as he looked at my mom and he just crumbled. I guess he had been trying to hold things together, but when he looked at Mom he couldn't. He had already lost his brother and sister-in-law, his mother was in surgery…it was just too much." Susan's voice was barely more than a whisper. "I had never seen him cry before."

Riley pulled Susan onto his lap and held her close, willing some of her pain to seep into him. When she looked at him, however, it was more than grief he saw in her eyes. It was fear. And then it hit him. Her family was on the road making their way back to Chicago. She needed to know they were okay but, at the same time, was afraid to find out.

"I'll be right here while you call."

The fact that he understood, that he knew her thoughts as well as she did, calmed her some. She wanted to hold on to him, to melt into him, and to pretend everything was fine. She'd tell herself it wasn't snowing and that her family was safe and sound back in Chicago. But she knew she needed to make the call. Incredibly grateful she wouldn't have to do it alone, she met Riley's eyes and nodded slowly. She stretched to reach the phone in her pocket, not wanting to move from the safety of his lap. With a shaky hand she pressed buttons and then, at her mother's carefree 'Hello', let out the breath she didn't realize she'd been holding.

She talked for a minute, even laughed a little, before hanging up and reporting to Riley. "Everything is fine, they're almost home and haven't seen so much as a snowflake. Mom just talked to Brad and their drive has been uneventful with the exception of frequent restroom stops for Mia." She sighed and closed her eyes, allowing her head to fall onto Riley's shoulder.

"I'm glad…that you called and that everything is okay."

"Thank you for listening and for helping me through that."

He gave her a squeeze in response. "Are you okay now? We should think about getting back to the house before we get snowed in here."

"I'm okay. And just so you know, I don't usually react quite like that and I almost never cry in front of guys. I find it makes most of them uncomfortable." She grinned at him. "You handled it quite well, actually."

He almost told her that he had been close to panic mode when she'd started to cry, that he'd briefly considered telling her to call Sam, or Karen, or his mom, or anyone that wasn't him. But he decided he'd let her think he'd had things under control the entire time. "Hey, Red, I'm not most guys." With that, he leaned over and kissed her, thankful to see the spark back in her eyes.

The kiss caught her by surprise. Just a moment ago she'd felt as if her world was spinning out of control due to fear. Now, her world was spinning for an entirely different reason. Her heart started to race and she reached a hand around his neck to steady herself. In an instant, the kiss went from friendly to passionate and she held on for dear life.

Riley had planned to plant a quick kiss on her lips to make sure she had moved past the worry and fear, but when she responded so quickly and wrapped her arm around his neck, he was lost. He grabbed her, fisted his hand in her hair, and let go with the feelings he had done his best to bottle up for the past few weeks. Part of his mind was telling him to back off, that getting involved with the woman he was working for was a bad idea. The other part was telling him she was like no other woman he had ever known, that he'd be crazy to let her get away. It didn't take long until he stopped listening to what his head was telling him and, instead, gave in to his desire.

Susan wasn't sure if she'd ever been kissed quite like Riley was kissing her. She knew she'd never wanted anyone else to kiss her like he was kissing her. When he gently grabbed hold of her hair she thought she heard a soft moan, but didn't know if it came from her or from Riley.

Riley's phone buzzed with a text. Susan half listened as he muttered an oath and said something about forgetting his promise to Jake. She was still dazed as he eased back from her and pulled out his phone. He showed her the screen. The text was from Frank telling him, in rather colorful language, that he was at their parents' house and would take care of the driveway once the snow let up.

Taking a moment to catch her breath as Riley returned the text, Susan stood up and looked at him. That was twice now that he'd kissed her and she'd been helpless to stop the desire that flooded through her. Her response to him left her rattled. She wasn't used to feeling out of control.

Riley stood too and, kissing the top of her head, took her hand and started to cross the room. "We need to get moving. I'll shut off these heaters and—"

Just as he reached for the switch, it shut off on its own and the room was pitched into darkness. Reflexively, Susan tightened her grip on his hand. Somewhere in the darkness the dog, who had been alternately sniffing and investigating every corner of the barn and napping, gave a little yip.

"Damn," Riley muttered. "Stay put for a minute."

Feeling his way along the wall with the help of the light from his phone, he moved back to the door where he had left a toolbox with a small flashlight inside. After some fumbling and a couple of scraped knuckles, he found it and clicked it on. He followed the small beam of light around the room and unplugged the heaters before again taking Susan's hand and leading her to the door.

Together, they shoved at the door to open it wide enough to get out. Gusto, thrilled to find a sea of white, bounded into the yard and jumped into a snowdrift only to find he couldn't get himself back out. Whining, he struggled and scratched, succeeding only in burying himself deeper.

Susan and Riley held onto one another and took exaggerated steps, raising their legs as high as possible over the drifts, and fought their way through the wicked wind and pelting snow to the dog. Riley scooped him up and they stumbled and staggered their way back to the house through the blinding, swirling snow.

Once inside, Susan began brushing snow from her jacket, pants, and hair and stomping her feet in an attempt to warm up. "I can't believe this. It's like a whole different world out there. I've heard stories of people freezing to death a few feet from their front door. I never understood until now. Look, you can't even see the barn from here."

Riley mumbled a reply but was already using the small flashlight to work his way around the house. When he returned, he had two more flashlights and a lantern. "It's almost dark," he said with a trace of worry in his voice. "We have decisions to make."

Before Susan could ask what he meant, his phone buzzed again with a text. His expression grew more worried as he read it aloud. "Jake says, 'Sam is okay, power out around most of lake, had report that tree branch came down on a power line so road between Sam's and Susan's is impassable. If you leave, have to go long way around. I say stay put if you can. Let me know.'" He looked at Susan. "Well, that sucks."

"What now? It's awfully cold in here."

"The heat is all running off electricity right now so without any power, we're without any heat. It's going to get colder. We can try to drive back to Sam's, but my truck is really blocked in by a drift and it sounds like it's going to be rough driving." He raked his hand through his hair and said, "We also have the pipes to worry about. Without any heat in here and with the insulation not finished around the pipes, I'm worried they're going to freeze. If we leave, we can shut off the water and drain the pipes. If we stay, I'll hook up the generator to keep at least some heat pumping and I'll keep the water trickling to try to keep the pipes from freezing. We can use the fireplace, that will help warm it up in here, too."

"Sounds like camping. I hate camping."

Riley chuckled. "That I believe. I'll leave it up to you. If you want to try to get out of here I'll do what I can to make that happen, but I have to hurry. I'm running out of any trace of daylight and doing everything by flashlight is going to be harder."

"And if we stay? Is there anything to eat or drink? Any firewood? Anything?"

"I keep some things in the mini fridge, it's easier than packing a lunch every day. There should be enough to make a couple of sandwiches. I know there's stuff to drink. We might even find some chips or pretzels. I'll find wood to burn."

Susan looked out the window. It was almost completely dark. "I guess the smart thing to do is to stay. I'll call Sam," she said on a sigh.

While Susan called Sam, Riley sent texts to Jake and Frank to let them know their plans. Riley connected the generator, turned the faucet in the temporary bathroom on low, and started a fire. Susan scrounged through the fridge and made a few sandwiches. Gusto was delighted with his meal of salami and ham.

"You know, I have a couple of blankets in the trunk of my car. They might come in handy. I suppose I could go get them…"

Riley rolled his eyes. "I'll go get them. Do you really think I'm going to sit here while you trudge through all that snow?"

"Thanks, I was hoping you'd volunteer," Susan answered brightly. "Here are the keys. Oh! I almost forgot. Brad and Mia gave Sam and me a bottle of wine as they were leaving today. I guess they had it in their bag all weekend but forgot about it. Anyway, I was busy hugging everyone goodbye so just tossed it in the car meaning to take it inside later. Sooo… it's still there. You may want to grab that too, it might help take the chill off."

"Anything else you keep in that car of yours? Maybe a hot pizza or a TV and some DVDs?"

"No, smarty-pants, I think that's it," she said, sticking out her tongue at him. "Just wait, you'll be thanking me for keeping blankets in there."

"Be right back," Riley laughed as he started to open the door.

"Wait, there is one more thing. I have a puzzle in

the back seat. You should grab that, too, it will give us something to do."

"A puzzle? Why do you have a puzzle in your car?"

"They just came in at the store. It's a picture of Misty Lake. I thought it was cute so I bought one. You'll be thanking me for that, too."

"Somehow I doubt it," he said as he forced the door open against the wind.

12

"*What* are you doing?" Susan asked, appalled. They were sitting in front of the fire, each with a blanket thrown around their shoulders, at a makeshift table Riley had put together using sawhorses and a piece of plywood. Gusto was curled up as close to the fireplace as he could get, contentedly dozing and oblivious to the storm that continued to rage outside.

"What do you mean, what am I doing? I'm doing this stupid puzzle you told me to do."

"You can't put inside pieces together until the border is done."

"These two fit together. Look, they make a flag," Riley said, holding it up for her to see. Why wouldn't I put them together?"

"Don't you know anything about puzzle rules? You have to do the border first. That's how it goes. I thought everybody knew that."

"You mean you have rules about puzzles, too? Is there anything you don't have rules about?"

"Well, it just seems to me if you're going to do something you may as well do it right," she grumbled.

"I can barely tell one color from the next in this light. It seems to me if I find pieces that fit together I should put them together regardless of whether the border is done."

"Well, if you want to do it wrong…"

"Oh, Red."

They worked in silence for a while, struggling with the colors in the weak light. Finally, Susan pushed back the stepladder she was using for a chair and stood. "This is hopeless. It's too dark. Where's that bottle of wine?"

"I left it by the front door."

"Oh, darn. I just realized we don't have a corkscrew."

"Now, wait a minute. Can you honestly tell me that you think I'm capable of building this place for you, working all the small miracles you are expecting, yet you think I can't manage to get a bottle of wine open without a corkscrew?"

Susan turned around quickly to look at Riley, afraid he was genuinely offended, and hurried to try to make amends. "I just meant *I* wouldn't know how to open it and since I was on my way to get it, I wouldn't be able to bring it back opened. I'm sure *you* can do it."

"Nice recovery, Red," he laughed. "Now, watch this."

Susan watched as Riley got a screw, a screwdriver, and a hammer. He used the screwdriver to twist the screw into the cork, leaving a little bit sticking out the top. Then, using the claw end of the hammer, easily removed the cork.

"Impressive, McCabe. I guess there really isn't anything you can't do."

They sat in front of the fire sipping wine from Styrofoam coffee cups and sharing stories about their childhoods. "I remember when I was a kid, I couldn't wait for winter. Once the pond by our house froze, we spent every minute we could out there skating and playing hockey. Well, Frank and I did, anyway. Jake and Joe could play and usually came along, but they weren't as crazy about it as Frank and I were."

"So they never played on the high school team?"

"No, they both quit before then, deciding to stick with football. And we all played baseball in the summer, of course."

"Of course," Susan grinned. "You must have kept your parents busy."

"At the time I didn't realize just how much they did, but looking back, yeah, they were busy, especially my mom. Dad's schedule could be kind of crazy, he worked nights and weekends sometimes, so most of the driving fell on her. And she became this sort of scheduling mastermind. She always had carpool arrangements worked out with the other parents. I'm pretty sure that's what got her to learn how to use a computer. She would put together schedules and make sure everyone was where they needed to be."

"I think that's part of being a kid. You're focused on yourself, you don't realize what everyone around you is doing. I hope you've thanked them now that you do realize it."

"I have, you don't need to scold."

Susan chuckled. "So did you and Frank always play together on a line?"

"Huh?" Riley asked, slightly confused.

"Did you always play together on a line?" Susan repeated. "When I watched you play, you two were always out there together with Frank centering the line. Obviously you're both good and you play well together, I just wondered if a coach ever tried to split you up…to spread out the talent, so to speak. Sometimes the theory is two good lines are better than one great line."

Riley was looking more intently at Susan. "I didn't realize you knew so much about hockey."

"Sure, it's a great game. I've been a fan my whole life. But you haven't answered my question."

"Oh. Well, we did have a coach once who decided we shouldn't play together. I don't know if his thinking was he could make two strong lines or if he just didn't like the fact that we were scoring most of the goals. His kid wasn't very good but Coach was convinced he was. He wanted him to skate with Frank so Frank could feed him passes the way he did me. It didn't work, his kid couldn't handle the passes, and no one was scoring. In the end, it was his own kid who told him he needed to put the lines back they way they were. That was the last time we were separated."

"I watched you two skate. If I hadn't known you before, I would have guessed you were twins. You both seemed to know where the other was, and would be, without looking. Kind of like watching the Sedin twins."

Now he flat-out stared at her. "You know who the Sedin twins are?"

"Oh, McCabe." She shook her head and looked up at him in the dim light. "Because I'm a girl it follows that I don't know anything about sports? Especially hockey?"

"No. Dammit, no, you're putting words in my mouth." He was clearly flustered and Susan had to bite her lip to keep from laughing at him.

"You do remember I'm from Chicago, right? Do you think I can be a Blackhawks fan and not know of the Sedin twins? We're not particularly fond of any of the Vancouver Canucks in Chicago, you know."

"Now wait just a minute." Riley got to his feet and started pacing. "You never said anything about being a Blackhawks fan. You're not serious, are you?" His eyes were wide and he was looking at her as if she were from another planet.

"Of course, I'm serious."

"Well…well, you never told me."

Now Susan was laughing out loud. "I didn't realize it was something I needed to disclose. Are you going to quit on me? I really don't want to have to find another contractor."

"What?" Seeing her laughing at him had him focusing. "No, I'm not going to quit. We may just have to discuss this further. If you're going to live in Minnesota it seems only right that you give the Wild a chance. I know, we'll go to a game," Riley said, his spirits lifting. "It's a lot more fun than a Blackhawks game, you'll see."

"Deal. Now sit back down, it's cold when you're not here." Susan patted the tarps they'd piled in front of the fireplace and Riley obliged, sitting close and throwing an arm around her shoulders.

"So, back to the McCabe twins. I'm guessing you didn't play in college since I didn't see any articles or pictures about it at your house. Why not?"

Riley looked into the fire. "It's incredibly competitive. There are so many hockey players, good hockey players, in Minnesota that it's tough to get noticed. I did have a few scouts show a little interest but…well, I guess I just didn't know if I'd be any good without Frank. He decided early on he wanted to study photography. That meant he wouldn't be going to a school that was looking for hockey players. He was okay with that. I wasn't sure what I wanted to do. For a while, I thought maybe hockey would get me into school and I'd figure things out from there, but in the end, I decided not to pursue it."

He sounded sad and Susan leaned in closer. "Do you regret it?"

"No, not really. Sure, there are times when I'm watching a college game and I start to think, but…no. I don't even know if I would have liked it as much without Frank. A big part of the fun was playing with him. And, like I said, I don't know what kind of player I would have been on my own." He shrugged and tore his gaze away from the fire to look at Susan. "I'm pretty happy with the way things have turned out. I'm doing something I enjoy and I'm still playing hockey for fun. Some of the injuries that come with the faster and more physical game in college could have made a job like mine impossible." Softening his voice he added, "And I may have never met you."

Riley gently ran his hand down Susan's arm, watching her intently. When the heat flashed in her eyes, he took her in his arms and kissed her.

Warm, Susan thought, as she snuggled against Riley. She was finally warm. Any chill she had felt in the drafty house disappeared when she was in his arms. He kissed her slowly, tenderly, and she knew her heart was his.

Riley tried desperately to make sense of his feelings. In the months he had known her, Susan had managed to both frustrate and amaze; she had left him puzzled one day and fascinated the next; she took him from teeth-grinding impatience to breathless desire in the blink of an eye. In the blink of her eye, he corrected himself. He looked into her emerald eyes, reflecting the flames from the fire but at the same time, darkening with desire. He pulled her closer, shifting so her head rested on his chest, and together they watched the flames dance until the logs burned low.

Eventually, Riley stirred. "I'd better get some more wood and check the pipes."

As he stood and the blanket fell, Susan shivered. "Hurry back."

Riley gave her a long look then knelt back down next to her. Taking her face in his hands he said, "I can't let you freeze, Red, even if you are a Blackhawks fan." He kissed the tip of her nose, whistled for the dog, and left her feeling warmer than ever.

Susan woke to hazy sunshine filtering in through the window. It took her a moment to remember where she was and why she was so stiff, but then the memories came flooding back and she inched closer to Riley.

He had been awake for a few minutes, watching her as she slept with her head nestled on his shoulder and her mittened hand flung across his chest. Her hair was a riot of tangles and curls and when the sun peeked through and touched it, it turned to flame.

"Hey, sleepyhead, we should get moving."

Slowly, Susan stretched and angled her head to face him. "Good morning to you, too," she yawned. "Did it stop snowing?"

"Looks like it. The power isn't back on yet, though. Are you cold?"

"Not really. What time is it?"

"It must be close to eight, the sun just came up. We got a few hours sleep, I guess."

"Mmmm," Susan murmured, fighting the light-headed, dazed feeling that comes with a nearly sleepless night. "I suppose we should go see what it looks like out there."

"I'm going to try to get in touch with Jake and see what he knows about the road. If it's not cleared of the power line we might have to stay put for a while."

"Okay." Struggling to her feet and stretching her arms over her head, Susan looked out the window. "Oh, look. It's beautiful."

Snow covered every surface, hung from tree branches, and glittered in the air as the wind swirled and the flakes caught the sunlight. For as far as Susan could see, there was white. Drifts easily six feet or more had formed by the barn and in front of her car.

"Beautiful, yes, but also a lot of work. We've got to try to clear a path to the driveway and then figure out how to get out of here."

Riley's phone rang and while he talked, Susan gazed out the window and found herself wishing it would start to snow again. The night had been magical. She and Riley had talked until they dozed off then, waking when it got cold, added logs to the fire and talked some more. She was sure she had learned more about him in one night than she would have in weeks under normal circumstances. As she rubbed at the kink in her neck, she knew she'd take it any day for another night like she and Riley had shared.

"Jake says the road is clear and the power should be back on soon. I guess he made it to Sam's some time after midnight so he's there now trying to get her plowed out. He just talked to Joe who's got a truck with a plow and said he'd be over to Sam's as soon as he could. Jake's going to send him this way when he's done there. So, it sounds like we'll be rescued."

"Wow, the McCabes really know how to rally."

"We're good at some things," he grinned. "Now, why don't we see if we can start clearing a path to the driveway?"

"I'm going to grab a bottle of water and pretend it's coffee. I'll meet you out there in a minute."

Susan watched as Riley trudged through snow that, at times, was thigh high. Bundling her jacket tighter around her and pulling her hat down over her ears, she headed out to join him. Then she smirked and rubbed her hands together. Following his footsteps, she moved as quickly and as quietly as she could, keeping her eyes on Riley's back as he worked to clear the area around her car. When she was close, she ran the last few steps, came up beside him, and throwing her hip out, sent him sprawling face-first into the drift.

Riley came up wiping snow off his face and

squinting up at her. "That's how you thank me for shoveling out your car?"

"You know, McCabe, it just seemed like it needed to be done." Then, throwing her head back, she howled with laughter at his appropriately chagrined expression.

The boy looked around him at the Christmas decorations that seemed to cover every surface in the small, dingy discount store. He saw people filling their carts with Christmas lights and candy canes. Nervously, he tugged on his mother's sleeve.

"Mommy, is it almost Christmas? You told Aunt Jenny we'd be back for Christmas, remember?"

His mother grabbed some cans of soup and tossed them in the basket she was carrying. She hadn't seemed to hear him.

"Mommy," he tried again, "you said we'd be home by Christmas time."

"Can't you let me concentrate? I can't worry about Christmas right now."

"But Mommy, we should go home," he tried to convince her.

"Home," she sneered. She wondered when she'd last had someplace she could call home.

The boy followed her as she moved down the narrow aisle. He tried again. "Aunt Jenny wants us to be there for Christmas, she told me when we left."

Sighing heavily, she stopped and turned to the boy. "Listen, I don't know when we'll go back there. I don't know if we'll go back there. You're just going to have to forget about Aunt Jenny's."

His chin started to quiver as he looked at her. His

eyes filling with tears, he said shakily, "But how will Santa find me?"

Rolling her eyes toward the ceiling, she opened her mouth intending to insist he stop badgering her. But, seeing his heart-broken expression, she softened and crouched down, drawing him close. "Oh, baby, Santa will find you. He knows how to find all the good little boys and girls. If you're real good and do what I say, Santa will find you. I promise."

Wiping his tears before she stood, she wondered how she was going to keep that promise. Then she wondered if Santa ever found mommies.

13

As Christmas approached, Susan threw herself into preparations for the holiday. She delighted in helping decorate Sam's house, all the while imagining what she would do the next year to decorate the inn. Since it was Sam's first Christmas in Misty Lake, the house was a clean slate when it came to decorating with no previous years' successes or failures to build on. Susan loved the challenge. She hung wreaths, draped garlands over the mantle and around the doors and banisters, and set the house, inside and out, aglow with thousands of white lights.

The best by far, however, was the tree. Following with the McCabe family tradition, Susan and Sam joined the pilgrimage to a nearby tree farm and spent the better part of the day enjoying sleigh rides, sipping cocoa, and trudging through fields in search of the perfect tree. Susan insisted they find a tree big enough that it would be worthy of the spot in front of the giant two-story windows facing the lake. Sam shared Susan's exuberance and the two searched until their toes were nearly frozen before finding a tree tall enough, wide enough, and straight enough to satisfy both of them. When it came time to trim the tree, it took Sam, Susan, Jake, Riley, and two stepladders to complete the job.

"How about now?" Riley groaned as he shifted the star ever so slightly to the left and waited for an okay from Susan and Sam. The two stood below, tilting their heads and squinting their eyes. "If you're not satisfied within the next thirty seconds, one of you is climbing up here," he grumbled.

"Just a tiny, tiny bit more to the left," Susan instructed.

Riley swore under his breath as he gently tapped the star and succeeded in moving it a fraction of an inch to the left. "How's that?" he asked, barely containing his frustration.

"Stop. Right there, don't you think, Sam?"

"I think you did it, Riley," Sam said. "Come on down and have a cookie. This is supposed to be fun, remember?"

"Fun. Right," he mumbled as he climbed down the ladder. But, he didn't turn down the invitation to have a cookie. "Do you have some of those peanut butter ones with the chocolate kisses in the middle?"

"Of course." Sam held out a candy cane platter filled with a dizzying array of cookies. She and Susan had spent hours upon hours baking all their favorites as well as some of the McCabe family favorites Sam had coaxed out of Jake.

Riley, cookies in hand and his mood improving,

stood back and studied the tree. "I guess it is a pretty amazing tree," he admitted, "even if it was a pain in the ass getting it in the house, in the stand, and decorated. I don't think I've ever seen a tree quite this big in someone's house before."

"I know," Susan said proudly, walking from one side of the tree to the other while holding up her phone. "We found just the right one for this spot." Frowning, she added, "We should get Frank over here to take a picture. I'm afraid my phone won't do it justice. Actually, unless I stand in the kitchen, I don't think I can even get the whole thing in the picture."

Jake stood with his arm around Sam looking at the tree. "I'm sure Frank would like nothing better than to come photograph your tree."

Susan gave Jake a withering look. "Fine. He doesn't have to make a special trip out here to take a picture, but I assume he'll have his camera on Christmas Eve. He can do it then." A satisfied smile crossed her face.

Lifting her head to look up at Jake, Sam asked, "So he's coming for sure? How about everyone else?"

Susan and Sam had talked, at length, guessing at how the McCabes would feel about spending Christmas Eve at Sam's house after having just been there for Thanksgiving. When the two had, somewhat reluctantly, decided not to make the trip to Chicago for Christmas, Sam had extended the invitation. It would be their first Christmas away from family, but since they both wanted to visit soon after Mia had the baby, making a trip at Christmas and then another in early January seemed like too much. They'd both felt hosting Christmas Eve, by far the cousins' favorite day—and celebration—of the year, and incorporating some of the Taylor family traditions, would ease the hurt.

Riley answered for Jake. "Sounds like they're all coming. Joe and Karen will be with Karen's family later on Christmas Day so they'll be here, too. Although, Joe said it will depend upon how Karen is feeling." He shook his head in disgust. "I'm telling you, Jake, I hardly recognize that brother of ours. I tried talking to him about Sunday's football game and somehow he turned it into a conversation about labor breathing techniques. When I asked him what he thought of Brady's touchdown pass he thought I was suggesting baby names. Pathetic."

"He does seem unable to focus on much else. I wonder what'll happen to him once the kid is born? Do you think he'll get worse?" Jake sounded slightly panicked.

Susan put her hands on her hips and scolded. "Geez, you guys make it sound like he's got some sort of terminal illness. He's going to be a dad in a few weeks, of course it's all he can think about. Cut him some slack."

"Well, I'm just glad everyone is coming. What about your great aunts? Do they usually spend Christmas with your family? Or do they have children or grandchildren nearby?" Sam had already moved on to planning for Christmas Eve.

"Rose never had children. Her husband died at a relatively young age and she never remarried. Kate has two kids, both out on the East Coast. They come home sometimes for Christmas and always in the summer, but from what I hear, neither is able to make the trip this Christmas so I assume both Rose and Kate will be here on Christmas Eve. Mom always makes sure they're not alone."

Sam smiled at Jake. "It's nice to have someone looking out for them like that. Anyone else? The invitation is open, I'd just like to have an idea of how many to expect. Do you get together with cousins at Christmas?"

"Remember when we used to?" Riley laughed. "When we were younger, the whole gang got together and it was a blast…at least for the kids. At some point we stopped doing that, I think there just got to be too many people. They all usually show up at the Fourth of July picnic, though."

Susan headed to the window and stared out at the darkness. The talk of family and holiday get-togethers had her feeling lonely and second-guessing her decision to stay in Misty Lake. She was grateful when Sam changed the subject.

"Hey, Suze, you never finished telling me what you learned about the history of your house."

"Hmmm?" Susan turned back to the group, trying to put thoughts of Christmas past from her mind and, instead, focus on the present. She knew what Sam was trying to do and she loved her for it. "Oh, the house. I learned some—it's amazing what you can find on the Internet—but there are still a lot of questions."

"Tell us what you did find. Since I read that journal, I've been plenty curious, too," Sam prompted.

Shaking off her melancholy, Susan dove into her story. "Well, I looked for information on Charlie—Charles—Walker and found that he did indeed marry one Martha Kane in 1950. He died in California so he and Martha must have gone there right after getting married and must have stayed there. I didn't find any record of them ever having children."

"I wonder if they were ever happy together? I agree with you, Susan, that his last entry sounded sad and not at all like it was written by a happy groom-to-be."

"We'll probably never know. I also found out that Charlie had one sister, Roberta, who married Edward Fuller and lived in St. Paul. Charlie's father, Thomas, died in 1970 in Misty Lake. His mother, Helen, died ten years later in St. Paul so at some point she must have gone to live with, or at least near, her daughter. Roberta and Edward had a son, James, and it looks like he ended up in Texas, which makes sense, because the person listed as the seller on the house was Sarah Fuller from Houston, Texas. Crazy how much you can learn with a few keystrokes."

Riley studied Susan suspiciously. "It makes me wonder what you've found out about me."

"Don't worry, McCabe, I've been too busy to Google you. So far." She wiggled her eyebrows and was rewarded with a pillow in the face.

"Were you able to find out any more about the house itself? Was it always in the Walker family?" Sam asked. "I know you were hoping to find some pictures."

"Actually, I did learn a little and I have you to thank for that, Jake. Bea over at City Hall is a treasure. She dug up all kinds of information for me and would probably still be talking if I hadn't finally claimed I had an appointment I needed to keep."

Jake smiled knowingly. "That sounds like Bea. She's a sweet woman. She probably could have retired ten years ago but she loves what she does."

"She found some old records that show the original owners of the house were the Baumgartners. Apparently the last family member died in 1929 and the house was abandoned. When taxes weren't paid ownership reverted to the county. Then in 1931 the house was sold to Thomas and Helen Walker, Charlie's parents."

"Did you ever come across any pictures?" Riley asked.

Susan's shoulders slumped. "No. Even Bea couldn't find anything."

"Then did you really learn anything? Was it just curiosity after finding the journal that had you doing all this research or were there some specific answers you were looking for?" Jake seemed perplexed.

"Oh, not really anything specific except for pictures. I was really hoping to find some that would give me an idea of how the place looked when it was lived in. It was mostly curiosity. I couldn't help but get hooked on Charlie's story. I guess I'm a sucker for romance."

"Well, let's hope he and Martha were happy," Sam said.

Susan talked everyone into watching a Christmas movie to wrap up the weekend. They settled on *Christmas Vacation*. Jake and Riley tried to outdo one another quoting lines and got into a shouting match seeing who could belt out Clark's tirade—when he finally loses his cool following one disaster after another—faster. Once the movie was over, Riley looked at the time and knew he needed to head out.

"I still have to stop by the house and drop off some revised plans. Cindy is going to be there early tomorrow morning and I'll be tied up in town for a while."

"I could drop them for you, I have to drive over there either tonight or tomorrow morning. I left a bag there with some things I need for work in the morning. I kept meaning to pick it up, but the weekend got away from me."

Sam and Jake were cozied up on the opposite sofa, whispering to each other and seeming to have forgotten Susan and Riley were still there. Riley cocked his head in their direction. "How about we drive over there together, give these two a little time alone."

"Good idea. I'll get my jacket."

The night was cold and clear and still, the kind of night when every squeaky step into the frigid snow is magnified a hundred times and when the lonely hoot of an owl carries for miles. As Susan and Riley made their way from the driveway to the house, Susan paused and breathed deeply. "I could get used to this. I don't ever remember this kind of quiet in Chicago."

"If it's quiet you want you've come to the right place. When I was a kid and I'd get sick of my family, I'd sneak to the park sometimes at night. In the winter, with nothing but silence all around, I could convince myself I was alone, that I didn't have to share a bathroom with three brothers and a bossy little sister, that no one was going to tell me it was my turn to dry the dishes. Of course, after a while I'd get lonely and head back to the chaos. I guess I'm just not cut out for too much quiet."

"Mmmm," Susan sighed and leaned into Riley. "I could have used a place like that when I was a kid. Being the only girl was…difficult at times."

"You and Shauna should get together and share stories. She was always complaining about us—that we were slobs, that we were noisy, that we were smelly. She was kind of a pain, really."

"It's not easy living with a bunch of boys. Trust me."

They made their way inside and while Riley set out the paperwork for Cindy, Susan ran upstairs to the bedroom where she remembered having left her bag. Riley was making a few notes for Cindy when he heard Susan.

"Riley? Riley…Riley!"

He made a mad dash for the stairs and was in the bedroom before she could scream his name again. "What? What's wrong?" He looked around wildly trying to figure out what had happened, but saw only Susan, stock-still and staring out the window.

"Look."

Coming up along side her, he looked out the window and over the lake. The sky was lit with a dizzying array of color. Shades of green, dark in some places, nearly yellow in others, swirled and danced across the sky. As they watched, the colors bent, expanded, and shrunk, ever fluid and changing.

Susan was mesmerized. It took her a while to find her voice and when she did it was barely more than a whisper. "I've never seen anything like it."

"The Northern Lights. It is a pretty incredible show."

"You've seen this before? Does it happen all the time here?"

"Yes, I've seen it before, but only a few times. It doesn't happen often that we get a show like this. You need to be farther North, usually."

They were silent for a while, just watching. Riley's hand found it's way up Susan's back and his fingers toyed with the ends of her hair. She rested her head on his shoulder for a minute then startled him by jerking away.

"Ha! I've got it. I knew it would come to me if I just waited. It always works that way, no use in forcing things like this, they just happen when the time is right." She bounced around the room, a triumphant gleam in her eyes.

"Care to let me in on the secret?"

"It's no secret. Remember that night when Jake asked about quilts or something, about designing a room around a quilt?"

Riley grinned mischievously. "Sure I remember. We talked about he and Mom sharing the honeymoon suite."

"I think you decided it was Cupid's Delight but that's beside the point. We never really finished the conversation about the rooms seeing as we got a little sidetracked by your story." Riley was laughing to himself but Susan continued. "I always planned on naming the rooms, giving them each a character of their own. I tried thinking of names a couple of times, even started to scribble ideas in my notebook..." At the mention of the notebook, Riley forgot Cupid's Delight and paid attention. "But I couldn't come up with the right names, the right ideas. I finally told myself that's not how it works. I can't just sit down and name the rooms. They have to name themselves."

Now he was confused. "Name themselves?"

"Sure. Something would happen in a room or there'd be something unique about it that would lend itself to a name."

"Okay..."

"So now I have the first name. This room will be Northern Lights. It's perfect. It sounds romantic and mysterious at the same time. Once in a lifetime, even. The kind of place where a couple may want to spend their first night together or spend a night commemorating the hundreds or thousands that have come before."

Riley considered for a minute then nodded his agreement. "I get it. Kind of like Jake talked about with quilts, but not with quilts. Each room will have it's own personality, so to speak. Maybe you can add the first room name to the website, start building more anticipation."

"That's a good idea, adding names and information one room at a time." She was grinning at him, pleased he understood and touched he showed so much interest in the future of the inn. "Now just six to go."

14

Susan found she had a few minutes to spare before heading to work so decided to take another look at her website. It had been live for a couple of weeks but it still gave her a little thrill to see it pop up on her laptop screen. She clicked through the pictures she had decided on and tried not to second-guess her choices. She'd leave the site alone for now, then add pictures as more construction was completed, she promised herself. She was anxious to start adding details about the rooms, especially since she had decided on the first name. Northern Lights. The more she thought about it, the more she loved it..

She daydreamed a little and imagined the special touches she could incorporate in the room. A deep blue rug was a must, she decided, as deep as the night sky. Maybe a cluster of white birch branches wreathed in tiny blue lights. Lit up at night with the lights reflecting off walls or off a mirror, the effect could be breathtaking.

She'd have to test it out. Glass tile in the bathroom, maybe with a bluish tint. It would give the illusion of moving, shifting light. She ran a couple of quick searches for examples of tile and was ecstatic when she discovered heat-sensitive glass tiles that started out dark then flowed through the color spectrum as warm to hot water heated them. Exactly like the Northern Lights. Perfect. She made a mental note to ask Riley to look into the product.

On a whim, she decided to check the email account she'd created for the inn. She didn't check it often as she didn't expect any activity yet, so it had been several days since she'd taken a look. It was a shock to see an email in her inbox. Well, she reasoned, she'd named a room the previous night, that was a step forward. This was another one, the first comment or inquiry regarding the inn. Glancing briefly at the subject line that read only 'owner,' she quickly opened the email. And froze. In large, red letters a three-word message screamed at her, 'You will pay.'

For a moment, Susan just stared at the screen. You will pay? She turned the words over in her head and couldn't make sense of them. The brief flash of fear at seeing the big, red letters was quickly replaced with disappointment. Her first email was nothing more than garbage. Probably someone stumbled across her website and thought he was being funny. Or thought he'd scare her. Whatever the case, Susan simply shrugged and deleted the email. Oh well, maybe tomorrow would be the day, she told herself as she headed out the door for work.

That afternoon Riley was hanging drywall when Jake and Joe clomped into the room. Funny how he knew it was them before he turned around. Years of living in the same house, listening to their footsteps on the stairs and throughout the house, left him able to detect the slight differences, the slight variations, in the sounds of their footfalls. Entirely too much time together, he told himself.

"Unless you came to help, you should probably turn right back around," Riley said, his back still to his brothers.

"A tad cranky this morning, little brother?" Jake asked.

"A lot busy this morning, big brother."

Looking around, Joe nodded his approval. "Haven't been inside in a few weeks, you're making some good headway."

Resigned to the fact that he was going to have to take time out to talk to his brothers, Riley sighed and stepped down off the ladder. "So…reason for this visit?"

"Nothing special, just wanted to see how things are coming along." Jake ran his hand along a section of drywall. "Are you on schedule? Ahead? Not behind, I hope."

"On schedule. Maybe a little ahead."

"Good. Sucks to get behind," Joe said matter-of-factly.

Riley looked from one to the other trying to figure out the real reason they were standing in the middle of his jobsite, wasting his time, and starting to piss him off. "Everything okay with Mom and Dad? The gift certificate for the dinner theater and the night in the hotel is all taken care of?"

"Yep. Karen got the gift certificate ordered and booked the hotel room. Guess she's having them put a bottle of champagne in the room, too. All wrapped up and ready for Christmas."

"Good. Thanks for handling that."

Jake looked out the window. "Saw Cindy on the way in, she's looking good."

"Yes, Cindy's fine. What the hell are you doing here? Don't you work?"

"Christmas vacation. One of the perks of being a teacher." When Riley narrowed his eyes, Joe continued. "Did you happen to catch the Northern Lights last night?"

Apparently this was going to take a while. "Actually, I did. Susan had never seen…" And then it hit him. They were there on a recon mission; sent, no doubt, by their mother. God love her, the woman didn't know what to do with herself if she wasn't busy poking her nose in her kids' lives.

Jake and Joe looked from one to the other as if both willing the other to speak first. As annoyed as Riley was, watching his brothers squirm almost made up for it.

"So," Riley began, "did she give you specific questions or is this just a casual fact-gathering mission?"

Jake ran a hand over his face. "Come on, Riley, you know how she is. You miss a couple of family dinners, she starts asking questions."

"Isn't she busy enough with your wedding," he waved an arm in Jake's direction, "and your baby?" He turned and pointed at Joe.

Joe simply shrugged. "She raised five kids. She knows how to multi-task."

When Riley scowled Jake said, "You're going to have to give us something. If we show up empty-handed she'll just send us back."

"Tell her I'm busy. Tell her this is a big job. Tell her whatever the hell you want."

"So we should tell her when you're not working here, you're spending time with Susan. And that even when you are working, you're spending a lot of time with Susan?"

"She hired me to do this job. Obviously I'm spending time with her."

"Then the dinners at The Brick, a few Saturday morning coffee dates, and the afternoon at the antique place were all just business?" Joe smirked.

"Yes. There are details to work out, questions that need to be addressed. If we do it over a pizza or a cup of coffee, what's the difference?" Letting Susan talk him into going to the antique shop to look at furniture was a little harder to explain so Riley chose to skip over it. "And how do you know every move I make?"

"Really?" Jake raised a brow. "It's Misty Lake. Do you honestly believe that you can go out with a woman and half the town won't comment on it? You're going to have to take Susan out of town—far out of town—if you want to keep it a secret."

"I didn't say I'm trying to keep it a secret. There's nothing to keep secret. There's nothing…damn, just…" With that he stomped out of the room. When he returned a minute later with a roll of drywall tape, his brothers were grinning like fools.

"I guess we've got enough to report back to Mom," Joe teased. "He seems to be at a loss for words."

"Bite me."

"Oh, and now he's getting mean. What are we going to do about that?" Joe asked, looking at Jake.

Jake casually lifted his hand and rubbed his knuckles. "We could take him outside and do the same thing we did when he was a bratty little kid."

Riley shook his head, called his brothers a list of inventive names under his breath, and turned back to the drywall.

"He sure is a touchy thing. I'd say Susan's got him wrapped around her finger and he doesn't quite know what to do about it," Joe said.

"I'd say you're right. And that's one determined woman. If she's made up her mind, he doesn't stand a chance."

Riley knew there wasn't much point in arguing, but his pride demanded he try. "You two may forget you have balls when those women of yours tell you what to do, but I don't. I make my own decisions."

"As long as those decisions fall in line with Susan's," Jake said and Joe hooted and nodded in agreement.

"You should talk," Riley said poking a finger at Jake then giving the bright red sweater he was wearing a tug. "Does Sam pick out your clothes now? Nice sweater. And what about the wedding? Are you sure you even need to show up? Sam and Susan seem to be making all those decisions, too."

"Weddings are girl's stuff…" Jake mumbled.

"And you," Riley turned on Joe when he started laughing. "Shouldn't you be home folding diapers or baby-proofing the house or reading some childbirth book?"

Joe looked slightly panicked and tried, unsuccessfully, to glance at his watch unnoticed.

"See? You've been away for what? An hour? And

all you can think about right now is getting back and doing more baby stuff. Pathetic." Riley shook his head in disgust. "Don't you two talk to me about being wrapped around a woman's finger. You two are the poster children."

Jake considered for a minute then nodded. "Yep. He's done. No one argues that hard against something unless he's trying to convince himself it's not true."

"Welcome to the club, Riles. How does it feel to finally admit it?" Joe asked.

"I haven't admitted anything! I...aw, hell." Riley raked his hand through his hair and, with one big sigh, gave up.

"It's going to be okay. It's all going to be okay," Jake said, patting him on the back. "Many men before you have survived this. You will, too."

Riley paced around the room unsure of how he felt. In a way, talking to his brothers was comforting. As Jake said, they'd survived. Thrived, actually, if he was being honest. Both were happier than he had ever seen them. Jake was head-over-heels for Sam and, for as much grief as he gave Joe, he knew Joe was thrilled with the thought of being a father and Riley knew he was going to make a terrific one.

But, on the other hand, was he ready to admit to everyone how he felt about Susan? He hadn't even really told her...well, not in so many words. What was he supposed to do about that? So many things to think about. Women were complicated, he decided.

Turning back to his brothers he said, "Just promise me one thing. When it's Frank's turn, I get to be part of the posse. Three on one will be fun."

"Deal," Joe chuckled. "And when it's Shauna's

turn, all four of us can gang up on her."

They all started to laugh but quickly froze, staring horrified at one another. They were silent, unpleasant thoughts racing through their minds. Finally Jake spoke.

"She's just a kid."

"And she's a girl," Riley added.

"And our *sister*," Joe said, a panic-stricken look on his face.

"I'm sure we won't have to think about it for years. And years," Jake said uncertainly.

"Right. Years," Riley echoed.

They were quiet again, glancing hesitantly at one another, and each waiting for the others to come up with a solution to what seemed to be an enormous problem.

"I know," Joe brightened. "Sometime down the road—and I'm talking years here," his brothers were nodding, their expressions hopeful, "we'll have Karen and Sam, maybe Susan and whoever else is in the picture, talk to her. It will be better coming from women, anyway. Right?"

"For sure," Riley said, nodding vigorously now.

"Absolutely," Jake agreed on a sigh of relief.

They all shifted, still somewhat uneasy. To break the tension, Riley said, "You know, if you guys are going to hang around you might as well give me a hand. I've got a lot of drywall to hang."

Joe glanced at his watch. "Actually, I need to get going. There's some ba—" Clearing his throat, he continued. "There's some stuff I need to take care of at home."

"Yeah, Sam asked me to pick up a few things at the store for her. I mean, she knew I was heading out so it's really not a big deal…"

Somewhat awkwardly, Jake and Joe bundled back into their coats and gloves and headed for the door. On some mumbled goodbyes and see you soons, they made their way to their cars.

Disgusted, Riley frowned and muttered, "Wimps."

15

On Christmas Eve the house was full, much as it had been just a few weeks before, but for Susan, nothing could match the excitement, the enchantment, the joy of Christmas Eve. By five o'clock it was dark already and the tree, set against the inky black windows, sparkled and twinkled brightly, as if it knew tonight was the night to give its all. Dozens of packages, carefully wrapped in glittering paper and topped with dazzling bows and ribbons, created a sea of color underneath. Next year, Susan thought, the tree and packages wouldn't be safe for a minute from the curious little fingers of Joe and Karen's son or daughter. The idea warmed her heart and brought a smile to her face. The same would be the case at her parents' house, she knew, with her niece or nephew. Again, a smile spread on her lips but a tiny pain tugged at her heart.

There had been a few moments earlier in the day

as she and Sam were hustling with their last minute preparations, when the melancholy threatened, but she had brushed it aside. Yes, she missed her family, and yes, Christmas would be different, but it was still Christmas and, she figured, there was no point in thinking about what could be or what should be. Instead, she'd focus on what was in front of her and surrounding her with the kind of love families provide on Christmas. Even if they're not your own.

She had called her parents and would again on Christmas. They had passed the phone around and she'd talked with everyone. If her heart had ached a little, that was okay, she told herself. If it hadn't, she'd have been more upset. As it was, she looked around her at the decorations, the food, the people she was coming to think of as family, and she was thankful. She had taken a big risk six months ago leaving behind her family, friends, career, everything she knew, to try something different. Crazy, even. So far, she couldn't be happier. And she had one person in particular to thank for that.

She spotted Riley across the room with Joe. It didn't take a genius to figure out he was doing his best to get Joe worked up about the baby again. As she watched, Joe paled and clutched at Karen's arm. Riley threw his head back and laughed while Karen patted Joe's hand and reassured. When Karen turned and said something to Riley, he was the one who paled. Curious, Susan paid closer attention as Riley began backing away, eyes zooming around as if hoping for rescue. Karen took a determined step towards Riley. Slowly, soothingly, she took his hand and placed it on her belly. Even from a distance, Susan could see every muscle in Riley's body tense. His eyes grew wide as Karen kept his hand in place. Susan's laughter bubbled over at the sheer terror on Riley's face. But then she saw him relax and slowly, ever so slowly, a smile spread across his face and lit up his eyes. She watched as he mouthed 'It moved' over and over.

Sweet, she thought. Riley and his brothers may act tough, but Susan knew they were almost as anxious as Joe for the baby to be born. The first McCabe grandchild was going to be loved—and spoiled—to pieces.

One who would be responsible for a big part of that spoiling approached Susan and caught her in a hug.

"I know I already hugged you and wished you Merry Christmas, but I expect you might be feeling just a little homesick right about now and I thought another hug might help."

"Thank you, Mrs. McCabe, it does help."

"Come sit down with me and tell me all about Christmas Eve with your family," Anna coaxed as she led Susan to the sofa.

Susan sat and clutched a cheery red pillow bedecked with dozens of tiny, glittery snowflakes to her chest. One of her favorite finds at It's a Lake Thing, she thought idly as she turned it over in her hands.

"Will they have a crowd tonight?"

"Just my parents, my brothers, and my sister-in-law. We don't have any other family around. Sometimes the Munsons, our neighbors for as long as I can remember, come over, but Mom said they're in Florida this year visiting some family. They don't have anyone close by either so we spend holidays with them sometimes."

"That's nice, I always think the more the merrier

at the holidays. Family or friends, it doesn't matter."

"I guess. Holidays were so different when I was a child, before…before everything. We were always at my grandparents' house, my grandmother did all the cooking, everyone was so happy, there were games, and laughter…it was Christmas. What Christmas was to me, anyhow. Then after, my mom started having the holidays at our house. The first couple of years were rough, even as a kid you notice the strain, the sadness, but it got better and we gradually made a new normal." Susan didn't realize she had stopped talking and was staring into the darkness until Anna put a hand on hers.

"No matter how much time passes, there's something about holidays, Christmas especially, that makes you remember. I guess it's because everyone is usually so happy. Those kinds of memories have a way of sticking with you when some of the not-so-happy ones fade. And that's how it should be, I think."

Susan nodded, grateful for the wise words.

"I was sorry to hear your aunts weren't going to be here tonight, I'm guessing they have an abundance of Christmas stories to share. Is Rose feeling better?"

"She is. I visited this morning, she's still got a bit of a cold, but she's a lot stronger than she was a couple of weeks ago…a few days ago, even. I'll admit she gave me a bit of a scare. I've never seen her so weak and run-down. And she just didn't seem to have the same fight in her that I'm used to seeing. I couldn't quite figure it out, but she and Kate were carrying on like normal this morning so she's definitely on the road to recovery."

"It must be nice for them to be in the same apartment building. They're able to see each other, to check on each other, without having to go outside."

"Yes, most of the time," Anna laughed. "Sometimes when I visit most of what I hear is how impossible the other one is. I guess that's sisters for you. But it's a nice place and it's a good thing they both moved in when they did. There's a waiting list now for the building. It's the only senior apartment building in town or within a number of miles so there's quite a demand. They're having a little Christmas Eve party tonight. Hopefully Rose feels up to going."

"I hope so." Susan caught sight of Riley pulling Sam under the mistletoe and leaning her back for a dramatic kiss in front of Jake.

Anna watched Susan watch Riley with the eyes of a mother who wants only the best for her child and who has just determined that's what is headed her child's way.

"I hear things are moving along nicely with the bed and breakfast."

Focusing her attention back on Anna, Susan answered, "They are. Riley is doing a wonderful job. If I'm not able to stop by for a day or two I'm always amazed at the progress."

"That's good to hear. He's quite something, Riley."

Susan couldn't miss the leading tone in Anna's voice. "Yes, he is," she answered tentatively, somewhat unsure of where the conversation was headed.

"He's always been one to throw himself into a project and not give up. He'll work hard until you're happy with the way everything turns out."

"I'm sure he will."

"You know, he's never brought a girl around for

Christmas. Not a one. Now, I realize he didn't exactly bring you as this is your home and you'd be welcome at our home tomorrow regardless, but I can tell that's kind of how it is for him."

Aha, Susan thought. Now Riley's mom was getting to the reason for their chat. She remained silent and waited.

"He's dated a few girls off and on but nothing serious." She let the idea hang for a moment before continuing. "And you? I realize I've never asked if you left someone behind in Chicago."

"Um, nope. No one left behind."

"I see." Anna was beaming. "You know what a small town Misty Lake is...I have some friends who like nothing better than to report to me on my children's comings and goings, so it's only fair to tell you I've heard you and Riley have been out together a number of times."

"I don't know if I'd say a number..."

"No matter. I just want you to know that I think it's wonderful. Riley is a special boy—man, I suppose I should say although he'll always be a boy to me—and I love seeing him happy. You make him happy, Susan."

"Well, I don't know...I think maybe I drive him crazy sometimes." Susan was starting to sweat. She didn't think she could have this conversation, didn't think she could handle discussing Riley with his mother. She looked around desperately, wishing someone would come over to talk to them, wishing Gusto would demand her attention, wishing Karen would go into labor, wishing the Christmas tree would spontaneously combust...

"Pardon me?" she realized she hadn't been listening as Riley's mother had continued to talk. She ordered herself to focus and to stop picturing a flaming Christmas tree.

Anna smiled knowingly. "I was just saying that I can always tell when Riley's thinking about a girl. He gets distracted and then he gets moody. It's not a bad thing, mind you, just his thing. He gets over it quickly as it usually doesn't take him long to decide if the girl is worth his trouble or not. Now with you, he's past the moodiness so I know he's made up his mind."

"Oh?" Susan managed.

"Look how he's smiling over this way. It's not hard to figure out what he's decided."

Smiling? Right. He was probably just trying to keep from busting out laughing. Evil, that's what he was, enjoying her obvious discomfort. Well, she'd show him. Gathering herself, she turned to his mother and leaned close. "Let's just hope his decision is the right one. I've done some thinking myself and I'd hate to have to tell him he's come to the wrong decision. Just between you and me, Mrs. McCabe, I've decided I'm quite taken with your son, but I don't think I'm ready to let him know quite yet. Nothing wrong with keeping a man guessing, I figure. Especially a man who has been looking pretty darn smug for the last few minutes. I'll tell him soon, but I hope you don't mind if I make him squirm for just a little while."

Anna drew back and studied Susan for brief moment before tossing her head and letting a laugh fly. "I knew I liked you, Susan. You're going to keep Riley on his toes, that's for sure. Good for you." She laid a hand on Susan's. "And I think you'd better call me Anna."

Susan kept one eye on Riley as she meandered across the room, stopping for a quick word with Karen to make sure she was comfortable, checking to see if Frank needed a refill, and patting her dozing dog on the head. By the time she made her way to him, the hint of concern she had seen in his eyes when his mother had first laughed was now full-blown alarm.

Riley saw them talking, figured Susan was sitting through a round of questioning from his mother. It was funny, really. Wasn't it usually the girl's dad doing the interrogating? Not with his mom in the picture. She'd probably know everything from Susan's favorite movie to her views on politics to details of her first kiss within a few minutes. For as self-assured as she liked to be, he could tell, even from this distance, that Susan was caving to his mother. He decided to relax and watch the show.

When Susan leaned in and started whispering to his mother, and when his mother got that surprised look on her face, the one that he'd seen only a few times, that's when Riley started to sweat. When they both looked his way and smirked he considered making a run for it. Now that Susan was in front of him, after taking her sweet time getting there, he wanted to appear unruffled.

"So, what were you two talking about," Riley asked, struggling to keep his voice impassive. "Is my mom making up stories about me?" He gave a weak, forced laugh that turned into a cough.

"Making up stories? I'm betting there are enough true stories that she doesn't need to resort to making things up."

"Well, I'm sure she embellished."

"Relax, McCabe. She wasn't in the story-telling mood today."

Now he was even more perplexed as he threw a glance his mother's way then focused again on Susan. "I doubt you were talking about the weather…what gives?"

"Just girl talk, you wouldn't be interested."

Not interested. Right. It was eating at him and she darn well knew it. Well, he'd get it out of her, or his mom, eventually. Time to change the subject. "If you say so." He gave a casual shrug and looked to the kitchen. "Let's go get something to eat before Frank and my dad clean us out."

Susan thoroughly enjoyed being with the McCabe family. They teased, debated, joked, and competed but above all, loved. And they treated Susan and Sam as if they had always been a part of the group. Later in the evening, when Shauna took control of the music that had been playing low in the background and insisted on a game of 'Name that Christmas Tune,' Susan was treated to a first-hand example of their competitive nature.

"Guys against girls isn't fair," Joe protested. "You know more Christmas songs than we do." His brothers nodded their agreement.

"But you have one more player since Shauna's running the iPod," Karen shot back.

"It's still not even. How about if we swap Dad for Mom?" Riley suggested.

"Well, thank you very much for your vote of confidence, son," Sean said with a long, slow look at Riley.

Anna chuckled and settled the argument. "We'll leave the teams as they are. You boys will just have to try your best."

"Okay." Shauna rubbed her hands together. "I'll

start out easy to get you warmed up, but pay attention because I won't necessarily start at the beginning of the song. When you know the answer, shout it out. First team to ten wins." With that, she started the first song.

A couple of notes in, Sam was on her feet, her hand in the air. "It's *Rudolph The Red-Nosed Reindeer!*"

"Right! That's one for the girls." Shauna smirked at her brothers.

Karen waved an arm in Sam's direction. "No one said anything about jumping to our feet when we know the answer. I can't do that. No way."

"It's not a rule. Apparently Sam just got a little excited," Shauna said.

"Yeah, I got a little excited," Sam said, then gave Jake a friendly punch in the shoulder when he laughed at her.

"Next song," Shauna announced.

The men were leaning forward in their seats, eyes focused on the iPod speaker, but this time it was Anna who shouted, "*Joy To The World!*"

"Good job, Mom, that's another for the girls."

Some mumbling started on the sofa where Frank, Jake, and Riley were seated. "You should have gotten that one," Riley grumbled at Frank. "Remember how he used to walk around the house shouting 'Joy to the World' at the top of his lungs all December long?"

"I remember," Jake said. "Annoying. Now pay attention, we're losing."

"Ready?" Shauna asked before starting the next song.

When Susan got *O Christmas Tree* out just a moment before Joe, there were some unpleasant looks exchanged on the men's team.

"You guys are getting your butts kicked," Shauna singsonged.

"Just play the next one," Frank grumbled.

A few notes into the song, Riley bellowed, "*Chris—Christmas Vacation!* That's *Christmas Vacation!*"

"Calm down, you only get one point regardless of how many times you shout the answer," Shauna admonished.

There were high fives and fist bumps all around as the men celebrated Riley's point.

"Don't get too excited, you're still down three to one," Sam cautioned.

"Getting nervous, are you?" Jake asked.

"Not at all, right ladies?" Susan said. They all chimed in.

"Right."

"It's probably the only one they'll get all night."

"Look at them, acting like they won the game."

"Moving on," Shauna said over the din.

It took Susan only a moment to recognize *O Holy Night*. "Hah! Guess you guys aren't so smart after all," she needled.

Sean just shook his head. "I don't know how you're answering so fast. I don't even have a chance to hear the song before one of you is belting out the answer."

To Sam and Susan Anna said, "Sean prefers games that don't require such quick answers. He's a whiz at trivia games provided it's not a race to answer first."

"Sounds like Granddad," Susan reminisced. "Remember, Sam? Remember how much he hated it when we'd play one of the dozens of board games with timers?"

"But he always played along…except when we asked him to play that game that was like charades. That one he only played once."

"He was a good sport. I miss him."

"I do too," Sam said and laid a hand over Susan's.

Before they could let themselves get too swept away in their memories, Shauna was starting yet another song.

This time, it took everyone a while. Anna was humming along, frustrated at not being able to come up with the title. Jake was mouthing the words, trying to sing ahead of the music to get to the title before someone else. Finally, it was Karen who announced, "*It's Beginning To Look A Lot Like Christmas.*"

"Darn it!" Jake pounded his fist of the arm of the sofa. "I was just going to say that."

"Well, you should have been quicker," Shauna chided. "You guys ready to give up?"

"We don't give up," Riley growled at his sister. "Just play the next one." He turned and scowled at his teammates. "Pay attention."

The women got the next three before Jake got *Grandma Got Run Over By A Reindeer* making the score eight to two.

"I've never liked that song," Anna frowned. "Why would anyone think it's funny that Grandma got run over by a reindeer on Christmas Eve? Christmas songs are supposed to be happy."

"How about that horrible Christmas shoes song? Why do we need to hear it on the radio ten times a day, I have to wonder? A song about a little boy buying shoes for his dying mom? It's awful." Karen's voice caught, her eyes started to fill, and Joe was on his feet and at her side in a flash.

"It's okay, honey," Joe soothed as he stroked her back. "I'm sure Shauna won't play that song." He glared at Shauna as if daring her to contradict him.

Shauna held her hands up in defense. "Don't worry, I'm not going to play it. I don't like it anyway."

Karen took a deep breath and seemed embarrassed by her behavior. "I'm sorry, sometimes these crazy hormones make me a little emotional," she muttered.

"A little?" Riley mumbled and earned a sharp elbow in the ribs from Jake.

After a couple of minutes Shauna asked, "How about one more song? There's no way the boys are going to catch up, but there's one more I want to play."

They agreed and Shauna started the music. There were some curious glances as no one could place the tune. Suddenly Sean announced, "*Christmas In Killarney*," his face beaming as he looked proudly around the room.

"Way to go, Dad!" Shauna congratulated him. "I knew you'd get it."

"Good choice, Shauna, this Christmas needed a little Irish," Sean said in the thickest brogue he could muster.

Anna checked the time. "We really need to start thinking about getting ready if we're going to make midnight mass."

"Midnight mass at ten o'clock, you mean. I wonder how many midnight masses I slept through as a kid? Ten o'clock is probably a smart decision," Joe said on a yawn.

They started gathering plates and glasses,

searching for coats and purses, and gradually made their way to the cars. "Go ahead," Susan said to Sam when Jake announced he had the car warmed up. "I'll lock up here and be right behind you."

When it was just the two of them, Riley called Susan over to the Christmas tree and handed her two brightly wrapped gifts. "I didn't feel like doing this in front of everyone."

"But we need to get going, we shouldn't be late."

"We have time. Mom always thinks we need to be the first ones there. Sit down for a minute."

"Well, okay."

"Here, open this one first."

Susan took a moment to admire the Christmas tree. Susan and Sam had added their names to the McCabe family gift exchange drawing so they'd all be opening gifts together on Christmas Day, but she had always preferred Christmas Eve. Opening packages in the glow of the Christmas tree made it more magical.

She began tearing the paper on the first box. When she opened it and saw a Minnesota Wild jersey and a pair of tickets to a game against the Chicago Blackhawks, she had to laugh.

"Oh, Riley, I don't know if I can wear this. It's asking a lot."

"Trust me, you'll be happy you did. It's no fun sitting in an arena wearing the opposing jersey when your team loses."

"And if my team wins?"

"Still no fun. Everyone around you will heckle you."

"I'll go to the game, it sounds like fun, but I'm not

committing to wearing the jersey just yet."

"Fair enough. The game's not until the end of January, you'll change your mind by then. Now open the other one."

"Why are there two? It seems excessive."

Riley huffed out an exasperated breath. "Just open it, Red."

"Okay, okay." She tore away at the candy cane striped paper, opened the box, and found layers of tissue covering whatever was inside the heavy package. Curious, she carefully pulled back the paper and caught her breath. Staring up at her was a dramatic photograph of the Northern Lights, just as she could still see the display in her mind.

Reverently, she ran a hand over the glass. The varying shades of green seemed to swirl before her eyes. Unable to speak, she picked up the frame and below found a second photo, as stunning as the first. This one was taken from a slightly different angle and the light seemed to dance on the frozen, snowy surface of the lake.

The photos had been expertly framed and matted and they were perfect—absolutely perfect—for her Northern Lights room. And Riley had known.

"Did Frank take them?"

"Yep. Turns out that while we were watching from the window, he was racing around the lake trying to find the perfect vantage point."

"Riley, I don't know what to say…I, I don't know how to thank you. These are incredible, beautiful, exactly what I wanted for the room without even knowing it. But you did, you knew, and you did this for me and it's so sweet and it's so thoughtful and…and…"

She felt her throat start to tighten and she couldn't go on. She didn't have the words and even if she had, she didn't think she'd be able to get them out. She carefully set the box aside then, putting her hands on Riley's face, kissed him.

"I guess I figured you'd like them but I didn't expect this. I hope Frank doesn't get the same kind of thank you."

Susan choked out a half-laugh, half-sob and put her head on his shoulder. "No, not quite the same. He did take some amazing pictures, though. How did you get these done so quickly?" She picked one up again to admire it.

"I really wasn't sure I'd be able to but Frank has connections."

"Hmmm, I might have to rethink my thank you for him."

"Very funny." He played with her hair, delighted with the way the curls coiled around this fingers, while she continued to study the pictures. "We probably should get going now or we will wind up late for mass."

Susan glanced at the clock on the wall. "They'll save a seat for us," she said as she wrapped her arms around Riley and kissed him again.

16

The boy rubbed his eyes and sat up. It was still dark in the room, but he thought it was probably morning. Christmas morning. Nervously, he looked around, his eyes slowly adjusting to the dark. His mom was still sleeping next to him in the hard, lumpy bed. The room was small, but even so, he couldn't quite see all the way to the corner...the corner where he had finally convinced his mom to put a tiny Christmas tree.

He squinted through the shadows, hoping he would see a gift under the tree, but at the same time, prepared to find the spot empty. His mom had assured him Santa would find him in the motel. She said Santa always found good boys and girls, but he wasn't so sure. He should be home at Aunt Jenny's, that's where Santa would look for him. What if Santa had a present for him but left it under Aunt Jenny's tree? His mom said they might not go back there. Sad and with the tears that always seemed to be close to the surface threatening again, he summoned his courage and carefully snuck out of the bed.

The rickety table that held the little tree was pushed tight into the corner of the room. The boy was pretty sure that when he'd gone to bed the table had been empty except for the tree. As he tiptoed closer, he thought he could make out other shapes on the table. Holding his breath and moving as fast as he dared, he kept his eyes locked on those shapes.

Easing the curtain back a little from the window, light from the parking lot spilled over the table. There was no colorful wrapping paper but he didn't care, Santa had found him. Spread out on the table he spotted a bright blue monster truck, some crayons, markers, and paper, and a Spider-Man action figure. Tucked under Spider-Man's arm he found a candy cane.

Unable to hold his excitement inside, he bounced on his toes and squeaked, "Mommy! Mommy! Santa was here! Santa was here!"

Groaning and pulling the blanket up over her head, the woman whispered, "Shhh, Mommy's sleeping."

"But look, Mommy, Santa was here and I got toys." He scrambled back to the bed, his presents all gathered tightly in his arms, and waited for her to look.

Slowly, she pulled the blanket back, washed a hand over her face, and squinted at the boy. "Whatcha got there?" she managed.

"Look! Some crayons and markers and stuff, and a monster truck, and look, Spidey! Isn't it cool, Mommy, isn't it?"

"Yeah, it's cool." She smiled and reached over to smooth her hand over his wavy, chestnut hair. Scooting back on the bed, she patted the mattress and he climbed up next to her, excitedly showing her one treasure at a time. When he got to the candy cane he decided to try his luck since his mom seemed to be in a pretty good mood.

"Santa left a candy cane, too. Do you think I could have it now?"

"It's too early in the morning for candy, you haven't even had any cereal yet."

"I know, but it's Christmas and Santa gave it to me…"

"Save it for this afternoon. We have to drive again today, you can have it in the car."

"Where are we going?"

Good question, she thought to herself. They had been in the dumpy motel close to Denver for nearly three weeks, but the money was running out. Quickly. The few bucks she'd made when they had stayed with Billy outside of Vegas were almost gone. She had to find work but without knowing anyone, didn't know what she'd do with the boy. She'd been thinking for days, trying to come up with a solution besides the one she dreaded. And the other one she wasn't sure she had the nerve to try.

She knew there'd be work in Omaha, just as there had been years ago. She'd have to beg, she knew he'd make her, but she'd do it.

She watched the boy plowing the truck over mountains made by pillows and blankets and hoped the cheap toys—all she'd been able to afford—would hold up, at least for a while. She should have left him in California. He was happy with Jenny and Jenny would have taken care of him like he was her own. But he was hers, the only thing she had left. She wanted to take care of him, wanted to be a good mother, but it was so hard. Jenny made it seem so easy, flitting from school conferences to soccer games to the gym. Well, Jenny's life was easy, hers wasn't. She was tired of being compared to Jenny, tired of the expectations, just tired.

"Watch, Mommy, Spidey's gonna rescue the truck cuz it's crashing." He staged a fantastic crash, complete with appropriate sound effects, into the pillow pressed up tight against the headboard.

"Okay, baby, just a minute, Mommy's head hurts. I'll be right back."

She watched his hands still and his face fall. She knew her headaches bothered him, knew her mood swings were hard on him, but didn't know how to stop them.

"Maybe we can call Aunt Jenny later and wish her Merry Christmas." She wanted to sound cheerful, wanted to put a smile back on his face.

"Really?"

"Sure, baby."

She grabbed her purse, pulled a ratty robe around her shoulders, and headed for the bathroom. Once inside, she dug through her purse with trembling hands. The fancy cell phone Jenny had given her when they'd left California, telling her she'd cover the monthly payments because she wanted to stay in touch, seemed to mock her and she shoved it aside. When her fingers tightened around the small vial, she relaxed. Shaking pills out into her hand, she filled a glass with water and washed them down. She leaned her head against the bathroom door and closed her eyes. She'd feel better soon. And then she'd start for Omaha because she had no choice.

17

Christmas was over, the new year well underway, and a long winter still ahead. Most years, Susan had to fight the blues that threatened once the excitement of the holidays was past, but this year there was simply too much to look forward to. The blues didn't stand a chance.

First, there were two new adorable, sweet, and perfect babies. Born just three days apart, Dylan Joseph McCabe and Lauren Elizabeth Taylor brought light to the long, dark days. Susan's only regret was that her niece was in Chicago and she wasn't able to stop in and visit on a moment's notice. Dylan helped ease the ache. He was a bundle of cuddly joy with the bright blue McCabe eyes, a mass of dark hair, and round, plump cheeks just made to nuzzle. On the day he was born the entire McCabe family had waited, anxiously pacing in the hospital waiting room, for the first of the next generation of McCabes to make an appearance. When Joe came out and announced his son had arrived, healthy and screaming at the top of his lungs, there hadn't been a dry eye in the room. Three days later Sam and Susan had hopped on a plane to meet Lauren, a fair-skinned, blue-eyed and blonde-haired beauty who already had her father wrapped around her finger.

Next, the progress on the inn was, in her opinion, incredible. The guest rooms were framed, most already covered with drywall, the bathrooms roughed-in, and her kitchen was starting to take shape. Riley had pulled down the rusted cabinets and the plaster that had covered the kitchen wall to fully expose the long-hidden brick. His best guess was that, at some point, a remodeling job involved updating the kitchen and the brick was deemed outdated. She loved the dark red brick that extended the entire length of the kitchen and, to her delight, another wall of the same brick had been uncovered in the parlor during demo. Susan couldn't wait to decorate the room around the deep red shades of the brick.

Online searches for ideas led her to a dizzying array of design options. She both praised and cursed the Internet. On the one hand, most anything she needed was at her fingertips. On the other hand, browsing the endless pictures and descriptions of the almost unbelievable homes others had envisioned and created left her feeling woefully inadequate. There was simply no way she'd ever match the spectacular displays she clicked through, one after the other. At times she found herself longing for the days when one's inspiration came from neighbors or from the one or two magazines devoted to home décor, and not from everyone in the world with a flair for the artistic and access to a computer.

Riley had stressed to her the importance of not

ordering too much too soon when it came to fixtures. Timing was important, he had explained, since there wasn't a great deal of space to store toilets, sinks, cabinets, and the like. To Susan, it became a challenge she embraced wholeheartedly. She devised intricate spreadsheets with expected completion dates, estimated shipping times, and ordering deadlines. She set up alerts to notify her as the dates approached. She was especially proud of the information she had built into the spreadsheet that spelled out not only individual item and shipping costs, but discounts based on quantity, where applicable. She would analyze the information to determine if it made more sense for her to hold off on ordering until Riley was ready for everything from a particular vendor, or if discounts either didn't apply or didn't outweigh the costs of waiting. Genius. She silently congratulated herself as she studied the data for the umpteenth time.

If she were being honest with herself, finding discounts wherever she could was becoming more of a necessity than merely just a challenge. She hadn't discussed it with anyone yet, but she was starting to worry about the costs and about her budget. She had known from the outset that the project was going to be expensive, but seeing the bills on a daily basis and knowing what was still to come had her worried. She didn't know if she could go back to the bank for another loan. Sam would help her out, she'd offered more than once and Susan knew she was sincere, but that would be an absolute last resort.

It was some of the changes and add-ons she had insisted upon and had convinced Riley to go along with that were killing her. Maybe she should have listened to him when he'd tried to talk to her about the price tag. But, she reasoned, they would pay off in the long run. Turning the barn into the event center would bring in more revenue, as would the additional attic rooms. She'd just have to figure it out.

"So, McCabe, what's so important that I needed to come over here on my day off, when it's twenty below zero, and when I really should be home doing laundry?" Susan asked as she hurried inside and rubbed her nose trying to get it to thaw. Gusto bolted in ahead of her, ran to greet Riley, then disappeared up the stairs.

"He sure makes himself at home here."

"Is he in the way? I don't have to bring him along all the time if it's a problem."

"Nah, he's figured out what he can and can't get away with and the guys all like him. He's getting spoiled. I think they've all started keeping treats in their pockets and sneaking him one when they think I'm not looking. If anything, he's going to need to go on a diet."

"He is a little mooch, isn't he?" Susan smiled and stretched on her toes to give Riley a kiss on the cheek. "Anyway, what did you want to talk to me about?"

"I had a call this morning…"

"And?"

"Remember Jeremiah?"

"The barn restoration expert? Sure. Did he finally get back to you?" Susan had been anticipating, and dreading, his report. If he felt it was possible to make the barn usable year-round she knew the price tag would be huge. But if he felt it didn't make sense, she'd be disappointed.

"He did, with details on how he thinks we should

finish the barn to make it usable all year, and he explained his reason for taking so long with his suggestions. You must have impressed him, or he wants to ask you out, or something, because he sure went to bat for you."

Susan grinned at the idea of sixty-year-old Jeremiah, father of eight, grandfather of fourteen and counting, asking her out. "He's a sweet man but what do you mean, went to bat for me?"

"Apparently there are grants available for the restoration and preservation of historical barns. He spoke with some of the right people, showed pictures, explained what you're doing here, and feels pretty confident that if you're willing to fill out some paperwork, you'll qualify."

Shock exploded like fireworks on Susan's face. "A grant? A grant, as in they'll give me money for the project?"

"That's what a grant is, sweetheart."

"Oh, my gosh. I can't believe this." She walked in circles as her mind raced. A grant would cover some of the expenses she had been fretting over. Everything happened in time and for a reason. She was overwhelmed.

"It would appear I owe you a huge thank you once again," she said turning to Riley.

"I didn't do anything, Jeremiah did the leg work on this one."

"Oh, I'll thank him, you can be sure, but you're the one who brought him here, the one who had the foresight to call in an expert, the one who explained to him what I wanted to do in a way that made sense, the one who made all this happen. Again. You have a way of making things happen."

When he just shrugged she went to him and slid

her arms around his waist. "In just a few months you've amazed me time and again. You pulled strings to get work underway far ahead of schedule, you rolled with all the crazy changes I suggested and made them a reality, you brought Shauna and Frank in to help with things I never would have been able to do myself, and now this. You're my hero, my knight in shining armor, my… miracle worker," she said dramatically.

When he chuckled and opened his mouth to argue, she laid a finger on his lips. "Don't. Just accept my thanks and know that it couldn't be more sincere or more heartfelt." Then she replaced her finger with her lips.

"If you're going to keep thanking me like that, I'll have to find more miracles to work."

"I don't doubt you for a minute."

Riley gave her an overview of what Jeremiah had suggested they do to winterize the barn to make it a year-round facility. Susan nodded, added a few comments, but was distracted. "You want to call Jeremiah, don't you?"

"Oh, I do. I have to thank him and I have a million questions for him. I don't want to get too excited before I know all the details of the grant. How long does the process take? Are there a lot of guidelines I'll need to follow as far as what changes I make to the original structure? What about the paperwork? How do I go about completing it? And on and on and on."

"Then go call him. I told him he should expect to hear from you today. I would imagine he's waiting."

"Thanks, Riley. Now, where is that silly dog? I haven't seen him since we walked in."

"I'm pretty sure I know where he is. Come on." Riley headed up the stairs and motioned for Susan to follow. They climbed all the way to the attic and found Gusto asleep in the corner of one of the attic bedrooms where the ceiling came closest to the floor and a narrow beam of sunlight snuck in from the dormer window.

"Look at him. I guess he's found his favorite spot."

"Ever since I did a little work up here one day and he followed me, he's been sneaking up here and hiding away in that corner."

A slow smile spread across Susan's face. She leaned back and crossed her arms over her chest, nodding.

Riley cocked his head and gave her a questioning look.

"That's it," she said simply. "The Hideaway."

Understanding dawned on Riley's face…the next name for one of her rooms. "I'd say it's pretty perfect. But you might have to add a disclaimer that the room comes with a dog."

That got a laugh out of Susan. "It is perfect. And this day just keeps getting better and better."

Omaha sucked. The crappy apartment she was sharing with three other girls sucked. And Dez really sucked. Even more than he had a few years ago when she'd worked for him. He had made her beg, that hadn't surprised her, but his anger had. He hadn't forgotten that she'd left town in the middle of the night without warning. He almost didn't take her back, but he was nearly as desperate as she was, so in the end, they'd worked out a deal. This time she'd made it clear she didn't plan on being around for long.

Now, here she was, squeezing into a short skirt, a tight top, and heels so high she'd had to practice walking in them. She didn't know why it mattered what she wore, none of them ever noticed. She studied herself in the mirror as she applied heavy makeup. Looking back at her was a pale, thin ghost of her previous self with stringy, faded blonde hair and haunted eyes. She tried to cover and forget. Forget the twenty-one-year-old with rosy cheeks over tanned skin, bright blue eyes full of secrets and laughter, arms and legs toned from hours spent swimming and water skiing, and sunny blonde hair that bounced on her shoulders and was the envy of all her friends. Forget that day over six years ago when she'd looked in the mirror and seen that twenty-one-year-old for the last time before making the decision that had changed her life forever.

She sighed as she grabbed her purse and started to head out. Before she closed the door behind her she glanced over at the boy sleeping on the stained sofa, a thin blanket tossed over him and Spider-Man clutched tightly in his hand. The girls said they'd look out for him while she was gone. She hoped they meant it.

She closed the door and tottered down the stairs in the sky-high heels. In the midst of trying to forget, she hoped she'd remember one thing. She hoped she'd remember how to block it all out, how to pretend she was somewhere else, how to close off her ears to the sounds, her nose to the smells, and just float away.

18

They'd decided to make a weekend of it and Susan was nervous. Excited, but nervous. The shopping she was looking forward to. They'd have Friday afternoon, all day Saturday, and part of Sunday to scour salvage shops and were hoping to find things to match existing pieces in the house. A couple of the glass doorknobs were no longer usable, a shutter was missing, and the stair rail and some floorboards needed replacing. On top of that, Susan was hoping to get an idea of what was available as far as fixtures for the bathrooms as well as kitchen equipment that met with food service regulations. They had a busy weekend ahead of them.

But first, she had to get over her nervousness regarding the hotel arrangements. Riley had asked her if she wanted a separate room. She had tried, desperately, to read his mind when he asked, tried to figure out what he meant, but he had kept his expression remarkably passive.

In the end, she had tried to remain cool when she'd said one room with two beds would be fine—they could split the cost, save some money—but she knew he had seen right through her.

She glanced at Riley, wondering how he was feeling about the weekend. Did guys ever get nervous about such things? Did they ever think that far ahead? As if sensing her stress, Riley took her hand and pulled it to rest under his on the center console. The simple gesture went a long way towards calming her nerves.

"I've been meaning to talk to you about that big pine tree on the southern corner of the house. I was working in the bedroom yesterday and with the wind blowing pretty hard, the branches were scraping against the window. You're going to have to decide if you want to take it down or see if it can be trimmed."

"I hate to take it down. Last fall when all the windows were open I loved going in that room. It smelled like Christmas…like heaven. It's a happy smell. I don't want to lose that. I'll check into getting it trimmed. You don't happen to know anyone, do you?"

"I can get you a name."

"I never doubted it." Then she grew quiet and stared out the window at the highway racing past, her lips moving and a crease deepening on her forehead.

Riley watched her for a minute before asking, "Care to share?"

She was slow in answering but finally turned to him and touching one finger at a time said, "Scotch Pine, Pine Woods, Big Pine, or…O Tannenbaum?"

"What?"

She responded with a long-suffering sigh. "You

really should have this figured out by now. A room name, you goof. What do you like?"

"O Tannenbaum?"

"It means Christmas tree."

"I know what it means, Red, it's just kind of weird, don't you think?"

"I don't know, it has a nice ring to it. I could keep a Christmas tree in there year-round. Maybe I wouldn't even rent it out, just keep it as my happy place."

"I'd go with Big Pine or...what was it? Pine Woods?"

She nodded thoughtfully. "You're probably right. A pine log bed and dresser, maybe a mirror framed in pine branches, a deep green rug. Pine scented potpourri and soaps, of course. It'll be gorgeous." She made a check mark in the air with her finger. "That's three. They just keep coming."

"We're getting close. Which place do you want to stop at first?"

"The big one, don't you think?"

"They're all big."

"The really big one."

Even really big didn't do it justice. The place was massive. Merchandise stretched as far as the eye could see. Warehouse after warehouse filled with everything she could have imagined, and then some. They had been there an hour before Susan realized there were four floors and an outdoor lot, too. And even though Riley had warned her it would be cold, she was freezing.

They made their way through row after row of doors until they found just the right one to replace a door that was, for some reason, missing from one of the bedrooms. One entire room was devoted to bathroom fixtures and the selection of clawfoot tubs was overwhelming. Susan walked the rows, considering and debating. Some were in bad shape, but several just needed a good cleaning. The prices on the tubs that were in at least fair condition were much higher than she wanted to pay. She asked Riley's opinion.

"You can probably talk them down some, they want to move the merchandise, but I don't know how we'll get everything back to Misty Lake. I still hope to find floorboards, a couple of windows, the stair rail, maybe some other stuff. It's not all going to fit in the truck. Maybe we hold off on the tub for now."

"Hmmm." She circled the tub she liked the best, leaning down to check the bottom and to examine the feet. Then she looked at the rows of similar tubs. "You're right. If I can't get this one, there will be another. We'll forget it for now."

As they headed off to check out the stock of stair rails and newel posts, Susan started shivering and felt her toes going numb. Her excitement was quickly waning.

They finally bumped into Jimmy, a muscled, bearded, red-faced giant who somehow seemed to know everything the salvage store carried, where it was located, and how to find it through the maze. When Jimmy saw Susan start to hop up and down in an attempt to get warm and took pity on her directing her to the employee office to warm up, he became her new favorite person.

While Riley followed Jimmy, Susan chatted with Francie over a blessedly hot cup of coffee and wiggled her toes, willing them to thaw.

"Where is this inn going to be?" Francie, who Susan learned had run the office for thirty-seven years, was a solid woman with tight grey curls, strong, capable hands, and a booming laugh.

"It's on Misty Lake. Do you know where that is? I'm still kind of new to the area so I don't even know how to explain where it's located."

"Misty Lake? You don't say." Francie slapped a hand to her thigh and grinned. "We used to go there when I was a kid. I have so many memories of fishing with my dad on that lake. We'd go out, just the two of us, before the sun came up. I loved those times when I had him all to myself. And I met my first boyfriend there...Teddy Franks. He kissed me one night on the beach with the moon and stars shining on the lake. I was fifteen and sure I'd found the man I was going to marry. Teddy had other ideas. Two days later I saw him kissing a blonde girl with big boobs. My heart was broken and I cried all night until my mom finally told me to snap out of it, a boy like that wasn't worth my tears, and when the right one came along, I'd know it. Four years later I met my Wally and I've never looked back."

"I hope some day people will remember their time at my bed and breakfast so fondly. That's my goal, really, to help people make memories."

"I get a little of that working here sometimes. I see people wander through and watch their eyes light up when they spot something that reminds them of grandma's house or their old school. I think it's knowing that we're making memories for those we love, or even for those we don't know, that makes things worth doing."

"I think you're right. I worked at a fancy hotel in

Chicago before coming here. I met couples on their wedding night, friends reunited after years apart, little kids staying in a hotel for the first time, and once, the sweetest couple celebrating their seventieth anniversary. Their family threw a party for them at the hotel and then booked the honeymoon suite for Betsy and Wilbur as a surprise. I escorted them to their room filled with flowers, sweets, and monogrammed robes. I've never seen anyone blush the way Betsy did when Wilbur teased her that they would need to make sure the kids' money was well spent. Times like those made all the long days and impossible guests worth it. The thought that, for those people, we were helping them seal a special time forever in their memories…you're right, that's what it's all about."

"I don't doubt your place will be the setting for many happy memories. What will you call it?"

"Do you know what's funny? With all the questions I've answered about the B&B, all the people who are curious and have asked everything from what kind of food I'll serve to how many towels I'll have in the bathrooms, not one person has asked me what I'm going to name the place with the exception of the one who helped me set up my website."

"Seems to me like a logical question."

"Doesn't it? I gave it quite a bit of thought and decided I'm going to keep it simple, old-fashioned, even. Rather than a cutesy sort of name, I'm going with The Inn at Misty Lake."

Francie considered for a moment, then a smile spread across her face as she winked her approval. "I think you're going to do just fine with that inn of yours, Susan. Sit tight for a minute." With that, she disappeared into a room off the office.

Susan looked around while she waited. The window in the office allowed her to watch people milling about, but there was no sign of Riley. She figured he must be close to frozen and felt a little guilty for taking refuge out of the cold.

Susan couldn't tell what it was Francie had in her hands as she came back into the office. She held it out in front of her and told Susan, "This came in a while back but I always thought it was too special to just throw out there with everything else. I've been hanging on to it for the right person. I've found her. It's yours if you want it."

Francie was holding an old-fashioned-looking wooden sign hanging from an intricate wrought iron bracket. The sign creaked ever so slightly as it swung gently when Francie held it out to Susan. It was beautiful and Susan fell in love with it even before Francie turned it around and she saw the carving on the sign. 'The Inn.'

"Oh, Francie, it's magnificent. I'd love to have it, name your price."

"No, honey, this is a gift. It was waiting for you."

Susan began to argue then told herself she needed to be gracious and accept a gift when it was given to her. "Thank you, Francie, that's incredibly generous of you. I happen to have a cousin who's a whiz with wood and I'm betting she can add another level to the sign that reads 'at Misty Lake.' I can't imagine anything more perfect. I'll tell you what. If you want to make another trip to Misty Lake you let me know. I'll have a room waiting for you."

"I just might take you up on that...make myself some new memories."

Susan was thanking Francie again when the office

door squeaked open.

"Head on in, Francie will ring you up," Jimmy said, holding the door for Riley.

As Jimmy went to give Francie a tally of what Riley had decided on, Susan rushed to Riley with the sign.

"Riley, oh, I hope you're not frozen." Before he could answer, she turned the sign to face him. "Look what Francie gave me. Isn't it absolutely perfect?"

He admired the artistry of the ironwork before he read the sign. "The Inn? Is that what you're going to call your place? I guess I never asked."

Francie scolded him. "How does it happen you spend every day working there and you've never asked the name of the place?"

"I'm not sure, ma'am, but it's definitely an oversight on my part. I'm sorry about that."

"Don't apologize to me, son. Those are words your lady needs to hear, not me."

Properly put in his place by a woman he hadn't even been introduced to, Riley turned sheepishly to Susan. "I'm sorry, I should have asked you a long time ago. And if I would have looked at your website like I keep meaning to do, I'd know. What do you plan to call it?"

"Well, since you've asked," Susan grinned, "The Inn at Misty Lake. What do you think?"

"I think I like it. It has a little bit of an old-time sound to it and from a marketing standpoint, it's a good choice. Anyone searching for anything related to Misty Lake will come across it. Very good choice."

"Thank you. I'm going to ask Sam if she can add a second tier to the sign so it displays the whole name."

"It will look right at home hanging from the front

porch." Turning to Francie, he tried to redeem himself. "That's a very considerate gift. It's very well made and Susan's lucky to have it. Almost as lucky as I am to be standing here next to her. You have a good eye, Mrs….?"

"Oh, call me Francie," she answered with a wave of her hand, Riley having already won her over. "And you're right, you are a lucky man. Don't you forget it. And don't you forget to tell her so everyday. A woman likes to hear those things."

"You can count on it, Francie."

They made a stop at the hotel to get checked in and to warm up and change clothes before the game. In the end, Susan agreed to wear the Wild jersey…but only after Riley promised—and crossed his heart—not to take a picture. Once there, she found herself in a dilemma. The arena was electric with excitement, it was hard not to be swept up in it. When the home team scored the first goal, the place erupted and, somehow, she found herself on her feet cheering right along. It wasn't until she caught Riley's 'I told you so' look that she realized what she was doing. Sheepishly, she sat back down and reminded herself she was a Blackhawks fan.

Watching the game seated next to Riley was exciting, amusing, and educational. He twisted and turned and deked in his seat right along with the players. He called penalties before the referees, saw plays setting up before some of the skaters, and questioned the coaches' decisions at what he deemed critical moments in the game.

"Have you ever thought about coaching?" Susan asked him during intermission.

"Interesting you'd ask that. I hadn't ever

considered it, but I got a call just this week from my old high school coach who's still sacrificing a little of his hair every winter in hopes of one day making it here," Riley swept his arm out in front of him to encompass the arena, "for the state tournament. His assistant had to step down mid-season due to health problems so he needs someone to fill in. He asked me to take the job. The season is winding down, it would be a short-term thing, but I know he's convinced I'll love it and agree to come back next year."

"What did you tell him?"

"I told him I'd think about it. He wants an answer by Sunday evening."

Susan studied him and couldn't miss the gleam in his eyes. "So you've thought about it and you want to do it, but…?"

"But I'm busy. Really busy. I'm putting in long days, working some weekends already. I don't want to risk getting behind schedule."

"Riley, if you want to do it, do it. I think you'd be an amazing coach. There have been times tonight when I thought you were going to head down to the bench to have a word with the coaches. And besides, I happen to know your boss will look the other way if you have to cut out early some days."

Riley's lip twitched and he snorted a quick chuckle. "Generous of you, but I don't know…it will suck up a lot of my time for a month or so."

"Only a month? How far behind can you get in a month?"

"Pretty far."

"Well, you've been saying you're ahead of

schedule so you can probably afford to slack off a little. I'll tell you what…I'm getting pretty good with that nail gun so I'll just take over when you have to leave."

"For that, I just might have to tell coach yes." He draped an arm around her shoulders and pulled her close.

Susan had more fun than she'd had in a long time. The game was a nail-biter and, more than once, she found herself on the edge of her seat. When Riley left for a quick trip to the concession stand and returned not only with popcorn and drinks but a giant foam Wild claw for Susan, she was delighted and promptly fit it on her hand and gave it a wave, giving in to the hometown fever sweeping the crowd. She rationalized that she could support two teams even though Riley argued the two were inherently mutually exclusive. Later, when the home team scored the winning goal with under a minute left in the game, she exchanged foam high-fives with the team of youth hockey players seated behind them and enjoyed every moment of it.

They made their way out of the arena and fought the crowd exiting the parking ramp. During the drive to the hotel, Riley rehashed the game, pointing out things that had gone right and things that had gone wrong. "Should have been an easy game but they were lucky to get the win," he grumbled. "I would imagine they got an earful in the locker room."

"Spoken like a coach. I hope you've realized you need to give it a chance."

"Yeah, I guess I came to that conclusion tonight. I'll call coach in the morning."

"Excellent. And I hope you're not going to tell me I can't come to these games because I'll come anyway."

"You can come, you can come."

Once the door of the hotel room closed behind them, Riley grabbed Susan and kissed her deeply.

"I've been wanting to do that for hours," Riley murmured in her ear as he inhaled the spicy, slightly woodsy scent that was Susan and that tied his stomach in knots. "I don't know what to make of you, Red...you're smart as hell, you're the most determined woman I've ever met, you get hockey, you somehow make shopping fun, and you smell so good. Are you real?"

Susan laughed as she playfully shoved him back and shrugged off her jacket. "I'm real. And you may want to hold off on your assessment of shopping until after tomorrow. I've got big plans, McCabe."

He watched as her eyes darted around the room and she rubbed her hands up and down on her thighs. "Why don't you take the bathroom first," he suggested.

"Thanks. I think I'll grab a quick shower."

Susan snatched her bag and darted into the bathroom, closing the door quickly behind her. She leaned against the door for a moment and took a deep breath. Then, chiding herself for being a fool, set about getting ready for bed.

She came out of the bathroom fifteen minutes later wearing blue and white plaid flannel pajamas buttoned up to her chin and fuzzy blue slippers. Riley scratched his head and laughed. "Trying to tell me something, Red?"

"No, just figured it would be cold in here," she lied.

Laughing again, Riley took his turn in the

bathroom.

Susan quickly chose the bed farthest away from the door, grabbed her book and her glasses, and climbed under the covers. She ordered herself to focus on the book and not on the man in the shower on the other side of the wall.

Riley showered, brushed his teeth, and decided he probably should have packed some sweat pants or a pair of shorts or something besides the boxers he was wearing. Wiping the steam off the mirror, he glanced at himself and ran a hand through his damp hair. He figured there was a comb somewhere in his bag, but decided searching for it wasn't worth the trouble. He opened the door wondering how Susan would feel about his dress, or lack thereof...and found her sound asleep.

She was propped up against a pillow, open book on her chest, and glasses slipping down her nose. Gently, he took the book and set it on the table, removed her glasses, eased her down to the bed, and tucked the blankets around her. He brushed the mass of wild red hair off her forehead and gently touched his lips to hers. "Night, Red," he whispered.

Susan stirred a little, snuggled down into the pillow, and in her sleep mumbled, "Night. I love you, Riley."

He froze. What? He whipped his head around as if he'd find someone who could tell him...tell him that he'd just heard Susan say she loved him. He knew he hadn't imagined it and he knew he was awake so he hadn't dreamt it. No, he was sure she'd said it. Huh. Of all the things he thought might happen, that wasn't one of them.

As he watched her sleep, he realized he hoped he'd hear the words again soon, when she was awake, but knew he'd never forget this first time. He ran his fingers down her hair and swore he knew exactly how the Grinch had felt when his heart grew three sizes that day.

"I love you too, Red."

Saturday was jam-packed with scouring salvage stores and hardware stores. Susan and Riley were able to find a few more things they needed and many more they hadn't known they needed. They stumbled upon a huge selection of drawer pulls that had been salvaged from an old hotel slated for demolition. Susan fell in love with a design that closely replicated that used on the antique armoire left behind at the inn. She scooped up enough to use on dressers, vanities, and cabinets throughout the inn and was delighted with her find.

Riley's favorite find, by far, was the reclaimed oak that fit exactly with what he had pictured for the bar top. It looked a bit rustic, had rough-hewn edges and a slightly weathered but not worn look to it…the kind of look that could only be created naturally, never in a factory. He bartered a bit with the shop owner and left with what he wanted at a fraction of what he had expected to pay.

They debated how to best get everything back to Misty Lake. Even with Riley's truck, they didn't have space for everything they had purchased. The shop owner who sold them the reclaimed oak gave them an estimate to have everything delivered, but in the end, they decided to rent a trailer and haul it themselves. Once the decision was made, Susan convinced Riley to go back to their first stop where she had seen the vintage claw-foot tub and they added that to their booty. By evening, they were tired, dirty, and hungry.

"I need a shower before we go anywhere," Susan complained. "I had no idea this would be such a filthy job." She took in her dusty, stained jeans and her greasy, blackened hands. Unable to find anything better to use to clean her hands, she wiped them on her jeans.

"You're starting to act like a contractor," Riley said as he watched her use her jeans to get all the dirt off her hands and out from under her fingernails. Good idea about the showers but I'm starving, let's make it quick."

On the drive back to the hotel, Susan caught Riley looking at her with the same strange expression he'd had on his face most of the day. She couldn't figure it out. It was as if he knew something she didn't and it wasn't sitting well with her. She had tried a couple of times to ask him what was going on, but he had simply smirked and claimed he was just enjoying the day. There was more to it, she was certain, but apparently she was going to have to wait him out.

Once they'd cleaned up and changed clothes, they decided against going back out into the cold in search of a restaurant and, instead, headed downstairs to the hotel pub.

The food was good, the live music better, and before Riley could figure out what was happening, he found himself on the dance floor.

"I don't dance," he hissed as Susan started to move to the beat.

"Everyone dances. Just relax and have fun."

"Fun is when I know what I'm doing. This is a particularly brutal form of torture."

"Oh, don't be such a baby."

She took his hands and led him along with her. He was right, she soon realized, dancing didn't come naturally to him but he gave it a shot, and for that, she loved him. A strange feeling of déjà vu struck her. Hard. Something about the way Riley was looking down at her and she saying she loved him. But she knew that had never happened. It had probably been a dream, she told herself, but that didn't feel quite right. She couldn't shake the feeling but couldn't put a finger on what she was trying to remember, either. Then the music slowed, Riley held her close, swaying with the rhythm, and she forgot everything but him.

19

Time seemed to move quickly, even during the typically long, endless months of winter. Riley found time between working, playing hockey, and coaching to teach Susan to ice fish and to take her snowmobiling and ice skating. She was a good sport, braving freezing temperatures on the back of a snowmobile, spending an entire Sunday in a fish house, and, to his surprise, keeping up with him on the ice rink. He had given her a good dose of heckling when she'd laced up bright white figure skates, but then stood shocked as she blazed onto the ice and cut a few laps around the rink before executing some kind of fancy jump and spin.

When she had skated fast up to him stopping on a dime mere inches from his face, his jaw had landed somewhere around his chest. He could still hear her laughter and teasing. Eventually, he had put a hockey stick in her hands and they had spent a couple of hours goofing off, even joining a pickup game when a group of middle schoolers were looking for more players.

As he prepped the walls in The Hideaway for painting, his mind wandered as it tended to do when the work didn't require his full concentration. He ran over his schedule and tried to estimate when the painting would be done. Susan had insisted from the outset that she would do, or at least help with, the painting. She'd be starting tomorrow. He was more than a little curious to see how quickly she moved. She had sworn she knew what she was doing. And he needed a final decision from her on ceramic tile, as it would go in soon after the painting was done. The thought of tiling eight bathrooms and a kitchen wasn't a pleasant one. Tiling was far down on his list of favorite jobs and just thinking about how long it would take for a job of such size had him wanting to reach for a beer. He made a mental note to call Travis that night to see if he and maybe one of his guys would be available to help. Travis did good work and would get it done quickly and correctly. Riley started to mentally rearrange his schedule assuming Travis agreed to the job but wouldn't be able to start right away.

Maybe he'd see if Susan wanted to grab a burger later. He could bring up the topic of the tile over dinner. He glanced at his watch and guessed she would be getting there soon; her shift would be ending in a few minutes and she had told him she'd be heading over straight from town.

They had become a couple over the last few months. Before meeting Susan, he had never given the idea much thought. Sure, he'd dated and sure, he supposed sometimes he and the girl were thought of as a couple, but it hadn't been the same. In the past it had been fun, but in all honesty, there had never been much closeness or affection, at least on his part. And there certainly hadn't been love.

He tossed around his idea again. It was starting to grow on him. Her birthday was coming up in April. He had already asked Sam to make sure Susan didn't make any plans and he had asked Emily to give her the weekend off. He wanted to take her away for the weekend—he had a couple of places in mind and reminded himself he needed to make a decision and a reservation soon—and then he would ask her to marry him. He had looked at rings, but was considering asking Sam to help him. He didn't want to screw it up.

He wasn't nervous, he realized, as he ran over plans in his head. Well, not too nervous, anyway. It felt right. Thinking about finishing up the job in a few months and then not seeing Susan nearly every day? That felt wrong. It would all work out. He'd ask her and she'd say yes. It was meant to be—they were meant to be—he told himself. And he mostly believed himself.

He finished up work in The Hideaway and decided he'd have time to tackle the floorboards in the corner bedroom downstairs. He had found some boards that were a close match at the salvage store and had kept them inside for a while to get the wood acclimated, so it was time to pull up the old ones and install the new ones. One more thing he could get installed and out of the way. He figured he'd have to remove a three by four foot section under the window. The boards had gotten wet at some point and the water had apparently gone unnoticed long enough to cause some pretty serious damage. The previous owners had pushed a bed over the damaged spot and apparently had done their best to ignore it.

Riley made some cuts then tugged at the warped and cracked boards, pulling out rusted nails and easing the boards away from the floor. When they were all up and he started to gather them, something in the floor caught his eye. Setting the boards down again, he reached his hand in the hole and stretched his fingers until they clasped something solid and smooth. Gently, he pulled until he was holding a tin box with a tobacco company logo on the lid.

He sat down on the floor with the box in his lap and was just about to open it when he heard Susan call his name.

"Up here," he answered as he carefully turned the box over in his hands.

"Hey, you, how was your day?" Susan asked brightly as she pulled off her coat and gloves.

"Look at this."

Susan sat down on the floor next to him. "What is it?"

"Some kind of box. I just found it under the old floor boards." Riley handed her the box and much like he had done, she examined the cover then slowly tilted it to see the bottom. Whatever was inside rattled and jangled as the box shifted.

"Someone hid something, I bet." Her eyes danced. "What do you think it is?"

"Well, there's one easy way to find out."

"Oh, we have to guess first!"

"Naturally. Well, I think it's a million dollars."

"A million dollars wouldn't fit in here," she

scolded.

"Okay, then it's a hundred dollars."

"You're no fun. I think it's another journal that's going to give me all the answers I didn't get from the other one. Oh, and pictures. Lots of pictures."

"Now who's not any fun?"

Susan laughed then leaned over and kissed him. "Anyway, hello."

"Hi. Now open it."

Susan eased the lid off the box and they both leaned forward to peer inside. "Look, it must have been someone's treasure box."

Susan lifted out a bag of marbles and a box of crayons. Clanking around the box were some rocks, buttons, and a few silver dollars.

"Morgan Silver Dollars," Susan said turning the coins over and looking for dates, "from 1899 and 1901." She handed them to Riley so he could get a better look. "I think these can be valuable."

"Are you a coin collector or something?" Riley took his turn studying the coins.

"No, not at all, I just know that these with Lady Liberty are called Morgan Dollars and since they're old, are made mostly of silver."

"Worth checking out. Too bad it's not full of them. What's on the bottom?"

There was still a piece of paper on the bottom of the box and Susan picked it up gingerly. It was folded in half and as she began unfolding it, cards fluttered into her lap. She heard Riley catch his breath before he shouted, "Don't touch them!"

A little taken aback, she shot him a questioning

look. Riley, however, wasn't looking at her. He was far more interested in what was lying on her legs and around her on the floor.

"They're baseball cards…really old baseball cards." There was a level of awe in his voice she had heard only once before—when he had held his nephew for the first time. She wondered how Joe would feel about that, but then decided Joe would probably be pretty darn excited about the cards, too.

"They look like they're in fairly decent condition. We shouldn't touch them or we'll get oil and dirt on them, and that can ruin them. I'll go find something to pick them up with and something to put them in."

Susan watched Riley dash from the room. When he returned, it was with surgeon-like precision that he used the long tweezers to pick up one card at a time by the corner.

"Ty Cobb? No way. And Frank Chance? Joe Tinker? Cy Young?" His voice was rising with each name. Susan just sat back and enjoyed the show. "Chief Bender? He was born right around here. Wow, some of these cards are incredible. I have to call Frank."

Ever so carefully, he laid the cards on a blank page of the open notebook he had brought back with him. He crawled around on the floor, leaning his head closer before pulling back, then laying his head almost flat on the floor and looking over the tops of the cards. Without taking his eyes off of the cards, he yanked out his phone and called his brother.

While Riley excitedly relayed his news to Frank, Susan examined the rest of the tin's contents as well as the tin itself. A small, cloth bag with a drawstring held a couple dozen glass marbles. They were beautiful with various colors in bright swirling designs. The box of Crayola Crayons looked to be well used; the writing on the box was faded in places and the eight crayons inside were all worn. Susan looked at the buttons and the rocks, wondering what sort of special significance they'd held for the person who had saved them.

The piece of paper that had been used to wrap the baseball cards caught her eye. She unfolded it and found a single line of meticulous printing on the inside reading 'This Belongs to Heinrich Baumgartner.'

The original owners of the house, Susan remembered, were named Baumgartner. Interesting. She turned the paper over again, but there was nothing else written to give her any more clues about Heinrich Baumgartner.

When Riley finished his call to Frank, she showed him the paper.

"He must have been a child when he hid this. I wonder if he left and forgot about it or if something happened to him."

"I might have to pay another visit to Bea, see if she can dig up anything on the Baumgartners. It's a long time ago, but I suppose there could be some records. Now I have unanswered questions about Charlie and Heinrich. This place is full of secrets."

Riley paused for a moment then a smug smile began playing at his mouth. "Sounds like it's time to name another room."

Her eyes flew to his and her surprise showed. "Aren't you the quick one? Thought of that before I did."

"What will you call it? Secret something?"

"I don't know." She looked around the room, studied the floorboards, examined the box and its contents again, then smiled. "How about Hidden Treasures?"

"That has a mysterious sound to it…I like it."

"Thanks, so do I. Maybe I can have surprises around the room…a special bubble bath tucked in a fluffy towel, a bottle of wine hidden in a drawer, a couple of vintage games in a little toy chest, maybe even some kind of wishing well…I'll have to think about it, but it could be some sort of different surprise all the time."

"That would appeal to people with a sense of adventure or those wanting to channel their inner kid. Make it a game…'You never know what you'll find in Hidden Treasures.'"

"That's good. I'm going to start adding more information on the website about the rooms so I need more teasers like that. Oh, and I'll put the claw foot tub in this room. I hadn't decided yet which room it would fit best with but definitely in here." She nodded as she spoke. She leaned over the cards to study them again, keeping her hands behind her back so she wouldn't be tempted to touch them. "And I think maybe I'll have the cards framed and hang them in here with the story of where they came from…a way of explaining the reason for the name."

Riley's gasp came fast and loud. "Frame them? And hang them in here? Don't you want to find out what they're worth? Talk to a collector?"

Susan started to chuckle, but saw Riley was dead serious. "How much do you think they're worth?"

"I don't know, I've never had any cards this old but since they seem to be in pretty good condition, I'm sure it's hundreds, maybe thousands for the lot."

"Well, in that case…you're the one who found them, they should be yours. Really," she added when Riley started to shake his head.

"No, Red, they came with the house. I just hope you'll at least look into the value before you decide to just stick them in a frame."

"Okay, I promise. But let me ask you…what would a collector do with them?"

"I don't know, I suppose for some it's an investment and they would hold on to them waiting for them to increase in value. Some probably just enjoy looking at them."

"Like maybe looking at them in a frame?"

"Touché, Red, touché."

20

After three solid days of painting, Susan was ready for a break. Her arms and back ached, she had a kink in her neck from looking up she was certain would never go away, and not only did she have paint all over her, Gusto had snuck into Northern Lights and knocked over a tray of paint on top of himself. Frightened by the noise, he had bolted and had tracked paint along the hallway and down the stairs before Susan had corralled him. So, by Sunday, Dylan's baptism was not only a cause for celebration but a welcome respite.

The McCabes were out in force for the service as was most of Karen's family. With Jake and Karen's sister Kelly serving as Godparents, the rest looked on as the priest baptized Dylan who, on cue, let out a wail as water was poured over his head.

Karen's mother and mother-in-law had overruled her and insisted on handling everything for the luncheon following the baptism. Anna had pushed to host it at her house and Karen's mother had agreed, so the group prepared to move from the church to the McCabe's house.

"'I told Mom I'd have Rose and Kate ride with us so she can get going faster and get home before everyone else arrives," Riley told Susan as they made their way out of the church. "They don't always move too quickly."

"Sure. I'd still like a chance to ask them a few more questions to see if they remember any history surrounding the house or the family that lived there."

"They'd be the ones to ask. They've lived here longer than just about anyone else in town."

The two made their way through the crowd and found the women chatting with the priest who, after greeting Riley and Susan, moved on to visit with a couple Riley didn't recognize.

"I'll pull the car up and meet you outside," Riley told his great aunts.

Kate started to agree, but Rose interrupted as her face went ashen. "You know, Riley, I'm really not feeling very well. I think I'd like to just go home."

"Are you sure? You could come over for a while, I'll take you home whenever you're ready."

"No, no, I think I'll just go home now. I'm tired and this bug I've been fighting all winter just keeps hanging on."

Kate looked disappointed but agreed with her sister. "It's probably for the best, a big crowd like that will tire her out. I'll head back with her and we'll have some lunch together."

Riley was concerned. Normally a big crowd did just the opposite for his aunt...she fed off the chaos and the more people, the more stories she could tell. He had hardly seen her since Thanksgiving with her bowing out of the Christmas Day celebration at the last minute, and now that he looked more closely he could, for the first time, see her age catching up with her.

"Okay, if that's what you want I'll get the car and take you home."

Rose seemed upset and started scanning the crowd. "Frank's right over there, I'll ask him if he can take us home. I need to talk to him about something anyway."

Rose walked away without so much as a goodbye and Kate, after giving Riley and Susan an apologetic shrug, followed.

"That was weird," Riley said. "I'm worried about Aunt Rose, I've never seen her like this before."

"Maybe she just doesn't feel well. It's been a long winter, spring will make everyone feel better."

"Maybe, but I think I'll talk to my mom, she always knows what's up with those two."

He did just that.

"I don't know, Riley, she seemed better the other day when I stopped by and took the two of them grocery shopping. She couldn't talk fast enough when she started telling me about the new woman who moved into the building and who likes to play her Elvis records well into the night. It's been a winter of ups and downs for her."

"She just seemed…old, I guess."

"Well, she is old and maybe that's all it is, but she's scheduled for a check-up next week. I'll mention to the doctor what's been going on and see what he has to say."

Riley nodded then noticed the grin blooming on

his mother's face. Turning to see what had her so pleased, he spotted Susan holding Dylan and fussing over him.

"She sure looks like a natural holding a baby," Anna sighed.

"Oh, no you don't. Jake's up before me...way before me." With that, he walked away leaving Anna to grin at his back.

Riley ended up asking Sam to help him choose a ring. He had been back to the jewelry store twice on his own but didn't trust his judgment on something so important. What did he know about rings? Sure, he could listen to the salesman tell him about cut and carats and so on, but that didn't help him figure out which one Susan would like best. Following the suggestion of the salesman who had helped him every time he'd been in, he had tried to get an idea of what type of jewelry Susan preferred. Did she tend to wear larger, flashier jewelry or understated, more traditional styles? Since he didn't know the difference, that hadn't gotten him far. And since so often when they were together they were working, she didn't wear much jewelry at all.

Sam had been a willing, even eager, assistant. Riley had sworn her to all forms of secrecy from pinkie swears to cross my hearts. He didn't doubt Sam's intent to keep the secret, just hoped that she didn't let anything slip. Sam insisted the ring they chose together was exactly what Susan would have chosen herself. It was simple with a single princess cut diamond that seemed, to Riley, to sparkle more than the others they had considered. And Sam had even thought to bring along a ring from Susan's jewelry box—one she swore Susan almost never wore and wouldn't miss in just one day—so the ring could be sized before Riley proposed. A woman didn't want to get a ring one day and then have to return it to the jeweler the next to have it sized, Sam had explained. With so much to ponder and consider, Riley found himself, on more than one occasion, helplessly deferring to Sam and thanking his lucky stars she had agreed to help him.

With the ring purchased and plans in place for a weekend away, Riley took to counting down the days like he had when he'd been a kid waiting for Christmas. Frank asked him repeatedly what was up when he was so distracted he forgot the frozen pizza in the oven until the smoke alarm went off, screwed up royally in their monthly poker game costing himself twenty bucks, and even forgot they were supposed to meet at Mick's Bar to watch a hockey game. Riley tried to brush it all aside saying he was busy making up for lost time after his coaching stint, but he was pretty certain Frank wasn't buying any of it.

She didn't want to ask Dez but she was desperate. She knocked on his door and tried to hide her desperation and her fear. When he growled 'come in' she took a deep breath, nervously smoothed her hair, and opened the door.

"Well, well, what brings you here, Lis—"

"It's Jasmine," she interrupted.

"Sure it is, Jasmine." When she just stood there staring he barked, "What are you doing here? If you're going to tell me you can't work tonight then you can walk out of here and just keep walking. I've put up with all I'm going to from you."

"I can work tonight. I, um, I wondered if you could do something for me," she stammered and broke out in a nervous sweat. Digging her hand in her purse she wrapped her fingers tightly around the vial and squeezed, drawing strength. Pulling it out of her purse, she held it in front of her. "Could you get my prescription refilled for me? I'm out and I, ah, I really need it." She couldn't meet his eyes as he started to laugh at her.

"Your prescription. That's rich, Jasmine."

"It is a prescription, see? My name's on the bottle." Her hand shook as she held it closer to him.

He snatched it from her and read the label. "Oxy, huh? Should have known. Oh, and would you look at that? It sure doesn't say Jasmine on the label."

"I hurt my back real bad. I need it, Dez. Please?" Her voice wavered as she begged.

Dez looked her up and down. "Right, okay, I'll get it for you but you're gonna work two nights for free. Take it or leave it."

She wanted to be mad, wanted to argue, but knew she wouldn't…couldn't. She just nodded and looked at the floor.

"Come back in an hour, I'll have it," he smirked.

"Thanks, Dez." She choked the words out as she turned and stumbled towards the door.

Once she was in the hallway, she forced herself to breathe deeply and tried to slow her racing heart. She checked the time on the cheap cell phone Dez had given her, ordering her to have it with her at all times. She'd be back in an hour. Exactly.

She'd turned off the phone Jenny had given her and had hidden it under the lining of her suitcase before coming to Omaha, figuring she could probably be tracked if she used it. She was sure Jenny had been texting and calling and was most likely plenty worried. Maybe she should try to find a computer and send a quick email. It would buy her some time, she figured, before Jenny did something. She wished she'd just leave her alone. She was never going to live up to Jenny's expectations—to her family's expectations—she'd stopped trying long ago.

When she got back to the apartment she made the boy a sandwich and sat him in front of the TV while she snuck away and counted the money she had managed to save. It wasn't much, but she was getting closer. She'd tried to figure how much she'd need before she could leave and move on to what she hoped would be the answer to her problems. What would have to be the answer because she was out of chances. A few months ago the idea had terrified her but she had managed to convince herself she could pull it off. She needed to do something. She couldn't go on like she was. She'd be in Dez's debt forever, or until he decided he was done with her.

She calculated and decided a month, at the most, and she'd be out of there. The weather would be warm enough that they could sleep in the car to save money. Once she got there she'd figure something out. It would be early in the season, maybe she'd be able to work out a deal for a cheap room. Some money was better than no money, surely someone running a business would realize that. It will all work out, she told herself again.

She checked the clock and paced for a few minutes until it was time to head back to Dez's.

"Can I please go with you, Mommy?" the boy pleaded.

"I said no. Can't you ever just listen to me?"

He seemed to shrink as he dropped his gaze to his

hands folded tightly in his lap. She turned away and pretended not to notice.

"Dina's here. Don't give her any trouble, you hear? I'll be right back."

She slammed the door and rushed down the stairs hoping Dez had followed through on his promise. She was sweating, her hands shaking, and her heart racing as she walked as quickly as she could to Dez's apartment. She knew he would make her beg again before he handed it over and she knew she'd do it. She hated him...but she hated herself more.

21

Susan fired up her computer and found three new emails in her inbox. She read the first, an inquiry regarding a family reunion. The group was interested in reserving all the rooms as well as the event center for a weekend in December and wanted to confirm the policy regarding children. Susan's fingers tingled with excitement as she typed a response and included links to caterers and restaurants in town. She highlighted some of the inn's selling points as they related to a large group and included a couple of her favorite pictures of the inn after last winter's big snow storm. She had given the subject of children a lot of thought and had decided if a group booked all the rooms, children would be welcome. She wouldn't be providing cribs or cots, but kids could bunk with their parents in sleeping bags. She figured if she wanted to attract groups for family reunions or weddings, kids were part of the package. Besides, she loved kids and as long as everyone in the group knew to expect them, she didn't foresee any problems. This was the third serious inquiry she had gotten and each one was thrilling. She already had two reservations penciled in and was crossing her fingers the Tanner family would like what they heard and would book their reunion.

The second email she opened was a good luck message. A bed and breakfast owner in Wisconsin had come across her website and had taken the time to send her best wishes along with a few words of wisdom. Susan was touched and immediately sent a sincere thank you hoping to keep the dialogue open between them.

Cheered by thoughts of the goodness of strangers, Susan opened the third email only to have those thoughts dashed. A cryptic, threatening message greeted her. 'Stay away from what's not yours.' She had no idea what it meant. Someone upset about the changes she was making to the property? That was really all she could come up with. The message she had received a few months ago and had promptly forgotten jumped back into her thoughts. What had that one said, exactly? 'You will pay,' that was it. It hadn't made any sense at the time and didn't make any more now, but that made two strange emails.

Susan noted the Gmail account used to send the email and considered replying, but quickly decided that probably wasn't a good idea. She didn't want to encourage communication with someone out to harass her. She had deleted the other email and didn't remember if it had come from the same address. She didn't even remember if she'd paid any attention at the time.

Somewhat stumped, she stared at the email for a few minutes before deciding to simply close it and wait and see if anything more happened. She wouldn't delete this one, though, in case more followed.

Moving on to happier things, she began adding details to her website, unveiling the name for another of the rooms with promises of more to come soon, and uploading pictures of the progress. She had decided on two more room names in the past week.

Lakeview named itself while she was painting and was continually distracted by the view from the room's window. The second floor room had, without a doubt, the best view of the lake. Even in the winter while still snow-covered, it drew Susan. She decided she'd decorate with a nautical theme and include Frank's photographs of the lake taken during all four seasons.

Sam ended up naming The Igloo, the second attic room, when she stopped by one day and, shivering while she chatted and watched Susan apply the white base coat, commented that she felt like she was in an igloo. Susan had immediately latched onto the name and the two had brainstormed ideas for decorating that included crisp, white linens, white and blue décor, and a Jacuzzi for two. Susan planned to promote the room as the perfect place to snuggle into in the winter or the ideal place to escape the heat in the summer.

That left her with one room yet to name, but she knew it would come in due time. She wrapped up her work on the website pleased with the way it was coming together...pleased with the way everything was coming together.

Susan's phone rang that evening and glancing at the display had her giddy with excitement.

"Hey, Cassie, how's it going?"

"How's it going? I'll tell you how it's going. Absolutely, craptastically horrible, that's how it's going."

Susan ached for her friend so had to tamp down her joy. Stephen must have done something especially stupid to finally convince Cassie it was time to leave and since she was calling, Susan was praying that meant she was headed to Misty Lake to get a look at the inn.

"What did he do?"

"He fired Jamie, that's what he did, the idiot."

"No. Even he's not that dumb."

"Oh, he is. Fired him yesterday in the middle of the dinner rush. He stormed into the kitchen, started pitching a fit about portion sizes, and fired him. Just like that."

"But Jamie's the best chef the Billingsley has ever had, he's got to know that."

"He doesn't think things through. When Billingsley Senior found out, he stomped into Stephen's office and slammed the door. Didn't matter, I could still hear the yelling. He demanded Stephen get Jamie back. Stephen tried, but Jamie told him to take a hike."

"Good for Jamie. He's not going to have any trouble finding another position, he's one of the best chefs in the city."

"Susan, I don't know how much more I can take. He's running this place into the ground and I don't want to be around to see it happen. So…I'm thinking about paying you a visit next week."

"Oh, Cassie, you have no idea how happy I am to hear that. Things are moving so quickly here, I've already booked a few reservations and I'm still months away from opening. I can't wait for you to see the place, you're going to love it. But no pressure or anything…"

"Sure," Cassie laughed. Then, growing more serious said, "I need to make a change. I almost gave my notice yesterday when he fired Jamie, but I need to have something lined up first. It's just depressing going into work, everyone is unhappy and on edge and the place is going downhill fast. I think Senior is starting to realize it and I get the feeling he's going to try to do something about it, but I'm afraid it's going to be hard to repair the damage that's already been done."

"You know, for as much as I couldn't stand Stephen, I feel sorry for Senior. He put his heart and soul into that place and it must be killing him to see his son run it into the ground. Too bad he doesn't have another son with a little more sense."

"He's been mentioning a niece to me lately. I wouldn't be surprised if he brings her in before long."

"A woman? Priceless. That will really send Stephen over the edge."

"So, are you available to give me the grand tour next week?"

"Sweetie, you just tell me when."

Susan had been working tirelessly trying to get the inn looking its best before Cassie arrived. Foolish, she told herself, as it was obviously still under construction and she couldn't possibly clear out all the mess, but she couldn't help herself. She was sweeping and straightening inside and doing what she could to clean up the yard outside. April had arrived and while there were still some piles of snow, grass was showing through in most of the yard. She picked up sticks and cleaned up after Gusto. As she stepped around the rotted boards on the porch, she wished Riley had gotten to it last fall as it definitely didn't make a very good first impression, but she knew the majority of the outside work would be tackled over the spring and summer.

Riley and his crew would also be shifting a lot of their focus to the barn soon. As with the outside work, most of the barn renovations were waiting until the weather warmed and there was more daylight to work with. Riley had made arrangements with Jeremiah to continue on a consulting basis and he assured Susan—every time she asked—that it would be ready for the wedding with plenty of time to spare. Susan would never admit it to Sam, but she was starting to worry.

As she finished sweeping out the last bedroom, Gusto wandered in and nudged her hand until she finally sat down on the floor with him.

"I'm sorry, boy, you've been neglected these past few days, haven't you?"

In response, the dog climbed into her lap as he had done when he'd been just a puppy. The fact that he now weighed nearly sixty pounds and he couldn't get much more than his head and shoulders in her lap didn't deter him in the least. They sat for a few minutes enjoying the sun shining through the window and warming them.

"I think I'll just rest for a minute before I get back at it," Susan mumbled as she leaned her head back against the wall and closed her eyes.

They were driving along a curvy, country road in a fire red convertible, the top down and her hair billowing in the wind. Riley reached over and took her hand. Lifting it to his lips, he pressed a kiss in her palm. They drove on and the road started to climb as they made their way up a mountain, past cows and wildflowers. Somehow Susan knew they were in Switzerland. She asked Riley how he had known to bring her there, but he just squeezed her hand and watched the road.

They stopped in front of a darling chalet complete with a balcony wrapping around the front and sides and with flower boxes beneath every window spilling over with brilliant red and yellow flowers. The grass was bright green and was dotted with cows as far as she could see. Susan could hear the lazy clanging of their bells as they meandered through the fields.

She wanted to go inside, but Riley took her hand and led her along a path made by countless hikers before them. She asked him where they were headed, but he just smiled. Susan longed to stop and look around, it had been so long since she'd seen the mountains, but Riley coaxed her on. Again she asked where they were going and why they had to hurry, but with a gentle tug on her hand, he urged her to keep moving.

The climb got steeper and Susan's legs began to burn. She looked at Riley and his eyes seemed to tell her to hold on, they were almost there. After a few more minutes, Riley stopped. Susan looked around her and felt as if she were on top of the world. She could see mountaintops and valleys. Tiny villages punctuated the landscape...clusters of houses and farms with nothing but green separating them. She spotted a waterfall and followed it with her eyes to a stream that flowed down the side of the mountain.

She could hardly tear her eyes away but needed to ask Riley why they were there. She was supposed to be meeting Cassie and she needed to get back. When she turned to look at him he was down on one knee holding a ring resting in a black, velvet box and he was asking her to marry him. Of course, she'd marry him, it was all she really wanted. She tried to tell him, but the cowbells were clanging loudly now and he couldn't hear her. Frustrated, she tried shouting but her words were drowned out by the bells that were getting louder and louder. The sound seemed to envelope her. She repeated herself over and over but he didn't hear her. Riley's eyes grew sad and he started to turn away from her.

Susan jerked and her eyes flew open. Gusto was on his feet licking her cheek and her phone was ringing. She took a deep breath and tried to gather her wits.

"Hello?" she managed.

"Hi, Susan. I'm almost to Misty Lake. Where should I meet you?"

Susan rubbed her eyes and tried to focus. Switzerland? Weird. But, she and Sam had just been looking at old photos. A red convertible? Maybe Riley had one hidden away somewhere. Eventually, she got her brain working and made plans with Cassie.

Struggling to her feet, she tried to shake off the feelings that she couldn't even really define. Part of her was deliriously happy with the idea of Riley asking her to marry him, but the fact that something got in the way of her answering him nagged at her. She couldn't get the sight of him turning away from her out of her mind.

Taking another deep breath, she ordered herself to shake it off. It was just a dream, it didn't mean anything.

Then she realized it did mean one thing...she had a name for the last room. Sweet Dreams. Because, she told herself, that's what it had been. If the dream had lasted just a little longer, she would have gotten through to Riley, he would have slipped the ring on her finger, and they would have planned their happily ever after. Satisfied, she headed out to meet Cassie.

"Now, keep in mind there's a lot of work yet to do and the place is a mess. The porch is in pretty rough shape, but it will be fixed up as soon as the weather gets a little warmer. I have sketches inside, I can show you what it will look like when it's done. And you'll have to imagine what it will look like inside once the tiling and woodwork is all done. It's going to be beautiful."

The words spilled out and Susan seemed unable to stop them. She was so certain Cassie was the perfect person for the job, her nerves and her desire to have Cassie love the place as much as she did had her babbling. She didn't slow down as she stepped carefully over the rotted boards on the porch and opened the front door.

"This is the parlor, one of my favorite spots. The fireplace is original and during restoration Riley uncovered this brick wall hidden behind the plaster. Isn't it gorgeous? I'm thinking I'll—"

"Oh, for heaven's sake, Susan, take a breath!"

Susan did just that and as she blew the hair out of her face said, "I just want you to love it, Cassie, but I'm going to shut up now and let you look around. I'll tell you whatever you want to know, but you need to make your own judgments. I don't want to pressure you. Really," she added when Cassie gave her a skeptical look.

They walked through every room with Susan explaining her plans in as much detail as Cassie seemed to want, but trying to keep her emotions in check. Cassie asked question after question and offered ideas and suggestions. The longer they spent talking and exploring, the more excited Susan became.

"I love the room names and the ideas you have for themes and décor. What about either stenciling 'Sweet Dreams' on the wall in here or…I saw something not long ago, it was oversized scrabble letters spelling out messages on the wall. You could write 'Sweet' horizontally and 'Dreams' vertically so they share an e. And maybe some star and moon shaped throw pillows. I bet you could find a comforter or quilt following the theme if you're going that direction."

Susan had to pinch herself in order to wipe the goofy smile off her face. "No, strictly duvets with white covers. I've spent enough time in the hotel biz to know I don't want to deal with spreads or quilts. Nasty."

"Good choice, I was going to suggest that but didn't want to step on your toes. What about the floors? The hardwood is gorgeous, you're not going to cover it with carpet, are you?"

"Absolutely not, maybe just a rug or two."

"Perfect. And window treatments? The same throughout or different for each room."

Cassie, whether she realized it or not, had slipped into work mode. Susan crossed her fingers…it had to be a good sign. "I'm not sure yet. I'll need something to block the light so maybe room-darkening shades with curtains that could vary from room to room fitting with the colors and themes."

"I have a few ideas, I'll show you later when we look at your website. Speaking of which, I assume you've already published prices? How did you determine them?"

"I did a little research, compared prices at nearby hotels and resorts. There aren't any other B&Bs in town, but I found some not too far away so used that data. Then there's always that fine line…don't go too high or you run the risk of scaring people away, but don't go too low that people think it's a dump."

"Okay, good. We can go over the pricing later, too, and I'll let you know what I think but since I don't know much about going rates in the area, I probably won't be much help without a little more research. Maybe we can look at offering different rates for peak season and off-season if you haven't already done that. Menu?"

"I have a few ideas. I may have borrowed a secret or two from the Billingsley's brunch menu but I'll put enough spin on them that they're my own."

"Hey, I'll never tell," Cassie laughed.

"I'll have one breakfast item a day—pancakes, waffles, French toast, quiche, whatever—with fruit, coffee, and juice, but I'm planning on having an alternate lighter option available every day, as well. It will be simple like fruit and oatmeal, but it will give people a choice in case of dietary concerns or restrictions."

"If you don't already, it might be a good idea to have a comment spot on the reservation page where guests can inform you ahead of time of allergies. That way, it will give you some advance notice and you can plan the menu accordingly."

"Good idea, I'll add it."

"Kids?"

Susan outlined the policy she had in place and got Cassie's approval.

"Now, tell me about the event center. I'll admit I'm intrigued but a little concerned at the same time. Usually at a B&B you're not responsible for your guests' entertainment during the day and you get some downtime between breakfast and check-in and then again later at night. It's what makes the whole thing doable. If you have people using the event center, won't you be on duty all day? Can you handle that?"

"Fair question. Yes, it will be more hours, but the fee I charge will allow me to bring in help if I feel I need it. In the case of a big event like a wedding reception, the group will be responsible for hiring their own caterer who will bring help for setup, serving, and cleanup. Of course, someone from the inn will need to be around to oversee things and handle any problems if they arise, but it's not going to be an every weekend kind of thing. I can handle it."

Cassie seemed a little skeptical but nodded. "Maybe we can talk more about it over dinner. I still have a million questions, but I've love to see the barn and then I need to get something to eat. I'm starving."

"Perfect, I have it covered. Riley is meeting us in town so you can meet him and ask him any questions you have. Sam and Jake are joining us and I think Riley's brother might be there, too. He wanted to talk to me more about taking some publicity photos and then maybe using them…well, it's a long story but you might meet him, too. And, you'll get to see Misty Lake in all its glory."

"Misty Lake sounds fascinating from what you've told me, but mostly I can't wait to meet Riley," Cassie said wiggling her eyebrows. "I've never heard you talk about a guy the way you talk about him. He's got to be pretty special."

"He is, Cassie, he is."

Susan had chosen For Heaven's Steak, her attempt to show Cassie that she could get an excellent dinner in Misty Lake. She figured if something was going to keep Cassie from taking the job it was likely to be the fact that Misty Lake was a far cry from Chicago. They pulled into the parking lot just as Riley did.

"There he is, that's Riley," Susan said and realized she sounded like a teenager.

"I…oh, um, okay," Cassie answered.

Susan studied Cassie, alarmed at the way she stammered and she seemed frozen in place, but before Susan could ask questions, Riley was at their car and she found herself making introductions.

"It's good to meet you, Cassie. Susan has been talking about you for months with nothing but good things to say. Welcome to Misty Lake."

Everything seemed to move in slow motion for Cassie as she lifted her hand to shake Riley's. She barely mumbled a hello as she stared. Then, as if his hand burned hers, she dropped it and started for the restaurant.

Susan looked between the two but could do nothing except follow when Cassie darted away.

Sam and Jake were already seated. They joined them and Susan began making more introductions.

"It's not quite Chicago, but what you do think of Misty Lake so far?" Jake asked Cassie.

"Well, I haven't seen much so it's a little early to say, but I'd like to think I'm open minded."

Jake laughed. "Ah, nicely played."

Cassie was looking at Riley again as Sam asked her about her trip. It took Cassie a minute to realize Sam was talking to her. Shaking her head and turning her attention to Sam, she said, "I'm sorry, I guess I'm a little out of it."

"No worries, I was just asking about your trip."

They chatted for a few minutes until Riley saw Frank come in and waved him over. Cassie turned to greet the newest arrival as he came up behind her. When she saw him, the color drained from her face and she gave a little gasp.

"Hey, Jake, before I forget, I have a box in the car Mom wanted me to—" As Frank glanced around the table and he caught sight of Cassie, the words died on his lips.

The two stared at each other, neither moving nor speaking. There were curious glances from everyone, but Frank and Cassie never noticed. Finally, Frank gathered his wits and whispered, "Cassandra?"

Cassie felt like she'd been slugged in the gut. She hadn't laid eyes on Frank McCabe in six years and thought she never would again. All at once the memories came flooding back, but she quickly shut them down as she managed to mutter, "It's Cassie. Just Cassie."

Susan was looking back and forth between the two. "You guys know each other? How?"

Jolted from their memories, both Cassie and Frank looked around the table then at one another as if wondering how to answer...and hoping the other one would answer first.

Cassie finally said, "It was a long time ago. We met back when I used to do some modeling, wasn't that it?" She remembered it as if it were yesterday.

"Yeah, when I was interning with Keith and I went along on that shoot in Chicago…" Frank added as if that would explain everything.

Sam broke the tension. "Small world. The waitress is giving us the eye. Should we take a look at the menu and give her our order?"

Once they were all seated and had placed their order, curiosity got the better of Susan. "I still don't get it. You two met in Chicago? Frank, you were working a shoot Cassie did?"

"Um…yeah. Keith had a few clients in Chicago, one was putting together some promotional material for a new line of outdoor furniture, wasn't that it?" he asked Cassie. She nodded but didn't say anything. "There were a few models there, Cassandra—Cassie, I guess—was one of them. We all got to know each other."

"And you haven't seen each other since?" Susan asked.

"No." Cassie replied. Not for six years.

"Do you still model?" Frank asked Cassie.

"No. No, I don't."

Cassie didn't know what to do. Part of her wanted to run and to keep running. Part of her wanted to just sit and look at Frank, to drink in everything about him, everything she remembered. When Riley broke the tension, she was grateful.

"Cassie, what did you think of the inn?"

Cassie pulled her gaze from Frank and turned her attention to Riley. Then she silently cursed the very idea of identical twins.

"I think it's going to have a lot to offer and should do well. And I think you do excellent work," she added, forcing herself to focus on business. Directing her comments to Sam and Jake, she said, "I understand you two will be the first to make use of the event center. Are most of your plans in place?"

Unconsciously, Sam reached over and squeezed Jake's hand as she answered. "We are and yes, most things are in place or at least in progress. Susan and I checked caterers and we've decided on one, we have a band lined up, a photographer," with that she gave Frank a wink, "and dresses, tuxes, flowers are all done. The only thing that still needs to be figured out is how to decorate. Susan has lots of ideas and the caterer we're going with will handle most of the decorating, but since the place isn't done, it's a little difficult to finalize the plans. And I probably just told you a lot more than you wanted to hear."

Cassie chuckled. "No, I'm interested. One of my...concerns, I guess you'd call it, about the inn in general has to do with the event center and how that's all going to play out. When a B&B branches out into something like that it becomes two businesses, really. I don't doubt Susan can handle it," she said with a nod at her friend, "but I want to help her look at it from an outsider's point of view...an outsider with experience in the industry."

"I would think that can only help," Jake said. "From what Susan has told us, it sounds as though you have quite a lot of experience. She said you've worked all over the country?"

"Well, not exactly all over but a few places. The first job I ever had was cleaning motel rooms. For some reason I've stuck with it so I've seen a lot over the years.

You learn what works, what doesn't." She shrugged as she looked at Susan.

"Well, I'm glad you're here. You know I'm going to try to get you to stay, but whatever you decide, we're friends and there's no one I'd rather take advice from when it comes to anything hotel related."

"I don't—"

Susan held up a hand and cut her off. "Nope. We're going to leave it at that. Tonight isn't about pressuring you into anything, we're supposed to be having fun. We're going to have dinner and then, if you're up for it, we'll show you around town. Saturday night in Misty Lake is not to be missed."

"Deal," Cassie said. Then she stole a glance at Frank who still had his eyes riveted on her and a look on his face like he was trying to solve a particularly difficult puzzle. He only looked away when Susan brought up the subject of the publicity photos.

After dinner they walked down the street to The Hideout. Along the way they all took turns pointing out businesses and sights they thought Cassie would find interesting. Cassie tried to focus but her mind, and her gaze, kept wandering back to Frank. They needed to talk, she supposed, but she didn't know where to start. Maybe he'd be willing to just let it go. But as he caught her eye and she saw the penetrating, questioning look, she sighed. She wasn't going to get off that easy.

They ran into Shauna at The Hideout. Susan made yet another round of introductions.

"Shauna, this is Cassie Papadakis, my friend from Chicago. Cassie, this is Shauna, yet another McCabe. I suppose Joe and Karen will show up any minute to round out the family."

As Shauna and Cassie greeted one another, Frank interrupted. "Pap...Papada...what?"

Susan and Shauna looked at him strangely, but Cassie grabbed him by the hand and said, "Let's dance." She didn't wait for him to agree, just pulled him onto the dance floor.

"What was that all about?" Shauna asked.

"I really have no idea. Apparently they met years ago in Chicago but haven't seen each other since. I don't know any more than that."

The rest of the group gathered around Susan when Cassie and Frank headed to the dance floor. The questions started flying.

"What's the deal with those two?" Jake asked.

"You didn't know they knew each other?" Sam said at the same time.

"No, I don't know any more than you do. Riley, what about you? Did Frank ever talk about Cassie? Or Cassandra?"

"Not that I remember but if it was years ago, who knows? He may have and I just don't recall. I do remember he went to Chicago when he was first getting started, but that's about it. He was living in Minneapolis at the time, we didn't see too much of him."

"Hmmm," Susan mumbled as she watched the two on the dance floor. They seemed to be doing more talking than dancing.

Frank stared at her and tried to figure out where to start. It hardly seemed possible, but she was even more beautiful than she had been years ago. Her hair was a little shorter but still jet black, thick, and wavy. He remembered the feel of it between his fingers. The full mouth that had smiled so readily now frowned a bit and her big, dark brown eyes seemed to hold more questions than answers. He wanted to run his hand along her cheek, to slide her sweater down and see the curve of her shoulder and to touch the smooth olive skin that used to heat so rapidly under his touch. He'd worked with dozens of models since. Not one could hold a candle to her.

"So, it's not Cassandra, it's Cassie. Fine. But Papa...whatever Susan said. What happened to Ray? Are you married?"

"No, no, nothing like that. It's my real name, Cassandra Rachel Papadakis. When I started modeling, my agency thought it was too ethnic sounding so convinced me to shorten it to Cassandra Ray. That's how I introduced myself to anyone in the business and, at the time, that's who I was."

"Okay." Frank waited but Cassie didn't offer any more. "So, what happened?" He fought to keep the anger out of his voice.

Cassie sighed deeply. "I'm sorry, Frank, I should have given you more than just that one email, I should have answered your calls. It wasn't fair of me to just...well, it wasn't fair. But I do remember telling you I had a policy not to get involved with photographers or anyone else in the business."

"Yes, you told me, but I thought you had made an exception." He remembered the exact moment she'd made that exception.

Cassie closed her eyes before answering. "It got

complicated. Right after you left I had some…trouble. I quit modeling, graduated, and left for New York. I just wasn't at a point in my life where I could handle anything else…anyone else. I really am sorry."

"I tried for a long time."

"I know."

"What kind of trouble?"

"It's not something I like to talk about, I hope you can respect that."

Frank gave a slow nod and was torn between respecting her wishes and demanding an answer from the woman who had stolen his heart all those years ago.

"Is everything okay now?"

"Yes, everything is fine. Do you think we can try to keep this between us? At least most of it?"

Frank looked over at the group watching them intently. "We can try."

The song ended and the band switched to a slower song. Cassie turned to rejoin the group but Frank took her hand. "Just one more?"

Cassie found herself in his arms. She squeezed her eyes shut tight and tried to stop the flood of memories, but as her heart fluttered they came thundering back. Two weeks. That's all it had taken for her to fall in love. Every moment they could steal between Cassie's school and work schedules and Frank's long hours in photo shoots, they spent together. By the second week, she had more or less moved into his hotel room with him. She studied while he worked. He waited up for her when she had a night shift at the hotel where she was working. When he left it was with promises from both of them that not more than three weeks would go by between visits. But then it had all gone wrong. So terribly, terribly wrong.

Cassie fought an impossible jumble of emotions. For six years she hadn't let herself think of what could have been. Now, she allowed herself a minute to hold Frank and to imagine. But just a minute because she knew there was no going back.

22

Susan hadn't asked Cassie any more questions. Cassie had seemed exhausted and, if Susan wasn't mistaken, sad, when they'd gotten home from town. But by Sunday morning she needed to find out if her friend was really all right.

They were sitting at Susan's computer with Cassie focused on the inn's website and offering opinions and suggestions. When they hit a lull in the conversation Susan tried to get her to open up.

"Cass?"

"Hmmm?"

"Cassie." She waited until Cassie tore her attention away from the computer and faced her. Cassie pulled the glasses from her face and rubbed her eyes. She still looked tired.

"I don't expect an answer from you yet, I want you to give it plenty of thought and be sure you know what you want, but I need to ask…what's the deal with

Frank? Is whatever history you two have going to affect your decision?"

Cassie turned and gazed out the window. She was quiet for a long time while Susan waited patiently. When she started talking it was with a forced nonchalance. She didn't meet Susan's eyes.

"We met six years ago but it was just a fling. We haven't seen each other since so it was something of a shock running into him last night and finding out he's your boyfriend's twin brother. The fact that he's here and that he's a part of your life and connected to the inn won't affect my decision."

Susan didn't believe her for a second. It hadn't been just a fling, of that much she was certain, but what had gone on between them that had Cassie so unwilling to talk stumped her. In the years they'd known each other they'd talked about all sorts of things. Susan recalled times she'd cried on Cassie's shoulder about a boyfriend, the times they'd vented and complained about their jobs, how Cassie had been there when Danny and then Susan's grandfather died. And then it hit her...Cassie was a good listener, ready and willing with comfort and advice, but their conversations were mostly one-sided. Susan was more and more ashamed as she realized she didn't know much at all about Cassie's past other than her work experience and the basics such as where she had gone to school. She needed to fix that.

"Cassie, is there more to it? If you want to talk, I'd be happy to listen. And I promise you, whatever you say stays between us."

Cassie hesitated and Susan thought, for a moment, that she'd open up. But then Cassie was patting her hand

and reassuring.

"There's nothing, Susan. Really. It's just been a shock. I guess I remember that Frank told me he was from Minnesota, but I never dreamed I'd run into him. No, there's nothing to talk about." She smiled and patted Susan's hand again before returning her attention to the computer.

Okay, she'd let it go. For now. But she promised herself she'd make an effort to get to know Cassie better. If Cassie needed a friend, it was going to be her.

After they had pored over the website, made some changes and updates, and discussed the best way to manage it, Cassie asked about inquiries and reservations.

"I have two firm reservations and one pretty serious inquiry about booking all the rooms and the event center. I've got my fingers crossed that one comes through. It's a little hard to sell it when there aren't even any pictures to show a potential customer. I'm waiting to hear back. Actually, I haven't checked email since you got here, let's take a look."

Susan opened the email account and found five new emails in her inbox.

"That's the most so far," she said excitedly. "Oh, look, this is from the group I was just telling you about." She quickly clicked to open the email and the two read it together.

They both shrieked at the same time. Susan jumped to her feet and danced in a circle. "All the rooms and the event center!"

"Awesome! That's huge, Susan. Congratulations."

Susan's heart was racing. "Oh, my gosh, I can hardly believe it." She started pacing around the room. "I'll have to keep in contact with…" she glanced at the email, "Jackie, and be sure I have the space configured to best fit their needs. Do you think I should just let each family or each couple choose their own room or do you think I should offer suggestions? If some will have kids I could try to steer them to the bigger rooms. It's still eight months away, but I have to make a note to have extra help that weekend. And—"

"And you should sit down before you pass out," Cassie laughed.

Susan fell into the chair and leaned her elbows on the table. "You're right. I need to calm down. But this is just so exciting!"

They celebrated and talked details for a few minutes before Cassie suggested checking the other emails. "Maybe you have another reservation in there."

Two were sales plugs, one from a linen supply company and the other from a cleaning service. She'd look at those more closely later. The next two were both reservations for early October.

Susan leaned back in the chair and shook her head in amazement. "Sometimes I still can't believe this is happening. I've gotten so used to the construction and the planning, it's hard to imagine that in six months that part will be behind me and I'll have guests. The fact that people are making reservations this far in advance for a place that's not even done kind of blows my mind."

"Some people love the idea of staying someplace new. When I was at the Catskills resort we opened up a section of new cabins. Once they were mentioned on the website the reservations started coming in even though the opening date was over a year away. A little different, I know, because the resort itself was established, but there's something about being one of the first to stay someplace that attracts people."

A new email popped up as Susan was taking down information from the reservations. She clicked to open it and was more disappointed than scared or angry. The thrill of getting two reservations and the hope that this would be a third quickly faded. This one said 'Enjoy it while you can.' As with the other two, she had no idea what the message meant. Enjoy what?

Cassie came up behind her. "Another reservation?"

"No, some weirdo has been sending emails, this is the third one. None of them make any sense."

Cassie sat down next to her and read from the screen. "Enjoy what?"

"No idea, I was trying to figure that out myself."

"Were the others the same?"

"No, they said, 'You will pay,' and 'Stay away from what's not yours' or something like that. I don't know what any of it means."

"Do you have the others? Are they all from the same email address?"

"I deleted the first one but kept the second. I moved it to this folder…" Susan clicked and pulled up the second email. "This one has a different Gmail address."

"Whoever it is must be creating a new email address every time. Have you told anyone about this?"

"No, I really didn't think anything of it. Do you think I should be worried?"

"Three emails, all with strange, threatening messages? I think I'd notify the police."

"I'll talk to Jake, see what he thinks. But let's not worry about it now and waste the rest of the time we have. What else do you want to know? Do you want to go back over to the inn and look around some more?"

"I would like to go back over there before I leave, get a little better look around outside, but first I have a question for you."

"Anything."

"What's your plan if I say no?"

Susan's heart sunk. She had been avoiding thinking about an alternate plan, desperately hoping Cassie would take the job. Now it hit her that she had no idea. "I don't know, I guess I'll start advertising. I might need to look further than Misty Lake...I don't know..."

"You've had plenty of experience interviewing, you know what you want, it's just a matter of finding the right person. Assuming that person comes through your door, you'll know he or she is right for the job."

"I suppose. Does that mean you're telling me no?"

"No, it doesn't. I want to tell you yes, but I have to take care of some things before I can give you a firm answer. Depending how it all goes, I should have a yes or a no for you soon. I just was hoping you had been thinking ahead in case this doesn't work out."

"Fair enough. You know how much I want you to say yes, but I understand it's a big decision for you. Think it through...be sure. And know that whatever you decide, we're still friends."

"I will, and I know. I promise. I don't know if I've told you but I appreciate you thinking of me for the job. This weekend has been all about you thanking me for coming and for the advice you think I've given you, but I want to thank you, too. It's flattering to be sought after like this. Makes a girl feel wanted."

Cassie grinned and seemed like herself again for the first time all day. Susan decided to take it as a good sign.

Frank stared at his phone for a full minute after hanging up with Cassie. She'd called, as he'd almost begged her to do, but he didn't know any more now than he had the night before. She'd asked him straight out if having her in Misty Lake would be a problem for him. He'd debated on how to answer, but in the end, had simply told her it wouldn't. That was about the extent of their conversation with Cassie avoiding all of his questions and claiming she needed to start the drive back to Chicago.

She hadn't told him whether she was going to take the job but he decided, this time, he couldn't sit and wait and wonder. He picked up his phone again and punched in the number for the magazine editor interested in his photos.

She was doing it. She was leaving Omaha. As sure as she had been the night before, as she loaded her son and their few belongings in the car and drove away, she saw her hands shake on the steering wheel.

It will all work out, she repeated over and over to herself. She'd made another call the night before to the one person there she could still call a friend and it had boosted her confidence. She thought she probably even had a place to stay, at least for a few days. She took a quick peek in the rearview mirror at the boy. He was vital to her plan and that worried her. She had never been one to put her faith in anyone…let alone a kid.

But it will all work out, she repeated again. And again.

23

Riley had been acting weird for days. Susan figured it had to do with her upcoming birthday and his determination to keep whatever secret he was trying to keep. She had tried to get him to spill the beans, but he had been remarkably tight-lipped. And if Sam knew anything, she wasn't talking either. Oh well, surprises were fun, Susan tried to tell herself. It was a lie. She hated surprises.

As she opened the birthday cards that had come in the mail, giggling at the ones from her brothers, her phone buzzed. Seeing it was Riley, she was smiling as she answered.

"Happy birthday, Red."

"Thanks."

"What are you up to?

"Opening some birthday cards that came in the mail. I'll have to show you the one I got from Kyle. You'll appreciate his twisted sense of humor."

"Can't wait to see it. Are you almost finished?"

"Finished with what?"

"With opening cards."

"Um, yes, it's not a big job."

"Good. Then start packing for the weekend. We leave at five."

"Huh?"

"I said, we leave at five."

"Leave for where? What are you talking about?"

Riley blew out a breath. "You're making this more difficult than it needs to be. I'll pick you up at five and then we leave. The destination is a surprise so don't even bother asking any more questions."

"Really? You planned a surprise weekend?" Susan's voice rose as she squeaked out the words. A whole weekend? Maybe surprises weren't so bad after all. She had known he was up to something, but she hadn't expected an entire weekend. Warmth spread through her as she realized, yet again, just how much she loved him.

"Yes, really. As long as that's okay with you."

He sounded nervous and Susan found it impossibly cute. "Of course, it's okay. It sounds pretty perfect, actually. I just can't believe you planned everything without me finding out about it.

"You didn't make it easy."

"Sorry about that. Are you at the inn already?"

"Just about there. Travis is going to start some tiling today, did I tell you that?"

"Really? I can't wait for it to go in, it will make the place look so much more put together. I was already planning on stopping by today, but now there's more than just your handsome face to get me out there."

Riley laughed. "Okay, then I'll see you later. Happy birthday."

Just as Susan hung up, Sam came in the kitchen followed by Jake who was carrying a huge bouquet of flowers.

"Happy birthday, Susan," he said as he handed her the flowers.

"Oh, Jake, they're beautiful. Thank you." She buried her face in them and inhaled. "They smell like spring."

"Glad you like them. Do you have big plans for your day?"

"Actually, I just got off the phone with your brother. Apparently we will be going away for the weekend, although I don't know where, since he insists on keeping it a secret."

"Well done, Riley," Jake said, nodding his head in approval.

"You don't happen to know where we might be headed…"

"I don't and I wouldn't tell you if I did. Sorry."

Susan turned her smile on Sam. "Sam? I really don't know how I'm supposed to pack if I don't know where we're going. If you'd just give me a hint I promise I won't tell Riley."

"Sorry, Suze, he didn't tell me either."

"So he really did this all on his own?"

"He didn't ask me for any help planning the weekend," Sam answered carefully.

Susan thought she caught a little glint in Sam's eye, but Sam turned away before she could be sure. Hmmm, maybe she did know something. Before she could ask any more questions, Jake noticed the mail on the table and commented.

"Looks like you got quite a pile of mail."

"Birthday cards from my parents, my brothers, a few friends. It's nice. I haven't opened this one," she said as she held up a bright yellow envelope. "It's from Cassie. I still haven't heard anything from her about taking the job. I don't want to pressure her, but I really expected an answer by now. The longer it takes, the more I'm convinced she's going to turn me down."

"It would be a really big change for her, Suze. It's a lot to think about."

Even though she hadn't come right out and said it, Susan knew Sam was thinking it was unlikely Cassie would say yes. Jake's expression told her he thought the same. She couldn't fault them.

"I know. I'm sure she's looking around to see what's available in Chicago before she makes a decision. A position in Chicago would mean a lot more money and the lifestyle she's used to. I shouldn't have gotten my hopes up so much after she visited," Susan said as she started to tear open the envelope. She read the card and grinned at the picture of two orangutans holding hands and hanging from a tree branch. The caption read 'Through it all, friends hang together.' Susan didn't read the rest of the card because the word 'job' in Cassie's handwritten note on the inside caught her attention.

Susan scanned the note then gave a little shriek. "She's coming! She's coming to Misty Lake!"

"Really? Oh, Susan, that's fantastic!" Sam pulled the card from Susan's hands to read it for herself.

"It is fantastic, she's the perfect person for the

job. What a relief," Susan said on a sigh as she fell into a chair. "I tried not to let myself think about it too much so, of course, it's all I could think about. I really don't know what I would have done if she had said no."

"Well, I'm glad you don't have to think about it," Sam said leaning over to give Susan a hug. "Cassie seems incredible from what I've seen." After a moment, Sam added, "I still wonder what the real story is with her and Frank, though."

Susan nodded thoughtfully. "She didn't tell me anymore than she and Frank told everyone, just that they knew each other in Chicago and had a fling, as she called it. I'm not buying it, but I have to wait until she's ready to talk, it's her business. Truthfully, I was afraid that's what was keeping her from taking the job." Susan gave Jake a questioning look through narrowed eyes.

Jake, in response, held up his hands. "Hey, I don't know any more than you do. Frank didn't say a word to me."

"Okay. I'm not going to think about it right now, I'm just going to celebrate the fact that she's really coming. I can't wait to tell Riley."

"It's nice when good news comes in the mail," Jake said.

Susan whipped her head towards Jake. "That reminds me of something. Do you have a minute, Jake? I'd like you to look at a couple of weird emails I've gotten."

"What do you mean, weird?"

"I'm not really sure. I think it's probably just someone goofing off, trying to scare me or upset me or something, but I promised Cassie I'd talk to you about it and I forgot until now."

Susan grabbed her laptop from her bedroom and brought it back to the kitchen. As she opened her email she told Jake and Sam, "There was one a few months ago and I didn't really think anything of it so I deleted it. Then I got two more that were similar so I saved those. Here, they're in this folder."

The email popped up on the screen and she turned the computer so Jake could get a better look. With Sam looking over his shoulder, he read the first, then the second, then went back to the first.

"What did the first one, the one you deleted, say?"

"Something like, 'You will pay.' I don't know what that's supposed to mean any more than I know what these two mean."

"Has there been anything else going on? Strange phone calls, anything in the mail?"

"No, just the emails. I'm sure it's nothing. Probably just someone who happened upon my website and thought they'd mess with me. Maybe it's someone who's worried I'll take their business away." Susan started to chuckle but quickly realized Jake didn't find it funny in the least when he looked at her with a furrowed brow and a frown.

"I hope that's all it is, but I don't want to just ignore this. After what happened with Sam last summer, I'm not writing anything off as a harmless prank."

"Oh, Jake." Sam seemed ready to argue that he needed to stop worrying, but changed tracks when she caught his worried expression. Instead, she leaned her head on his shoulder and rubbed her hand up and down his arm.

"The emails didn't come from the same email

address, but I'd still like to have our tech guy do a little checking, see what he can find on where they originated. If they're from the same place, we can be pretty sure they're from the same person. If you're okay with it, he can probably dig into your computer's memory and pull up the first one that you deleted and see where that one originated, as well."

More concerned now than she wanted to be, Susan nodded her agreement. "Take it, I don't need it this weekend. I can use my phone for most everything."

"Okay, I'll let you know what we find. In the meantime, you be sure to let me know if anything—and I mean anything—out of the ordinary happens…you get any strange phone calls or mail, you notice someone who seems to be hanging around watching you, anyone you don't know shows up at the B&B…anything, Susan."

"All right, I promise. Geez…you're sure putting a damper on my birthday and my good mood," she frowned.

"Sorry, I just don't want to ignore something that's right in front of us."

Susan nodded again then decided she'd had enough of the unhappy thoughts. "I'm going to get back to enjoying my day. First, I'm going to call Cassie to celebrate and talk details. Next, I'm going to go try to pack for a trip for which I don't know what I'll need, and then I'm going to go see Riley and check out the tiling work that's starting today. What I'm not going to do is worry about this anymore right now. Happy birthday to me," she sang as she danced her way out of the kitchen.

Later, as she walked into her ever-changing inn, she did so with a bounce in her step. Her talk with Cassie had gone well. They'd decided Cassie would start towards the end of the summer. Susan hated forcing Cassie to stick it out that long at the Billingsley, but she really couldn't afford to start paying her until she was closer to her opening date. Cassie had seemed fine with it saying that just knowing her days were numbered would make heading into work every day and putting up with Stephen Billingsley a little easier.

Susan checked out the tile work in the kitchen and was surprised to see it in place in over half the room. She met Travis and his assistant, Will, and after complimenting them on their work, went in search of Riley. She found him laying the bathroom tile in Lakeview.

"I thought Travis was doing the tile."

Riley hadn't heard her come in and jumped a little at her voice causing him to push a tile out of place. Grumbling to himself, he reset it before turning to Susan.

"Since I'm so good at it I thought I'd help." He stood and bundled Susan in a hug. "Happy birthday again," he said as he landed a kiss on her upturned lips.

"Thank you," Susan answered breathlessly as her stomach fluttered the way it always did when Riley kissed her. When he tucked her head under his chin, she just closed her eyes and enjoyed. There was no place she'd rather be.

When she finally stepped back, it was to survey Riley's progress. "It looks great and I love the color. It's a relief to see it in here and find out I still like it. I have to admit I've been doing some worrying ever since I made the final decision."

"You made a good choice. It's neutral but has enough color that the room won't look washed out. You'll be able to use different colors to decorate since anything will go with the beige hues in the tile."

"Are you an interior decorator now, too?" Susan teased.

"With as much time as you've made me spend looking at tile, fixtures, paint, towels, furniture, and a thousand other things, I probably am by now."

"Oh, poor Riley," Susan soothed as she went back to him, extended her arms, and laced her fingers behind his neck. "How can I ever make it up to you?"

Riley grinned and his brows rose. "I bet I can think of something. I might even come up with something this weekend."

"Speaking of this weekend," Susan said as she pushed away from him, "are you ready to tell me where we're going?"

"Not a chance."

"But how am I supposed to pack if I don't know where we're going and what we'll be doing?"

"I'm sure you'll figure it out."

"Hmpf. You're no fun."

"Oh, I'm lots of fun. You're just nosey."

"I'm not nosey." When Riley gave her a sidelong look, she added, "Well, maybe I'm a little nosey but this hardly qualifies. I just need some information in order to be properly prepared."

"Like I said, I'm sure you'll figure it out."

"Fine. Actually I'm already packed, I just hoped you might give me a hint because I could always repack."

"Oh, Red."

Giving up for the moment, Susan changed the subject. "Guess what?"

"You're really going to stop badgering me for

details?"

"Very funny. I was going to tell you that I heard from Cassie and she's going to take the job, but if you're going to be mean..."

"I'm not being mean. Congratulations, that's a pretty nice birthday present. I'm happy, Red, I know how much you want her here."

Susan beamed. "I really do, I just know she's going to be a perfect fit. One more example of everything falling into place."

Riley walked her around, showing her the latest progress and verifying her decisions on a few minor points.

"When will you install the color-changing tile in the Northern Lights bathroom? I can't wait to see it."

"It will go in next week, but I'm going to have Travis do it. It's too expensive...I don't want to screw it up."

"I'm sure you could do it. Look around, you can do anything."

"Thanks for the vote of confidence, but that's why Travis is here. Trust me, he's better at this than I am."

They spent a few more minutes walking through the inn then made their way back to the bathroom where Riley had been working.

"I'd like to get this room done before I wrap up for the day and I told the guys we'd cut out a little early this afternoon. That way I can get home and get showered and we'll be on our way by five."

"And where are we headed again?"

Riley just shook his head. "Nice try."

Susan frowned. "We're not going to Switzerland,

are we?" she asked, almost more to herself than to Riley. The dream she'd had suddenly came back to her and she was scared. She remembered the helpless feeling she'd had in her dream when she'd been unable to get through to Riley and she'd sensed she was going to lose him. A shiver ran down her spine.

Riley turned to look at her with his eyebrows knitted together in confusion. "Huh? Did you say Switzerland?"

Feeling foolish, Susan ordered herself to shake off the feeling. "Never mind, I'm just kidding. And okay, I give up, it'll be a surprise. I'll let you get back to work. But first…" She put her hands on his face and, rising up on her toes as she gently pulled him toward her, found his lips with hers. "Thank you for such a wonderful, thoughtful birthday gift." She paused a moment then looked him in the eye. "I love you, Riley."

Riley froze, his heart flipping in his chest. He'd been waiting to hear the words for months, had wanted to say them to her, but had wanted to make sure she was ready to hear them. Finally, was his only rational thought.

"Susan, I—"

"Hey, Riley, there's someone here to see you," a voice shouted from downstairs.

Riley let out a huge sigh as he rested his forehead against Susan's and silently cursed whoever it was that had managed to ruin the moment.

Susan huffed out a laugh. "Nice timing."

"Don't move, I'll get rid of him and be right back."

"It's okay," Susan answered as she turned to

follow him down the stairs. "I need to get going anyway so you can finish up and we can start our weekend. You know, there's still time to repack if you want to give me an—oof!"

Susan walked into Riley's back as he stopped short and stared at the woman in the doorway.

24

The drive from Omaha was miserable. She was tense and crabby and the boy was whiny. She knew he was scared and that he hadn't had any sense of security, or home, since they'd left California so she tried to be understanding, but the whining got on her nerves and she snapped at him often. Eventually, he stopped saying much of anything except for the mumbling she heard occasionally from the backseat as he drove his truck or staged some sort of dramatic scene for Spider-Man.

She glanced at the odometer every few miles and couldn't decide if she wanted it to move faster or slower. She wanted to get there, but she was scared. She thought she had everything figured out, but knew it could easily fall apart.

As she finally pulled into town, she looked around and tried to remember. Main Street looked about the same. She recognized the bars and restaurants where she had spent some time years ago. But there were just as many places she didn't recognize. Whether they had been there before and she just hadn't noticed or didn't remember, or whether they were new, she couldn't be sure. She drove carefully through town, not wanting to attract any attention. She followed the directions her friend Courtney had given her and in a few minutes found herself in front of an apartment building. Gripping the steering wheel tightly, she took a deep breath and told herself again that she was doing the right thing.

By the next afternoon, she was feeling more confident. She'd talked with Courtney well into the night and had gotten caught up on town gossip. Not that she'd remembered most of the people Courtney talked about, she hadn't, but she thought she had done a good job pretending to care. She had really only paid attention when Courtney brought up the one name she was waiting to hear.

Courtney had offered to let them stay with her for a few days, much to her relief. Thankfully, Courtney had taken a liking to the boy—that had been one of her biggest concerns—she really hadn't been sure what she would have done if Courtney hadn't offered. The money was running out quickly. So was her prescription. Dez had filled it once, but had refused the next time she had asked. Knowing she was leaving soon had left him in a less-than-generous mood. After finally working up the nerve the night before, it had taken only a few carefully worded questions to Courtney to lead her to the run-down cabin on the lake she was now looking at.

With strict instructions to stay in the car and to

stay quiet, she closed the door on the boy and called on every ounce of courage she had to set her feet in motion towards the cabin. She made her way across a rutted yard littered with empty beer cans and countless cigarette butts. The place looked deserted, but Courtney had assured her someone would be there…they didn't dare leave the place unoccupied. She raised a shaky hand and knocked on the scarred door.

It took so long she was just about to turn around when she heard a gravelly voice shout, "Yeah, who's there?"

"Um, I'm a friend of Courtney's, she said you'd be expecting me?"

It took a few more minutes until the door finally squeaked open. Squinting into the dark room, she was able to make out a figure walking away from the door, his back to her. Unsure what to do, she started to follow, and with a quick glance back at the car, pushed the door closed behind her.

"You got the money?"

"Yes, I have money." She fumbled in her purse and pulled out the wad of bills Courtney had assured her would get her what she wanted.

"Court said Oxy. Anything else as long as you're here?"

Her eyes had adjusted to the dim light and she could see a short, skeletal man with a heavily pock-marked face and stringy, greasy hair sneering at her, his eyes moving up and down her body.

She was desperate to leave. "That's all."

"You sure? Got some good stuff here, comes with my personal guarantee." He wheezed out an evil-sounding laugh that ended in a cough that he couldn't seem to get under control.

"No, thank you, not today."

"All right, suit yourself. Gimme the money."

She handed over the bills and watched as he slowly counted them, holding each up to the little bit of light that was coming in through a grimy window. Her heart was pounding and her hands shaking as her eyes darted around the room. She was afraid...not so much of him as she was that he'd change his mind. Finally, he seemed satisfied and handed over a small plastic bag. She snatched it from his hand and turned for the door.

"Ya'll come back now, ya hear?" he cackled at her back as she shut the door behind her and stumbled to the car.

Once inside, she locked the doors and let go with the breath she'd been holding. She greedily swallowed two of the pills and once the shaking slowed enough that she could start the engine, backed out and spun her wheels in her desire to put him, his house, and the entire experience behind her.

She drove for a while until the pills did their job and she felt reasonably calm. Their next stop was going to be even more important than the last and it was imperative she was ready. She glanced in the rearview mirror at the boy. What to tell him? Too many instructions and he'd get confused. Not enough, and who knew what he'd say. She decided to keep it as simple as possible.

"We're going to stop and visit one of Mommy's friends. I want you to be nice, okay?"

"Okay." She could see the hesitation in his eyes.

"He's a busy man so I don't want you talking a lot

and wasting his time."

"Okay," he repeated.

"If he talks to you, you can answer but that's all, understand?"

"Yeah."

She was almost certain he didn't, but she didn't know what else to do. She flipped over the piece of paper with directions, this time following a route to a different house on the lake, a house where Courtney had assured her she'd find him.

25

Susan rubbed her forehead on the spot where she had walked straight into Riley's back as she peeked around his shoulder to get a better look at the woman standing in front of them. She was tall and thin with faded, stringy blonde hair. As Susan studied her closer, she realized she wasn't just thin, she was alarmingly so. Her collarbones jutted out under the cotton blouse she wore and the wrists extending slightly past the end of the sleeves seemed to be nothing but bone. She had applied makeup with a heavy hand, most likely in an attempt to hide the dark circles Susan could still detect under her eyes and to smooth the rough complexion. However, her high cheek bones, narrow, straight nose, and huge, wide-set, brilliant blue eyes told Susan she had been beautiful—stunning, most likely—before. As she watched the woman's hands shake and her eyes flit around nervously, Susan suspected the woman was a drug addict. She had spent enough time with

Danny, had attended enough group sessions while he was in various treatment centers, to know the signs.

Susan was so focused on the woman and on trying to figure out why she was there, she didn't immediately notice the young boy peeking out from behind her legs. Now she was even more confused. When she looked at Riley, he was staring. She didn't think he'd moved a muscle with the exception of his jaw that she watched open and close without him ever making a sound.

Finally, the woman spoke. "Hi, Riley. It's been a while." She forced a laugh that came out shrill and died quickly on her lips as Riley stayed silent and motionless.

Susan stepped forward and extended her hand. "Hi, I'm Susan Taylor." Susan dropped her hand after a moment when the woman ignored her.

Susan's voice jolted him out of his stupor. He watched Susan try to shake Lissa's hand and figured he must be having some sort of out of body experience. What in the hell was Melissa Cosgrove doing in Misty Lake? He hadn't seen her in...how many years? Six? Seven? He couldn't remember. Then he noticed the young boy. Lissa's kid?

He watched as the boy gazed around the yard, looked toward the lake with curiosity, then caught sight of Gusto tied out near the barn. The boy started to bounce on his toes and tug on Lissa's arm.

Turning his attention back to Lissa, Riley finally answered. "It's been a long time, Lissa. How have you been?" He hardly knew what to say to her, he hadn't heard from her in years, not since she'd left Misty Lake at the end of that summer years ago.

"Good, I'm doing good." But she didn't seem good.

"How did you find me out here?" Riley knew he was being rude, but he couldn't come up with a logical reason why she was in Misty Lake, let alone tracking him down at the inn.

"I ran into Courtney, she told me you've been working out here."

Susan softly cleared her throat. Riley jerked and looked at her, his eyes wide in his pale face. "Oh, um, Susan, this is Melissa Cosgrove. Lissa, Susan Taylor. Susan is…I'm working…she owns this place."

Susan gave Riley a questioning look but he didn't notice. His eyes were back on Lissa and the boy. "Is this your son?"

"Yeah, um yes, yes it is. This is Ryan." Looking down at the boy she nudged him and said, "Say hello, Ryan."

Ryan squinted up at Riley and gave a quick, "Hi," before turning his attention back to the dog.

Riley didn't know what to say to her, they'd never had much in common. "When did you get here? And what brings you back to Misty Lake?"

Lissa seemed uncomfortable as she nervously looked from Riley to Susan then back to Riley. "That's kind of a long story."

Riley was wondering how to respond when the boy looked up at him with wide, deep blue eyes. "Is that your dog?" He looked and pointed to the barn before turning his gaze back on Riley.

"Actually, he's my dog. His name is Gusto. Do you want to meet him? If it's okay with your mom, that is." Susan smiled at the boy who looked hopefully at his mother.

"Sure, fine," Lissa answered with barely a glance at Susan.

Giving Riley a long look, she held her hand out for the boy. When he eagerly grabbed hold and started pulling her along towards the dog, she followed, glancing back at Riley as she did so.

Riley watched for a minute as the two crossed the yard, still trying to work out what Lissa could possibly be doing in Misty Lake. He centered his attention back on her as she took a few shaky steps across the porch and sat on the stairs.

Riley followed but didn't sit, instead paced a little in the yard in front of the steps. He didn't know why, but the fact that she had shown up out of the blue left him with a very uneasy feeling. He studied her a little closer and was shocked to see how different she looked from the beautiful, carefree girl he remembered. Her hair was dull and hung carelessly around her face, a far cry from the bouncy, sunny ponytail that had so often been pulled through a baseball cap after a day on the water. She was frighteningly pale. Granted, winter was just ending so she wouldn't have the same tanned complexion she did when she'd spent the summer working at the resort, but she looked unwell. And her eyes, while still the brilliant blue that had always made him think of the lake on the clearest, sunniest day, had lost their sparkle and laughter. Now, they looked tired, haunted, and desperate.

"So, did you just happen to be in the area or did you have a reason for coming back?" He tried to sound friendly, but knew the question came out sounding critical.

"I came to talk to you, Riley. I've been thinking about you lately." She shook her head and looked at the ground. "That's not really right. I've been thinking about you ever since I left."

"Oh?" What the hell was he supposed to say to that? If he was being honest, he hadn't given Melissa Cosgrove a thought since she'd left town.

"I should have called you years ago. Actually, I shouldn't have left. I need to tell you something."

Riley's heart thudded painfully. Without knowing what was coming, he somehow knew it wasn't going to be good. He waited while Lissa fidgeted and grabbed her purse. He wanted to yell, wanted to demand she tell him why she was there. And why now when everything was going so perfectly with Susan?

"It's Ryan. He's your son."

Riley didn't exactly know what it felt like to be hit by lightning, but guessed it had to be pretty close to what he was experiencing. For a moment, it was as if every inch of his body was electrified and he could feel a current running from his head all the way to his fingertips and to his toes. And then he went numb and couldn't feel anything.

He didn't know how much time had passed, didn't know how he had gotten to the lakeshore, and certainly didn't know what the hell to do. He felt like he was going to be sick, so he staggered to the nearest tree and leaned against it. He tried to breathe deeply when his breath wanted only to come in short, quick gasps. When the nausea finally passed and he looked around, he saw Susan and the boy still near the barn playing with Gusto. He was alone so apparently Lissa hadn't followed him, and since he couldn't see her, guessed she was probably still on the porch.

He looked back at the boy. His son? He forced himself to concentrate and to try to figure out when it was he had last seen Lissa. He knew he had been done with school and had already started working for Howard, the man who had mentored him and had taught him more than school ever had, so it was probably six years ago, close to seven. Many of his buddies had already moved away, but those that remained were, like him, working full time and finding themselves with a pocket full of money come the weekend. They had been wild and carefree, hanging out in the bars, and more often than not, looking for some girls to hang out with them.

That's where he had met Lissa, he remembered now. He'd been with a big group at The Hideout when she'd come in. He'd recognized one of the girls she was with so invited them to join their table. Lissa had been the classic All-American girl...long blonde hair, blue eyes, glowing, sun-kissed skin, and a smile and personality that lit up the room.

He blinked hard and forced his thoughts back to the present. He had a son? A son he was just now finding out about? The shock started to turn to anger and after glancing once more at the boy, he began striding furiously back to the porch.

"How can you show up here after all this time and just announce that I have a son? Where the hell have you been for the last six years? It never occurred to you to tell me about this before now? Damn, Lissa, if he's mine I had a right to know!"

He wanted to shout but fought to keep his voice

low enough that Susan and the boy wouldn't hear him. He could feel his face heating and his hands trembling. Lissa seemed to shrink before him but he didn't care. He deserved an explanation.

Lissa crushed out the cigarette she'd been smoking. "I'm sorry, Riley, I should have let you know about Ryan long ago, but try to imagine how it was for me. I was back in Denver, supposed to be starting my senior year of college, and I find out I'm pregnant. I couldn't tell my family, my dad would have killed me. He was up for reelection and news of his twenty-one-year-old unwed daughter turning up pregnant wouldn't have done much for his campaign. You were back here, busy with your work, and surrounded by a family and a town that expected more from you than winding up with a kid. I considered an abortion but I kept putting it off and the next thing I knew, it was too late." She shrugged and clutched at her purse once more.

Riley stared at her through narrowed eyes. Did she really believe that was a reason? An excuse for keeping his son from him?

"Sorry, Lissa, you're going to have to do a little better than that. You've had years to tell me about him. How can you say I was too busy? What the hell is that even supposed to mean? If he's…" Suddenly Riley froze. When he started speaking again the words came out slowly and ominously. "How do I know he's even mine?"

Tears pooled in her eyes and she shook from head to toe, even after she grabbed the porch railing to try to steady herself. "That's not fair, Riley. You and I had something special. There wasn't anyone else."

Riley ran his hand roughly through his hair and

turned away. It was a lie, plain and simple. There hadn't been anything special about their relationship. They'd been casual friends, they'd hung out together with a bigger group on the weekends, and a couple of times, when they'd both had too much to drink, they'd been stupid and careless. And there had almost certainly been others. He wanted to tell her that, but no matter how angry he was, he couldn't stand to see her cry. And what would be the point of lying to him? If he wasn't the father, why would she be there? She'd tracked him down, she could have just as easily tracked down someone else.

"Okay, Lissa, this isn't the time or place to do this. I have people inside working, the boy is right across the yard, and Susan…" At that, he sunk down onto the steps, closed his eyes, and dropped his head in his hands. How was he going to tell her?

"Maybe we can meet later and talk?" Lissa asked. She was already inching toward her car.

"Yeah, okay. Give me your phone number and I'll call you to arrange something. I'm supposed to be going out of town this weekend…" He didn't know how that was ever going to happen now. He'd have to tell Susan what was going on and didn't expect she'd feel much like going away with him after she heard the story.

"Um, I'll give you Courtney's number, I'm staying with her. My cell phone is, ah, broken." She hadn't used the phone Jenny had given her for months, she didn't want Jenny to be able to figure out where she was, and she'd returned the phone Dez had given her. She dug the slip of paper with Courtney's number out of her wallet and copied it onto a gum wrapper. Her hand trembled as she handed it to Riley.

Riley shoved it in his pocket without looking at it as he stared across the yard at Susan and the boy. His son, he corrected himself. So many emotions were ripping through him he didn't know which one to hold on to. With nothing more to say to Lissa, he started for the barn.

Susan was taken with the boy. He was polite, sweet, and absolutely in love with Gusto. She had learned a little about him, that he had an Aunt Jenny and that he and his mom had driven a long time to get to Misty Lake, but he was reluctant to talk too much. Every time Susan asked him a question, he glanced toward his mother before giving a brief answer.

When it came to Gusto, however, he couldn't talk enough. He asked if the dog was a boy or girl, how old he was, what his name meant, where he lived, what he ate, and if he knew how to swim. Susan found an old tennis ball and let Ryan throw it repeatedly for Gusto. The two chased and wrestled and hugged one another and Gusto planted countless sloppy kisses on Ryan's cheeks, which delighted the boy to no end.

Susan kept stealing glances over at Riley and Lissa. She couldn't make out what they were saying, but it wasn't difficult to figure out that Riley was upset. She watched as he staggered towards the lake, paced some, and then stormed back to the house. As much as she wanted to know what was going on, she sensed it would be best to keep Ryan away from the tension. When she spotted Riley coming their way, she couldn't miss the turmoil in his expression.

As Riley approached Susan and Ryan, he searched

the boy's appearance for resemblances. His hair was brown, lighter than Riley's, but brown, and a little wavy. Riley didn't know how tall an almost-six-year-old should be, but he studied the boy and tried to figure out if he was tall, short, or average for his age. Riley had always been tall. He seemed very coordinated and athletic, Riley thought, as he watched him run and jump with the dog. When he sent a tennis ball sailing through the air, Riley couldn't help but feel a sense of pride as he watched it soar.

"Is everything okay?" Susan asked as Riley clung to her and buried his face in her hair.

He couldn't answer, knew he wouldn't get the words out, and didn't want to get into it until they were alone. Instead, he moved slowly away from Susan and crouched down to eye level with Ryan when the boy came barreling back towards them, the dog hot on his heels.

"Hey, Ryan." The name seemed to catch in his throat and he coughed to cover the emotion. "Are you having fun with Gusto?" Riley studied the wide, deep blue eyes and tried to decide if they looked like his. The shape was all Lissa, but the color was most definitely a deeper blue than hers. He had high cheekbones like his mother but a full mouth that, when he broke into a big grin, looked frighteningly familiar.

"Oh, yeah, he's awesome! Once Aunt Jenny said—" He seemed to catch himself and darted his eyes quickly toward his mother who was starting to make her way to the car. When Gusto licked his face, he forgot all about what he could and couldn't say and collapsed in a heap of giggles.

"Ryan, come on, we have to go now," Lissa called from the car.

Ryan fought his way out from underneath the dog and jumped to his feet. Giving a little wave, he was off like a shot. About half way to the car he seemed to remember something and stopped short. Turning back, he yelled, "Thanks for letting me play with your dog!" Grinning from ear to ear, he resumed his dash to the car.

Riley and Susan watched as Lissa loaded Ryan into the back seat and drove off.

"He's quite a kid," Susan said smiling. I guess I haven't been around kids for a while, I've forgotten how much fun they are…and how much energy they have. I think it's safe to say Gusto's worn out." The dog had flopped down at Susan's feet and was lying on his side, legs extended and tongue hanging out.

Riley didn't answer, just stood watching the car drive away. He didn't know where to begin, how to begin, or how to keep from hurting Susan. He could see the concern and worry building and wished he knew how to stop it.

"Is Melissa an old friend?"

Riley's shoulders slumped a little before he finally answered. "I knew her some years back. She spent a summer here working at the resort on the lake."

"And she's just visiting?"

"Something like that." He scraped a hand roughly through his hair and leaned his head back, drawing a deep breath and praying the words would come out right. "We need to talk, Susan."

Now she was scared. It must be an old girlfriend. The one he'd always wished hadn't gotten away? The one he'd been hoping would come back? Her stomach roiled and she realized she was shaking her head and mouthing 'no' over and over.

The pain in his chest was almost crippling. Apparently your heart really could break, he thought to himself. As he watched Susan, the only thought he had was that he didn't want to hurt her. With every ounce of his being he wanted to comfort, to reassure, but he knew that wasn't going to happen, at least not now. Trying to ignore the pain, he took her hand and led her to a stack of bricks piled against the side of the barn.

"Will you sit down for a minute?"

"What's going on, Riley?"

"Lissa came back to Misty Lake looking for me. I don't know why she waited this long—I didn't get many details from her—but she said…she came to…she told me Ryan is my son."

Susan pulled her hand back and her body tensed. Riley's son? She tried to process the information and found she really couldn't. Had he known? Had he at least suspected? How could he not? She'd guessed the boy was around five so Riley knew Lissa long before she ever met him. She tried to tell herself the hurt, the betrayal, the jealousy…all the things she was feeling weren't fair, weren't warranted, but she couldn't convince herself. A son…it would change everything. Selfishly, all she could focus on was how it was going to affect her and what it would mean for her relationship with Riley.

Riley waited for Susan to respond—to yell, to cry, to do something—but she sat as if frozen in place. He reached for her hand but she snatched it away from him and jumped to her feet.

"So what now? She left with you barely speaking to Ryan. Are you going to meet her…meet them?" Her words came out clipped.

"I don't know what's next, Susan, I've hardly had time to process all of this. I told her I'd call, that we could talk later…I don't know how this works, what I'm supposed to do…I just don't know." He began pacing and raking his hand through his hair again. The ramifications were starting to hit him…he'd have to tell his parents, his siblings, hell, the whole town would know soon enough. He didn't know where Lissa had been living. If it was far away, how would he see the boy? Would she move them to Misty Lake? Did he want her to? So many questions swirled in his mind he felt almost dizzy. Desperate for some understanding, some support, some calm, he turned to Susan but was met with a stony stare.

"Well, then I suppose you'd better wrap things up here so you can go talk to her." She turned to head for her car.

"Please don't go, Susan. Just wait a few minutes while I run inside and tell the guys I'm heading out. Travis can lock up for me. It'll just take a minute. Please." He felt like he was losing her now when he had been so close to asking her to stay forever.

"No, I have to go and you have to take care of…of everything you have to take care of." She started to hurry away before he could see the tears.

"Talk to me, Susan. Please don't leave like this."

She stopped but kept her back to him. "Okay." Drawing a deep breath and swiping at her eyes, she slowly turned to face him. "Did you love her?"

"No. No, I never loved her. Believe me, it was never like that. We weren't close, we didn't even really date, we just sort of—"

Susan held up a hand to stop him. "I get it, I don't need the details."

"I didn't love her, Susan, I've never loved anyone until—"

Again she stopped him. "Not now, Riley, not like this," she said shaking her head.

This time when she turned and walked away, she didn't stop until she got to her car. After a quick whistle for the dog, she opened the back door for him, climbed in the front, and drove away without looking back.

Riley watched her leave and knew he had never felt more helpless. The woman he loved was driving away and there was no guarantee that anything would ever be the same between them. A woman he barely knew was waiting for him with his son. He reached his hand in his pocket and as he tightly gripped the box that held the engagement ring he had planned to give to Susan later that night, all he could do was wonder if he'd ever get the chance.

26

Sam was locking up the shop and heading for her car when Susan pulled in. "Hey, Susan, I'm just heading out. In case I don't see you before you leave, have a wonderful weekend." She tossed her bag in the car and looked up to wink at Susan. Then she saw her face.

"Susan! What's the matter?" In a flash, Sam was next to Susan, holding her tight. Just as fast, she took Susan's shoulders and pushed her back, examining her to see if she was hurt. "What happened? Are you okay?"

Between sobs Susan managed, "Yes, I mean no...I mean yes, I'm okay, nothing's wrong." She tried to pull away.

"Obviously something's wrong. Tell me."

Susan shook her head and didn't say anything.

Sam studied Susan's face, the eyes red and swollen from crying, the pale complexion, the trembling lip, and knew it was definitely something. "Please talk to me,

Suze."

"You're on your way someplace. It can wait."

Sam stole a quick glance at her watch. She was due at an appointment with a client looking to have some cabinets built and installed in a mudroom. It was a lucrative job, but her cousin was more important. "My appointment can be rescheduled. Come on inside."

Sam took hold of Susan's arm and led her to the house. Once inside, she settled her in a chair at the kitchen table and asked, "Is this a tea problem or a wine problem?" She hoped to get a least a smile from Susan but Susan just stared out the window, the tears continuing to trickle down her cheeks.

"Okay, give me just one minute, I have to make a call. Don't go anywhere. Promise?" When Susan gave a short nod, Sam dashed back to her car for her purse and quickly called her client with her apologies and the offer to reschedule at any time.

Susan was where Sam had left her, still staring out the window without seeing. Sam sat down next to her and took her hand. "Now, tell me what happened. We'll figure it out, whatever it is."

Susan turned to face Sam and tried to start. "It's Riley…"

"I thought it might be. What did he do?"

"He didn't really do anything, at least not recently." Susan rubbed at her eyes and sucked in a deep breath. "A woman showed up today while I was with him over at the B&B."

"Who?"

"Her name is Melissa…Melissa something, I can't remember."

"A friend of Riley's? An old girlfriend?" Sam guessed.

Susan swallowed a sob. "I don't really understand what she is to him. They knew each other a few years ago, apparently."

Sam waited but Susan didn't offer any more. "And?" she prompted.

"And, she had a little boy with her and...and...told Riley he has a son." Susan dropped her head on the table and stopped trying to hold back the sobs.

Sam closed her eyes and blew out a breath. "Oh, honey." Then she leaned over, hugged her cousin, and held on while the sobs wracked through Susan.

When Susan was finally cried out, she lifted her head and took the handful of tissues Sam offered. Wiping her eyes and her nose she asked, "What am I supposed to do?"

"Well, I guess that depends. What is Riley going to do?"

"I don't know, I don't think he knows. They didn't talk too long this afternoon, he's going to meet her later and talk things out. There goes my birthday weekend."

"I'm sorry, sweetie."

Susan gave a wave of her hand. "No, it's okay. I need to stop thinking about just me. I know this isn't easy for Riley and I was no help whatsoever. He needed a friend and I just walked away."

"I think that's understandable. It's a lot to deal with for you, too."

Susan lifted her shoulders and let them fall. "I'm

just afraid, Sam. I don't know what this woman wants of him. And I don't know how Riley really feels about her. I do know him well enough to know that he's not going to just turn his back on his son. What if he decides he needs to try to make things work with her? What if he thinks they should try to be a family? I'm not so sure I could even argue with that. The boy deserves a father."

The desperate look in Susan's eyes had Sam wishing she had magic words to make everything better, but she found she didn't know what to say. "I'm afraid you're just going to have to wait a little while and see what happens. There are ways for him to be a father, to be in the boy's life, without being in some kind of relationship with the mother. Riley cares about you, Susan, he's not going to just walk away from you."

"Maybe, maybe not."

Part of Sam wanted to tell Susan that Riley had bought a ring, that he loved her and was going to propose, but aside from her promises to Riley to keep it a secret, she was afraid knowing would only make things worse for Susan.

"I really think you and Riley are going to be able to work this out, Susan. There will be some things to figure out, of course, but it will work. Do you know where this woman lives?"

"I don't know. I got the feeling Riley hadn't seen her in a long time."

"Well, then I'm sure it's not someone he's been pining after for years. Give it a little time. Things have a way of working themselves out."

Sam watched Susan wrestle with the doubt, the insecurity, and then quit fighting and give up. "I guess I'm not going to solve anything right now."

It was all Sam needed to hear. She grabbed Susan for one more quick hug then announced, "Forget about the tea and the wine, it's your birthday. I'm making margaritas."

Riley didn't know what to expect as he walked into the diner. They were meeting a little ways out of town, both of them agreeing it was best to attract as little attention as possible at this point. Riley had rehearsed dozens of questions on the drive, everything ranging from where Lissa had been for the past seven years and why she hadn't contacted him until now to when Ryan had learned to walk, what his first word had been, and if Lissa had ever told him who his father was.

Since Lissa had shown up at Susan's door and given him the news, he had struggled to wrap his mind around the fact that he had a son. Could he be a father? A good father? It seemed to him that parenting skills probably developed as one's kid did. A guy wasn't expected to know how to handle things like first days of school, setting curfews, and knowing what advice to give for a first date from the beginning. He would learn as he went and those things wouldn't seem so daunting. For Riley, though, he had been cheated out of almost six years of experiences and the learning that came with them. So he was just supposed to jump right in and know what to do? He was pretty sure he wasn't ready for that.

He had to swallow his anger at Lissa when he spotted her sitting in a corner booth. He wouldn't get anywhere if he approached her angry from the outset. He noticed she was alone, and while he figured they'd be able to talk easier if it was just the two of them, couldn't help being concerned about Ryan. Who was watching him? Probably Courtney, he figured, but what did she know about kids? A story Riley had read recently about a young boy who died after eating a snack given him by a friend that contained peanuts and that had triggered an immediate allergic reaction popped into Riley's mind and for a crazy moment he wanted to race to find the boy and make sure he was safe.

Lissa spotted him and he ordered himself to calm down before joining her at her table. He again noticed how pale she was, how her eyes seemed somewhat unfocused and vacant, how sick she looked. If he had passed her on the street, he was sure he wouldn't have recognized her. He considered the possibility that she was seriously ill and that's what had finally prompted her to contact him regarding his son.

Riley didn't say anything right away, all the rehearsing on the way over turning out to be useless. Lissa sunk in her seat under his gaze.

"I don't really know where to start, Lissa, except I'm wondering why now? Why keep my son from me for years then show up here out of the blue?"

"Ryan has a right to know his father. I guess I just decided it was time."

"Yes, he has a right to know his father just as I had a right to know my son. You seem to conveniently forget that this goes two ways."

"I know, I guess I was just afraid."

"Afraid? Afraid of what?"

"Afraid you wouldn't want anything to do with us…with him. Afraid of your reaction, your family's reaction…I don't know."

A waitress approached their table with menus so Riley bit back his retort while he ordered a soda. Once they were alone again he tried another approach.

"Does he know I'm his father? What have you told him all these years about why he doesn't have a dad around?"

"No, he doesn't know you're his father. I thought that's something we should tell him together. If you're willing, that is," she added as Riley's eyes hardened.

"Has he asked about his father? About where he is?"

"Not much. It's always been just the two of us. That's life as he knows it, I guess. Lately, though, he's been asking a few more questions. I think it's just part of growing up."

At the mention of Ryan growing up, Riley felt a little pang. He should have been a part of it…of all of it. "Tell me about him. What does he like, what doesn't he like, is he healthy, does he go to school yet…just tell me about him."

Lissa seemed to relax and soften somewhat as she started talking about her son. "He's a good boy, he always has been. And he's healthy. Aside from a cold now and then, he's never really been sick. He likes pizza, Cinnamon Toast Crunch cereal, and, if you can believe it, broccoli. He doesn't like hot dogs or carrots. He loves cars, trucks, and action figures. He's particularly fond of Spider-Man. He's very athletic, things like riding a bike and throwing a ball came naturally to him."

Riley couldn't stop the emotion that welled up inside him. Rationally, he supposed the things Lissa mentioned would apply to most boys Ryan's age—well, maybe not the broccoli—but hearing them used to describe his son left him feeling proud…and cheated. He should have been the one to teach him to ride a bike and to throw a ball. He should have been there when Ryan had his first bite of pizza. Riley liked carrots. Maybe if Ryan had seen him eating them he'd like them, too.

He was surprised at how strong the feelings were that coursed through him. Until he'd decided Susan was the woman he wanted to spend the rest of his life with and had started thinking some about the future, he had never really given a thought to children or to being a father. Even when he'd thought about the kids he and Susan might have one day, he'd never felt anything like the pull he felt now towards Ryan.

Thinking about Susan brought on a whole new set of emotions. He had tried calling her several times since she'd left him earlier, but she hadn't answered her phone. As much as he had wanted to drive to Sam's and beg her to talk with him, in the end he'd decided it would make more sense to talk with Lissa first so that he'd have more to share with Susan. He rested his elbows on the table, dropped his head onto his fisted hands, and closed his eyes as he thought about how radically different the evening was from what he'd planned.

When he looked up again, Lissa was staring at him. She still looked nervous and almost sickly but, if Riley wasn't mistaken, there was a small spark in her eyes that hadn't been there before. Not knowing what to make of it, he asked another question even though he was afraid to hear the answer.

"Where have you been living? And what are your

plans?"

"We haven't been real settled lately. We stayed with my sister for a while, but she's got her hands full with her own family and she made it clear she didn't want us around any longer. As far as my plans, I guess that depends partly on you," she said, tossing the ball back in his court.

"I want to know my son, Lissa. One way or another, I want to make that happen." Riley hesitated. Did he want her to stay in Misty Lake? What would that mean for his relationship with Susan? "I guess there are some things we're going to have to work out. I hope you can stay around until we can make those decisions."

"I, ah, don't know how long I can hang out with Courtney so I might have to look for somewhere to stay…it would have to be pretty cheap, I don't have much money right now, so if you know of some place…" Lissa tensed and held her breath as she waited for Riley's response.

"Oh, well, I don't know, I could ask around, I guess."

"Okay, and I'll try to get an idea of what Courtney is thinking. Like I said, though, there are expenses and I'm not sure how long I can stick around."

She wanted money. How had he not realized that sooner? "Listen, Lissa, if you need some money to get you through for a while, I can try to help."

"I guess I wouldn't say no, kids are pretty expensive…"

"I'll help out with Ryan." It came out angrier than he had intended, but he was starting to feel like she was playing him. Was money the only reason she came back to

Misty Lake? "I'll help," he repeated, forcing his voice to stay calm. He reached in his pocket and pulled out his checkbook. Scribbling a check for her, he slapped it on the table.

Lissa watched as he wrote the check. She reached for it and shoved it in her purse, but not before stealing a glance at the amount.

"You can take it to First National, they'll cash it for you. When can I see Ryan again? I'd like a chance to spend some time with him."

"Tomorrow," she said a little too eagerly. "I have some things I should take care of, maybe you could spend a couple of hours with him tomorrow afternoon?"

Alone? he wanted to ask but settled for a long, hard look at Lissa. Granted, he was the boy's father, but Lissa barely knew him. He had to believe most mothers would be more protective. He could tell Lissa was growing restless, she had started to shift in her seat and play with the straw in her soda.

"Sure, tomorrow afternoon would be great. Do you want me to pick him up?"

"No, how about I meet you at the park in town. He saw it earlier today and he's been asking me to take him there. It will keep him busy and you won't have to bother with him too much."

"He won't be a bother," Riley said as his forehead creased and he studied Lissa.

"Well, I didn't mean a bother, really, I just meant that there will be plenty for him to do. You can see how he loves to climb and what a little daredevil he is when it comes to swings. He'll tell you to push him higher and higher until you're sure the swing is going to flip right over the bar."

"What time?"

"One o'clock?"

"Sure. Great. I'll see you then." Riley dropped some bills on the table and left as quickly as he could. Something didn't seem right, but he couldn't quite put his finger on it. Maybe she was just nervous, it would make sense. Right now, though, he knew he needed to head to his parents' house. It was a conversation he wasn't looking forward to.

As Lissa watched him leave, she relaxed. A little. It had gone reasonably well, she thought. She snuck another peek at the check in her purse and breathed a sigh of relief as she started calculating. It would get her through for a while. She couldn't put off new shoes for Ryan much longer, his toes were almost poking through the ones he'd been wearing since they'd left California. She would probably need to pick up a few shirts and pairs of pants, as well. The boy seemed to grow overnight. That shouldn't use up too much of the check. She'd have to help out with groceries if they were going to stay at Courtney's. But there'd be enough left over, she'd make sure of it. And it meant the cash she had in her purse right now was hers to do with as she chose.

She got in her car and followed the same directions she'd followed earlier that day. This time when she parked and made her way across the yard, she did so with more confidence. She knocked on the door, answered when he demanded to know who was there, and when the door finally opened, squared her shoulders and spoke clearly.

"You mentioned you might have something else I'd be interested in?"

He snorted in reply. "They always come back," he laughed as he unlocked a cabinet and reached inside.

It took only the briefest glance at her son as he walked into her kitchen to know that something was wrong. Dispensing with the silly greeting she still used when it was just the two of them, Anna instead slipped straight into mother hen mode.

"What's the matter, Riley?" She didn't want to think about the possibility of there being problems between her son and the woman she knew in her heart was the right person for him, but the look on his face told her that was most likely the case.

"Hi, Mom." He gave her a hug and, Anna noticed, held on a little longer than normal.

Anna hugged back while her heart ached. He didn't behave like this unless something was really bothering him. As much as she wanted to ask again, demand even, she knew she needed to wait until he was ready to talk.

"Is Dad home?"

"Yes, he's out in the garage playing around with the lawn mower. He's convinced it's going to be dry enough and warm enough to mow before long." Anna shook her head. "You know your dad."

"Yeah." Riley attempted a smile but it didn't reach his eyes. "I think I'll go see if he can take a break."

When Riley headed to the garage, Anna put the kettle on the stove. Before long, Sean followed Riley into the kitchen, wiping his hands on a rag and, Anna thought, blessedly oblivious to the fact that upsetting news of some sort was headed their way.

"Maybe you guys can sit down for a minute, I need to talk to you," Riley said.

"How about a cup of tea first?" Anna asked. Keeping her hands busy would help. Her mind seemed to want to focus on something other than the problem staring her in the face, and images of the countless times over the years that she had brewed a pot of tea, sat one member of her family or another down at this very kitchen table, and listened, counseled, and sometimes cried, flashed through her memory like some wild movie on fast forward.

Anna settled Riley and Sean at the table, set tea in front of them, and added a plate of cookies. She had just baked peanut butter cookies, Riley's favorite, and when he didn't immediately reach for one, her concern deepened.

"I got some news earlier today. It came as quite a shock to me and I'm still trying to figure out how to deal with it, but I wanted to tell you before you heard it from someone else."

Anna paled. "Are you sick, Riley?" Her voice was barely more than a whisper.

"No. Geez, Mom, I'm sorry, it's nothing like that. I'm fine, healthy as a horse."

The vice around Anna's heart loosened somewhat. She knew her son better than anyone. He was telling her the truth, but, as she watched him fidget, she knew that there was difficult news to come.

"A girl I knew some years ago came back to town today. She showed up out at the inn this afternoon." Riley reached for a napkin and twisted it into a knot. "She had a boy with her. She told me he's my son."

One of Anna's hands flew to her mouth as the other reached for Sean's. Squeezing his hand, she looked at her son through dazed eyes while trying to process what he was telling them. It was silent for a long time.

Sean was the first to speak. He leaned back a little in his chair and fixed his eyes on his son's. "Who is this girl?"

"Her name is Melissa Cosgrove. I don't think you ever met her. She spent a summer here about six—I guess almost seven—years ago. She worked at the resort, hung around town when she had time off."

"And you never knew about the child until today?"

"No, Dad, I had no idea. Lissa showed up out of the blue. I hadn't even heard from her since she left at the end of that summer."

"Where has she been? Why didn't she let you know?"

"I don't know too much. I'm just getting back from meeting with her. We talked a little, but I feel like I don't know much more than I did before. She told me she lived with her sister for a while, but also said she and Ryan have been on their own for some time. The details are kind of fuzzy. I'm not really sure where she's been for all these years and why she decided to tell me now, except she said Ryan had started to ask questions."

"His name is Ryan?" Anna managed. She felt a tear escape and drip to her cheek.

"Aw, Mom, don't cry. Please."

"I'm sorry, Riley, this is just a lot to take in. You have a son? We have another grandson? He's almost six years old and we've never laid eyes on him?" Her voice shook with emotion and she dabbed at her eyes with a napkin.

"What happens now? Is she here to stay?" Sean boomed.

Anna understood, and almost appreciated, Sean's barely contained anger. Shoot questions at Riley, try to piece together the answers. His methodical approach to problem solving had served him well in his years as Misty Lake's sheriff, as well as his years as a parent. Now, having something concrete to focus on would mean less time to think about all they had missed, about all that could have been.

"I'm going to spend some time with him tomorrow afternoon. Lissa is going to stay around for a while…I don't know how long. We have some things to work out."

"I'll say you do," Sean snapped.

Anna spotted the hurt in Riley's eyes and knew Sean did, too. His tone softened.

"Listen Riley, the situation may not be ideal, but it's nothing that can't be figured out. What are you thinking right now? What do you want?"

"I just don't know, Dad. I haven't had much time to really think about it."

"I'd like to think we raised you to do the right thing. This girl may have not handled things in the best way—you had a right to know about the child from the start—but since you know now, you have a responsibility and we expect you to take that responsibility seriously."

"I know that. I intend on doing what I can…trying to be a part of his life, I guess."

"You guess? I think you'd better do a little more than guess." Again Sean's voice rose and again he tamped it back. On a sigh, Sean started again. "Riley, if this child is yours—" He stopped suddenly and pursed his lips. "Are you certain he's your child?"

Riley seemed to grow even more uncomfortable. "Lissa said he's mine. I asked the same question and she seemed genuinely hurt and started to cry. I didn't want to push and upset her more than she already was." Riley looked down at the table. "It's not impossible that he's mine," he mumbled.

"Well, not impossible and for certain are two very different things. Don't you think you should insist on some proof?"

"Yes, and I will. But I just keep wondering why she would lie about it. Why say I'm his father if I'm not?"

Sean shook his head. "That I can't know. I just think it would be wise to be sure before you get too deeply involved."

It was Anna's turn to speak up. "You're going to see him tomorrow? Do you think we could meet him?" She was almost desperate.

"Maybe the next time, Mom. I think I need to get to know him first. I don't know if he's shy around new people...I don't want him upset or scared right from the start."

"I suppose you're right. But you've seen him already...what does he look like?" She needed something.

Riley nodded, as if understanding the need. "He's got brown hair that's a little wavy and dark blue eyes." Riley focused on a spot in the distance and his forehead creased as he concentrated. "He's got a few freckles on his nose, he runs like he could keep going all day, and when he smiles it seems to fill his whole face. He seemed very polite, I heard please and thank you, and he loved Gusto…"

At this he stopped and Anna figured she knew why. His voice, his posture, his expression, all told Anna that, whether he realized it or not, Riley already thought of the boy as his son. But aside from the overwhelming shock and the confusion, there was more going on.

"How is Susan taking the news?"

Riley sunk lower in his chair, his head falling back and his shoulders sagging. "Not so well. She was there when Lissa showed up. I tried to talk to her but…I don't know, I guess I didn't do a very good job of it. She left, I had to go meet Lissa. I've tried calling her but she's not answering."

"It's a shock for her, too, Riley. I know you have a lot on your mind, but if you care about Susan the way I think you do, you're going to have to make a special effort to include her in some of the decision making. Give her a little time, but not too much."

"Today's her birthday. I had made plans, a surprise, and now…" He raised his hands and let them fall.

"I'm sorry, that's lousy timing." As she'd done when her children had been young, Anna longed to take away the pain, wished it could be given to her, instead.

"Yeah. So what am I supposed to do now? I'm sure by tomorrow half the town is going to know my business."

"We can't tell you what to do, Riley, you're going to have to figure that out for yourself. Just put that boy's best interests first," Sean answered. "As far as the people in town, you know how things work. Sure, there will be talk, but there will also be plenty of support from those who matter. As for the rest, let them talk. Words can't hurt you. You'd do well to remember that."

"Thanks, Dad, I will."

27

Riley figured he'd slept about an hour total. Every time he'd closed his eyes, images of the boy appeared. He saw him as a toddler learning to walk, at the park in one of those baby swings that held kids in place, swinging a big plastic bat at a wiffle ball. When he did drift off, the images turned dark. The boy was falling from the top of a slide and there was no one there to catch him. He waded out into the water and stumbled, his head bobbing up and down in the waves and him screaming for Daddy, but no one came. His chubby fingers reached for a cherry. He turned it over in his hands for a moment before stuffing it in his mouth. He started to choke; his face turned red and his eyes grew huge, pleading for help. No one noticed.

At three o'clock, Riley had finally given up and brewed a pot of coffee. He'd sat staring out at the darkness for hours but not finding any answers.

Now, as he sat at a picnic table and scanned the area for Lissa and Ryan, he was jumpy and tense, the result of not nearly enough sleep and far too much caffeine. He spotted them walking from the parking lot and had to smile as he watched Ryan pulling on his mom's hand, trying to get her to hurry, while never taking his eyes off the playground. Riley walked to meet them.

"Hi, Ryan."

The boy looked up at him and recognition slowly dawned. "Oh, hi. Did you bring your dog?"

"No, the dog isn't here today, sorry about that."

"Oh well, that's okay." Turning his attention to Lissa, he asked, "Can I go play?"

"Sure," she answered, and he darted off.

"Thanks for bringing him today. I was a little worried you might change your mind."

"Hmmm? Why? I mean, it will be okay. He shouldn't be too much trouble."

"I'm not worried about him being any trouble, Lissa."

She seemed calmer than she had the day before...almost too calm. Her movements were slow and her eyes didn't completely focus when she turned to look at him. "Are you feeling all right?"

"Oh, sure. Just a little tired. Didn't get much sleep on the pullout at Courtney's." She attempted a crooked smile.

"I didn't get much sleep, either," Riley muttered. "We need to talk some more. I have more questions and there are a hundred different things we are going to have to figure out."

"Sure, sure, we'll talk. But later. Right now I need to go." She turned to walk away, but Riley reached out and grabbed her arm.

"Lissa, what about right now? How long will you be gone? Where do you want to pick up Ryan? Has he had any lunch?"

"Oh. I guess I'll pick him up here in a few hours. And no, I don't think he's had any lunch."

"You don't think?" When she gave him a confused look he added, "Never mind. I'll let him play for a while then take him to get some lunch. Here's my cell number in case you want to reach me." He handed her one of his business cards which she absentmindedly shoved in her pocket.

"I'm sure he'll be fine. He's a good kid. Have fun." With a little wave at Riley and without a word to her son, she was off.

Riley watched her for a moment and wondered again if she was ill, but he quickly turned his attention to Ryan who was racing around the playground in a game of tag with the half dozen friends he seemed to have already made. Since he didn't know what Lissa had told him, Riley caught up with Ryan.

"Hey, Ryan, I'll be sitting right over on that bench if you need anything."

Ryan looked up at him, confused for a moment but then accepting the plan. "Okay," he answered easily before tearing after a boy in a purple jacket.

Riley watched him run, jump, climb, and, best of all, laugh. The boy appeared to be overjoyed with the park and with the kids. After about thirty minutes, a few of the kids left and the group grew smaller. Ryan made his way through the sand to Riley.

"How long are we stayin' here?"

"How long do you want to stay?"

Apparently it wasn't the response Ryan had expected. He looked positively ecstatic. "You mean we can stay a long time?"

"If you want."

"Cool!"

"Are you hungry? Your mom said you didn't have lunch."

Ryan seemed to consider. He turned back to the playground then back to Riley. "I'm kinda hungry. Can I eat and then play more?"

"Sure. What do you want to eat?"

Ryan pressed his luck. "Pizza?"

"Sounds good, pizza's my favorite."

Ryan seemed delighted with the news and his face broke into a wide grin. "Mine too. But I don't like any green stuff on it."

"No green stuff then, I promise," Riley answered with a grin of his own.

As they headed across the park and towards The Brick, Ryan reached up and took hold of Riley's hand. Riley's heart swelled with the simple gesture. When Ryan sheepishly asked if he could have orange soda with the pizza, Riley could only nod over the lump in his throat but he knew he'd give him the moon, if he could.

Their waitress was Megan, the younger sister of one of Riley's buddies. She looked at Riley questioningly as she delivered their menus. "Who's your friend, Riley?"

"This is Ryan. He's visiting for a few days."

"Hi, Ryan." She was curious, but Riley's look

made it clear he wasn't anxious to answer any more questions. "Can I get you guys something to drink?"

"Two orange sodas, please. And we'll have a large pepperoni."

"Coming right up." She smiled at the two before bouncing off to fill their order.

Riley watched as Ryan held a blue crayon tightly in his hand and concentrated on tracing the outline of a pizza on the kids' menu Megan had placed in front of him. His tongue slowly worked its way out of his mouth and moved from one side to the other as he drew. Riley couldn't help but wonder if he'd done the same thing as a child.

When he finished his task and was choosing another crayon, Riley asked him, "Do you have a big playground at home?"

"Um, yeah, I think so."

"How about friends? Did you have a lot of friends by your house?"

"You mean my cousins? They're older than me."

"You live with your cousins?"

"I used to. Mommy said we might not go back." He seemed sad as he thought about it and Riley was curious.

"Why not?"

"I dunno. Sometimes Mommy and Aunt Jenny fight."

Riley felt a little guilty pressing the boy for details, but he was curious. And, he felt he had a right to know what his son's life was like. "What do they fight about?"

"Dunno. Mommy leaves sometimes and Aunt Jenny gets mad, I think."

Riley watched as Ryan chose a red crayon and

went back to work on the placemat.

"Did you leave your Aunt Jenny's house a long time ago?"

Ryan pulled his attention from the placemat to Riley. He seemed to mull over Riley's question and Riley wondered if he didn't remember how long it had been since they'd left, or if he just didn't want to answer. Maybe was afraid to answer.

"Yeah, it was a long time ago. I wanted to go back so Santa could find me, but Mommy said we couldn't."

Again, Riley thought Ryan looked sad when he talked about his Aunt Jenny's house. Lissa was going to have to do some explaining whether she liked it or not. Riley figured if Ryan was worried about Santa not finding him if he wasn't at his aunt's house, they must not have left too long before Christmas or he probably wouldn't still consider it his home. He couldn't help but wonder what kind of life Lissa had been giving him.

"Where does your Aunt Jenny live?"

"She lives at her house." Riley could almost hear the unspoken 'Duh!' and it was clear Ryan was starting to wonder how smart Riley was.

"Right. I just wondered where her house is. Do you know?"

"Um…." His eyes looked to the ceiling and his forehead wrinkled as he concentrated. "I think Cal…Cal-for-na?"

"California?"

The big grin was back in place. "Yeah, that's it," he answered, clearly pleased Riley had figured it out.

Their food arrived and Riley dropped the interrogation. He couldn't remember the last time he'd been alone with, and responsible for, a kid during mealtime. Never, he decided, he would have remembered. Between cutting and trying to cool the hot pizza, cleaning up spilled soda, wiping messy hands, and flagging down Megan three times for more napkins, Riley barely managed to feed himself. It was alternatingly hilarious and terrifying. At one point Ryan tried to get to his knees to watch a dog passing outside the window and managed to fall right out of the booth. Riley was sure he was going to start to scream as his head knocked against the side of the table, but Ryan just rubbed his head and looked around as if trying to figure out what had happened.

Once Ryan had eaten his fill and Riley had done his best to clean him up, Ryan announced he needed to go to the bathroom. As Riley guided him to the restroom at the back of the restaurant, he couldn't miss the curious glances from some of the other diners. Riley did his best to ignore them, keeping his attention on the boy who had started to squirm. Recognizing the sign, Riley doubled his pace. Quickly ushering him into a stall, Riley pulled the door closed and, holding the top, said, "I'll be right here."

"But there's no step."

"Huh?"

"There's no step. I can't reach."

Riley opened the door to find Ryan staring at the toilet. The squirming had escalated. Not knowing what he was supposed to do, he started to panic.

"How do we do this?"

"You have to lift me."

"Lift you?"

"Yeah. And hurry. Please?"

How many times had he let Megan refill their

glasses? Probably too many, he decided, as he finally just unbuttoned, unzipped, then lifted Ryan and sat him down on the toilet.

Ryan looked at him and wrinkled his nose. Clearly Riley had done something wrong, but at the moment he was just thankful their next stop wouldn't have to be a clothing store.

"You're spose to put toilet paper on the seat," Ryan said shaking his head at Riley.

"Sorry, I didn't know that."

"Mommy says there's germs."

"She's right, I should have put toilet paper down."

"I guess it's okay. I won't tell."

"Thanks."

Once they had everything buttoned and zipped, hands washed and dried, and shoes retied—because apparently when you use the bathroom you also need to take off your shoes and make sure your socks aren't twisted—they headed back to the park.

Once again, Ryan took hold of Riley's hand as if it were the most natural thing in the world and once again, Riley's heart swelled. He couldn't help but think about his brother Joe and about all he had to look forward to with Dylan. Joe grumbled at times about the sleepless nights and unexplained crying, but Riley found he was envious of even those not-so-great parts. How could a few hours with this little boy have changed his perspective so drastically? He recalled how he had mercilessly teased Joe about having to deal with all the things, that now, he found himself longing to have experienced. Weird.

"Can you push me on the swing?" Ryan asked, yanking Riley back to the present. Ryan was looking up at him hopefully.

"Sure I can."

"Yes!" Ryan shouted victoriously as he made a beeline for an open swing. Riley chuckled and jogged after him.

They played on the swings, climbed on the pirate ship play structure, and joined in on a basketball game on the kid-sized court. Lissa was right, the kid was a natural and feelings of pride coursed through Riley. Ryan dribbled the ball around kids Riley was sure were older and made more shots than he missed. And he loved every minute of it.

Riley checked the time and figured they had about another thirty minutes until Lissa arrived. "Is there anything else you'd like to do before your mom gets back?"

"I kinda need to go potty again."

Riley surveyed the park and spotted the port-a-potty but after the experience in the restaurant, decided to try to find something that would hopefully be a little cleaner. Unless this was another emergency.

"Do we need to hurry?"

Ryan pursed his lips and considered. "No, I don't think so."

Riley swallowed his laugh. "Okay, then let's take a walk."

They wandered down Main Street for a few minutes with Riley thinking they could duck into The Whole Bean and use the bathroom. Before they made it there, Ryan stopped in his tracks. The Toy Box's current window display featured just about every super hero Riley had ever heard of, and then some. It was hard not to be impressed even if his days of action figures were behind him.

In one corner, Captain America was wielding his huge shield while Thor stood along side him with his hammer held high. Iron Man and Hulk were doing battle with a slew of evil-looking bad guys. Batman was rushing to the scene in a Batmobile that appeared to be equipped with all the latest gadgets befitting such a venerable crime fighter. High above the fray, Spider-Man was swinging into action on the end of his web.

Ryan's eyes were huge, and as Riley watched, he began to move his lips and weave from side to side, clearly imagining joining in the on-going fight against evil. Riley almost felt like doing the same. It didn't take much for Riley to make up his mind.

"How about we go inside and take a look around? I bet they have a bathroom, too."

"Really?"

"Really. But the bathroom first."

Riley got Ryan's nod of approval on how he handled the bathroom trip the second time around. He congratulated himself for being a quick learner.

The store was filled with games, art supplies, and all sorts of toys, but Ryan only had eyes for the action figure display.

"Who's your favorite?"

"Well, I like Spidey a lot, he's cool cuz he can shoot webs." Ryan mimicked blasting a web to the ceiling. "Capin Merica is cool, too. I like his shield. Did you know Hulk turns green when he gets mad?"

"I did," Riley said with the appropriate amount of respect.

"Sometimes they used to be on TV but I don't think they are anymore. Maybe it was only in Calforna." He looked as if he were trying to work something out but quickly gave up and returned his attention to the scene in front of him.

Riley felt an inexplicable urge to buy him everything in sight, to make up for all the missed birthdays, Christmases, trips to the doctor or dentist as, he remembered, his mom would sometimes reward them with a small toy or treat after particularly harrowing visits. Easter was only a week away. He'd have to see what Lissa had planned and hoped she didn't balk when he stuffed the biggest basket he could find with everything he thought Ryan would like.

"Do you have any of these guys?"

"I have Spidey, Santa brought him."

"Why don't you pick two more? Spidey can't always fight the bad guys by himself."

"You mean you're gonna buy them? For me?"

"Yeah. Spidey definitely needs some helpers. Who do you want?"

Ryan was eyeing him suspiciously. "Are you my mom's friend?"

"Yes, I am."

"Did you ask her if I could get one?"

"No, but it will be okay."

Ryan still looked unsure, but it didn't take long for excitement to win out over doubt. He carefully considered, rejected, and reconsidered before settling on Thor and Captain America. He was bouncing with excitement as they began heading for the register. Riley stopped.

"You know, I'm thinking you probably need a

couple of bad guys, too. Who are these guys going to fight?"

This time Riley didn't have to do much convincing. "Okay!" Ryan almost shouted as he dumped Thor and Captain America into Riley's arms and dashed back to check out possible villains.

In the end, they left with bad guys Loki and Ultron, good guys Thor and Captain America, as well as a Spider Cycle for the Spider-Man figure Ryan already had, and a Spider-Man glove that fit Ryan's hand, shot webs, and made all sorts of sounds that, Riley figured, would drive Lissa crazy. Ryan seemed a little dazed. Riley wondered if he'd overdone it, decided he probably had, and then decided he didn't care.

They returned to the park just in time for their scheduled meet-up with Lissa, but she was nowhere in sight. Riley didn't mind. They took a seat at a picnic table and he began unboxing and assembling and soon the two were engaged in an epic battle between good and evil complete with a surprise attack from behind a garbage can, a close call when it looked as though Loki might be able to wield Thor's hammer, and a dramatic rescue featuring Captain America leaping from the top of the picnic table to save the fine citizens of Misty Lake who were in danger of being vaporized…and who were being portrayed by a pile of pinecones. Riley hadn't had so much fun in years.

Riley checked his watch and realized Lissa was over forty minutes late. He was just considering loading Ryan into his truck and taking him home as he'd noticed Ryan starting to yawn, but spotted Lissa idly wandering in their direction.

Ryan spotted her too, and any signs of tiredness

vanished as he sprinted for her, his arms loaded down with his treasures. The look on Lissa's face when she reached the picnic table was less than pleasant.

"What's all this?" she asked, waving her hand at the pile of toys.

"Just some things we found at the toy store in town. Is there a problem?" Riley knew his tone was frosty, but it irked him to have to defend his actions where his son was concerned.

"Ryan, put your things down here and take another turn on the slide before we have to leave," Lissa ordered.

Ryan looked between the two but did as his mother said.

"What are you trying to do? Swoop in and be some sort of hero? Buying him a pile of things that I couldn't possibly afford?"

"A hero? No, I'm not trying to be a hero. And I wasn't trying to show you up, if that's what you're implying. I haven't been able to buy him a thing…ever. Consider this a start at making up for lost time."

"It's too much."

"He said he doesn't have many toys. I'm not judging or trying to change the way you've been parenting, I just wanted to buy my son a few things. I don't think that should be a problem."

"Fine. Just clear it with me the next time. There are things he needs more than a pile of toys."

"What sort of things?"

"He's a growing boy, Riley. He needs shoes, clothes, haircuts, he hasn't been to the dentist in a while…it's all expensive."

Riley figured she was probably right, but at the moment his frustration and anger won out. "If I'd known about him years ago I would have helped, I would have done what I could to see that he had what he needed. As it is, I felt like buying something he wanted and that he'd enjoy…enjoy a hell of a lot more than a shirt or a trip to the dentist."

Riley's tone said it wasn't the time to push. "Sorry, you're right. Thanks for the toys, I know he'll have fun with them."

"About the other stuff, if there's something he needs right now I can help with the expenses."

"You gave me the check, that's enough for now. Maybe we can try to work something out…I don't know, some kind of arrangement?"

"Sure. Have you talked to Courtney about staying at her place for a little longer?"

"She's okay with us hanging around for a while. We didn't talk specifics, but she seems cool with us being there for now."

"My parents would like to meet Ryan. Is that all right with you?"

Lissa tensed and was slow to answer. "I don't know, he's been through a lot already. Maybe we can give it a little time? Let him get more comfortable with you before we spring too many more people on him?"

Riley wanted to argue. Ryan seemed like a pretty well adjusted kid. He hadn't balked in the least when Lissa left him at the park, and he had seemed plenty comfortable at the restaurant and the toy store, talking when spoken to. But giving him some time probably wasn't the worst idea.

"Okay, we can take it slow. Next weekend is

Easter. How about if I bring him over to my parents' house for dinner? You're welcome too, if you'd like," he added.

"No, I'm not ready to meet your family." She was emphatic. "I'll let you introduce Ryan without me. It will probably be easier for your family that way, too. Easter will be fine."

"I'd like to get him something...an Easter basket, some candy, toys, and, if you give me sizes, I can add in some of the things he needs."

Lissa nodded. "Okay." She looked over to the playground where Ryan was climbing the slide again. "We should probably get going, it's been a long day and I'm guessing he's tired."

"There are some more things we need to discuss." Riley was uncomfortable, but it was a talk they needed to have. "I don't know any details of when and where he was born. When is his birthday? Do you have a copy of his birth certificate? I'd like some proof he's really my son."

A shiver shook Lissa and Riley eyed her warily, afraid she was going to crumble...or run.

"I don't carry his birth certificate with me, but his birthday is May eighth. The math works. You may not remember dates, but I do. We were at a big bonfire out at the lake. The music was loud, there were people everywhere, but we just wanted to be alone. We snuck away far enough that we could barely hear the music, the moon was full and it was all so romantic, we had that crappy bottle of wine..." She gave a small laugh and turned away.

Riley didn't remember it quite the same way but didn't see the point in sharing his version just to hurt her.

Lissa had a far away, almost dreamy look in her eyes and the hint of a smile on her lips. Her tension seemed to melt away and for a moment he could see the girl he remembered, the girl who had always smiled, the girl who had always seemed to have the world by the tail. But then she gave her head an almost imperceptible shake, turned to face him, and the moment passed. Her eyes, once again, had a haunted, defeated look and she seemed to shrink before him until she looked so frail Riley was again afraid she was going to collapse.

He didn't want to push when she looked so fragile but couldn't just let it go. "I'd like to have a copy of his birth certificate. Is it possible to have someone mail it? And I want a paternity test."

"Riley!" she gasped.

"Look, Lissa, it's something I need. You show up here out of the blue with a child and tell me he's mine. It's possible, yes, I'm not arguing that. But you need to understand it's quite a shock. I can't get past the fact that I hadn't heard a word from you in years and now…this. I don't think wanting some proof is too much to ask."

She sighed heavily and leaned a hip against the picnic table. "I don't know when I can get a copy of his birth certificate. It's in a safe deposit box and my dad is the only other person authorized to access it. He's out of the country, I think."

"Then I'll wait on that but I want to get the paternity test done. I did some checking, it's a pretty simple procedure."

"Ryan's afraid of needles. I want to give him a little time to get settled before I spring a doctor visit on him."

"There are no needles involved, it's just a swab on the inside of the cheek."

"It's still a doctor's office. He won't like it. Just give him a little more time, we'll take care of it soon."

He didn't know Lissa or Ryan well enough to know if he should believe her. What kid liked the doctor? But, if it was going to be a traumatic experience for him, it could wait a few days.

"A little time then, but not too long. I want everything verified before we tell Ryan I'm his father and I'd like to be able to do that as soon as possible." Riley watched her sway and stagger. She needed to get some rest. "When can I see Ryan again?"

"Soon, whenever you want. Just call."

Riley gave her a long look. "Are you sure you're okay? Are you sick?"

"No, just tired. It's been a long few days...few months, really. I need to go." She scanned the park and called for Ryan.

"Do we have to go, Mommy?"

"Yes, you've had plenty of time to play."

Ryan kicked at the dirt and mumbled to himself but didn't argue.

"I'll see you later, Ryan," Riley said as he mussed the boy's hair.

Ryan looked up and his forehead creased as he studied Riley. He seemed unsure of something. "Is my mom going to leave with you like she did—"

Lissa grabbed him by the arm and started pulling him away. "It's time to go, Ryan. Right now. Grab your things."

"Thanks for all the stuff." Ryan waved as Lissa

herded him towards the parking lot.

Riley waved back. As they drove away, Riley already missed the sound of Ryan's voice, his laugh, his exuberance. And he worried about Lissa. If they'd had more than a few blocks to go, he would have insisted on driving. Lissa seemed in no condition to be behind the wheel. He told himself that when they spoke next he was going to demand some answers. She was hiding something from him and he was afraid if it was a health problem, it could mean a dangerous situation for Ryan. Making a quick decision, he jogged to his truck and took off after Lissa's car. He was going to make sure they got to Courtney's safely.

28

Later that evening, Riley strode purposefully to the door at Sam's house, his arms loaded down with flowers and a huge, brightly wrapped box for Susan as well as a bag stuffed with dog toys and treats for Gusto. At this point, he wasn't above using the dog to get to her. Susan hadn't answered his calls or texts. He'd made up his mind he wasn't going to take no for an answer any longer. They needed to talk.

"Oh, Riley," Sam's face fell when she saw Riley at the door. "Susan's not here and I'm guessing that's not all for me."

"Where is she? I stopped by the inn, she's not there."

"She's in Chicago."

"Chicago?"

"Come in." Sam took the box and led Riley into

the kitchen. "Can I get you something to drink?"

"Why is she in Chicago?"

Sam went to the fridge and pulled out a beer for Riley then sat at the table and waved for him to do the same. "She left early this morning. She already had the weekend off and she called Emily to switch a couple of things around on the schedule so she could stay a few days." Sam shrugged helplessly. "I think she just wanted to get away for a while, wanted to see her family."

Riley's head dropped. "I suppose she told you?"

Sam reached a hand out and covered his. "She did. I was here when she got home yesterday. She was pretty upset. We talked."

"And?"

"And I don't know. She was a little calmer by last night. We had a couple of margaritas, ate some of her favorite chips and salsa, and I tried to get her to enjoy her birthday, but she was distant. She didn't really talk about it after...after she told me."

"Have you heard from her? Did she make it to Chicago okay?"

"Yes, she called. She's there, visiting with everyone. She sounded better."

"I really want to talk to her, Sam. I need to fix this." Riley got up and walked to the window. He stared at the lake, defeated.

"I know. It will do her good to be home for a few days. Once she's back I think she'll be ready to talk." When Riley just continued to stare out the window, she added, "How about you? Do you want to talk?"

Riley turned to Sam. His eyes were wet and his voice was raspy. "I can't lose her, Sam. I just can't."

Sam closed him in a hug. "You won't. She loves you. She just needs some time to sort things out. I think she's afraid she's going to lose you."

Riley drew back and raked his fingers through his hair. Sam took his hand and led him to the sofa. "This is really a mess and I don't know how to fix it."

"Tell me what's going on. Where do things stand with you and the boy's mother?"

Riley huffed and looked at the ceiling. "I wish I knew. She's…I don't know, strange, I guess. I think she may be sick—really sick—and that's why she's here now, after all this time. She doesn't look well, she seems to have trouble concentrating. I haven't gotten too many answers out of her and I don't really know what her plans are."

"Is she going to stay in Misty Lake, for a while at least, so you have a chance to get to know your son?"

"It sounds like it. She's staying with a friend. I don't know how long that will be possible and I don't know what will happen after that. She's made a few comments that make it seem as though she doesn't have a lot of money and I think that's a big concern for her right now. I've offered to help—have helped some." He shrugged.

"What about your son? What's he like?"

Riley's whole demeanor changed with the change in subject. "He's pretty great. He's full of energy, he's polite." Riley thought back to the trip to the toy store. "He loves to play and he appreciates it when someone does something for him."

"He sounds like a great kid. Susan said the same."

"She did?" Riley was surprised…and pleased. He'd been afraid Susan's opinion would change after finding out Riley was his father.

"She said a lot of the same things you just said. She was crazy about him."

Riley nodded. "That doesn't really fix the problem though, does it? There's still the fact that, out of the blue, I have a son and my life is going to change drastically."

"It will change, yes, but change doesn't have to be a bad thing."

"But in this case it's a sudden thing. It's not the direction things were headed...not the path I saw us taking. And we both know Susan. She's a planner, she likes to have things under control, in order. She doesn't particularly care for surprises."

"You're right about that, but don't sell her short. She's got a big heart. Right now, though, Susan is worried that maybe you're in love with this woman, that you always have been, and now that she's back, you'll try to work things out."

"That's crazy. I told Susan it wasn't like that."

"Okay, but it's not me you have to convince. Try to understand Susan's point of view. Obviously you had some sort of relationship with...what's her name? Melissa?"

"Yeah, Lissa."

"Okay, Lissa. Obviously, at some point, there was something between you and Lissa. For a woman, it's never easy to come face to face with a former girlfriend. In this case, it's a lot harder. It's a lot more complicated. Susan's fear is that the feelings you once had will come back...maybe because of the child, but maybe they would have regardless. She has to get past that. She needs you to convince her it's not going to happen."

"But it's not. I told her that." Riley was frustrated. If that's all it was then it should be simple. He told her, she should believe him.

"You have to try to think like Susan. Her confidence has been shaken, a lot of doubt is sneaking into her head. She didn't expect that there was no one in your past, but she also didn't expect to be blindsided by not only a former girlfriend, but a child, too."

"Okay, I can do that. If she'll talk to me, that is."

"She'll talk to you. Try her again tomorrow. I think a day at home will make a big difference."

"I don't know…"

"Have you talked to anyone else about this? Your family?"

"I talked to Mom and Dad last night. It was tough. But no one else." He looked at Sam and mentally calculated. "I've been kind of out of it for the past twenty-four hours or so. Does everyone know? Does Jake know?"

"I didn't tell him. I thought it should come from you."

Riley didn't know what he preferred…telling Jake and the rest of his family himself, or having Sam or his parents break the news and letting some of the initial shock wear off before he had to face them. It was all so much to deal with. He fell back into the sofa and threw his arms over his face.

Sam drew him into another hug. "It will get better."

Jake walked in and found Sam and Riley embracing on the sofa. "Making a move on my fiancé, Riles?" He laughed until they both turned and he saw their faces. "Aw, crap. What happened?"

29

Susan didn't answer Riley's calls until Tuesday and didn't return until Wednesday. It was Friday before they saw one another. Susan was busy making up for the extra days off from work and used it as an excuse to avoid stopping by the B&B. In truth, she was afraid. No matter how often she heard she didn't have anything to worry about, that the fact that Riley had a son didn't mean the relationship between the two of them had to change, and no matter how often she nodded and agreed, she couldn't quite convince herself it was true.

They'd talked a few times, but Susan had kept the conversations short and the topics mostly business. She had asked about Ryan, whether Riley had seen him again and how it was going, but hadn't encouraged many details. And she hadn't asked about Lissa.

So on Friday evening when she pulled her car into the driveway and parked behind Riley's truck, her nerves got the better of her and she sat for a long time. She knew she couldn't keep avoiding Riley, it wouldn't solve anything and, besides, she didn't want to. She missed him but she worried things would be different. Of course they'd be different, she corrected herself. How different remained to be seen.

The first thing she noticed as she gathered her courage and made her way to the inn was the porch torn apart and the front door blocked off. She couldn't stop the smile that spread across her face. She'd been anxious to have the old, rotting porch replaced, but knew it hadn't been on the schedule for another month so couldn't help but wonder if Riley had moved things around to please her. She took a moment to imagine how it would look when the work was completed and pictured the sign that Francie had given her, Sam had worked her magic on, and that now read 'The Inn at Misty Lake' hanging above bushel baskets full of flowers. It would be beautiful.

With renewed purpose, she wound around to the back door and peeked slowly inside to make sure the coast was clear before barging in and upsetting work in progress. Seeing no one, she stepped inside and gasped. Her kitchen was done. Not only was the tile work finished, but the cabinets were hung, the stainless steel work counter and sinks were in place with the ceiling-mount racks hanging over them, and even the appliances had been installed. Susan could only stand and stare. The room glowed, clean and shiny.

Slowly, she turned in a circle and took it all in. She ran her hand along the cool, smooth surface of the stainless steel refrigerator before opening it to look inside and marvel at the size. She walked to the range and examined the gas burners, opened the oven doors, and touched all the knobs and dials. She went to the sinks and played with the handle and the huge spray attachment. Not expecting the water to be connected, she got a surprise when she turned the nozzle and water gushed from the faucet. Giggling, she used her sleeve to wipe the droplets, not wanting anything to sully the appearance. She examined the brick wall on the far side of the kitchen facing the lake. It was clean and glowed a soft reddish brown in the late afternoon sun. She loved how it softened the look of the otherwise somewhat sterile, industrial looking room and made it homier. The room was, in a word, perfect.

How in the world had Riley gotten it all done? A week ago the floor was only about halfway completed, the cabinets were still packaged and in the barn, and the appliances hadn't even been delivered.

Riley watched for a minute without Susan noticing him. All the tension and exhaustion built up over the past week seemed to melt away as he watched Susan walk through her kitchen, happier than she'd been in days. If only it could stay that way.

"Welcome back."

Her first reaction was genuine. She heard his voice and turned, beaming and anxious to share her excitement with the person who mattered the most. She almost ran to him, but then she remembered. Remembered the wedge that had been driven between them and remembered that things weren't quite the same.

"Thanks," was her only response.

"What do you think?"

"It's incredible. Perfect. How in the world did you get all this done in a week?"

"I haven't been sleeping much."

She looked closer and saw the dark circles under his eyes and the hollow cheeks. Apparently he wasn't eating, either. "Riley…"

He waved aside her concern. "Are you sure you like it? I wasn't positive on where you wanted all the overhead racks. I think this is what we talked about, but I can change anything you want."

"It's exactly how I wanted it. I can hardly believe it's done. And you started on the porch. Seriously, Riley, have you done anything but work?"

Again he deflected her concern. "I just started on the porch today. The weather's been decent so I decided to get going. Having it done will make it easier to move things in. Maneuvering around the broken boards was getting old."

This time she went to him and looked him in the eyes. It was even worse close up. "Riley, you need to slow down. I'm thrilled with everything you've gotten done, but you can't kill yourself. There's time."

Ignoring her concern, he said, "We need to talk, Susan."

"I know. We will. First show me around?"

Riley nodded. A little longer wouldn't hurt.

He showed her the tile work in the bathrooms and the wood floors he'd refinished in Pine Woods and Lakeview. In the bathroom in Northern Lights, he pressed his palms against the shower tile and gave her an idea of how the color-changing tile would look when the shower was running. Susan was delighted and Riley seconded her opinion when she deemed it super cool. Susan played around for a bit before they made their way back downstairs to the kitchen.

Riley eased into the conversation with something safe. "So, you had a nice visit with your family?"

"I did. Lauren is getting so big, I could hardly believe it. I guess I should have expected it since she's the same age as Dylan but since I hadn't seen her in a few months, it was a shock. She smiles all the time and has the most adorable dimples." This she could talk about.

"I'm looking forward to meeting her. Do they have any plans to visit this summer or will they wait until the wedding?"

"I don't think they'll be here until the wedding. Mia is back at work and life is pretty crazy for them right now."

When there was a lull, Susan realized that, before, silence between them had always been comfortable, not tension-filled as it was now.

Eventually, Susan broke that silence. "Have you spent much time with Ryan?"

"Yes, I've seen him just about every day. He's really quite a kid." Riley's feelings were written all over his face.

"I thought so after the time I spent with him." She waited but Riley didn't offer any more. "How are things with his mother?"

Riley began to roam around the kitchen. On a sigh, he said, "It hasn't been easy."

"Oh?" It was all she could manage.

"She's, well, she's making some decisions about

the future…about whether she's going to stay in the area or head back home, wherever that may be."

Susan just stared at him, her heart pounding in her chest. Something told her she wasn't going to like what was coming.

"She's talking about leaving, saying she's not comfortable in Misty Lake, that people are talking behind her back, and that no one has made her feel welcome."

"Small town, she probably should have expected that."

Riley shrugged. "I'm worried about her leaving with Ryan. I don't think she's well and I'm not convinced she's capable of taking care of him. She seems to be in a daze sometimes, she's moody, forgetful, she doesn't show much interest in Ryan's well-being…I can't help but worry."

Susan thought back to her first impression of the woman and being fairly certain Lissa was an addict. It had only been a few minutes, though, and it was possible she had read Lissa wrong. While she didn't feel any sense of loyalty to the woman, she didn't want to falsely accuse her, either. "So what are you saying?"

"I don't really know what I'm saying. I don't want to leave here…I can't leave here. My business, my family, my life is here. But I don't know how I can let her take him away."

"Leave? You're thinking about leaving?" She could hardly get the words out.

When Susan's eyes widened and the color drained from her face, Riley rushed to explain. "No, I'm not. I'm just trying to figure out what to do and she's not making it easy. I don't want to be thousands of miles away from my son. I've tried to convince her to stay somewhere nearby. Even if she's not in Misty Lake she could be in Minnesota. She argued that she doesn't know anyone and I guess I understand that." Susan remained stony and Riley continued hesitantly. "She's hinted that the only way she'll stay in Misty Lake is if we are in some kind of relationship. She thinks that will keep people from talking and maybe even begin to accept her. I told her—"

"What?" Susan interrupted. "What do you mean, a relationship?" The words burned in her throat and came out shrill.

"There's no relationship. There's not going to be a relationship. I'm just trying to figure out how to keep my son in my life. Can you understand that?"

It was Susan's turn to pace. Could she understand? She honestly didn't know. Everyone she'd talked to—Sam, her mom, Mia, Cassie— had all said the same thing. The fact that Riley had a son didn't mean their relationship had to change. They'd all told her, over and over, that things would work out, that she just needed to give it some time and be patient while Riley figured things out with the boy's mother. Easy for them to say, they weren't in the middle of it. They weren't listening to the man they love talk about moving across the country or working on a relationship with another woman. She was supposed to understand that? And be patient? How? She turned back to face him.

"I don't know, Riley. It's a lot to process."

"I know and I wish I could tell you more but things are just very unsettled right now."

She didn't like his answer, but his appearance worried her and she didn't want be the cause of even more stress. "How's Ryan handling everything?" It seemed easier to focus on the child.

"He doesn't know what's going on...at least I haven't told him anything. I've just been trying to spend as much time as I can with him."

"Did he know before they came to Misty Lake that you were his father? Is he old enough to understand what that means?"

"He doesn't know. I'm not certain how he'll take the news, but based on how he's dealt with what sounds like quite a bit of disruption in his life up to this point, I have to assume he'll take it in stride."

"He doesn't know you're his father? They've been here for a week. Why not?"

"Lissa wants to wait until he's comfortable with me, I guess. Although, like I said, nothing much gets to him. I agreed to go along with it until the paternity test is done."

Susan snapped to attention. "Paternity test? You're not even certain he's your son?" Susan's voice was rising and she was unable to stop it. The absurdity of the situation struck her, and forgetting her earlier concerns, now wanted to scream sense into Riley.

"It's not that I doubt it, I just want something official to prove it. Lissa doesn't have his birth certificate or any other documentation with her so it seems like the logical thing to do."

"Logical? I would say so," she scoffed. "Why haven't you done it yet?"

"Lissa said Ryan is terrified of the doctor and she wants him to get settled here before springing it on him. He's due for a check-up, I guess, so she's going to combine the two. She said she made an appointment for next week. She's taking him to a clinic out of town to avoid gossip."

"She's taking him? Don't you have to go along? I assume a sample is needed from you, too."

"She's taking him to a pediatrician. They will collect the sample there and send it to the lab that does the testing. I guess I can have a sample collected anywhere and forwarded to the lab."

"Hmmm…"

"Listen, Susan, it's just something to make things legal. If it comes down to a custody battle, I'll need that on my side."

Susan didn't answer, just eyed him skeptically.

"Can we talk about us now? I've missed you so much. Can't we try to get things back to the way they were before?"

"I've missed you, too," she conceded, "but it seems like you have a lot to deal with right now. I think you need to take care of that before we can think about anything else."

"No. It doesn't have to be that way. I'll admit there's a lot going on, but that doesn't mean I don't have time for you…for us."

She studied him. "When's the last time you had a decent night's sleep, Riley?"

He merely shook his head at her concern. "I'm fine."

"No, you're not. You look like you're ready to fall down where you're standing. Are you eating?"

"Of course, I'm eating." He scratched his head as if trying to remember. "I had an energy bar this morning…maybe that was yesterday…I know I had an ice cream cone with Ryan last night..." he continued muttering and looking confused.

"Go home, have something to eat and get some sleep."

"I'm picking up Ryan in about thirty minutes. Come with me? Please? He asks about you and about Gusto, I know he'd love to see both of you."

"No, not tonight."

"What about Sunday? It's Easter. You'll be at my parents' house, right? We had that planned."

"I don't know for sure…"

"Please, Susan? I want to spend some time with you. Promise me you'll be there on Sunday."

"I'll try." It was the best she could do.

Riley glanced at his watch. "I really need to get going. Are you sure you won't come with me?"

"No, you go. We'll talk later."

Riley moved to hug her and while she hugged him back, it was strained. Riley looked as though he wanted to say more, but just kissed her and left without another word.

Susan watched him leave. She waited five minutes after his truck pulled away before she let herself cry.

30

It took until Easter morning for Sam to convince Susan to go to dinner at the McCabe's. Susan had told herself she wouldn't. She didn't want to face Riley, his son, his family, and most of all, the questions. Even worse was the thought that everyone would try to act as though nothing had changed. She was certain her being there would add to the tension for everyone, but Sam wouldn't relent and she finally agreed.

They went to the McCabe's straight from church. Since Lissa wouldn't let Riley take Ryan to church, arguing that she didn't want him on display for the whole town to gawk at, Riley had gone to pick him up and Susan found herself with his entire family, except for him.

As she had expected, they all went out of their way to chat with her. They asked about the inn, about her trip to Chicago, about her family, about everything except Riley and his son. Susan was surprised to learn that none of them had yet met the boy. She watched as one after the other, they glanced at the door, out the window, and down the street anxiously waiting for them to arrive.

When they did, Susan was glad she'd let Sam convince her to be there. No matter her feelings, it would have been impossible not to be touched by the scene. When the door opened, the room grew silent. Anna and Sean reached for one another's hands and held on tightly. Susan saw Anna's lip began to tremble. Riley's brothers' conversation about the start of the baseball season came to a halt. Shauna and Karen, who had been on the floor with Dylan, jumped to their feet, eyes wide. Even Rose and Kate quieted and looked curiously toward the door.

Ryan looked from one person to the next, holding securely to Riley's hand. When he spotted Susan, he brightened and asked, "Is your dog here?"

"No, sorry. He had to stay home today."

Anna stepped forward. "Hi, Ryan. I'm glad you're here." Susan knew it took everything Anna had not to grab the boy and wrap him in a hug. As it was, she reached a hand out and ran it tenderly over his hair.

"I think there's something for you in the kitchen, Ryan," Riley said.

Ryan looked up with interest. "What is it?"

"Well, I didn't look too closely but it is Easter…"

"You mean the Easter Bunny was here?" Ryan asked skeptically.

"It looked like it. Let's go check it out."

Riley led Ryan to the kitchen with most everyone following. Ryan's eyes grew wide as he spotted the giant

Easter basket on the kitchen table.

"Come take a look," Anna encouraged.

Ryan climbed up on a chair and began unloading the contents. "Can I eat some of these?" he asked, holding up a handful of jellybeans.

"I think that would be okay. It's Easter after all," Sean answered as he took in the scene in front of him.

"Whatsis?" Ryan managed with his mouth full of jellybeans.

"It looks like a mini hockey set. My brothers and I had one when we were kids. It's pretty fun."

Ryan cocked his head. "You have brothers? I don't."

"Yeah, these guys are all my brothers." Riley pointed at Frank, Joe, and Jake. "And that's my sister," he added with a wave in Shauna's direction.

"I'm Shauna. Can I take a look at your stuff from the Easter bunny?"

"Kay."

Shauna snuggled in next to Ryan on the chair and began sorting through his basket with him.

Susan watched from a distance. Riley's family was wrapped up in his son, as they should be, but she felt like an outsider looking in. With Ryan busy with Shauna, Riley went to Susan.

"Happy Easter."

"Thanks, you too."

"He seems pretty happy, don't you think?" Riley asked with a nod toward Ryan.

"I'd say so. Your family, too. Look at your parents."

Riley looked over to see his mom and dad in an

embrace, his mom's face buried in his dad's shoulder. When she picked up her head and looked at Sean, both had to wipe away the tears.

"Why isn't Lissa here?" Susan knew her tone was bitter, but she found she couldn't mask her feelings.

Riley sighed. "Like I said, she claims she's not comfortable around my family, or anyone else for that matter, as long as there's nothing between the two of us." Susan started to turn away but Riley grabbed her arm. "It's not like I begged her to come along if that's what you're thinking. I don't have any feelings for her, Susan. You have to believe that."

"It looks like your son needs you," Susan answered as she turned again, and this time walked away.

Ryan was struggling to lift the box holding the hockey set and looking around the room. When he spotted Riley he asked, "Can you open this?"

Riley watched Susan walk away from him, his pain apparent. Unable to be two places at once, he headed for Ryan.

"What do you say we get a couple of my brothers and go downstairs and give this game a try?"

Susan wandered into the living room where Rose and Kate were chatting by the window.

"How are you, Susan? How's that inn of yours coming along?" Kate asked as Susan sat down next to them.

"Very well, thank you. It's a lot of work, but the changes are incredible. I hope you can both come see it one of these days."

"That would be nice," Kate smiled while Rose gazed out the window and didn't respond.

"What about you, though, how are you? Anna has filled us in on what's been happening with Riley and his boy. It can't be easy for you." Kate patted Susan's knee and studied her with kind eyes.

"Oh, I'm doing fine." Susan forced a smile but figured she wasn't fooling anyone. She needed to change the subject. "Rose, how are you feeling? I know it was a rough winter, are you feeling better now that spring seems to finally be here?"

When Rose didn't respond, Kate nudged her. "Rosie! Susan asked you how you're feeling?"

"Fine, fine," she answered, but determinedly kept her gaze out the window.

"I think she's still miffed about the new gal at the beauty parlor. Rosie went in for her regular appointment yesterday and someone was filling in for Geri. Rose was angry that no one had told her and that she had to try to explain to someone new how to fix her hair."

That seemed to get Rose's attention. "Hmpf," she snorted. "You'd be miffed too if you had someone named Aphrodite telling you you've been mistreating your hair for sixty years. What sort of nonsense is that?"

"Her name was Annalise, not Aphrodite," Kate corrected.

Rose rolled her eyes. "Regardless, she was a foolish thing, hardly old enough to drive herself to work, and she's going to tell me what to do with my hair? I don't think so."

Susan watched the volley between the sisters and felt herself relax for the first time in days. Dinner preparations continued but when her offer to help was gently brushed aside by Anna and Karen, saying things

316

were well under control, she busied herself playing with Dylan and checking in periodically with Kate and Rose. When the men were called up from the basement and appeared, sweaty, red-faced, and mumbling about penalties and cheap shots, Susan joined the crowd and took her seat at the table.

Dinner was pleasant enough with most of the focus on Ryan. That suited Susan fine. She didn't feel up to fielding questions. As soon as the meal was over and the dishes washed, she started to look for an excuse to leave. She had insisted on driving knowing Jake would probably drive Sam home anyway, so there was nothing keeping her at the McCabe's.

Before she could start to make her exit, Rose approached her.

"Susan, I wonder if you're planning on leaving soon? I'd like to head home and thought maybe you'd be able to give me a ride."

It wasn't hard to spot the unease in Rose's expression and in her voice.

"Aren't you feeling well?" Susan asked.

Rose shot a quick look around the room before answering. "I'd just like to leave. It's been a long day."

"Of course. Let me just say a quick goodbye and grab my purse."

Susan wasn't sure what to make of the desperation she was sensing from Rose, but was grateful for a way out without having to dream up an excuse. Riley tried to convince her to stay, but Susan and Rose made a quick exit.

"Would you please walk me in?" Rose asked when they arrived at her apartment building. "Maybe you would like to stay for a cup of tea?"

Curious and more than a little concerned that something was wrong, Susan agreed. Once they were inside and seated with cups of tea in front of them, Rose seemed to become even more agitated. Without saying anything, she got up quickly and disappeared into the bedroom. She returned shortly carrying a small box.

"I've been avoiding you since last fall," Rose admitted. "It wasn't right."

"Avoiding me? Why? I hope I didn't do something to offend you."

"Oh, no dear, nothing like that. I just wanted to avoid dealing with some things and, in turn, that meant avoiding you. I'm sorry."

"There's no need to apologize. Truthfully, I wasn't aware you were avoiding me specifically. I know you've missed some family gatherings, but thought it was just due to the illness that seemed to want to hang on."

"I'm afraid I used that as an excuse. I was rid of the cold within a week or so…it was the rest that wasn't so easy to get rid of."

Susan was utterly confused. "I'm not sure I follow."

Rose didn't meet Susan's eyes, instead stared intently at her hands clasped tightly in her lap. "Of course you don't, I'm not making any sense."

"If there's something I can help you with I will certainly try," Susan offered, grasping at straws. She was starting to worry and wonder if she should try to contact Anna.

"I'm the one who can help you." She was silent for what seemed like a long time as she gingerly fingered the box in front of her. "I haven't opened this in years."

"What is it?"

Again Rose paused, but then seemed to steel herself and met Susan's eyes.

"I have something to tell you, Susan." She took a deep breath. "I'm Rosemary. Charlie's Rosemary," she said firmly.

For a brief moment Susan was confused. Then she gasped. Charlie Walker's true love. Rose was the Rosemary in the journal.

"I…you…you are?"

"It was so many years ago. I've done my best not to think about Charlie or those days so when you brought up his name and his journal, it was quite a shock. There aren't many people left in town who remember Charlie. Certainly no one has mentioned him for a very long time."

"What happened?" Shocked and fascinated by the information, Susan spoke without thinking and regretted her words. "I'm sorry, that's none of my business," she added, hoping Rose would forgive her insensitivity.

"If I didn't want to answer any of your questions I wouldn't have brought you here today," Rose snapped. "I know you've been asking around town trying to learn more about Charlie and his family, about the history of the house. I can help you with some of that if you're still interested. But then I need you to listen to me about something else."

Unsure and somewhat hesitant, Susan nonetheless nodded her agreement.

"I have a few pictures." She opened the box and tenderly removed a small stack of faded black and white photos. Susan leaned forward in her chair to get a better look as Rose spread them out on the table.

"A couple of these were taken at his house…your house. Charlie had purchased a camera and loved to play around with it. Here's one he took of me on the front porch." Rose smiled nostalgically at the picture. "I remember this dress. It was light pink with a dainty white pattern around the skirt," she explained as she ran her finger carefully along the hem. "Shoulder pads were popular and, of course, a lady had to wear a belt. Charlie loved me in that dress."

Susan studied the younger version of Rose, smiling brightly and waving at the camera. She appeared happy and carefree. The porch and front door of the house were visible in the shot. The door was the same but there was an ornate lever and a fancy doorknocker, neither of which were still there. A few wicker chairs sat on the porch along with baskets of flowers. Susan moved her gaze back to the image of Rose.

"You look lovely, and so happy. May I ask what happened?"

"Charlie and I were so much in love and so happy together. He was a year ahead of me in school so after he graduated, he went to work and told me he was going to save up enough money to marry me. We spent as much time together as we could, but I had school and he was working, sometimes out of town." Rose picked up another picture and stared at it, lost in her thoughts.

"One day, shortly before I was set to graduate, he came to my house unexpectedly. He said we needed to talk. I knew right away something was wrong. We walked and he told me how he had met a girl one night when he had been away working. He apologized, telling me he had made a horrible mistake, but the girl was pregnant. He had only seen her a few times and had forgotten about her, but once she was no longer able to hide the pregnancy from her parents, her father dragged the truth out of her then dragged her to Misty Lake and to the Walkers' home. He demanded Charlie take responsibility for his actions."

Susan heard the pain in Rose's words, pain that seemed to have barely faded in spite of the years that had passed. She knew her words wouldn't provide any real comfort, but had to try.

"I'm sorry, Rose. That must have been incredibly difficult."

"You have to understand that it was a much different time. Women didn't have as many choices, they weren't raising children by themselves. Charlie told me he was going to marry her. He cried. I cried even more. I watched him walk away from me that day and I never saw him again."

"He moved to California right away?"

"Yes. There was that stigma regarding pregnancy out of wedlock. I think he just wanted to try to make a fresh start."

"I did a little research after I found the journal," Susan admitted. "I never found any record of a child."

Rose looked away, but not before Susan spotted the tears in her eyes. "A few months after they left I heard that she miscarried. It must have been fairly late in the pregnancy. Perhaps today something could have been done, but back then…" She just shrugged and shook her head. "Divorce wasn't as commonplace as it is today, either."

The ramifications hit Susan. Charlie had given up

the love of his life to marry the woman who was going to have his child. When there was no longer a child to consider, he had stayed with a woman he probably didn't love. A sense of duty and of responsibility kept Charlie and Rose apart. It was heartbreaking.

"I didn't share all this with you to get your sympathy." Rose seemed to strengthen and her eyes focused intently on Susan. "I need you to listen to me. I let the man I loved walk out of my life and I have regretted it ever since. There may not have been anything I could have done to change his mind, but ever since, I've had to live with myself knowing I didn't try. I didn't fight for him. I cried, yes, but I didn't fight. You have a choice and I expect you to make the right one. You fight for Riley. Don't let him walk away from you the way I let my Charlie walk away from me. Don't make the same mistake I made."

By the time she finished, her voice was powerful and she looked almost fierce. Susan shrunk before her. "I don't know what I can do. Riley has to make up his own mind."

"True, but you make sure he knows your feelings before he does so. He needs to hear from you exactly how you feel about him. Things are so different today. There are ways to make it work for everyone involved. That little boy is precious. Don't misunderstand me, I want the best for him. But, in this case, the best isn't necessarily a mother and a father who are together. If you feel about Riley the way I felt about Charlie, and I'm fairly certain you do, then you fight for him. Promise me, you'll fight for him. Don't let history repeat itself."

Susan listened but found it difficult to maintain

eye contact as the intensity in Rose's eyes seemed to bore right into her. It was all Susan could do not to crumble.

"I love him but I don't want him with me if he's always going to think he made a mistake. That, I think, would be worse than losing him."

"It's never a mistake when two people love one another. Really, it's quite simple. We were put on this earth to love. Don't you forget that."

Susan left with a stack of photos after giving Rose her word she would talk with Riley and let him know her feelings. More than that, she promised she'd fight. She only hoped she could follow through on her promises.

31

A few days later, Susan opened her laptop. Jake had returned it shortly after she had gotten back from Chicago, but she hadn't been motivated to do much work. As it was, she hadn't checked the inn's email or done any work on the website for almost two weeks. Jake's tech expert had determined the two most recent emails had originated from a library in Omaha. After some digging, he had also retrieved the first email and found it had been sent from Denver. Since Susan didn't know anyone in either city, she hadn't been too interested in pursuing the issue, and as far as she knew, Jake had let it drop, as well.

Now, as she sat and stared at her website, the images blurred in front of her eyes. She hadn't been able to concentrate on anything since her conversation with Rose. She'd kept the information to herself, figuring it was up to

Rose to share if she chose to do so. She hadn't talked much with Riley, either. She felt guilty about not keeping her promise to Rose, but she didn't know how to approach Riley. He was engrossed in his work and in his son. Susan didn't begrudge him the time he was devoting to Ryan, but she didn't know how to feel about the fact that he had stopped trying to convince her that nothing was going to change between the two of them. Truth be told, he had stopped putting much effort into trying to do anything that involved her.

Susan tried not to read too much into it…he was busy and had a lot on his mind. She had spoken briefly with Frank who had confirmed her suspicions. Riley was barely eating, barely sleeping, and, in Frank's opinion, barely holding on. Susan couldn't help but wonder if he was trying to speed up progress on the inn so he'd be free of that obligation should he decide to leave town with Lissa and Ryan.

She ordered herself to stop imagining the worst and to focus on her work. She scanned the website, uploaded a few new pictures, and highlighted Northern Lights now that the bathroom was completed. She hoped that anyone browsing the website would find the shower tile as intriguing as she did.

Clicking over to the email account she was surprised, and pleased, to find eighteen new emails. She worried for a moment that she may have lost potential clients by neglecting the emails for so long, but pushed past the worry and told herself better late than never.

She sorted through the list and found several reservations. Each one thrilled and delighted. She still found it a little unbelievable that people were booking stays at her bed and breakfast. Again, there were solicitations for business from suppliers of everything from mints to cleaning supplies. It was overwhelming and she promised herself she'd weed through and start making some decisions soon. Then she found herself longing for Cassie's help. Too bad she was still months away from having her wise friend at her side.

The second to last email on the list stopped her cold. She drew in a sharp breath and even looked over her shoulder, she was so startled. The wording was similar, short and to the point, but this one had a decidedly more threatening feel to it. 'I warned you. You leave me no choice.'

Her heart racing, she got up to see if Sam was still home. She wanted to show the email to someone and, she admitted, she didn't want to be alone. But Sam was gone. Susan remembered Sam had told her she was heading to a meeting with a client and would most likely be gone several hours as she had a number of stops to make after the meeting. Susan paced and gave the computer a wide berth, peeking at it and frowning. In spite of her unease, Susan decided she was more annoyed than anything.

"If you don't like what I'm doing here, have the nerve and the decency to sign your name," she muttered as she marched back to the computer.

"Hmmm, two days ago." She continued talking to herself as she looked closer at the email. Sent from yet another Gmail account, this one had arrived in her inbox fairly recently. She picked up her phone to call Jake knowing that if she didn't, she'd never hear the end of it. But then she set it down again, deciding to just drive into town and talk to him since she had a few errands to take care of anyway.

Lissa stared out the window of Courtney's apartment and watched the traffic on Main Street. She hated Misty Lake...hated the little shops that lined the street, hated the fake smiles on the people who walked and waved to one another, and hated the ridiculous giant fish statue that greeted everyone who drove into town.

She wanted out and desperately hoped it wouldn't be too much longer until she got her wish. She knew Riley was crazy about Ryan and that he didn't want her to take him clear across the country. They still hadn't reached an agreement, but she felt fairly confident they would soon.

Right now, she needed to make another trip to the run-down cabin on the lake. She pulled the plastic bag from her purse, and even though she knew exactly how many were in there, counted the pills again. Courtney was at work and would be home in a couple of hours, but Lissa didn't want to wait that long. And she didn't want to take the boy. He was starting to get familiar with the area and she was afraid he'd tell Riley they'd been at the lake. She couldn't risk it.

She paced, twisted her hair around her finger, smoked one cigarette after the other, and decided she needed to go.

"Hey, Ryan, I need to go somewhere."

Ryan looked up from his toys. "Okay." He got up, grabbed Spider-Man, and went for his shoes.

Lissa's heart softened a little watching him. He was such a good boy. She knew she'd put him through a lot, but he rarely complained. He tried hard to make her happy, harder than a little boy should have to try. She went to him and snuggled.

"I have to go alone, Ryan. I'll be back in just a few minutes and Courtney will be home real soon, too."

"Oh." He dropped his shoes. She knew he didn't like to stay alone.

"I promise I'll be back soon." She squeezed him once more, but then hurried out the door before he could beg her to stay.

Susan got herself ready, stashed the laptop in her bag, and, at the last minute, decided to take Gusto with her. When Rigi danced in front of her as she held Gusto's leash, she relented and loaded both dogs in the car after scribbling a quick note to Sam.

On the drive, she tried to come up with a reason someone could be so angry with what she was doing in Misty Lake and with the inn that they would send threatening emails. It didn't make sense to her. There weren't any other bed and breakfasts in town so she couldn't imagine another B&B owner was put out enough to threaten her. Maybe the resort owners? Did they think she'd take away too much business? It seemed unlikely. From what she'd heard, the resort was well run and was always booked solid. Other local businesses? Again, it didn't really make sense. If anything, her business should be good for theirs.

Deciding she wasn't going to solve the mystery just then, she pulled into a small gallery in town that provided framing services. She had dropped off the baseball cards after deciding she wanted to frame them. She'd done as Riley had asked and checked in to their value. While she probably could have sold them and made several hundred dollars, she had decided she'd get far more enjoyment out of having them preserved and displayed at the inn. She had been excited to show Riley what she'd decided to do with the cards, but now she had to wonder if he'd ever see them.

Next, she stopped by the sheriff's department. Jake wasn't in so she dropped off her computer and left an explanation with the deputy at the front desk. Jake was due in later that evening, he could call her then and ask whatever questions he had for her.

Lastly, she needed a few groceries. She parked her car, but decided to stroll down the street with the dogs and maybe grab a cup of coffee before doing her shopping.

Jake hadn't liked the way Riley sounded when he'd called earlier in the day. Something was wrong, Jake was certain, but Riley wouldn't get into it over the phone. The fact that Riley was home in the afternoon when Jake knew he'd been working almost nonstop was another red flag.

Riley answered before Jake could knock. The dark circles under his eyes that Jake had noticed on Easter were worse…much worse. Riley hadn't shaved and Jake wasn't certain he'd even changed clothes recently.

"Riley, what in the world is going on with you?"

"I need your help, but you've got to keep it quiet for now." Riley grabbed him by the arm and pulled him inside, kicking the door closed behind him.

Riley's eyes were strangely focused and bored into Jake. It was the sort of look Jake had seen often in his line of work. It belonged to those who were desperate for help and didn't know where else to turn "What is it? Are you in some kind of trouble?"

"No, no, it's not about me. Well, not really. It's about Ryan. I need to sit down."

Riley moved unsteadily to the nearest chair and fell into it. Jake followed. "You need to tell me what's going on, Riles."

"Yeah, okay." He was quiet for a minute and Jake thought he'd lost his train of thought, but then he started again. The words came out fast.

"I was with Ryan last night. We were talking and he said something about liking hockey. I asked him if he's ever played and he said his Aunt Jenny told him he had to be six before he started. I mentioned his birthday coming up and not having to wait much longer. He gave me this look like he thought I was pretty dumb or something then said he's going to be five on this birthday."

Riley paused for a moment and Jake tried to catch up. So the boy was younger than Riley thought…

"So I said to him, 'Ryan, you're going to be six.' He looked at me again and this time figured he needed to show me. He held up his hand and tried to show me four fingers saying he was that many and when he had his birthday he'd be a whole hand." Riley was demonstrating with shaky hands.

Jake stared at Riley. If the kid was really younger than Riley had calculated…or had been told…then that meant he couldn't be Riley's.

"Don't you get it, Jake? If he's only four, he's not my son." The words came out like a loud whisper and Riley dropped his head in his hands. "I don't know what to think. I don't know if he's mixed up or what. I was going to ask Lissa for an explanation, but when I dropped off Ryan, Courtney said she was sleeping. The more I thought about it, the more I decided I don't want to confront her until I'm sure. Something's not right with her and I'm worried for Ryan. If she takes off with him, I'm not sure he'll be safe."

"Okay, Riley, you've got to calm down." Riley's voice was hoarse and Jake spotted the tremor in his hands. "What do you want me to do? Do you want me to try to talk to her?"

"No! She'll freak out for sure." Riley stood and walked to the window, pulling back the heavy curtain just enough to peek outside. He looked up and down the street as if expecting someone to be watching his house, watching him. "I want you to try to contact her family."

Jake looked quizzically at Riley. "Contact her family? Why me?"

Riley leaned forward in the chair, elbows planted on his knees and his chin resting on his knuckles. His voice took on that of one devising a scheme with his co-conspirator. "I've been thinking about it. What reason would they have for talking to me or answering any of my questions? If you call, you can explain Lissa's in town with her son and there's some…I don't know, make something up. Just try to figure out what the story is with her."

"Riley, I can't just call, say I'm the sheriff in Misty Lake, and that I want to know everything there is to know about this woman. They'll be under no obligation whatsoever to answer my questions. Think about it…would you answer questions from someone claiming to be in law enforcement? There's got to be a better way to go about this."

Riley was on his feet again. "Dammit, Jake, I don't have time! I have to know if he's my son. Do you know what the past ten days have been like for me? She shows up out of the blue with this kid, tells me he's my son. I've been trying to wrap my head around that, finally felt like I got there, and now this? I can't take much more, Jake!"

Jake couldn't recall ever seeing Riley quite as upset. "Calm down, Riley. We'll figure something out."

"I won't be able to calm down until this is resolved. Don't you get that?"

"Yeah, I think I do. I'll try to call the family. I can't guarantee anything, but I'll try. What do you know about her? Where is her family?"

Riley took a deep breath, steeling himself for what was coming next. "Her name is Melissa Cosgrove, she's from California. Her father is Senator Cosgrove."

"Ah, man, Riley. You can't be serious. I can't call a senator and demand information."

"I know, but Ryan keeps talking about an Aunt Jenny. Can you do a little searching and see if Senator Cosgrove has another daughter? I'm hoping that's the Aunt Jenny he's been talking about. Maybe you could get in touch with her."

Jake shook his head then lifted his hands and let them fall. "I'll give it a try," he said on a sigh.

His mom had been gone a long time. He had already played with all his toys and she still wasn't back. Ryan looked out the window and watched the people walking on the sidewalks. He didn't see her. He was getting hungry.

He watched for a little longer, slouched in the chair closest to the window. Suddenly, he jumped to his feet. He was pretty sure he saw the lady with Gusto, but she had two dogs. When the lady stopped and talked to someone, he squinted his eyes to try to get a better look. He was sure it was the lady who knew Riley.

Ryan wanted to play with the dogs. If he ran real fast, he could probably play for a little while before his mom got back. Deciding quickly, he grabbed his shoes, shoved his feet in, slapped the Velcro straps in place, and dashed out the door.

Funny how many people smiled and even stopped to talk when you walked with a couple of dogs, Susan thought as she strolled down Main Street. She watched as a young girl tugged on her mother's arm and pleaded with her to let her stop and pet the doggies. The mother obliged after clearing it with Susan, and the two chatted as the girl got a double dose of puppy love.

When she heard footsteps racing up behind her, she slowed and turned, expecting another child wanting a turn petting the dogs. She was surprised when the child turned out to be Ryan.

"Hi, Ryan," Susan said brightly, looking past the boy for either Riley or Lissa. When she didn't spot either, she asked him, "Where's your mom?"

Ryan was already on his knees in front of the dogs, wet tongues and cold noses eagerly greeting him. He giggled and hugged before finally managing, "I dunno."

Susan did her best to calm the dogs and to get Ryan's attention. "Who are you here with?"

"No one," Ryan answered as he stroked Gusto's head.

Susan scanned the street again, sure there must be someone looking for the boy. She didn't see anyone. "How did you get here?"

"I saw you from the window." He looked up at her now, a hint of fear in his eyes. "Are you mad?"

"No, I'm not mad. Did you come outside all by yourself? Did you tell your mom?"

"She's not there. She left."

Susan was growing alarmed but tried to keep her voice easy. "When did she leave?"

"I dunno. A long time ago."

"Who was there with you when she left?"

"No one. She said Courtney was coming back but she didn't."

Ryan didn't seem concerned but Susan certainly was. Maybe something happened to Lissa. Her earlier suspicions about the woman's drug use came roaring back. She'd have to discuss it with Riley, but right now her concern was Ryan. She grabbed her cell phone and tried Riley. No answer. Not wanting to worry him unnecessarily, she left a message simply asking him to call. Now, what to do with the boy? She supposed the logical thing to do would be to go to the police, but she knew Jake wasn't in and figured his deputies would have to follow protocol which would most likely mean calling in a social worker and who knew what else. She didn't want to put Ryan through all of that.

Knowing it probably wasn't the best decision and guessing she'd probably catch some heat later on, she decided to just bring him home with her and keep trying to get in touch with Riley.

"Do you think you'd like to come to my house for a little while and play with the dogs some more?"

Ryan seemed to hesitate and Susan assumed he'd probably been taught to not get in a car or go anywhere with a stranger. Susan could almost see him trying to decide if she was a friend.

"I'm sure it would be okay with your mom. We'll wait there for her to get home. And we can call Riley, too."

"Okay." Ryan was already hugging the dogs again.

The shack was starting to feel familiar. Lissa parked and marched to the door, a far cry from the petrified, trembling mess she'd been less than two weeks ago. This time as she knocked on the door, she called out her name and demanded the man hurry.

When he opened the door, Lissa pushed her way in and sat at the table. "Tell me what you've got today."

Jake found Susan's computer waiting for him when he got back to the office. He glanced at the note about Susan receiving another threatening email and immediately called Ian, their tech specialist.

He fired up his own computer and ran a quick search to see what he could find about the Cosgrove family. It didn't take long to learn that Senator Cosgrove did, in fact, have a daughter named Jennifer. A few more keystrokes and he learned Jennifer was married to Randall Westbrook and lived in Oceanside, California. He easily found a phone number and dialed.

"Mrs. Westbrook, this is Sheriff Jake McCabe calling from—"

"Oh, God, it's Lissa, isn't it? Is she okay? How about Ryan?"

"She's fine, Mrs. Westbrook, and so is Ryan. I didn't mean to alarm you. I was just calling to try to verify some information."

"Oh, thank goodness, you can't imagine how worried we've been. So she's there? Right now? We've been trying to find her for months." The relief was evident in her voice. "Did Mr. Patterson contact you?"

"Yes, she's here. Mr. Patterson?"

"Oh, I just assumed he traced her and was working with you. Mr. Patterson is a private investigator. We just hired him a few days ago and I know he was heading to Denver."

"Denver? Mrs. Westbrook, I apologize for all the confusion. I haven't been in touch with a Mr. Patterson and I'm not calling from Denver, I—"

Again Jenny interrupted. "She's back in Omaha, isn't she?" She sounded defeated, as if she knew she wasn't going to like Jake's answer.

The mention of Denver and Omaha set off warning bells in Jake's mind. It was too much to be a coincidence. "She's in Minnesota, a town called Misty Lake."

"Minnesota? What in the world is she doing in Minnesota?"

"I'm afraid that's something you'd have to ask her, Mrs. Westbrook." The conversation wasn't going at all as Jake had expected.

"She told us she was going to Denver. The last time we heard from her she said she was there and her cell phone records confirm that. I don't understand what she's doing in Minnesota. You said Ryan is with her? You're sure he's okay?"

"Ryan is here and, as far as I know, he's just fine."

"Then I don't understand, Sheriff McCabe. Why are you calling me?"

Jake knew he needed to tread carefully. "It has to do with Ryan, as a matter of fact. Melissa came here to see Ryan's father and Ryan's father contacted me…he has some concerns—"

"I'm sorry, Sheriff, I'm just not following you at all. You say you're calling from Minnesota and that Lissa is there to see Ryan's father? That can't be. Lissa told us she was going to Denver because that's where Ryan's father lives. She left California months ago. She never said anything about Minnesota."

Jake leaned back in his chair and looked at the ceiling. It seemed as though Riley really wasn't Ryan's father, at least not according to Jenny's information. Then what was Lissa doing in Misty Lake and what was she after?

"Mrs. Westbrook, you are under no obligation to answer any of my questions, but if you're willing, I have a few. It seems as though there's an awful lot of confusion regarding your sister."

"That, Sheriff McCabe, I believe. I just want her and Ryan safe. I'll answer your questions, but I need your word that it goes no further. I'm sure you're aware of who our father is. He's spent years trying to help Lissa and at the same time, keep her name out of the news. Given his position, it hasn't been easy."

"You have my word, Mrs. Westbrook. I have something of a personal interest in this matter, as well, and would really like to unravel some of the mystery."

"Well then, it sounds as though we have some things to talk about." Jake heard her sigh and heard the sounds of her footsteps before a chair scraped across the floor and he could tell she fell into it. "I think you'd better call me Jenny, Sheriff."

Once Jake left, Riley flopped face down on his bed. He was exhausted, his head was pounding, and he simply didn't know what to do. He had come to love Ryan. If his suspicions were correct and the boy really wasn't his son, he didn't know how he'd feel. He prayed Jake would learn something…soon. He felt himself drift off. A phone rang, but he was too tired to care.

32

Susan got Ryan and both dogs inside, and as she watched the tangle of arms and legs as boy and dogs wrestled and rolled around on the floor, wondered what to do next. She nervously drummed her fingers on the table as she considered. She figured Jake would call once he got to the office and found her computer. She'd fill him in and see how he wanted to handle things. She dug her phone out of her purse and tried Riley again but like before, there was no answer.

Lissa might be years removed from a place of honor at her father's side, but that didn't mean she'd forgotten the lessons he'd drilled into her. 'It's all about self-confidence, Melissa. If you believe in yourself, others going to believe in you, too.' She'd heard that one over and over.

'Speak like you mean business. If you come across as weak or undecided, the vultures will circle.' She hadn't understood that one for a long time, but today it had come in handy.

Slick, as she'd decided to call him—she had no idea what his real name was—never knew what hit him. She'd demanded he give her his best stuff…and at a price she decided on, not him. Not that she'd cheated him, that had never been her intention, but she had made sure he didn't cheat her.

And best of all was when she'd asked for a little something more. She knew he'd have it, everyone like him did. He'd denied it at first, afraid of the change in her and, she'd figured, afraid she was going to rat him out. But, in the end, she'd gotten what she wanted.

As she drove, she patted her jacket pocket again and felt the heft. She was past the first hurdle, but that had been the easy one. Her confidence started to wane a bit, but she gave herself another pep talk and tried to stay focused on the prize at the end.

Slick really did have some good stuff, she thought dreamily as she drove to the other side of the lake.

When Jake hung up, his head was spinning. He'd learned things from Lissa's sister that had left him shocked, curious, and more than a little angry. Jenny had been cooperative, wanting only to get her sister and her nephew back home safe and sound, and willing to give Jake whatever information he needed in order to make that happen.

Jenny had said she was going to book a flight to Minneapolis as soon as they finished their conversation.

Jake had given her his contact information and Jenny had said she'd be in touch as soon as she was in Minnesota. Jake had offered to help make arrangements to get her to Misty Lake as quickly as possible, but Jenny had brushed his offer aside saying she could handle it. After talking with her for twenty minutes, Jake didn't doubt it. Apparently one didn't grow up the daughter of a senator without knowing how to get things done.

Now, Jake needed to get back to Riley's and tell him what he'd learned. He didn't know how Riley would take the news, but suspected not well. His assistant had put a note on his desk letting him know Ian had called back and would be in shortly to take a look at Susan's computer. He was almost certain Ian would find that the most recent email was sent from Misty Lake or somewhere close by. He needed to get in touch with Susan, as well, but decided he'd wait until Ian confirmed his suspicions.

Riley was trying to lay tile in a bathroom, but the high school marching band wouldn't stop practicing. The drums got louder and louder, so loud that the floor shook and tiles slid out of place. He tried to block out the sound, but it was everywhere and he couldn't escape it. Frustrated, he started to shout. His own yelling woke him. He looked around and struggled to focus. It took him a minute to realize he was lying on his own bed and he'd been dreaming. He rubbed his eyes roughly and tried to quiet the pounding in his head. He sat up when he realized the pounding was coming from his front door.

Still dazed and more than a little pissed off, he staggered to the door and ripped it open. He was ready to launch into his brother when he remembered he'd asked

Jake for help.

"What did you find out?" he asked in a gravelly, sleep-deprived voice.

"Let's go inside." Jake pushed past Riley and headed for the kitchen where he grabbed the coffee and started to make a pot. Even though his brother would likely prefer a beer, Jake needed him clear-headed. And awake.

"Sit down," he said to Riley who was leaning against the doorjamb, blinking and trying to clear his eyes. "We need to talk."

Lissa pulled up to the house thinking how easy it was to learn just about anything from the Internet. Months ago, after she'd first reached out to Courtney and had fished around for information on Riley, she'd searched for details on the sale of the lake property and had easily learned about Susan Taylor's plans for a bed and breakfast. Finding her website had been simple. Just this past week when she'd searched through articles for details about the Taylor house she'd been hearing so much about, figuring there was most likely a connection to Susan, she'd easily determined its location on the lake. It was nice, she admitted, as she scrutinized it, obviously some money behind it. Searches led her to Samantha Taylor and figuring out that she and Susan lived there together was so simple Ryan probably could have done it.

She'd come this far, now she just needed to finish the job. A little something as a reward for handling everything up to this point, she told herself as she reached in her purse and grabbed her latest purchase.

A few minutes later, she was leaning her head

back on the seat, feeling as if she could conquer the world. She drew on the strength she'd harnessed when dealing with Slick as she opened her car door and strode to the house.

Susan heard the knock and guessed it was Riley. Opening the door, she was surprised to see Lissa.

"Lissa. How did you know he was here?" It wasn't the most polite greeting, but Susan's displeasure at seeing the woman at her door and taking in the glassy eyes and twitching fingers had her feeling less than gracious.

"Who's here?"

Susan briefly considered trying to keep Lissa outside and away from Ryan. She had no idea why Lissa was there if it wasn't to collect Ryan, and it was clear that Lissa was in no condition to care for her son. Before she could step out to the porch and close the door, Ryan came barreling toward his mother.

"Mommy!"

The force of Ryan grabbing her legs had Lissa stumbling and almost falling. Then, her entire demeanor changed in an instant. She whipped around to face Susan, her eyes blazing.

"What in the hell are you doing with my son?" she screamed.

"Nothing," Susan shot back. "I'm just keeping an eye on him for the time being."

"You have no business having anything to do with my son," Lissa hissed.

"He was alone. I was just trying to see that he was safe."

The dogs had followed Ryan out onto the porch

and were standing close to Susan. Lissa was smart enough to know she needed to lower her voice or risk the dogs, sensing something was wrong, trying to protect Susan.

"Ryan," she turned to her son who was looking at her with wide eyes. "Why don't you go in the yard with the dogs and play for a while?"

"I don't wanna," he whined as he looked from his mother to Susan.

"Ryan, I told you to go," Lissa said.

"The dogs have been in the house for a while, I'm sure they'd like to run a little. Just make sure you stay close to the house and far away from the lake." Susan was terrified at the thought of leaving the child outside alone so close to the thawing lake, but was equally terrified of the anger and hatred she sensed coming from Lissa.

Susan watched as Lissa's face grew red and knew she was struggling mightily to hold her tongue until Ryan was away from the house. Once he was running through the yard with the dogs at his heels, she whirled on Susan.

"Who do you think you are telling my son what to do? You are sadly mistaken if you think you are going to have anything to do with him."

Susan chose to remain silent, waiting her out.

"And the same goes for Riley. Do you really believe he's going to choose you over his son? You may think he loves you but blood is thicker than water. The two of them have become even closer than I hoped during the past couple of weeks. When I leave town, Riley will be coming with me, mark my words."

That was Susan's biggest fear, and by the look of triumph in Lissa's eyes, it was apparent Lissa knew it. Her expression turned downright evil as she spoke slowly to

Susan.

"Just so Riley's decision isn't a long, drawn out one, I've decided you're going to help him along. You're going to make sure he's convinced any feelings you may have had for him are gone."

Lissa was sneering now and Susan was becoming more and more frightened, but thoughts of her conversation with Rose and the promise she had made had her standing her ground.

"No, I'm not going to do that. I love Riley and I'm going to make sure he knows it."

Lissa laughed cruelly. "Oh, I don't think so…not when I explain the consequences."

"What are you talking about?"

"Well, first off…this little bed and breakfast of yours? I have someone ready to torch the place. All I have to do is give him the word. And if you think I'm kidding, just try me."

"You can't be serious. You'll never get away with it."

"Oh, Susan, how naïve you are. It's cute, really. I can almost see why Riley thought he might care for you. But, I will get away with it. You see, my connections run deep. Very deep. I know people in places and with power you can only imagine. I didn't grow up the daughter of a senator and not learn a thing or two."

Now Susan was terrified. She still didn't believe Lissa would get away with it in the long run, but if what she said was true, the damage she could cause would be catastrophic. Susan knew recovering from it could be impossible. Desperately trying to come up with a plan, she worked to keep Lissa talking.

"My business is important to me, but Riley is more important. You aren't going to scare me away with your threats." It was a struggle to keep her voice steady and Susan knew she was failing.

Lissa blew out a breath. "Threats? No, not threats. Facts. But if that wasn't enough to have you reconsidering, let me throw this at you. If you try to convince Riley to stay, I'll start talking. I will tell this whole pathetic little town the real story of how I ended up pregnant with Riley's child. Believe me, it's not pretty."

Anger replaced fear and Susan's voice rose. "Now you're lying. Your word won't mean anything in this town. People here know and respect Riley."

"That may be, but things change. When I explain how Riley tricked me into following him into the woods that night, far away from the party and from anyone who could hear me, and then proceeded to force himself on me, opinions will change."

"You can't be serious! That's nothing but a lie and you know it."

"No, it's not. Why do you think I was so afraid to tell him about the baby when I found out and then so afraid to come back here for all these years? I was afraid of what he'd do to me. It wasn't until Ryan started asking about his father and I felt I owed it to my son to let him know his father, that I worked up the nerve to come back."

Susan just stared. She didn't believe a word of it but had to give the woman credit. A rumor, a lie, could be just as damaging as the truth. There would be people who would choose to believe Lissa and Riley's reputation, likely his business, would suffer. She began to shake with rage and fear and grabbed onto the porch railing to steady herself. She needed to get to a phone without Lissa realizing what she was doing, but didn't see any way that was going to be possible.

"So, it looks like you're starting to believe me. That's good. It will make things so much easier. Why don't we head inside right now and you can make a call to Riley? You can tell him you've given it a lot of thought and your feelings have changed knowing that he has a son. You can explain to him that you don't want to see him any more and that you think the best decision for everyone is if he tries to give his son a real family. Trust me, he's already leaning that way. Hearing it from you will be the last little push he needs to make up his mind."

She was crazy, plain and simple. Susan considered trying to make a break for it, trying to get inside the house and lock the door behind her before Lissa could react, but she glanced across the yard at Ryan running and laughing with the dogs and knew she couldn't risk his safety. With as unstable as Lissa appeared, Susan had no idea how she'd react. Maybe she could call Riley and find a way to let him know something was wrong without Lissa realizing what was happening. Her mind raced with possibilities but she couldn't seem to piece together a logical plan.

"Shall we?" Lissa said with a wave towards the door.

The last thing Susan wanted was to be inside with Lissa. "You can't leave Ryan out here alone. He's only yards from the lake on one side and the road on the other. It's not safe."

"I told you to keep your mouth shut regarding my son. I'll worry about what's safe and what's not safe. Now, inside. Or do you need a little encouragement?"

Susan watched as Lissa reached into her pocket and pulled out a gun. Susan's heart thudded wildly and every nerve stood on end.

Lissa waved again toward the door, this time with the gun in her hand, and Susan had no choice but to do as she said.

"I tracked down Lissa's sister Jenny and spoke with her. She told me…well, a lot." Jake watched Riley closely, not liking the look on his face.

"And?" Riley barked.

"And, there's no way Ryan can be your son."

Riley fell back in the chair and closed his eyes. He was still for a long time before slowly sitting up and looking Jake in the eye.

"Tell me what she said."

"We had a long conversation and it's a complicated story, but I'll start by telling you Ryan is only four years old. Jenny confirmed his birth date and he will be turning five shortly."

"Oh, God. So it's all been a lie? Everything she's told me? Why?"

"I don't know, Riley, but from what Jenny said, Lissa has had a lot of trouble over the past seven years. When she left Misty Lake after that summer, she returned to Colorado and to school, but didn't last long. I guess she got pretty involved with drugs and ended up dropping out of school and taking off with a group of no-good hooligans—Jenny's words. She didn't have much contact with her family until she showed up with a baby a couple of years later. It sounds like she lived with Jenny off and on, sometimes she'd disappear and leave the boy there. I think Jenny has done more to raise him than Lissa has, and she's worried sick about him…about both of them."

"So why the lies? I don't get it."

"Jenny didn't really know either, but figured it probably has to do with money. Their father has tried to get her to turn her life around, to be the daughter who will stand by his side on the campaign trail, but Lissa hasn't cooperated. Jenny didn't come right out and say it, but I got the feeling the father finally had enough and cut Lissa off. When she took Ryan and left California last fall, she was angry and said she was never coming back, that she was going to live with Ryan's father."

"Who is his father?" Riley breathed, slow and deep, trying to ward off the nausea.

"She told Jenny he lived in Denver but after our talk, I don't think Jenny believes that any longer. I'm pretty sure she thinks Lissa doesn't even know who the father is. It sounds like she spent some time in Omaha, um, earning money in a less-than-respectable way."

Riley let everything sink in. Ryan may never know who his father is. He rubbed at his eyes and tried to focus. "So, what now? Am I supposed to confront her? I'm afraid she'll take Ryan and run and then who knows what will happen to him. I don't think he'd be safe."

"Jenny is on her way to Minnesota. She asked me to try to keep them here until she can get here. No one had heard from Lissa in months, they'd just hired a private investigator to try to track her down. It sounds like Jenny's been very worried. She's determined to get Lissa to come back to California with her."

"Okay. So I'll wait until her sister gets here, but I

will have a chance to talk to Lissa before she leaves. She has some explaining to do."

Jake's cell phone rang. Taking a look and seeing it was Ian, he turned away and answered. Riley didn't pay any attention. He was lost in his own thoughts. Part of him felt like a fool for believing Lissa, for falling so completely for Ryan. Another part of him felt as if his heart had been ripped out, as if he'd lost his child. Now what? He had been so focused on figuring out how to care for Ryan and how to keep him in his life, he felt directionless.

"Riley."

Jake's voice jolted him to attention. Riley immediately noted the intensity, the urgency, and while he didn't think there could be any bad news left to hear, was suddenly afraid that there was more coming. He waited and braced himself.

"I don't have a lot of time to explain, but I'm worried about Susan."

"Susan?" That wasn't at all what Riley had expected to hear. "Why?"

"Have you talked to her recently?"

"No," Riley answered sounding guilty.

"Try to call her, make sure everything is okay. Now, Riley," Jake added when Riley stared blankly.

"Jake, what's wrong?" Riley asked as he ran in search of his cell phone. When he found it, he saw two missed calls from Susan and his heart started to race. He frantically dialed her but didn't get an answer.

"No answer?" Jake asked.

"No. Tell me what's going on," Riley demanded. He couldn't take much more.

"Let's go, I'll tell you on the way."

Lissa pushed Susan in the door and closed it behind them. "Get your phone and make that call. I'm running out of patience."

Susan watched as Lissa carelessly waved the gun. She didn't seem to know how to handle it and that scared Susan more than anything. Susan was still trying to come up with some way of getting a message to Riley as she looked through her bags, wondering where she had dropped her cell phone. She waited for Lissa's next demand, but as she watched, Lissa seemed to become distracted and started rummaging through her purse, almost seeming to forget Susan was there.

Just as Susan was working up the nerve to try to text Riley and Jake, she froze and stared in horror. Lissa dug a small bag out of her purse, and without a thought to Susan just a few feet away, proceeded to carefully pour something onto a small mirror she produced. Susan turned away, unable to watch.

At that moment, the door opened and Ryan peeked in, the dogs close behind. Susan saw him look to his mother who, with her back turned, hadn't noticed him, then saw him grin as the dogs pushed past him. She acted fast, her only thought to protect the child. Drugs, a gun, and an unstable woman made a lethal combination. Rushing forward, she scooped Ryan up in her arms and ran out the door.

Ryan's eyes were like saucers as he twisted in her grasp trying to figure out what was happening, but Susan kept running. She had almost made it across the yard when she heard Lissa scream. Willing her feet to move faster,

Susan lowered her head and charged forward. She considered ducking into Sam's shop, but guessed the door would be locked and stopping to check would just slow her down. Instead, she headed across the road and into the woods.

Lissa heard Susan's footsteps pound on the wood floor. Whirling around, it took her a moment to focus and to realize Susan had Ryan in her arms. Steadying herself as she fought a wave of dizziness, she shouted, "Put my son down, you bitch!" When Susan didn't slow, she grabbed the gun, slammed the door on the dogs, and started after her.

"Tell me what the hell is going on with Susan," Riley barked as Jake backed out of the driveway and began tearing down the street.

Jake didn't answer right away as he was on the radio instructing his deputy Marc to head over to Courtney's apartment and see if Lissa was there. Riley nervously tapped his foot and drummed his fingers on his thigh.

When Jake ended his call with Marc, he asked, "Did she tell you she'd received some strange, threatening emails?"

"No. What kind of emails? What kind of threats?" Riley could barely wrap his mind around everything that seemed to be happening all at once.

"She's gotten a few over the past few months, another one just recently. She mentioned it to me and I had the department's tech guy look into them. The earlier emails came from Denver and from Omaha. The most recent one came from the library here in Misty Lake."

Riley tried to make sense of what Jake was saying. "I don't get it. You mean people from around the country are sending her threatening emails? Who? And why?"

Jake stole a quick glance at his brother as he picked up speed now that they were out of town. "According to Lissa's sister, she has ties to Denver and Omaha. And now she's here. I'm almost certain she's the one who has been emailing Susan."

Riley just stared. It didn't make any sense…nothing made any sense. "Why?"

"I don't know for sure, but my guess is she's after something—most likely you—and she sees Susan as an obstacle. I can't claim to know what she's thinking, but it seems like she's been planning for some time already."

"Oh, God. I had two missed calls from Susan earlier today. Do you think she's in trouble?" Riley yanked his phone from his pocket and struggled to steady his hands enough to dial. When he didn't get an answer he shouted at Jake, "Hurry!"

Susan was deep in the woods and finally had to stop to catch her breath. She put Ryan down and leaned over, hands on her knees, and tried to calm her nerves and her racing heart. She knew she didn't have much time. She patted her empty pocket, her mind knowing she had left her phone on the table, but her heart willing it to be there.

"Why are we running?"

Ryan's voice was shaky and Susan could tell he was fighting tears. She took a deep breath before crouching down in front of him. She needed to choose her words carefully.

"Ryan, I need you to listen to me. Your mom isn't feeling well. She's going to be okay, but for right now, she can't take care of you."

Susan saw his chin begin to tremble and his eyes dart wildly in every direction. She gently placed her hand on his arm.

"Ryan, I promise everything is going to be okay." She stopped when she heard Lissa yell again and knew she was in the woods looking for them. "This is going to seem weird, but I want you to hide. Do you think you can do that?"

The tears started to roll down his cheeks and Susan had to bite her lip to keep her own at bay. Slowly, he nodded.

"Good." Susan scanned the area, not sure what she was looking for, but also not knowing what else to do. When she spotted a downed oak tree about twenty yards away, she took Ryan's hand, and as fast as she dared, headed for the tree.

"Look, Ryan, there's a spot for you right here." Susan pointed and silently thanked God for the storm that must have brought the tree down. There was an indentation in the ground…far too small for her, but just right for a little boy. "Crawl down and see if you can get under the tree," she encouraged.

Ryan was obviously scared, not knowing why he needed to hide, but wanting to do what Susan asked of him. Susan's heart swelled when he got down on his belly and slithered under the giant tree.

"That's good, Ryan, really good. I can hardly see you." Susan breathed a small sigh of relief that the boy had been willing to cooperate, but she knew she had a bigger task in front of her. "I need to go check on the dogs, but I need you to stay right here. You have to be quiet and you can't come out for anybody but me. Do you understand?" Susan hoped using the dogs would help convince Ryan to follow her instructions.

"I want to check on the dogs," Ryan answered shakily.

"No, not right now. I'm going to go get them and then they can try to find you. It will be like hide and seek."

Ryan brightened at the idea. "Okay. But will you hurry?"

"Oh, honey, I'll go as fast as I can, I promise. Just make sure you stay here and be super duper quiet. We don't want anyone to find you except Gusto and Rigi."

Susan attempted a smile and hoped she could convince the child. When he nodded his agreement, she gave him a quick kiss and ran before she could change her mind. She knew the only way to ensure his safety was to keep him from Lissa. Terrified, but determined not to let it show, she headed for the sounds of Lissa crashing through the woods.

"I hope we made the right choice," Jake said as he took the turn for Sam's house.

"She's got to be there. She hasn't been spending much time at the inn since...well, she hasn't been there much lately," Riley answered, fighting the crippling fear that threatened when he let his thoughts wander to what could be happening with Susan.

"There! That's her car," Riley shouted as they got close enough to see the driveway. "Oh, God, that's Lissa's car," Riley managed as he opened the door and jumped out before Jake could come to a stop.

Riley raced to the house, ignoring Jake's instructions to wait. He threw the door open a moment before Jake caught up with him. Gusto and Rigi didn't stop to greet him as they shot past and out the door.

"Dammit, Riley, wait!" Jake shouted as he watched his brother race from one room to another without a thought to his safety.

"There's no one here! Where is she, Jake?" Riley was frantic.

Jake let his years of training take over and attempted to ignore the fact that this involved family. "Let's go look outside. She can't be far."

The two made their way to the yard and stood for a moment, searching in all directions. There was no sign of Susan. Or Lissa.

"Check the shop," Riley shouted as he started running for the woods.

"Riley! Stop. We'll go together."

After a quick check of the shop, the brothers headed into the trees. It didn't take long until they heard the yelling.

Susan stayed back but made sure Lissa saw her. Once Lissa spotted her, she began screaming.

"What did you do with my son? If you hurt him, I'll kill you."

Susan watched as she raised the gun, but struggled to hold it steady. Susan's heart thudded so hard it hurt in her chest. She moved slowly, but steadily, away from Ryan's hiding place praying Lissa would follow and that Ryan would stay put.

"What did you do with my son?" Lissa screamed even louder.

"He ran. I think he's trying to get back to see the dogs," Susan improvised, desperate to convince Lissa that Ryan was far away.

Lissa dropped the gun down to her side and turned in the direction of the house, seeming unsure of what to do next. "Get over here," she said as she raised the gun once again.

"Listen," Jake hissed at Riley. He heard a woman yelling but couldn't quite make out the words.

Riley stilled and strained to hear anything that may give him an idea of where Susan was. The next time Lissa screamed, the words were clear.

Jake pointed. "This way. You stay behind me. I'm not asking, Riley," he said with a firm hand on Riley's shoulder.

Riley nodded, his face drained of all color, and followed Jake deeper into the woods.

Susan didn't know whether to follow Lissa's orders or to try to stall. The fact that Lissa was waving a gun in her direction made it almost impossible to think. Just as she was about to start to make her way toward Lissa, she caught a flash of color off to Lissa's right.

"She has a gun, Jake." Riley could barely get the words out, his fear was paralyzing. He could see Susan start to head in Lissa's direction, moving slowly with her hands held up near her shoulders.

Jake grabbed Riley's arm and yanked him to the

ground. "Stay down and let me handle this, Riley." His tone left no room for negotiation.

Swamped with utter helplessness, Riley watched Jake snake his way through the trees towards Lissa. He tasted salt as the sweat dripped off his forehead. Riley knew the moment Susan detected someone else in the woods. Her head shifted slightly in their direction before she focused her attention back on Lissa. What he didn't know was whether she knew who else was in the woods. He ached to signal her somehow, to let her know she was going to be okay. Knowing Jake would probably want to kill him, he crouched low and started in the opposite direction Jake had gone, planning to circle around and come up behind Susan.

The flash was there and then it was gone. Susan knew someone else was sneaking around in the woods but didn't know who. Her thoughts wanted to focus on the threat Lissa had made about having someone ready to torch her inn, but she did her best to beat those thoughts down. She couldn't let herself believe that Lissa had someone so close and ready to jump into action.

Carefully, she started in Lissa's direction, but walked at an angle away from Ryan's hiding spot, forcing Lissa to turn slightly to keep Susan in sight and to keep the gun pointed at her.

"Hurry up," Lissa ordered. "We're going to find Ryan and then you're going to make that call. I've had enough of your stalling and, frankly, I'm getting tired of you all together. Dragging me out into the woods is making me very angry."

Lissa swiped at some leaves caught in her hair and

looked disgusted as she swatted at a fly buzzing near her head. When she looked up to follow the fly's path, she stumbled and nearly lost her balance. She reached out to catch herself on a tree trunk and the next thing Susan knew, the world exploded.

Susan threw herself on the ground. Something hit her, but she was too frightened to try to figure out what. She stayed as still as she could, unsure what was happening since she couldn't hear anything over the ringing in her ears.

Lissa looked dazed when Jake reached her. She stood holding the gun limply in her hand, studying it as if trying to figure out what it was and how it had gotten there. Jake simply put one hand on her wrist and used the other to ease the gun from her grasp. She barely moved.

When the shot sounded, Riley forgot all Jake's warnings and began hurtling through the woods. There was no way he was going to wait in the background if Susan was in danger.

Gingerly, Susan reached a hand to her shoulder where she had felt something strike her. Warm, sticky blood met her fingers as pain shot through her. Her only thought was that she must have been shot. She began to shake.

Riley saw Jake take the gun away from Lissa but when he scanned the area, there was no sign of Susan.

"Where is she? Where's Susan?" he demanded. He was vaguely aware of the sounds of dogs barking somewhere behind him.

His eyes locked on Lissa's but she gave no indication she heard him. Riley lunged at her, half crazed and determined to get an answer out of her. Jake's arm stopped him.

"Riley! Enough," Jake said.

"She hurt her, Jake, I know she did. Make her tell us what she did!"

"She didn't shoot her, Riley. The gun went off when she stumbled. I think the bullet hit a tree."

"Then where is Susan?"

They both looked again and this time spotted Susan lying on the ground, slowly lifting her head.

As the ringing in her ears gradually subsided and Susan heard Riley's voice, she started to get to her feet. She saw Jake handcuff Lissa who, for her part, barely seemed aware of what was happening around her. Susan looked at her hand and saw a smear of blood. Never one to handle the sight of blood very well, she wavered, but the sounds of the dogs barking had her refocusing. She had to get to Ryan. If he'd heard the gunshot, he had to be terrified.

Ignoring the pain in her shoulder, she turned and ran in the direction of the fallen tree where she had left Ryan to hide.

"Susan, wait!" Riley called after her.

She didn't stop. She'd told Ryan to hide. If he'd left his hiding place when he'd heard the shot, he could be anywhere. Fear had her tearing through the forest, oblivious to the branches scratching her face and arms.

The barking got louder as she got closer to where

she'd left Ryan. When she spotted the downed tree, she figured out why. Gusto and Rigi were standing side by side next to the tree, directly in front of the dugout area where she'd told Ryan to hide. When she looked closer, she spotted a small hand poking out from under the log, slowly stroking Gusto's hind leg.

Susan fell to her knees. All at once, relief engulfed her and, with her head in her hands, she began to sob.

33

The bandage on her shoulder prickled, the stitches itched, and the whole thing was driving Susan crazy. She'd been trying not to think about what had happened in the woods, but the wound was a constant reminder. Thankfully, it hadn't been too serious. When Lissa's gun had gone off and the bullet hit the tree next to her, a chunk had broken loose and connected with her shoulder. It had taken a good dose of painkillers and the doctor's steady hand to remove the wood splinters and then to stitch her back together. The pain was mostly gone, but she was starting to think the healing was worse than the injury.

Right now, though, she almost welcomed the annoyance as it provided a distraction from what was coming next. Susan stared out the window of her nearly completed bedroom but didn't see anything. Riley would be there any minute and she didn't know what to expect. They had spoken some on the phone, but Riley had been busy trying to straighten things out involving Lissa and Ryan and she had given him time. But they had things to straighten out, too.

She jumped when she heard his footsteps.

"Hi," Riley said. He sounded stiff.

"Hey. Everything settled with Lissa and Ryan?" She sounded just as stiff. She hated it.

Riley sighed deeply and Susan noticed that the circles under his eyes hadn't faded. In fact, they were probably darker.

"I guess so. Lissa's sister, with a little help from her father, I assume, managed to take care of the charges against Lissa and hustle both Lissa and Ryan out of town this afternoon. I had a chance to talk to her, she's determined to get Lissa back into a treatment facility. She's bringing Ryan back to live with her again."

"How is Ryan doing?" Susan hadn't had time to do much other than make sure he was unharmed after he'd crawled out from under the tree before things had become fuzzy. Ryan had hugged the dogs, waved goodbye to her, and then Riley had whisked him away before he'd had any idea of what had happened with his mother. Marc, one of Jake's deputies, had shown up by that time and had helped Susan out of the woods and to a waiting ambulance.

"He's a little confused, but he was happy to see Jenny. Thankfully, I don't think he understands what's going on. He just knows he's going back home to California with Jenny. And she promised him a puppy so he's been talking nonstop about colors and names. Right now, he's thinking a black dog named Gusto. Go figure."

Susan smiled at the image. "He really loved Gusto. And Rigi. I'm telling you, Riley, when I saw the two of them standing in front of that tree and his little hand reaching out petting Gusto, well…" She had to blink back the tears and swallow over the lump in her throat.

"I know. I've tried not to think about what could have happened had he left his hiding spot. He could have gotten lost, he could have wandered back to the lake and out onto the thin ice, he could have been there when the shot was fired. Those dogs knew he needed them, didn't they?"

Susan nodded, still unable to talk.

They were quiet for a few minutes, both lost in their thoughts. When Susan spoke again, she did so carefully.

"How are you doing, Riley? Really doing. Have you come to terms with everything that happened over the past few weeks?"

He turned and walked to the window. "Look how dark the ice is, it's almost thawed. Ryan would have enjoyed watching it go out." Then, focusing on her question, he said, "I think so. I don't even know how to describe the range of emotions. I really cared about him, you know? I believed he was my son and I feel…empty. But at the same time, I feel like a fool…like I should have known he wasn't mine. I had a hard time saying goodbye to him, but I'm not sure why."

Susan went to him, and placing her hands on his shoulders, began kneading at the tension. "You have a big heart, Riley. The fact that you let Ryan in never surprised me. It would have surprised me if you hadn't."

Riley turned to face her. "Lissa played me for a

fool. I let her."

The pain in Riley's eyes had Susan reaching for him. "You choose to see the best in people, not the worst. That's admirable. And you didn't let her do anything. You made a choice to accept life-changing news and to figure out how to make it your new normal. She didn't win, you did."

"I let her come between us. Whatever else I did that may have been right or wrong, that's something I never should have done. I'm not sure how I let it happen and I'm not sure how to apologize to you."

"I've had a lot of time to think. Things may have gotten off track between us, but it wasn't all your fault. I pulled away when I should have dug in. Someone very wise made me aware of my mistakes and I made a promise to try to correct them. I'd like to think I would have if things hadn't come to a head the way they did."

"Aunt Rose," Riley said knowingly.

"She told you?"

"Just this morning. I guess saying I was surprised is an understatement."

"I've had a little more time to get used to the idea but, yeah, it was quite a surprise. I can't believe she's Charlie's Rosemary and she's been living with that heartache for so many years. I talked to her yesterday. I told her I'd like to give her the journal. She said she'd think about it."

"The similarities are crazy." Riley shook his head and gazed out the window again.

"Did you have a chance to talk to Lissa? Do you know why she did what she did?"

"I hardly talked to her, she really wasn't in any

shape to talk. I feel like a fool for not realizing she had a drug problem. I thought she was sick."

"She is sick, Riley. It's a terrible sickness. I suspected from the start, but I've had experience with it. That's another mistake I made. I should have said something about my suspicions."

A shadow passed over Susan's eyes. The pain of losing her cousin to drugs would never completely go away. Riley reached out, took her hand, and held it tightly.

"I did talk to her sister for a long time, though. She seems to be a good person and I know she'll take care of Ryan…and do what she can for Lissa. Her best guess is that Lissa needed money and somehow convinced herself I was the answer to her problems. Jenny figures Lissa thought she could convince me to marry her and then she'd have access to anything that was mine." Riley gave a helpless shrug.

"Using her son as a pawn…she must have been desperate. I'm glad Ryan has Jenny."

"It was hard to say goodbye to him. I asked Jenny if she'd consider a visit to Misty Lake sometime down the road…I'd like to see him again. Do you think that's weird?"

"Of course not. It may have been only a few weeks, but you built a relationship with him. There's nothing weird about wanting to see him again, wanting to make sure he's doing all right."

Riley just nodded.

"How are your parents doing?"

"It's been tough, so many highs and lows in such a short amount of time. They were thrilled with the idea of another grandchild and then…"

"I think everyone who met him feels a sense of loss. He's a pretty great kid."

Riley was quiet, lost in his thoughts for a moment, before his eyes suddenly brightened. "I almost forgot, she sent something for you."

"Who did?"

"Jenny."

"Why?"

"She insisted. When she heard the story of what happened with Ryan and how you did everything you could to keep him safe, she wanted to thank you."

"She doesn't have to thank me," Susan said emphatically.

"I know, and I told her that's what you'd say, but like I said, she insisted. She wanted to meet you to thank you in person but there wasn't time." Riley handed Susan an envelope.

"What is it?"

"I'm not sure, she didn't tell me. Exactly."

Susan kept her narrowed gaze on Riley as she opened the envelope. Inside, she found a check along with a handwritten note. She glanced at the check and when she saw the amount, the check fell from her fingers and fluttered to the floor.

"Oh, no. That's ridiculous. She can't give me a check like that." Susan began backing away from it and shaking her head.

Curious, Riley picked up the check and gave a low whistle. "Wow. I guessed it was a check, she mentioned something about a reward they were getting ready to offer for information on Lissa and Ryan, but she never mentioned an amount."

"You have to give that back to her. I can't possibly accept something like that."

"Read the note," Riley suggested.

Again, Susan narrowed her eyes at Riley, suspecting he knew more than he was letting on, but she unfolded the note and began to read. When she finished, she threw up her hands in exasperation.

"Well, now what am I supposed to do?"

"What did she say?"

"She thanked me for watching out for Ryan, said that Ryan kept talking about me and told her that I was nice and let him play with my dogs. I guess he told her how I had him hide in the woods and about how Gusto and Rigi 'guarded' him. She also mentioned hearing about the inn," at this she raised a brow at Riley, "and that she hoped the money that was going to be used as a reward for the safe return of Lissa and Ryan would help me with the renovating costs. She said she'd be hurt if I didn't accept it."

"I don't think there's much point in trying to argue with her, Susan. She's a kind, good person but, I think, used to doing things her way. And in her circles, money talks. It's her way of thanking you. Really."

"But this is too much," Susan argued. "And I don't need her charity."

"She's not thinking of it as charity, that much I know. She was truly grateful for all that you did."

"What about you? You did more for Ryan than I did."

At this, Riley looked down and dragged his foot through the sawdust on the floor.

"McCabe," Susan said, her voice dangerously low,

"she tried to give this to you, didn't she? Didn't she?" Susan said again when Riley didn't answer.

"Not really. I mean, she tried to give me something, I don't know what she had in mind, but I sort of convinced her it should go to you."

Susan gaped at him. "You *sort of convinced her*?"

"Well, I may have had an ulterior motive."

"What is that supposed to mean?"

"Sit down, Red, this isn't going at all like I'd planned."

"I don't know what you're talking about, but I'm not keeping this money if she wanted to give it to you…" Susan kept muttering as Riley led her to a scaffolding bench in the corner of the room.

"Will you listen, for just a minute?"

The quiet desperation in Riley's voice—and the way he'd so easily used his nickname for her, something he hadn't done in weeks—had her settling down and studying him.

"I made some mistakes during the past few weeks. I can get past most of them, except the ones that involve you. I never wanted to hurt you. I managed to ruin your birthday and I barely apologized. I closed myself off. I let myself get too caught up in what was happening and spent too much time worrying about how it was going to affect me without giving near enough thought to how it was going to affect you."

The sadness on his face and the regret in his eyes tugged at Susan's heart. She loved him, nothing had changed for her. "It was a lot to deal with, Riley. You did what you had to do."

"No. I made a mess of things. You have every

right to be angry with me."

"Angry? No, I have no right, no reason, to be angry. I was, though, for a while, and that's part of what I did wrong. I should have made more of an effort to support you, but I turned my back. I was busy feeling sorry for myself when, instead, I should have been talking with you and trying to help you. Help us."

Riley rested his forehead against Susan's. "Let's agree we both made some mistakes and try to put it behind us?"

"Deal," Susan smiled.

Riley breathed a sigh of relief. He hadn't been sure how Susan was going to react, but he realized he hadn't given her enough credit. She was, in a word, amazing. And he needed to let her know.

"So, back to that check," Riley started.

"I don't want it. It's yours."

"Hold on, Red. Remember I said I had an ulterior motive?"

Susan crossed her arms and waited.

Now that he had her attention, his nerves got the better of him. Three weeks ago he'd thought he had it all figured out. A romantic weekend, a fancy dinner, some champagne, and Susan would be swept away. But now, he realized he'd had it all wrong. He'd learned a lot about her…over the past nine months and especially over the past three weeks. She wanted real, not flashy. And while she may come across as rash, flighty even, he knew there was more to her. A lot more. Sure, she drove him crazy dreaming up one wild idea after the next, but he'd come to learn her ideas were always well thought out. Deep down, she knew exactly what she wanted. Everything she did, she did for a reason. It was all building towards the future she had planned out for herself. He just prayed she would like the part of the plan he wanted to add.

"Red, I didn't want her to give me anything because I wanted her to give it to us. You and me together."

"Well, then you should have had her split it if she insisted on doing something with it," Susan said reasonably.

Riley looked up to the ceiling and exhaled deeply. "Oh, Red, don't you get it? I want there to be an us. I want there to be an us forever. If you'll have me, I want to spend the rest of my life listening to your crazy ideas, realizing they're not so crazy after all, and figuring out how to make them happen. We make a good team, you said that once. Most of all, I love you. I've wanted to tell you that for a long time, but I was afraid you didn't want to hear it. Now, I want to tell you every morning when we wake up and every night when we go to sleep."

Susan stopped breathing as Riley got down on one knee in front of her, reached into his pocket, and pulled out a black velvet box. Everything seemed to slow as she watched him open it and settle it on his palm. It was like her dream, but, then, not at all like her dream.

"Will you marry me, Susan? I promise to love you with everything I have and to do whatever I can to keep that beautiful smile on your face and those green eyes of yours dancing."

Her breath whooshed out. Nothing existed but the two of them. It was as if the world had stopped spinning and everything had frozen in time. Susan wanted to hold on to the moment forever.

The words wouldn't come at first, she couldn't seem to get her thoughts from her brain to her tongue. "I can't believe this is happening," she finally managed. "Wait, that's not what I meant to say," she quickly corrected herself. "I meant…Oh, my, Riley, you've…I'm…I mean yes! Yes, I'll marry you. Of course, I'll marry you. I love you, Riley."

She joined him on the floor, wrapped her arms around his neck, and then the words wouldn't stop. "You're everything I've always wanted, Riley. You're smart and funny and you know how to do everything and you're patient with all…well, with most of my ideas and, of course, you're gorgeous and you're kind and you're generous and you play hockey, for crying out loud and—"

Grinning, Riley silenced her with a kiss.

Susan was lost in the kiss. How could it feel so different than it ever had before? Because no moment had ever been like this before. Nothing had ever been this wonderful, this perfect. Suddenly, she pulled away.

"Wait, wasn't there a ring?" she asked, her eyes alive with anticipation.

Riley slipped it on her finger.

Susan looked at it from every angle. It was exquisite and it fit as if it had been made for her alone. She leaned back into Riley's chest and his arms came around her. Another perfect fit.

In a moment, though, she sat up straight, a look of triumph on her face.

"What is it?"

"The last room name."

"But you've already named all of them. Wait a minute...you don't have another one of your ideas, do you?"

"No. Well, actually I have lots of ideas but that's not what I'm talking about."

Riley breathed a sigh of relief. "Then what room are you talking about?"

"This one, of course."

"This is your room. You're going to name your room?"

"I am now...now that it's going to be our room."

A slow smile spread across Riley's face. "I have some ideas."

"Just stop," she ordered, laughing.

"Okay, okay, I'm sorry. Tell me what you've decided on."

Her expression softened and she looked him in the eyes. "Forever."

Riley took her in his arms. "I like the sound of that."

Watch for Cassie and Frank's story

Misty Lake in Focus

Book Three in the Misty Lake Series

By Margaret Standafer

Coming Soon

Margaret Standafer lives and writes in the Minneapolis area with the support of her amazing husband and children and in spite of the lack of support from her ever-demanding, but lovable, Golden Retriever. It is her sincere hope that you enjoy her work.

To learn more about Margaret and her books, or to sign up for her email list, please visit www.margaretstandafer.com

Made in the USA
Lexington, KY
06 August 2016